THE WORLD OF
DARKNESS

Prince of the City

a sequel to Dark Prince

Based on Vampire: The Masquerade

Keith Herber

WHITE WOLF
FICTION

For Lorraine and Shirley, mother and aunt,
two sides of the same coin.

Note: Although this tale is based upon historical events, people, and places, certain details have been altered to suit dramatic needs. This is, after all, a fantasy.

1

1849: Gold Rush

The hot California sun beat down on the black man standing on a dusty rise overlooking the broad American River below. Riley lifted his battered hat and mopped his brow with a red handkerchief, revealing black hair speckled by gray. His shoulders were broad, his neck thick and powerful. His clothes were dusty and dirty, his buff-colored broad-brimmed hat stained with sweat. He wore a revolver on his left hip; a broad knife hung at his right. In his left hand he carried a shotgun.

He stood next to a mule hitched to a wooden wagon. On the wagon rode a large wooden box more than seven feet long, three feet wide, and two feet deep. Solidly built of oak, it was carefully and securely lashed to the wagon's bed. Riley had hauled the box all the way from Texas to California, crossing deserts and mountains in a trip that had taken months. Tonight he would reach his goal: the city of San Francisco.

Near the riverbank he saw hundreds of men milling about, raising clouds of dust, shuffling back and forth between the crowded, hastily constructed docks and the wooden fort called New Helvetia on the slopes above. Men hurriedly unloaded boats, bartering and selling mules, equipment, and supplies to the mob.

Some wore work clothes; others dressed in fashionable waistcoats and cravats; still others were garbed in foreign attire. In all directions men streamed away from the fort, singly and in groups, heading upriver, toward the nearby eastern foothills and the mountains beyond, all in search of the same thing — the gold discovered lying in the stream beds and washes in the recently acquired American territory.

With a soft cluck of his tongue, Riley got the mule moving, leading it down the gentle slope toward the riverbank. He looked straight ahead as he made his way toward the docks, moving against the tide of humanity streaming away from the riverbank, avoiding the looks of the white strangers all around him. But only a few took notice of Riley, and none said anything: most were either too busy with their own plans or fearful of the well-armed negro with the set look on his face. A few wondered what supplies he carried with him.

Reaching the riverbank, Riley accosted the first boatman he saw, a youngster standing next to an unpainted twelve-foot skiff of rough construction. The gangly, towheaded boy did not look a day over sixteen.

"I need passage downriver," Riley said. "How much?"

The kid rubbed his peach-fuzzed jaw, sizing up the customer. A paying passage back to the coast was rare, and he was unsure how much to ask. Coming upriver the gold-hunters were willing to pay nearly anything. The occasional prospector who'd struck it rich and was headed back to San Francisco also had a good deal of money to spend. But this man didn't look like a prospector.

"Just you?" the boy asked the stranger.

"I got some freight, too," Riley said, pointing to the heavy box stowed aboard the wagon. "I want to get into San Francisco — by tonight."

"Ten dollars for you, five for the box," the boy finally said.

Riley's eyes narrowed at the price. The cost should have been no more than a tenth of that. But even as he stood there he overheard men paying three dollars for a shovel and two for a blanket.

"You can sell the wagon and the mule for more than that," the boy suggested, hoping to persuade his customer. "You'll get enough to pay for your passage, with something left over."

"All right," Riley said, pulling off his hat and wiping the sweat from his brow; the temperature was still rising. "How soon do we leave?"

"Sooner the better," the boy said. "We want to get off the river by nightfall if we can. Bandits hole up along the bank at night, waiting to pick off small boats heading down to San Francisco," he explained. "But if we can reach the bay before sunset we won't have no problems." They shook hands on the deal. "Welcome aboard," the boy told Riley. "My name's Davey Foster."

Riley's wagon and mule sold quickly, as Davey had promised, but before allowing the new owner to lead it away Riley had to unload the box. He dropped the wagon's tailgate and began sliding the heavy crate off the bed. Davey came round to help, catching hold of the other end of the box as it slid off the end of the wagon. He groaned as he caught the full weight of the box, his knees buckling slightly.

"Christ, Mister! What do you got in here? Rocks?"

Riley, carefully walking backward along the dock, smiled back at Davey but said nothing. Davey staggered along after him, arms straining. Riley carried his half of the load easily, showing no sign of effort.

Davey's skiff was flat-bottomed and square-prowed, built for the shallow, gentle river that wound through California's central valley. They carefully lowered the box into the boat. Riley tossed his bedroll and few meager belongings in after it, then followed Davey aboard. While the young man cast off the lines, Riley lashed the crate down tightly, securing it aboard the craft. Once free of the dock, Davey poled them out to midstream. The lazy current began carrying them west and south, toward the Pacific coast and the new town of San Francisco. Riley, finally nearing the end of his long journey, wondered what he would find there.

It was near the end of summer — the dry season — and the river was shallow, exposing countless mud-capped sandbars.

"The river's down this time of year," Davey explained, now seated near the center of the boat, the muscles of his face tightening with each pull on the creaking oars. "The rainy season 'round here don't start till November."

Riley sat in the stern, saying nothing, his shotgun placed between his feet. He watched the banks of the broad river as they slid by — a rolling land colored golden brown and covered with dry scrub and a few oaks — far better farmland than any Riley had seen in Texas. The soil was rich and Riley judged you could raise anything here you wanted — fruit, wheat, cotton, whatever. And, if the weather was as good as he'd been told, a farmer could raise crops year round, pulling harvest after harvest out of the fertile soil.

"You up from the south somewhere?" Davey asked his silent passenger. He recognized the accent.

"Yeah," Riley said. "From Texas."

"Alone?"

Riley hesitated, then answered: "Yes."

"So what is it that brings ya to these parts?" It was obvious the man wasn't here to prospect.

"I've got a business opportunity in San Francisco," Riley told him, adding: "With a partner."

"That's the best idea," Davey said, stroking steadily at the oars. "It's the businessmen that are gettin' rich — not the prospectors."

Riley smiled at the boy. "You seem to be doin' all right," he chided. "Chargin' a man ten dollars for a ride down the river."

Davey grinned nervously, glancing at the shotgun between Riley's feet. What if the man decided to kill him here on the river? He hadn't thought of that when he agreed to take the job on. His passenger seemed nervous, apprehensive. Davey wondered what he had in the box.

"Here," Riley said, sensing the boy's concern. He got up off his seat. "Give me a spell on those oars."

The two switched positions; Davey now sat in the stern near the shotgun, while Riley pulled at the oars.

The conversation loosened up and an hour later the two were talking freely. Riley told Davey of his long trek up from Texas and over the Donner Pass while Davey told Riley all he knew about the gold rush and the burgeoning town of San Francisco on the bay.

"What did you used to do in Texas?" Davey asked Riley later on, the sun now creeping down toward the western hills. Davey was back on the oars, Riley once again seated in the stern.

"I was a farmer," Riley told him. "Had a family."

"Where are they now?" Davey asked innocently. "Did you leave 'em at home?"

"They're dead," Riley replied flatly, his expression growing dark.

"Oh," Davey said. Noting the look on Riley's face, he inquired no further.

They were within a few miles of San Francisco Bay and less than an hour from sunset when the travelers spotted a dense column of dark smoke rising up from somewhere downstream. Its source was hidden by the steep round hills now surrounding the river.

"A steamer," the boy said, looking over his shoulder. "We gotta pull over."

Entrepreneurs had already shipped steamboats around the Horn, hoping to cash in on the heavy traffic now flowing up and down the river between the gold fields and the coast.

Davey began turning the skiff toward the distant bank on their right. The river was very broad and shallow, and Davey had been keeping to the middle, where the channel was deepest, away from the sandbars and low spots nearer the banks.

"We got to make room — and in a hurry," Davey said, now pulling frantically at the oars. "They'll be heading straight up the middle of the river when the water's this low."

They could hear the steamer now, the chug of its engine, the splash made by its great stern paddle wheel. Davey pulled hard to starboard, trying to get them out of the way, but then the steamer suddenly appeared huffing around the bend, bearing down on them, its engines thundering as black smoke poured from its single tall stack and the great stern paddle wheel churned the muddy waters to a froth. The steamer sounded its whistle. In a few seconds the great boat would be upon them.

"Shit!" Davey shouted, scrambling to his feet, pulling one of the oars free from the lock. "Grab an oar, Riley. Quick!"

The steamer continued to pound toward them, its broad bow splitting the waters. They would have to stave themselves off.

"Hey! Hey! Ahoy!" Davey shouted, waving his oar in the air, trying to get the steamboat pilot's attention.

But the man in the pilot house high above the deck paid them no heed. He wasn't about to risk beaching his steamer simply to avoid two men in a small boat. Small craft would have to learn to pay heed to the steamers. He blew the whistle again: a long, mournful blast.

"Look out!" Davey shouted to Riley as the great boat bore down on them. "Try to push off!"

The cleaving bow missed them by a few feet, its wake splashing over their gunwales, but then the great wooden hull loomed up, a waterborne wall that threatened to overwhelm and crush them. They laid into it with their oars, trying to push themselves away, but then the steamboat struck the skiff's stern, spinning it around, knocking Riley off his feet and nearly pitching him overboard.

"Hang on!" Davey shouted as the skiff's bow swung round and crashed into the steamboat, and another wave washed over the craft.

"We got to get clear of the paddle wheel!" Davey shouted. The great threshing blades of the wheel thundered nearer while the two men scrambled to shove the skiff out of the way. If they were sucked in by the wheel, they would be chewed to bits.

While Riley regained his feet, Davey desperately thrust his oar against the hull of the passing steamship, trying to push the skiff clear; but the suction of the passing steamboat kept drawing them back in. Meanwhile a curious crowd of passengers — would-be miners — were gathering at the rails above, gazing with interest on the drama unfolding below them.

"Look out!" Davey screamed as the paddle wheel crashed down on the front of the skiff, splintering its square bow, nearly capsizing the boat before releasing it and sending it spinning away.

The steamboat's wake carried the skiff over a sandbar, where it snagged, leaving the two of them stranded ten yards offshore, half-swamped and stuck fast.

"Bastards!" Davey swore at the steamship as it headed up and around the bend, never slowing its course. "Shit!" Davey said, now talking to Riley. "We nearly got it, for sure."

"Is the boat okay?" Riley asked. He was already checking the ropes holding down the soaking wet box, making sure it was still secure.

"It looks okay," Davey announced after checking the damage.

Despite the splintered bow and some opened seams, the skiff still appeared seaworthy. Provided they bailed a little, Davey reckoned they could make it to San Francisco safely enough. "Once back in town I'll have to make some real repairs to her, though," he added.

The sun was now sinking below the line of hills in the

west, and Davey grew anxious to depart the area. He kept searching the deepening shadows along the banks, looking for signs of bandits.

"Let's bail her out and push her free," he said, grabbing up a worn leather bucket and scooping water out of the boat. "We don't want to stay here too long."

Riley placed his shotgun atop the box to dry and joined him, forced to use his sweat-stained hat in lieu of a bucket.

The boat was but half-emptied of water when a gunshot rang out from shore and a bullet splashed in the water next to the boat.

Davey stood up and looked toward shore. "What the he—" he began; then a shotgun roared and the boy fell backward into the river. More gunfire erupted; bullets crashed into the boat, sending splinters flying. Riley dove for cover behind the great box, shielding himself from the unseen attackers on shore. Spotting Davey floating motionless in the water near the boat, Riley snatched the boy's body out of the river, lifting him with one hand and setting him down in the bottom of the half-swamped boat.

"Come on out!" someone shouted from the shore.

"Give yourself up," called another voice.

Carefully, Riley reached up and slipped the shotgun off the top of the box, provoking another eruption of gunfire.

"Give up!" someone shouted again.

Trapped behind the box and unable to return fire safely, Riley knew he couldn't hold out long. The bandits on the bank would soon spread out and catch him in a crossfire. He squinted toward the sun sinking below the line of hills. It was nearly dark. His charge would be ready to awaken. He pulled out his heavy knife and, reversing his grip, beat the hilt against the side of the box.

"Wake up!" he hissed. "It's time to rise. The sun's nearly set."

He then began sawing at the ropes holding the crate, cutting through them one by one while the gunmen on shore kept up a steady fire.

"Come on. Give it up," they demanded. "We promise you can go free, unharmed." Riley knew they were lying.

"It's nearly time," Riley said, whispering again to the box, glancing at the setting sun, checking its position. Something inside the box stirred. Riley felt relieved.

The gunfire momentarily ceased and the evening fell quiet. Carefully, Riley crawled forward, peeking around the end of the crate in an attempt to catch sight of his attackers. He saw three men positioned behind a fallen tree on the riverbank. One of them spotted Riley and shot at him with a pistol. The bullet whined off the end of the crate as Riley ducked back out of sight.

It was now dusk. Riley whispered to the crate: "There are three of them. Behind a dead tree on the riverbank to your right."

More movement came from within the box: something battering at the lid. Boards split and nails wrenched free as the top of the box splintered, then broke apart. A tall, lean man stood up, knocking aside the shattered boards as he rose to his feet. Riley took advantage of the bandits' distraction to take a shot at them from behind the box. He hit one of the bandits; the man went down even as the two remaining attackers prepared to return fire. Before they could squeeze off a shot, the newcomer leapt from the boat and splashed toward them through the knee-deep water. As he ran he drew a short cavalry saber from the sheath on his hip, swinging it above his head.

The bandits fired on him, and though they were sure their shots hit him, the man never slowed his pace.

With no time to reload, the bandits turned to run but the stranger was already upon them. One of the bandits drew a revolver from his belt but the stranger slashed at it with his sword, severing the bandit's hand at the wrist. Another powerful stroke caught the man across the throat, silencing his screams as he fell to the ground, nearly decapitated.

The second man swung his empty shotgun at the swordsman, breaking the wooden stock across the man's back. The stranger barely flinched. Turning around, he knocked away the bandit's broken weapon with a backhand blow, disarming him. Realizing escape was impossible, the bandit fell to his knees, hands clasped for mercy, but before a word escaped his lips the blade fell again. The bandit flopped face first in the grass, dead.

The dark stranger wiped the blood from his sword on the fallen man's shirt, then replaced it in its sheath. Riley's voice came to him from the dark of the river.

"Are you all right, Vannevar?"

"Yes," Vannevar answered. "I'm fine." The two bullet wounds he'd suffered were painful, and his shoulder was badly bruised by the bandit's assault, but the wounds were minor and would quickly heal.

"We got a man hurt out here," Riley called through the gathering darkness. "He's still alive, but he needs attention."

"I'll be there in a moment," Vannevar said.

Kneeling beside the nearly beheaded bandit, he bent over the gaping wound, lapping the warm blood welling up from the man's severed throat.

The man named Vannevar Thomas returned to the stranded boat a few minutes later, leaving the bandits' bodies hidden beneath the tangled roots of a scrub oak that leaned over the bank. He had relieved them of their weapons, bringing them back to the boat, along with a small quantity of minted cash and several small bags of gold dust the bandits had undoubtedly stolen from earlier victims.

Vannevar Thomas was tall — nearly six feet — slim and well proportioned. His long chestnut hair was kept tied back with a ribbon in a short queue that lay over his collar. He was still handsome at the age of forty-five, though fine lines around his eyes and at the corners of his mouth betrayed his age. His eyes were dark brown, nearly black, and his nose like the beak of a hawk. Despite his pale complexion his skin showed a ruddy quality from the thin strain of American Indian blood that ran through the veins of his aristocratic Virginia family. His clothes, though worn and filthy from months spent on the trail from Texas, were well made and of fine material. He carried himself with his head held high and shoulders squared. He had the bearing of a well-bred man.

"How bad is he?" Vannevar asked as he waded to the side of the boat. Stashing the loot on board, he hauled himself in over the side, dripping wet.

"They got him in the shoulder," Riley said, kneeling at the boy's side, examining the wound. "It's not too bad, just a couple pellets, but he needs a doctor." The boy's shoulder blade was fractured. The wound bled steadily, staining the water in the bottom of the boat with red.

"Let's move on, then," Vannevar said, stooping to bail out the rest of the water in the boat.

They placed Davey on what remained of the wooden crate, up out of the water that kept leaking in through the skiff's opened seams. The two of them bailed as much water as they could; then Vannevar hopped back out of the boat and began pushing the skiff free while Riley seated himself at the oars. Once off the sandbar, Vannevar hauled himself back in over the stern and sat down on the narrow seat.

"How far are we from San Francisco?" he asked Riley, pulling off his tall black boots and pouring river water out of them over the side.

"The boy said another half-hour to the bay," Riley told him, pulling steadily on the oars. "And then another half-hour to San Francisco."

It was almost pitch dark now; only the sliver of a rising quarter-moon provided a pale light. They followed the current downstream toward the coast, taking turns manning the oars and bailing water. They had nearly reached their goal.

2

Earlier Years: Other Lives

The vampire Vannevar and the ghoul Riley had come to the West Coast on orders from their superiors. Gold had been discovered in the newly acquired California territory, a matter of great interest to the Texas elder whom Vannevar obeyed. People were flocking to the area from all over the world, and the once tiny village of Yerba Buena — now renamed San Francisco — appeared destined to play a key role in the country's future. The bay upon which the city was located was perhaps the greatest in the world: safe, secure, and large enough to hold the combined navies of the entire world. Vannevar's elders believed the city would someday be a great port, providing a gateway to the Pacific and the world beyond.

Vannevar Thomas had been born in Alexandria, Virginia, in 1732, the eldest son of a family of tobacco farmers and horse breeders. Educated and refined, he seemed the proper heir to the family fortunes. But in 1776 he left the family home to join the American revolutionary cause.

An expert horseman, he was commissioned a captain in the cavalry and distinguished himself in several campaigns before receiving a field promotion to the rank of major. A few weeks after his promotion, while on a nighttime ride through a heavy woods on his way to headquarters, he fell victim to the Tories.

He was galloping his horse at full speed through the moonlit woods when a shadowy figure suddenly stepped out onto the trail in front of him. The man raised his hand as though to bar the way but Vannevar spurred his horse on, not deigning to stop for a stranger on a midnight road while on an errand of military urgency. But then the man made a series of strange passes with his hand and Vannevar's horse suddenly reared, screaming in terror, throwing Vannevar out of the saddle to the hard forest floor where he struck his head and lost consciousness.

When he awoke, Vannevar found himself lying on the dirty floor of a rocky cavern. A single candle sitting atop an oblong rock gave off a feeble, yellow light, revealing limestone walls streaked by water. The air was damp and still, tinged with a musty odor. Next to the rock and candle squatted the older man who had waylaid him in the forest.

He was dressed darkly, in a civilian's coat, breeches, and buckle shoes. His linen was dirty, his stockings torn — one lay crumpled around his ankle, the garter broken. The man stared coolly at the slowly awakening Vannevar, waiting.

Vannevar recognized the stranger's face, or at least thought he did. The man looked exactly like Quincy Cullen, an uncle of one of his family's neighbors, the Cullen family. But Vannevar knew that Quincy Cullen had died some twenty years ago, shortly after coming to this country to live with his American cousins. Vannevar had attended the funeral. He had once been close friends with the Cullens, Vannevar's relationship with his neighbors had, over the years, soured as the debate over colonists' rights went on, growing increasingly heated with the years. The Cullens were loyal Tories, opposed to the revolutionary views held by Vannevar and most of his family.

"Who are you?" Vannevar asked the stranger.

"Ye know me, Vannevar," the mysterious man answered. "It's not likely you could forget 'old uncle Quincy' that easily, now could you?" The man's sneering tones were familiar to Vannevar's ears.

"Quincy Cullen died years ago," Vannevar told the man. "You can't be him."

The man laughed — a dark chuckle, chilling and cold. He smiled, revealing a row of long, yellow teeth surrounded by pale, shrunken gums.

There was no doubt about it, Vannevar thought. It was indeed Quincy Cullen, but what was he doing here? Why was he not dead? He remembered the funeral and the closed coffin. He had never actually seen the old man's body. Perhaps, he thought, the man had not died, but lost his mind, and the Cullen family, out of shame, had locked him away, staging the mock funeral to allay suspicion. The coffin had never been opened, Vannevar recalled. Old Cullen was supposed to have died after falling from a horse, and the corpse to have been badly mangled after being dragged through the woods.

"I did not die," Quincy told him, as though reading his thoughts. "Oh, no," he added. "Old Quincy won't die that easily. I can promise you that."

Vannevar, convinced now of the man's identity, felt sure he was mad. Vannevar knew the Cullen farms had been swept by the war more than once, and rumors held that most of the family had either been killed or captured by the Continental Army. Old Quincy must have somehow escaped his captivity and now roamed the countryside, lost and helpless.

"I am what some have called 'undead,'" Quincy continued. "A predator, a scavenger, a stalker of the innocent." His voice grew excited as he spoke, his eyes taking on a strange glow in the feeble light of the candle. "I am called by some a *vampyr*."

Vannevar did not recognize the word, but his terror grew as Quincy explained it to him: how he roamed at night, killing and drinking the blood of humans. Quincy then told Vannevar that he too was now a vampire, an undying blood-drinker, one of the legion of undead.

"I have chosen you to help me, young Vannevar," Quincy said. "The war has made existence precarious and I need a friend."

More than ever, Vannevar believed the man was mad. "I can help you," he assured Quincy. "But we must leave here right away." Vannevar's urgent message to headquarters was still undelivered. He struggled to get up, his body aching. He felt weak, dizzy, and wondered how long he'd been unconscious.

Quincy sat watching as Vannevar got to his feet. "Then go on," he told Vannevar. "See for yourself." Quincy pointed toward a bend in the cave a few yards away where a gray light could be seen, spilling in from outside. Whether dawn or dusk, Vannevar could not guess. "But don't tell me I didn't warn you," Quincy cackled.

Quincy remained seated on his rock, watching Vannevar as he staggered unsteadily toward the cave's entrance, bracing himself against the damp stone walls.

But when Vannevar reached the bend and saw the opening before him, he shrieked in pain. The pale morning sun burned his eyes and seared his skin, forcing him back inside. Quincy sat waiting for him.

"See?" the old man smiled maliciously, chuckling softly, as Vannevar collapsed on the cold, hard floor of the cave, sitting down with his back against the wall. "You'd best stay out of the sunlight, now, like I told you. If you want to survive this war — if you want to survive at all — you and I will have to work together."

In life, Vannevar had been only mildly fond of the elder Cullen, a hard-line Tory who'd made his fortune in the slave trade. In death Vannevar found the old man repulsive. But he soon found he was unable to resist the demands of the one who now called himself "Master."

"You are bound to me," Quincy explained to him. "And must do as I say."

Not only had Quincy made Vannevar a vampire, but he had stolen Vannevar's will from him. After draining Vannevar of his blood, killing him, Quincy had then revived Vannevar with an infusion of blood from Quincy's own veins. Had this been all, Vannevar would have awakened a vampire, but free. But Quincy had taken advantage of Vannevar's weakened condition to nourish him twice more with his own vital blood, establishing a permanent bond between them that left Vannevar as Quincy's unwilling slave.

"You are my childe," Quincy told him. "We are one."

And it was true. No matter what Cullen demanded of him, Vannevar found himself compelled to obey. He would have killed himself, had not Quincy forbidden him this escape.

Two days later, after Vannevar had regained his strength, the pair left the cave at nightfall. They began moving west, away from the ravages of the war, seeking quieter ground where they would be safe. With the Cullen family dispersed, Quincy had no one to protect him during daylight hours while he lay helpless and vulnerable. His plan was to head deep into the wilderness, far from the unpredictable conflict.

Holing up by day in caves and dark glens and traveling by night, they avoided roads and inhabited areas, living on the blood of raccoons, opossums, and squirrels. They eventually left Virginia behind them, wandering south into near-virgin territory later known as Tennessee. Traveling deep into the mountains, they found fewer and fewer white men. At last they entered wilderness beyond the limits of all but the most daring trappers. Throughout their long journey Vannevar obeyed his master unfailingly, doing all that was asked of him — for he could not summon the will to refuse. Existence became a dark, stumbling dream from which he could not awake.

They finally discovered a cave in a high rocky face overlooking a river winding through a wooded valley. This, Cullen hoped, would serve as a permanent refuge. But a few days later they awoke to discover a small band of Cherokee Indians camped on the riverbank below. Vannevar felt it foolish to disturb them, but Quincy, after weeks of living on small animals, longed to feast on human blood.

"It is time you learned," he told Vannevar.

They raided the encampment that night, entering the pole huts silently and drinking only slightly from one or two victims, thus satisfying their undeniable thirsts while leaving their victims essentially unharmed. Vannevar was initially hesitant to drink of human blood, but Quincy forced him to it, and he soon discovered the deep and undeniable pleasure of feasting on one's own kind.

The next night Quincy lost control, leaving his Indian victim a pale corpse without a drop of blood in its veins. To avoid suspicion, they hauled the body to the river and tossed it in, watching as the current carried it swiftly away. The next morning the Indians were mystified by the disappearance of one of the band, but had no inkling of what had actually happened.

The following night, despite Vannevar's pleas for restraint, Quincy killed again, this time twice. They again used the river to dispose of the bodies but later, back in the cave, Vannevar discovered Quincy had borne something away from the Indian camp. As Vannevar watched transfixed, Quincy unwrapped a tiny papoose he had spirited away from the side of its sleeping mother. Lifting the softly crying infant toward his mouth, Quincy bared his fangs. Vannevar turned his back, but could not fail to hear the crunching sound as Quincy's fangs fastened themselves in the infant's throat, nor could he avoid hearing the baby's suddenly throttled cries.

Quincy carelessly tossed the little corpse aside after he'd finished. As dawn broke, the two vampires retired to their separate corners in the cave. Vannevar sat awake into the morning, his soul blasted and blackened.

The band of Indians awoke the next morning to the cries of the distraught mother, who, upon awakening, had discovered her missing infant. Two more members of the tribe had also vanished. Later, when one of the bloodless bodies was found downstream, snagged on a tree root, the Cherokees knew they had stumbled into a place of evil spirits. While most of the Indians hastily broke camp, a small band of warriors, after painting themselves with protective symbols known to their wisest men, ascended the cliff overlooking the river, following the almost invisible trail left by the two vampires.

Vannevar awoke with a start as the first of many tomahawks buried itself in the sleeping Quincy's chest. Vannevar struggled to his feet as Quincy's roars of pain and rage echoed throughout the cave. Driven by the Blood Bond between them, he was prepared to sacrifice his own life in order to save his master. Even as he gained his feet, however, the deadly weapons found their mark, sundering Quincy's heart, severing his head and destroying him.

The undeniable compulsion to sacrifice himself for Quincy left Vannevar with a rush. His head now clear for the first time since the fateful encounter with the old Tory, his only thought was to preserve himself, to escape the cave and the maddened Cherokees who'd come to slay him.

Brushing aside the warriors attempting to block his path, Vannevar dashed out of the cave into the sunlight. His skin immediately began to blister and char. Howling in pain and terror, he plunged deep into the shadowy woods, the vengeful Indians in hot pursuit. Running blindly through the woods, dodging from one dark glen to another, avoiding the occasional pools of golden sun that found their way to the forest floor, Vannevar was finally able to outdistance his pursuers.

Now free of Quincy's influence, Vannevar began making his way back east. Only after days of travel did he reach the first white settlements scattered along the frontier, and it took weeks before he finally saw the familiar towns and farms of his native Virginia.

As he drew closer to home, his hopes and expectations rose but, once back in Alexandria, he hesitated to make his return. Forced to exist as a night-stalking predator, how would he explain to his family what had happened to him? How could they possibly accept him?

Entering the town after dark, he made his way to the deserted town hall. Slipping inside, he found the casualty lists posted on the wall. On them he saw many names he recognized, including his own. Vannevar was listed as killed in action, believed taken prisoner by the British and shot as a spy. His family had been told he was dead.

He knew then he could never return to the life he'd once known. Even if his family did accept him, would he someday become another Quincy? He turned his back on Alexandria that night, leaving his past and his home behind forever.

The next few decades Vannevar maintained his existence on the fringes of the ever-expanding new America, establishing temporary residences in booming towns as they sprouted up along the frontiers, moving on whenever he felt his existence might be exposed. He fed regularly on human blood but rarely killed. Only the occasional victim deemed too criminal or corrupt failed to survive a late-night encounter with a black-clad Vannevar in a dark street at night. Throughout all these years of lonely wandering, Vannevar never encountered another of his own kind.

By 1832 he'd reached Texas, following in the wake of the thousands of American settlers invited by the Mexican government to take up residence in this underpopulated, formerly Spanish northern territory. It was in the small town of San Joaquin that Vannevar encountered Samuel Travis, a vampire who would become the most important contact Vannevar would ever make.

Vannevar was hovering near the fringes of San Joaquin's plaza when he noticed a tall, lanky man walking toward him across the tiled square. Vannevar was standing in the shadows, nearly invisible to most, but it was plain the man had spotted him. He thought of fleeing, but instead held his ground, deciding to await the man's approach.

Stepping up before him, the man offered Vannevar his hand and asked: "You are new to the area?"

Vannevar hesitated a moment, then stepped out of the shadows. "I am from the East," he said. He took the man's extended hand and shook it. "My name is Thomas, of Alexandria, Virginia."

"Samuel Travis, originally out of North Carolina," the stranger introduced himself, his Southern accent cultured and aristocratic. "What brings you to these parts, sir?"

Vannevar did not answer at first. Other than mad Quincy, Vannevar had known no other of his kind. He assumed all vampires were as cold and cruel as Quincy had been, but Travis's lined face seemed kinder. To Vannevar, he seemed nearly human.

"You have nothing to fear," Travis finally told him, noting Vannevar's reluctance. "You are among friends."

Travis invited Vannevar back to his haven, a secure room in the rear of an adobe *hacienda* that faced out on the plaza. Vannevar feared a trap, but the opportunity to meet and converse with another — even a vampire — was too great a temptation to resist.

Travis was an educated man who, like Vannevar, could read Latin and Greek, and, thanks to several tours of Europe, was proficient in a half-dozen modern languages as well. Vannevar was initially cautious but within an hour or two came to trust this elder vampire, a creature he instinctively recognized as wiser and more powerful than he was.

Travis took Vannevar under his wing, establishing a haven

for him in a small town just a few miles from San Joaquin. Quincy had left Vannevar sadly unprepared for his new life and Travis now saw to it that Vannevar learned many of the things he would need to know in the future.

And he introduced Vannevar to other Kindred. Many American vampires dwelt in the territory, all united under the leadership of Sam Travis. Vannevar learned they were part of a secret society of vampires called the Camarilla. An ancient organization of Kindred formed centuries ago in response to the terrors of the Inquisitions, the Camarilla regulated the activities of vampires worldwide, establishing codes of behavior that allowed the race of vampires to move and survive, unseen and unknown, among the world of humans.

"It was not easily achieved," Travis explained to Vannevar one night in the back room of the *hacienda*. "Many old grudges had to be set aside in order to accomplish this cooperation. And even to this day many of the more powerful members intrigue constantly against one another in an endless struggle for power and control."

The world of mortals knew little of vampires' existence, Travis told him, but few things transpired in the realm of humans that were not in some way influenced by the secretive Camarilla. The organization held subtle strings to governments and industries, and pulled them as they would, instigating and controlling many major events in human history. Travis claimed the American Revolution was the result of a split between certain American and European factions of the Camarilla.

"But there are other vampires who exist without us, and who threaten our cause," Travis told him. "I speak of the Sabbat."

The Sabbat was a dark and bloody cult of vampires who, though much smaller than the Camarilla, opposed the Camarilla's aims in nearly every way. Travis warned that a bloody war would soon break out between the Camarilla forces in America and the Sabbat-influenced government of Mexico.

Sabbat forces had gained an early foothold in the New World, following on the heels of the Spanish Inquisition. The sect had established itself in Mexico and parts of South and Central America. Travis told Vannevar the Camarilla was currently inciting the Texans — Americans and Mexicans — to revolt against the Mexican authorities, declaring their independence and forcing the Mexican government out of the area. Other parts of Mexican territory, including California, would be absorbed in the course of the conflict as well. Neither the U.S. nor the Mexican government knew anything about the secret forces that were forging their destinies.

"Who exactly are the Sabbat?" Vannevar questioned Travis.

"The main body of the group consists of two rebel clans of vampires — the Tzimisce and the Lasombra — as well as many others drawn from the ranks of the disgruntled and dissatisfied."

The Sabbat were everything Vannevar feared vampires to be: rapacious, predatory killers who believed themselves the natural superior animal. Given free rein, they would make humans their slaves, reigning over them in a bloody regime. The Camarilla, though dedicated to the survival of the Kindred, envisioned a world of peaceful coexistence with the human race — a world wherein their presence would never be revealed. Seven major clans charted the destiny of the Camarilla. Vannevar learned that he was of the Ventrue clan, long a major force within the organization.

In the few months he had knew Travis, Vannevar came to trust him in all things. Thus it was without hesitation that he volunteered to help the Camarilla effort in Texas. Swearing allegiance to both Travis and the Camarilla, Vannevar joined the secret forces already fostering revolt in the Mexican territory.

It was in 1836, after the Alamo had fallen and been retaken, that Vannevar found Riley and saved his life. A Texas cotton farmer, Riley was the son of slaves escaped from Georgia and had been raised a free man. Finding themselves caught in a war not of their making, Riley's family managed to survive first the Mexican army's advance and later, its subsequent retreat. But when the Texans came through, the family fell afoul of a gang of whites who, offended by the idea of a black landowner, took the opportunity to destroy the farm. They shot the family, burned the buildings and hanged Riley by the neck from a tree, bound hand and foot, his toes barely touching the ground, leaving him to strangle slowly as the sun set in the west.

Vannevar came upon the ruins a half-hour later. Rising at sunset, he had followed the advancing Texans in a mop-up operation intended to destroy any Sabbat vampires left behind by the hasty Mexican retreat. Vannevar was not shocked by the burning ruins when he came upon them — he had seen much destruction these last weeks — but when he spotted the silhouette of the hanged man against the deepening evening sky, he broke into a run.

Reaching the unconscious man's side and quickly cutting him down, Vannevar laid him gently on the ground. The man still breathed, but laboriously. Vannevar checked his throat for injuries and found the windpipe crushed. The man would not live long. Already his lips were turning a cyanic blue.

Vannevar had seen a great deal of death these last weeks: soldiers shot or otherwise slain, left lying at the sides of trails, their bloated bodies providing food for the buzzards. He had even occasionally fed upon the recent dead when no other nourishment presented itself. But the man now dying in front of him awakened a sense of compassion he'd thought long ago turned dead and cold. If Vannevar fed the man with his own unnatural blood, he would survive, his devastating injuries quickly healing under the influence of the vampire's vigorous blood. With a knife Vannevar opened a vein in his forearm and, as the thick red fluid oozed forth, he pressed the unconscious man's mouth to the wound.

Within days Riley had recovered from his injuries; by the time the two were moving about, the war for Texas' independence had been won. They returned to Vannevar's lair and, working together, soon became inseparable. Riley, though now infused with some of the strength and vigor of Vannevar's vampire blood, was not a true vampire but rather what was called a "ghoul" — a blood-linked creature of unnatural abilities, but not bound to sleep by day, nor required to drink the blood of the living to sustain its life. The ghoul's occasional need of sustenance was satisfied by blood drawn from the vampire's own veins.

In the years that followed, Riley became Vannevar's eyes and ears during the day, protecting Vannevar while he lay asleep. In return, Vannevar extended Riley his protection and influence. Those foolish enough to threaten or insult Riley quickly learned that retribution was swift, coming by night as Vannevar visited the offenders in their homes and made his wishes known. Few dared cross Riley a second time.

By the spring of 1849, after Texas had been annexed by the United States for more than three years, Travis invited Vannevar to meet with him in the city of San Antonio. Vannevar agreed to come and, accompanied by Riley, arrived at Travis's adobe *hacienda* a few days later, near midnight. The building was large and trimmed with wrought-iron railings. A pair of oil lamps mounted on either side of the heavy wooden front door lit the entrance.

Travis met the pair at the door and invited them in. A member of a vampire clan known as Toreador, Travis, as usual, was dressed well. Attired in a suit of soft tan buckskin, expertly tailored, with tall, high-heeled boots of exquisitely tooled leather, he looked the part of a successful Texas rancher.

Breezing through the formalities of greeting, Travis invited the two to sit down at the table. Travis lit one of his favorite small black cigars, then got down to business.

"We haven't heard anything from McNaughton in several months," he said, frowning, then blowing a small blue smoke ring. "We suspect he is dead."

Brendan McNaughton, a Scotsman and part of the Texas group, had been sent to northern California a few years ago, right after the territory had fallen into the hands of the invading Americans in June of 1846. Sparsely populated, this northernmost outpost of Mexican territory had been seized without a shot being fired. McNaughton arrived in the area in the summer of 1847 and found little to report regarding the tiny, sleepy village of Yerba Buena on the edge of San Francisco Bay. By early 1848, however, rumors of gold found in the hills and mountains began reaching the coast. These rumors were soon confirmed and, by the end of the year, news of a great gold strike had spread across the country, touching off an exodus as thousands upon thousands of hopeful prospectors. But then nothing more was heard from McNaughton.

"We need to move fast," Travis told them. "It is essential that the Camarilla take control of the area, and soon. There is too much at stake."

Vannevar nodded, knowing already he was to be sent.

"San Francisco is the spot," Travis said. "Used to have about a hundred people living there. Now it counts three, maybe six thousand, depending on whom you believe. Most of the area's shipping docks and departs at the town's bay, and the miners flock to the area to spend their gold."

Vannevar nodded his comprehension.

"Other Camarilla representatives are already being dispatched," Travis told him. "I want us to get there first."

"We can leave the day after tomorrow," Vannevar told him. It was understood that Riley would accompany him.

"Good," Travis smiled.

And so the long journey began.

3

1849: Boom Town

The journey was now nearing an end. The river finally emptied into the broad expanse of the northern bay where Vannevar and Riley turned south, guiding their leaking boat in the direction of the city of San Francisco. Ten miles later they rounded a point of land and spotted their destination.

Still miles away, they could see the lights of the city burning along the shore, glowing softly in the thin fog that shrouded the bay. Even at this distance they could hear the sounds of men working on the docks, hammers pounding, and music jingling from the saloons. Knowing they were within reach of San Francisco, Vannevar eagerly anticipated their arrival. It had been a long and hazardous journey. Riley was anxious, too, but also nervous. They were a long way from his home in Texas.

An hour later they neared the shallow cove around which much of the town was built. They saw long wooden docks reaching out from the shore, beckoning them to tie up, but found their route partially blocked by a veritable forest of ships, dark and silent, riding at anchor out in the bay.

Ship after ship had arrived in port the last few months, only to be abandoned by their crews and sometimes even their captains, all anxious to make their fortunes in the gold fields. Left stranded in the port with little hope of hiring a crew to sail them out, these crewless ships were towed away from the docks and anchored out in the bay, left to rot. Nearly a hundred such ships now stood idle and waiting.

Picking their way through the floating hulks, working their way around anchor chains and lines, Vannevar and Riley finally reached one of the wooden wharves — the longest of the dozen or more on the cove — and carefully guided the skiff into a berth, tying up next to a greasy-smelling New England whaler. They secured the skiff, then climbed the ladder to the high dock, where they were greeted by a watchman with a lantern.

"There's a docking fee here on Long Wharf, you know," the man said, challenging the two.

"It's not our boat," Vannevar explained coolly. "And there's an injured boy aboard. He was shot by bandits. We're just paying passengers."

The watchman looked over the edge of the dock, holding his lantern high to see what lay in the boat below.

"My lands!" he exclaimed. "It's Davey Foster. Is he hurt bad?" he asked Vannevar.

"The wound isn't serious, but he needs a doctor," Vannevar said. "Here." He handed the watchman one of the bags of gold dust taken from the bandits. "See that he's taken care of."

"Of course," answered the watchman. "Yes, sir." And he hurried off to find a physician.

Leaving the wharf, Vannevar and Riley strolled north along the waterfront, the busiest section of the town. Though it was nearing eleven o'clock, the docks hummed with activity; ships were being unloaded by oil lamps as swearing teamsters hauled the goods away on horse-drawn wagons. The sounds of hammers and saws echoed from the dozen or more streets running west from the waterfront, as the construction of new hotels, restaurants, and dance halls continued nearly round the clock. Now and then they heard gunshots, and they noticed many of the inhabitants openly displayed weapons. The population seemed entirely male. Neither saw a single woman.

Saloons were as common as any establishment, and most of them were packed to the doors, the sound of tinkling pianos and voices raised in song spilling out into the streets. Here they spotted a few women, mostly saloon girls hired to entertain the miners. A few others around town worked as waitresses in the dozens of restaurants, or as laundresses charging as much as two dollars to wash a man's shirt. The whole town catered to the prospectors; gold dust was plentiful and prices were ten times as high as in the East. A sign advertised fresh eggs for a dollar apiece.

Though predominately male, the population was hardly homogenous. News of the gold strike had quickly spread across the Pacific Ocean and eventually spanned the globe. Everywhere they turned they saw men dressed in exotic garb and heard the babble of foreign tongues. They saw Germans, Frenchmen, Scotsmen, Swedes, and Englishmen; Russian trappers in tall, furred boots; Mexicans wearing broad sombreros and serapes; Kanakas from the South Seas; robed Chinese who had crossed the Pacific in crowded ships; South Americans from Chile, Peru, and the Argentine. Everywhere they encountered crowds, shouts, unbridled excitement and expectation.

Many wore plain work clothes but others, less appropriately attired, had arrived in California wearing whatever clothes they had at the time. Vannevar had been concerned about his and Riley's appearance, but he soon discovered that an elegant Virginia aristocrat with a sword buckled to his hip, accompanied by a black man carrying a shotgun, drew little notice in this half-wild place. Regardless, they were filthy from their long, cross-country trip, and Vannevar's boots, still soggy from the battle on the riverbank, were already coated with dust. His clothing, though washed by the river, was stiff and foul from the months he'd spent sealed away in the wooden crate on back of the wagon. Riley also felt the need for a bath and a clean bed. They needed a place to stay.

They trooped north along the edge of the cove until reaching a street called Pacific, near the northern limits of the settlement. If anything, this area seemed rowdier and more lawless than the sections they'd passed through earlier. Saloons lined both sides of the street and men shouted loudly while women screamed and shrieked. A large brown bear chained near the entrance of one of the establishments growled at customers as they went in and out through the front door.

They turned back south, eventually passing Long Wharf, the place where they had docked the boat. They spied a group of men standing near the end of the dock. A physician was attending to Davey, now laid out on a stretcher.

"We'll have to keep an eye on him and make sure he comes out of this all right," Vannevar told Riley as they passed.

"He's a good kid," Riley agreed. He knew Vannevar remembered those who had done him a favor.

A block further south they turned west on a thoroughfare whose handpainted sign proclaimed it "California Street." Like the rest of the city, the dusty street was paved with hastily laid timbers and lighted by oil lamps nailed to building fronts. Only two blocks long, the street ended abruptly at the foot of a steep, nearly barren hill that climbed more than three hundred feet into the night sky. Near the end of the street they found a relatively quiet area where Riley thought he spotted a suitable dwelling.

"How about there?" he asked, pointing out a fair-sized, three-story hotel. Like most of the buildings, it was newly constructed of fresh-sawn redwood indigenous to the area. In a burst of extravagant pride, the owner had slapped a coat of yellow paint on the building, setting it apart from its neighbors.

They crossed the street and stepped inside, Vannevar leading the way. A clerk with thinning hair and pince-nez glasses stood behind the counter.

"We'd like a pair of rooms, please," Vannevar said, speaking with the clerk. "With a bath."

The man behind the desk hesitated a moment.

"Ah...for you and the gentlemen?" he asked. The clerk tipped his head toward Riley, peering knowingly over the top of his glasses at Vannevar. He hoped he did not have to explain to this stranger that Braxton House was a quality hotel, not catering to people of color.

Vannevar felt, rather than saw, Riley tense. He signaled him to remain quiet.

"My associate will pose no problem," Vannevar said, his voice flat but somehow beguiling. He stared straight into the clerk's eyes, his gaze unwavering.

"Of course, sir," the clerk replied, now suddenly placid, subordinate.

"You will check us in immediately," Vannevar added, casting a wink at Riley.

"But of course, sir," the clerk answered obediently. "Braxton House is honored to have you and your friend as its guests."

He spun the register book around for Vannevar to sign, handing him a pen. Vannevar dipped the pen in the inkwell and signed for both of them, then paid the man in Texas gold pieces taken from a large pouch tied to his waist. The clerk squinted at the unfamiliar currency, held it up to the light, then weighed it in his hand. Finally, after biting it to assure himself of its authenticity, he dropped it in the till and turned back to his guests.

"Thank you, sirs," the clerk said. "We hope you have a pleasant stay in San Francisco."

Vannevar smiled back at him, then followed the bellhop upstairs to the rooms.

The next evening, refreshed, relaxed, and outfitted in new clothes, Vannevar sought out the owner of the hotel and within an hour had purchased the place lock, stock, and barrel. His first action as new owner was to fire the sniveling clerk behind the counter.

■

The pair spent the next week familiarizing themselves with the town and gathering what information they could. Vannevar was now dressed in new clothes: soft buckskin trousers, a linen shirt with stiff collar and cravat, topped by a fashionable waistcoat of black velvet. His new black boots were worn under the trousers and he adopted a short cape to ward off the cold nighttime fogs that blew in over the city from the Pacific Ocean during the summer months. Riley wore a collarless work shirt, heavy shoes, and a pair of the stiff blue denim work pants he'd purchased from a local Jewish tailor named Levi Strauss. The tailor had guaranteed Riley the riveted pants would "last a lifetime," a promise that had made Riley smile.

The heart of the small city lay wrapped around Yerba Buena Cove, the best anchorage on the bay, and consisted of no more than a few dozen streets laid out in square-grid fashion. But day by day the city kept growing as new streets were laid out and timbered, and nearly overnight lined by stores, hotels, and saloons. Vannevar, already convinced they would be staying here a while, began planning how best to invest the money they'd brought with them from Texas.

San Francisco was a lawless town, growing so quickly it enjoyed neither a viable government nor anything resembling a police force. Murders and disappearances were commonplace, and, with tens of thousands of hopeful gold miners continually passing through the city, it was nigh impossible to keep track of what went on. Disputes and bloody gunfights were everyday events.

But nowhere was violence more a way of life than on the north side, at the foot of a steep, rocky 250-foot hill. This area, known as Sydneytown, was inhabited by a large contingent of transported Australian criminals who had found their way to San Francisco by legal or illegal means. Pacific Street formed the heart of Sydneytown, a rowdy strip that ran west several blocks from the waterfront.

It was in this area that Vannevar and Riley first discovered evidence of at least one other vampire inhabiting the town. Too many deaths in the area bore the unmistakable signs of vampiric thirst, and Vannevar guessed the unknown vampire was probably behind McNaughton's disappearance. Vannevar and Riley sought more information, maintaining a low profile as they frequented the Pacific Street saloons and dives night after night, buying drinks and talking to local residents.

They had been in San Francisco nearly a week when Riley made their first solid contact. Vannevar was in the Beef and Bear Saloon on the corner of Jackson and Dupont Streets when Riley found him. Vannevar had lately become a frequent visitor to the Beef and Bear, smitten by a dark-eyed Chilean barmaid named Doña. Olive-skinned, with full lips and raven hair, she lived in the Chilean encampment on the hill overlooking Sydneytown, sharing a small house with her aged father, Ferdinand. Vannevar had flirted with many women over the years, but Doña he found particularly attractive. She had been raised a Catholic girl and was shy and chaste, qualities that endeared her to him.

Riley pulled Vannevar away from his conversation with the young woman.

"What have you learned?" Vannevar asked impatiently.

"I think I turned something up at Donovan's Hall over on Pacific Street."

Donovan's was a saloon run by one of the Australians of Sydneytown — a dance joint where the girls entertained customers upstairs as well as on the dance floor. Unlike most of the saloons, Donovan's girls drank real beer rather than colored water; Donovan claimed it made them "livelier." Donovan's Hall was a favorite hangout of the Sydney Ducks, the Australian gang that terrorized and nearly controlled the northern part of town.

"I come across a guy in there named Burt," Riley explained. "One of the Ducks. He's a real loudmouth — with rotten teeth — claiming 'big connections' up around that part of town. He pretends to be human but I think he's probably a ghoul. Anyway, I started talking this jackass up, finally getting around to the point, but he claims he and 'his boss' know nothin' about McNaughton. He says there's some Spaniard living down south of town somewhere, supposed to be behind some of the 'funny deaths.' I don't believe him, but I pretend like I do. Pretty soon he leaves and I follow, not lettin' him know I'm behind him. He went into a boarding house off Broadway. I think it's probably our man's lair."

Vannevar nodded approval. "Show me where," he said.

The boarding house was located on a dirt-paved alley running south off Broadway, a street one block above Pacific and forming the city's current northern boundary. Riley and Vannevar stood out on the street, looking down the alley.

"He's up there, I think," Riley said, pointing to a third-floor window lit by yellow light. "I think it's where his 'boss' lives."

"All right," Vannevar said. "I'll investigate. Meet me in the alley behind the Beef and Bear in an hour."

Riley nodded and slipped away, silently disappearing into the foggy street.

Stepping into the narrow alley, Vannevar stared up at the dimly lit window and saw shadows moving behind the cheap, unstarched curtains. The window was open and his sharp ears detected a pair of voices engaged in conversation. But their words were indistinct. Vannevar turned to the building across the alley. By scaling the wall he could gain a vantage point level with the window but still remain at a safe distance.

Slipping out of his boots and laying his saber on the ground, he took hold of the rough clapboards of the nearby building and crawled quickly and surely up its face. Reaching a height nearly even with the window across the alley, he paused, clinging to the wall like a lizard, craning his neck around to look in the window. His dark cape helped him blend into the shadows, making him difficult to spot.

Vannevar saw a man he assumed was Burt, seated in a battered wooden chair. Even from a distance he could see the man's rotten green teeth. Burt was speaking with someone out of Vannevar's line of sight. The conversation, however, was clear.

"I tell you, Choker, something's goin' on," Burt said to his unseen companion. "This stranger waltzed in last week and bought up the Braxton House on sight," Burt said. "He's got some nigger working for him, too — he was lurking around Donovan's tonight asking all kinds of funny questions. I seen him snoopin' 'round the waterfront earlier this week, too."

"Do you think he's one of the others?" the unseen man named Choker asked. His accent was Australian, his voice a growl.

"He might be. He's throwin' money around the same way as that McNaughton bloke."

The man out of sight stood up and walked across the room. Vannevar caught sight of him through the gap in the curtains. Tall, strong-looking, and rawboned, Choker was a big man, his face marked with the scars of smallpox. He scowled as he talked.

"I ain't worried 'bout him," Choker said. "Delfonso'll find out soon enough, then I suppose he'll go the way of the other."

Burt laughed heartily and Choker joined in. The vampire

walked away from the window and once again out of sight.

Who was Delfonso? Vannevar wondered. Another vampire perhaps?

He stayed a few minutes more, listening as Choker and the ghoul discussed future plans for the Ducks — robberies and extortion rackets they intended; then, deciding not to press his luck, he slipped back down the wall and out of the neighborhood.

Vannevar arrived at their meeting place behind the Beef and Bear a little late and was surprised to find Riley not already here. Taking up a spot in the shadows of a back doorway, he waited patiently for Riley to arrive.

The dead-end alley was dark and deserted, chosen by Vannevar because of its secluded location a good distance from the heart of town. A wispy fog settled over the city, blown in from the ocean to the west, sparkling in the moonlight.

Soon, he heard the sound of a horse clopping slowly along the street beyond the alley, hooves ringing on the wooden timbers. Tuning his ears to the sound, Vannevar listened as the horse stopped, hesitated, then turned down the alley where Vannevar was waiting.

Pulling himself tighter into the doorway, blending into the darkness, Vannevar peered through the misty fog, trying to see the approaching horse and its rider. The animal's black head appeared first, emerging out of the mist like a spectre, bobbing up and down, proud, wearing a finely tooled bridle decorated with silver. The man riding the horse appeared next, dressed all in black, with tight trousers cut wide at the ankle and a short, tailored jacket of the kind favored by the local Mexican *Californios*. Like the horse's tack, the man's clothing was embroidered with silver. On his head he wore a broad, black sombrero of matching design.

He was an older man, perhaps in his middle fifties, with a black, cleanly trimmed mustache and tiny pointed beard. His flesh was pale, nearly luminescent in the dark. On his side hung a heavy rapier with gold wire pommel and finely carved guard.

The man stopped his horse in front of the doorway where Vannevar was hiding.

"Buenos noches, señor," the rider said, looking straight at Vannevar.

His Spanish was pure Castillian, clipped and precise, unlike the Mexican drawl more familiar to Vannevar's ear. Realizing concealment was futile, Vannevar stepped out of the doorway, into the comparative light of the dim alley.

"Good evening," Vannevar said, looking straight up at the stranger.

The two vampires sized each other up; Vannevar immediately sensed the stranger's power.

"Welcome to San Francisco, amigo," the man said, swinging his right leg over the saddle and sliding smoothly off to the ground, his wicked spurs jingling as his heels struck the earth. Looking Vannevar up and down, the shorter Spaniard began circling him, inspecting him carefully as he walked around Vannevar.

"You are Americano, yes?" the man asked, his casual stroll now taking him behind Vannevar's back, out of his range of sight.

"Yes," Vannevar answered, forcing himself to stand steady. "My name's Vannevar Thomas — lately out of Texas." He kept his eyes looking straight ahead, resisting the urge to turn and face the other vampire.

"There was another Americano here," the Spaniard said, now finishing his inspection tour to take up a stance in front of Vannevar. "He is gone now, though, I fear." He smiled wickedly.

Vannevar knew now he was facing McNaughton's killer.

"Where is Riley?" Vannevar asked him, guessing the Spaniard had something to do with his friend's failure to appear at the proper time.

"He is safe, my friend. Do not fear. We take care of our guests well." He winked. "Though I must admit, he put up quite a struggle."

Vannevar, moving carefully so as not to betray himself, sought the hilt of his sword. The Spaniard caught the movement.

"A swordsman, eh?" he said, stepping suddenly back and drawing the sharp rapier from its scabbard with a ringing sound. "You would test me, eh? Please draw your weapon, señor."

Vannevar, realizing he had no choice, drew his saber. Although first among his peers in use of the short, heavy weapon, he'd never actually fought a serious duel with the blade. His was the heavier, slower weapon — the stranger's, a lighter sword designed for thrusting.

The two matched blades, saluting each other, then the Spaniard attacked, unleashing a flurry of thrusts and cuts that drove Vannevar back, barely able to defend himself. The Spaniard, using his lighter weapon to great advantage, forced Vannevar to give ground, mercilessly driving Vannevar back toward the wall of the building behind him. Left without retreat, Vannevar raised his blade only to have it knocked aside by a powerful blow from the Spaniard's rapier that left his wrist numb and throbbing. Then the Spaniard went to point, driving the tip of his blade into Vannevar's chest and forcing him up against the wall. Vannevar knew that if he tried to move, his opponent would impale his heart.

"Concede?" the Spaniard asked.

"Concede," Vannevar answered warily.

The Spaniard dropped the point of his sword, bowed, then introduced himself.

"I am Diego don Delfonso," he said. "I wish to know why you are here, señor."

"I was sent by others," Vannevar told him.

"Others? What others?"

"By the Camarilla, of course," Vannevar said, expecting some sign of recognition from the Spaniard.

Delfonso knit his brow, obviously not understanding. "And what would these 'Camarilla' do if I killed you, like I did the other? I have lived here since 1777 and this place is mine. No one shall come in and take it away from me. I know not whom you represent, but I am afraid, señor Thomas, that you have not proved any more worthy than McNaughton." He winked at Vannevar. It was becoming obvious to Vannevar that Delfonso knew little or nothing about other vampires. Like Vannevar, he had been left to fend for himself soon after being Embraced and had no idea of the powerful forces he intended to stand against. Vannevar saw in Delfonso a fellow outcast. He reasoned with him.

"There will be others. Some are already on their way," Vannevar told him, trying to make him understand.

"Then I shall be forced to kill them as well," Delfonso said haughtily.

"There are too many," Vannevar told him. "And they are too powerful. Eventually, you will fall."

Delfonso looked at Vannevar warily, recognizing the ring of truth in the vampire's words. He had lived here unmolested nearly seventy-five years, but now, with the discovery of gold, Delfonso knew this sleepy stretch of coastline would never be the same. Other vampires would inevitably be drawn here. Already Delfonso had reason to fear the growing power of Choker Barnes.

"You would be well advised to ally yourself with us," Vannevar told him. "There is more than enough to share, and I believe more yet to come."

Delfonso sheathed his sword. "I have lived here a long time," he said. "Since the coming of the missionaries. It has long been mine, but I know that you speak the truth. Tell me," he said. "If I should agree to ally myself with your people, what do I gain?"

"The cooperation and resources of the Camarilla," Vannevar told him. "And as original resident of the territory you may lay claim to the title of prince. I would back your claim, sir."

Noting Delfonso's honorable nature, Vannevar thought he might have the makings of a prince. By backing Delfonso early, Vannevar hoped to gain his confidence, an advantage if the Spaniard successfully claimed the throne.

"I would be prince?" Delfonso asked, intrigued by the thought. He had been born of Spanish nobility but as a third son had no right to inherit his family's property. He had come as a human to the New World, seeking his fortune, hoping to lay claim to a kingdom of his own.

"Yes," Vannevar told him. "Though your rule would not be absolute. You would have to answer to a council of elders. You would not be allowed to take certain actions without their consent and approval."

Delfonso considered the proposition for a few moments, further questioning Vannevar about the details of the arrangement. Soon they struck a deal, agreeing to meet the following night and discuss the proposal in depth. Vannevar was glad to avoid the bloody conflict that would have resulted had Delfonso refused to listen to reason. Though the Spaniard would have assuredly lost any war against the Camarilla, peaceable methods were always preferred. And Vannevar had succeeded in gaining the Spaniard's confidence. If Delfonso was seated on the throne, Vannevar and his family would benefit greatly from the friendship he had gained.

Delfonso then led Vannevar to a nearby warehouse where two swarthy Mexicans stood watch over a bound and gagged Riley. Released, Riley flew into a rage at his kidnapers.

"If either one of you ever touches me again," he promised, throwing off the now loosened coils of rope that held him, "I'll break both your necks. You understand."

Delfonso's two Mexican ghouls cautiously stepped back from the fuming Riley.

"Calm yourself," Vannevar told him. "I want to introduce you to our new friends."

4

1851: The Vigilantes

Vannevar later learned that Delfonso had been born in
Spain and had come to the Americas in 1519 as a
conquistador in the company of Hernan Cortez. The story of
the Spaniard's Embrace, and his early life as a vampire,
Delfonso kept secret; moreover, his true bloodline was
obscure, his clan unknown. Nonetheless, he was a powerful
vampire who, having existed here as long as he had, could
make fair claim to primacy over the vampires lately arrived
in the city. Vannevar supported Delfonso's claim and helped
convince Camarilla representatives arriving later to follow
his lead.

Vannevar's arrival in San Francisco had been fortunately
timed. Delfonso, until then the undisputed master of the
entire area, had been worried about the Sydney Ducks, a
gang of Australian humans and Kindred led by a powerful
and particularly vicious vampire known as Choker Barnes.
Gangsters, thugs, and murderers, they raped and pillaged the
northern parts of the city almost at will. For a time they
had restricted their depredations to the northern
neighborhoods, but now they were foraging farther south.
Alliance with the vampires of the Camarilla was thus to
Delfonso's advantage.

By 1851 the city's population had exploded to nearly

40,000 people. There were more women seen around the city these days, and even a few children. Real estate was at a premium and, in an attempt to create additional salable land, the shallow cove along the waterfront was being steadily filled in with sand, unwanted cargo, and the hulks of abandoned ships. Wharves that once extended as far as a quarter-mile out into the bay were now city streets surrounded by dry land, lined with stores and shops. Any number of sailing ships had been engulfed by the landfill project and, left where they were tied up, now served as stores and restaurants; one even functioned for a short time as the city's jail.

The city's center was still along the waterfront, but streets, shops, and dwellings had spread in all directions and were even beginning to climb some of San Francisco's steepest hills. Numerous fortunes had already been made and the city's most wealthy residents had begun building atop steep Rincon Hill, south of the main thoroughfare of Market Street. The hill, now bristling with mansions, had become San Francisco's most desirable neighborhood and provided its residents with splendid views of the harbor.

Vannevar himself had done well the past two years, investing his funds wisely, buying real estate and occasionally financing special building projects. For a time he had entertained the idea of building his own manse atop Rincon Hill, but his hopes were dashed when the vampire ruling that part of the city, the Brujah primogen Snake Whitcomb, refused to grant him permission. Disappointed, Vannevar had continued to reside at the downtown Braxton House, a few blocks south of Sydneytown. He remained here, in the heart of his domain, sandwiched between the lucrative part of downtown controlled by the Tremere clan south of him, and violent Sydneytown to the north. Aside from the shops, hotels, and office buildings in his domain, he also controlled a substantial portion of the northern waterfront.

And he continued to see Doña, the two growing ever

closer despite frequent objections from her sternly Catholic father, Ferdinand. Doña had long known Vannevar's secret but Ferdinand had never been told. Nevertheless, Vannevar believed the old man entertained suspicions about him. Vannevar had considered Embracing Doña, making her one like him, but had discarded the idea. He did not wish to bring the curse upon her. He had never broached the subject with her.

One night, Vannevar and Doña trysted in a private dining room at the rear of an elegant restaurant on Washington Street. Vannevar owned the place and paid Doña a handsome salary to manage it for him.

It was now after eleven o'clock and Vannevar was walking Doña home, strolling up Dupont Street, an area already becoming known as the Chinese Enclave. "The Celestials" — as the newspapers continued to call the Chinese — had been emigrating to San Francisco in sizable numbers ever since the discovery of gold. While many went prospecting in the gold fields, others had chosen to stay in San Francisco. Chinese laundries washed shirts for only a dollar apiece, driving most of the female laundresses, who charged two dollars apiece, out of business. The laundries were a boon to San Francisco, where the long-time shortage of such facilities had forced Vannevar, like many other men, to ship his dirty linen all the way to Hawaii in order to get it properly cleaned and starched.

Doña still dwelled among the other Chileans inhabiting the slopes of what was now called Telegraph Hill — named for the tall, wooden semaphore station that had been erected on its flat summit to announce the arrival of ships coming into port. She and her father occupied a large house, built for them by Vannevar, near the top of the hill.

"Has your father expressly forbidden you to see me?" Vannevar asked her as they strolled along the raised wooden sidewalks.

"No," she said. "I don't think he would ever do that."

"He enjoys the extra income, no doubt," Vannevar said, somewhat cynically. He saw to it that Doña and her father regularly received extra money.

"It's not that," she protested mildly. "That would make no difference to him. It's simply that he would never presume to tell me what to do."

"Not even if he thought you risked damnation of your soul?" Vannevar asked her with a bitter grin.

"Not even then," she said firmly. "He believes a person must be free to choose."

Vannevar himself agreed with the sentiment, but found it hard to believe that Doña's withered old father could be so liberal regarding his own daughter's welfare. Vannevar wasn't sure he agreed.

"And you?" Vannevar asked. "You don't fear for your soul?"

She gripped his arm a little tighter and laid her head on his shoulder.

"With you," she told him. "I fear nothing."

He dropped her off at her home, leaving her at the door to avoid meeting old Ferdinand, then turned back toward the city. He planned to meet another member of the primogen, a Frenchman named Montelaine, at the Braxton House tonight. Montelaine was the Tremere clan's representative in the city whose domain lay just south of Vannevar's. Together they planned to ride out to Mission Dolores, where a meeting of the primogen council would be held.

Vannevar was behind the Braxton House, in the stables saddling his horse, when Montelaine rode up the gravel drive. The silver-haired Frenchman sat straight in the saddle, cutting a dashing figure in gray coat and matching trousers. A tall felt hat of the same color sat atop his head. He carried a gold-headed walking stick in the same hand he held his horse's reins.

"Ready, *mon ami?*" he asked, watching Vannevar as he tightened the cinch on the big black Morgan he rode.

"All set," Vannevar told him, then swung himself up into the saddle. Together they rode out and turned south on Kearney Street, which was still busy with traffic. Side by side, they talked as they rode along.

"You know the purpose of the meeting tonight?" Montelaine asked, as they headed south.

"Only that the Ducks are to be the main topic of discussion," Vannevar answered.

The Sydney Ducks, led by Choker Barnes, had continued to run riot in the northern part of the city, which was now known as the Barbary Coast. Murders and robberies had increased, the Ducks having lately grown brazen enough to commit their crimes in broad daylight. The week before a shop owner had been beaten and nearly killed by two members of the gang who escaped with no more than six dollars from the till. Worse still were the fires. Six major conflagrations had swept through the town in the past year and a half, all of them believed to have been set by the Ducks, who used the smoke and chaos as cover while they robbed and looted at will. The last of these fires had been the worst, burning down nearly two thousand buildings and killing several dozen people. The citizenry was outraged and the people of San Francisco were demanding action.

Reaching the end of Kearney, the two crossed over broad Market Street, then rode two blocks farther to the dirt road called Mission Street. They would follow this road out of town for nearly a mile before arriving at the adobe Mission Dolores, the city's oldest building and the site of tonight's meeting.

"It must be clear to Delfonso by now that Choker is out of control," Montelaine said. "If we don't put a stop to him, the people of the city will, and that would risk our exposure."

A group of five hundred concerned citizens had recently

formed a Committee of Vigilance and had publicly threatened to treat future malefactors with summary trials and hangings. Both Montelaine and Vannevar feared that such actions might expose Barnes as a vampire, putting the rest of the Kindred at risk. Vannevar and Montelaine had both argued long and hard for eliminating the wild Australian from their midst. But Delfonso was hesitant to decree a Blood Hunt.

"Perhaps it is time we consider a new prince," Montelaine said, looking straight ahead.

It was no great secret that Montelaine coveted the throne, and Vannevar had to admit the Tremere was far better suited for the position than Delfonso. But plotting the overthrow of a ruling prince was a dangerous business. If a plot failed, the repercussions could be disastrous. Such plans were kept grave secrets, the players in such dramas careful never to tip their hands. Besides, there were other would-be princes. Vannevar made no comment regarding Montelaine's suggestion and kept his thoughts to himself. Tonight he planned to make his own special request of Prince Delfonso. He wanted formal permission from the prince to create a childe.

A half-hour later they arrived at the front of the old Mission. Built in 1791, Mission Dolores was constructed of adobe bricks; its walls were nearly four feet thick. Closed down by the Mexican Secularization Act of 1834, it was no longer a church but instead a cantina frequented mostly by the local Mexican *Californios*. Although the Mission was still considered 'out in the country' by most San Franciscans, the growing city was rapidly expanding and Vannevar knew it would not be many years before the Mission was engulfed by new streets and the homes built along them.

But for now the Mission stood alone, pale in the moonlight, a long narrow edifice with peaked, tiled roof and columned facade. It was a humble building, constructed of sun-baked mud by Indians working under the orders of the Franciscan monks. Next to the Mission stood a small cemetery containing the graves of monks and a few Spanish and Mexican officials unfortunate enough to die while posted here.

Two dark-eyed Mexicans — ghouls working for Delfonso — waited near the Mission's front door, watching Vannevar and Montelaine as they dismounted and tied their horses to the rail in front of the building.

"Good evening, Emilio, Rodriguez," Montelaine greeted them, tipping his hat as he stepped through the doorway. Vannevar followed him.

"*Buenos noches*," the two mumbled, touching the brims of their sombreros with their hands and nodding as the pair passed through the front door.

The meeting was to be held, as usual, in a small room on the second floor of the Mission, away from the noise and racket of the customers on the ground floor. The cantina's Mexican clientele lined the bar and sat crowded around small tables. In the corner a man softly played guitar. Montelaine and Vannevar appeared distinctly out of place in this setting, but none of the cantina's customers paid them any attention. Most guessed that the men meeting frequently upstairs were important, but none was foolish enough to ask questions about it.

Upstairs, Vannevar and Montelaine found Delfonso and the city's two other seated primogen already in attendance and waiting for the two late arrivals. Delfonso occupied the head of the short table; Snake Whitcomb slouched in a chair to his left, while the Nosferatu primogen, a Russian named Sergei, sat at his right.

"Good evening, gentlemen," drawled Snake as Vannevar and Montelaine entered. He wore a white suit. His hair was black and slick, his mustache long, curling, and carefully waxed. "We thought you might not make it," he chided them.

A Southerner up out of New Orleans, Whitcomb pretended to an aristocratic heritage, but Vannevar knew the man had once earned his living as a cardsharp working the riverboats. He was an oily figure, as slick as his greased hair. A member of the Brujah clan, he was the most disruptive of the city's primogen and, Vannevar knew, a secret aspirant to Delfonso's throne.

"Come, come, Snake," Delfonso responded with good humor. "We must make time for romance now and then."

Snake knew the prince referred to Vannevar's love life. "Still with the Virgin Doña, Thomas?" he asked snidely.

Vannevar didn't bother to answer, taking a seat on Delfonso's right, next to Sergei and across the table from Snake.

"Good evening, Sergei," Vannevar said to the shadow-shrouded Nosferatu.

The figure leaned forward, into the dim light, revealing a hairless head, swollen beyond normal proportions. The wrinkled flesh stretched over the tumorous skull was a putrid shade of blue. The man was one of the Nosferatu, the cursed clan of vampires, and several centuries old.

"Good evening to you, too," Sergei rumbled good-naturedly, a thick Russian accent coloring his words.

Sergei had come to San Francisco from somewhere in eastern Russia, crossing the Bering Strait and making his way down the Pacific coast on foot. His hideous appearance masked a gentle, thoughtful soul. "Please do not feel you have delayed us. Snake arrived but a moment ago himself," Sergei apologized for the presumptuous Brujah primogen.

Vannevar thanked him for the kindness while Montelaine took the chair across the table, sitting down next to Snake.

"We are all here now," Delfonso said. "What is the first order of business?"

Snake was first to speak. "It is time we moved against Choker Barnes," he said. "There's no reason to put it off any longer."

Montelaine agreed. "He threatens us all. The Committee of Vigilance will move against the Ducks soon. They may discover Barnes' secret. We do not want the people of this city to know we are in their midst."

"Agreed," Delfonso said. "But I fail to see why we must rush to a decision. I believe there is still time. I suggest we move cautiously and carefully."

As always, Delfonso argued against an immediate decision. It was a habit Vannevar had found increasingly exasperating. Though elegant, intelligent, and charismatic, Vannevar was discovering that Delfonso lacked the decisiveness required of a prince. He enjoyed too much the pleasures of unlife and was always ready to put off a decision to another time. Vannevar joined with Whitcomb and Montelaine arguing for Choker's extermination. Even gentle Sergei joined in, pressing the prince to take some kind of action.

Two hours later they were still deadlocked.

"Good God, man," Snake argued. "How long do you intend to let that damned Australian carry on like this?"

"It's not like he hasn't been invited to join us," Montelaine added, for once siding with Snake.

"Gentlemen, gentlemen," Delfonso pleaded. "No more. I have made my decision. There is no need to act hastily. We can wait and see what comes about, then decide what to do. I trust that is all to be said of the matter tonight," he concluded. "We may speak of it more at our next meeting. Now, before we adjourn, is there any other business to discuss?"

This was Vannevar's chance. He would make his request.

"I would ask that I be allowed to take a childe," he told Delfonso. "I have need of another in my service."

Vannevar wanted to make a vampire of his own, an offspring he could trust, a loyal retainer. Not a Blood Bound slave like he had been to Quincy, but an honest and loyal apprentice with a free will. He had a candidate in mind.

"Do you wish to embrace Riley?" Delfonso asked, thinking Vannevar wanted to convert the ghoul to a fully undead being.

"Shit, hell, yes," Snake interjected. "Ain't nothin' we need around here more than some nigger vampire thinkin' he's king-shit. I suppose you want him drinkin' blood from white women, as well?"

Enraged by Snake's comments, Vannevar choked back the urge to confront him, ignoring him instead. "No, it is not Riley," he told Delfonso calmly. Vannevar had long ago offered the opportunity to his ghoul, but Riley had turned him down. He was not anxious to give up his freedom to move about by day. Vannevar continued: "There's an ex-sailor working up on the Barbary Coast right now, a man named Sullivan — a big Irishman. I think he would prove useful to me." Sullivan, without family or connections, had seemed a perfect choice to Vannevar. Unrefined — almost brutal — Sullivan nonetheless showed a streak of loyalty that Vannevar admired. He would be a good man, he felt, if given the proper guidance.

"What makes you think him right?" Delfonso queried. "Is he intelligent, careful, subtle, particularly useful to us in any way?" Delfonso was teasing Vannevar. Familiar with the candidate, the prince knew that Sullivan was none of these things.

Vannevar thought for a moment. "He's very honest and loyal, I believe," he finally said.

Delfonso smiled. "Permission granted." He was happy to grant this simple boon after a long night of wrangling about Choker Barnes and the Ducks. Delfonso enjoyed the opportunity to be magnanimous.

Later, outside the cantina, Vannevar said goodnight to Montelaine. The wizard-vampire was heading south to check on a field of special herbs he had sown on the slopes of the city's central mountains. Sergei had left the meeting by the back door to avoid being seen by any of the patrons still lingering in the taproom. Snake remained upstairs with Delfonso, claiming he had private business to discuss with the prince.

"It's too bad we can't make the prince move on this," Montelaine told Vannevar. "The time may come when we find it necessary to force him to abdicate."

Vannevar agreed, adding that he hoped it would not be necessary.

Montelaine rode away to the south as Vannevar turned and headed back to the city. He was halfway back to Market Street when he saw the first flames erupting on the southern face of Telegraph Hill. The Ducks were attacking the Chilean encampment, he realized, and he spurred his horse to a gallop.

By the time he reached the city his horse was in a lather, but he didn't slow the Morgan, driving him on, through the heart of town, hooves ringing off the wooden streets while pedestrians scattered out of his path. He reined up briefly at the foot of steep Telegraph Hill, then dug the spurs deeper, driving his panting beast up the slope toward Doña's house.

On top the hill Vannevar found madness: houses in flames, Chileans fleeing in panic, and everywhere the Ducks — humans and otherwise — beating and robbing, pillaging and raping. Flames leapt skyward as one home after another was put to the torch, the winds spreading the fires. Vannevar guided his horse through the carnage, ignoring the horrors around him, intent on finding Doña before it was too late. Nearing the flat summit of the hill, he finally saw her.

In the mouth of an alley twenty feet away, two of the Ducks held her down while another raped her. Pock-faced Choker Barnes stood by watching, arms folded across his broad chest, laughing at the sight. Doña, screaming, her clothing half torn away, struggled futilely against the men violating her.

Vannevar reined his horse around and, as it reared and turned, pulled out his saber, shouting: "Choker!"

The men raping Doña turned to look, as did Choker. He leered when he saw Vannevar.

Then someone leapt from out of nowhere and crashed into Vannevar, knocking him out of the saddle. Vannevar landed on the ground on his back, struggling with his assailant, who pressed his elbow into the vampire's throat. Next to the struggling pair, a flaming house suddenly collapsed into its own basement with a roar, sending a shower of sparks into the air.

"Hey mate," the attacker grunted down at Vannevar, his breath reeking and foul. "Come to join the party, have we?" It was Burt, Choker's ghoul, his face turned demonic by the dancing flames of the burning house behind them. Burt opened his mouth wide, revealing rotten green teeth. He hissed.

But Burt was no match for Vannevar, who easily tossed the ghoul off and scrambled to his feet, looking around for his fallen saber.

Someone else hit him from behind — one of the humans who'd been attacking Doña. Vannevar kept his feet and, driving his elbow back with all his strength, smashed several of the man's ribs. The attacker grunted in pain and let go of Vannevar. Spinning around, Vannevar grabbed him by the hair and bent him backward over his knee, cracking the man's spine before dropping him to the street, paralyzed from the waist down.

Then Burt was back on him, grabbing him from behind. A tough, stringy arm wrapped around Vannevar's neck. Vannevar reached up and pulled the arm down, snapping the bone. Breaking loose of Burt's grip, Vannevar turned on the ghoul, wild with rage.

Burt quailed as Vannevar sprang at him, picked him up and lifted him high above his head. Burt struggled vainly, screaming as Vannevar tossed him down into the inferno of the flaming basement. The burning ghoul's howls of agony were soon drowned out by the roar of the flames that consumed him.

Vannevar turned back to rescue Doña only to find Choker had already fled the scene. A large, dark form now hovered over the prostrate Doña, a misshapen man whose features were hidden by the shapeless brown cloak he wore. It was Sergei.

But even as Vannevar hurried forward, Sergei backed away from the fallen woman, motioning to Vannevar to stay away.

Doña's aged father hurried up and knelt beside his injured daughter, followed by the local priest. The priest carried a large crucifix, which he kept carefully trained on the retreating Sergei and Vannevar. The device had no effect on either of the vampires, but they backed off anyway, not wishing to interfere.

Sergei took Vannevar's arm. "I think she will live, my friend," Sergei whispered in his deep, hollow voice. "And she was not bitten."

"Thank you, Sergei," Vannevar told him. He watched helplessly as the old man and the priest got the dazed Doña to her feet, doing the best they could to cover her with the scraps of clothing still left hanging on her bruised and battered body.

Sergei looked around quickly. "I must go," he told Vannevar. "I do not wish to be seen more than necessary."

The priest was now helping Doña back toward her house. Ferdinand followed behind them, now carrying the crucifix. Then the old man stopped, turned and faced Vannevar and Sergei, still standing together near the flaming ruins of the house. Staring at Vannevar, Ferdinand quickly made the sign of the cross, then turned and scurried after the priest and his daughter.

"There's your man," Sergei said before he left, pointing down the street, across the hill. Then he slipped away, disappearing quickly into the shadows.

It was Riley, hurrying toward Vannevar, reloading his revolver as he ran. A white scarf was knotted around his arm, the badge worn by the Vigilantes to identify themselves. "You gotta get out of here," Riley told Vannevar when he reached his side. He snapped the revolver closed, then waved it in the direction of the bottom of the hill. "The Vigilantes are coming. They're after the Ducks, swearing this will be the end of them. They want the city back. We better not get caught here."

Already they could hear the shouts and cries of the angered citizens of San Francisco. Near the foot of the hill they saw men racing through the streets, guns drawn, in pursuit of fleeing Ducks and other gangsters.

Vannevar allowed Riley to lead him off the hill, away from the danger, and away from Doña.

The next evening Vannevar tried to visit Doña but was not allowed in the house. Old Ferdinand rebuffed Vannevar at the front door, accompanied by the physician attending to Doña's injuries. Outside, the doctor explained to Vannevar that Doña was still in shock and only semiconscious. He judged most of her injuries fairly minor, and felt sure she would recover in the next few weeks. But he was concerned about her eyes — Doña was apparently blind. There were no signs of injury, and the doctor judged it a hysterical reaction to all she had suffered.

"I'm confident she'll be all right in a week or two," the kindly doctor told Vannevar, then said goodnight.

Not wishing to force his way into the house, Vannevar decided to go look for Sullivan. Delayed by the Ducks' riot and the subsequent Vigilante raid, Vannevar had been forced to delay the taking of his would-be childe. Tonight he would remedy that.

Vannevar had never created another before — excepting the conversion of Riley to a ghoul — but now the time had come. The city was growing rapidly and he needed a family to help him control the domain he ruled. Delfonso already had a childe, drawn from one of the local *Californio* families, and Snake had at least one offspring of his own, probably more. Montelaine had established a chantry and already a young Italian apprentice was on his way, stowed aboard a ship bound from Europe.

The city was quiet tonight, the streets not so busy as usual. The Vigilantes were patrolling the streets in gangs, and while they did not interfere with those who appeared to be law-abiding citizens, they were quick to bring suspected criminals to justice, making liberal use of clubs, guns, and knives. Vannevar was careful not to draw attention to himself.

He first visited the Barbary Coast, looking for Sullivan among the dives and dance halls. He checked in at Maggie's Poorhouse, where Sullivan was employed as one of Maggie's best crimps. As a crimp, it was Sullivan's job to befriend sailors coming into port, luring them to stay at one of Maggie's boarding houses. Here he supplied them with liquor, drugs, and women, quickly separating them from their seaman's pay and leaving them in debt to him. Once fleeced of their money, he would then sell them to the first ship leaving port in need of a crew, all usually within a day or two of the time they first set foot in port.

Asking around, Vannevar discovered that no one had seen Sullivan since the night before. He left the Coast, heading south, keeping his eyes and ears open for any sign of the lumbering Irishman. Down on Mott Street he checked with some of the low-priced prostitutes operating out of the flimsy 'cribs' lining the narrow, dirty street. Most of them knew Sullivan, but none of the women had seen him tonight. Perplexed, Vannevar turned back north, wandering through the western reaches of the city, still searching for his quarry.

He was on Dupont Street, passing through the exotic Chinese Enclave, when he finally spotted his man. Sullivan, dressed in his usual seaman's cap and peajacket, was standing casually on the other side of the street, leaning against a building, watching the Chinese passing in front of him with an odd, blank stare. He looked pale. As Vannevar watched, Sullivan left his spot on the sidewalk and, turning down a dark alley, walked slowly out of sight. The man's gait was unsteady, Vannevar noted, and he wondered what might be wrong.

Vannevar followed after him, entering the dark alley just as Sullivan reached the end and turned a corner, disappearing from view. Vannevar heard a door slam and guessed that Sullivan had entered a building. He hurried after him, wondering what the man was doing in this part of town. Then a tall shadow stepped out of nowhere, blocking his path.

The man was Chinese, taller than Vannevar and dreadfully thin. His dry skin was stretched tightly over his skull, giving him a cadaverous appearance. He was dressed in long flowing robes of red silk. Vannevar guessed he was probably a ghoul.

"No, no," the tall, thin ghoul told him, gesturing at Vannevar with his clawlike hands. "You go home now." He spoke in stuttering pidgin-English. "You no come here no more. Sulliman with *us* now. You please to go home." He shooed at Vannevar with his hands.

Vannevar could have easily pushed the ghoul out of his way but then another figure appeared out of the darkness — another Chinese, quite young and much smaller than the cadaverous ghoul. Vannevar sized the newcomer up and immediately recognized a vampire. Dressed in black silk trousers and shirt, the short man — hardly more than five feet tall — looked up at Vannevar with a dangerous glint in his eyes. In his hand he held a small hatchet made of silver. He said something to the ghoul in Cantonese, calling him Chi.

Vannevar then realized his intended childe was lost — that he had been taken and embraced by this strange and unknown family of Chinese Kindred. Bowing slightly,

Vannevar backed out of the alley and left Chinatown to its mysterious undead inhabitants.

Though Vannevar accepted the loss of the childe, he was for several days afterward haunted by a dark dream: the lost Sullivan standing near a huge, shadowed figure with glowing red eyes.

Within days the Vigilance Committee had arrested and hanged one of the Ducks, and loudly threatened more of the same. During the short time of the Committee's existence, several more of San Francisco's most notorious criminals were captured and hanged in downtown Portsmouth Square. Others were forced to leave the city, and the few that dared to remain stayed out of sight, fearing for their lives. Choker Barnes left town a few nights later. No evidence of vampirism was discovered and when the Committee finally disbanded a few months later the city was a markedly safer and quieter place.

During this time Vannevar repeatedly visited the ailing Doña at her home. Her aged father grudgingly permitted Vannevar to call, though he always kept a safe distance from the man he now felt sure was some agent of the devil.

Although Doña's injuries healed quickly, her mind did not. The doctor could find no physical cause for her blindness, prescribing nothing but further rest and quiet, hoping she would eventually recover. But Doña remained sightless, her mind unhinged and rambling. For her own safety she was kept locked away in the house on Telegraph Hill.

5

1859: Winds of War

"I see we are all here now. The meeting shall begin."

It was Montelaine speaking. He had called a special meeting of the primogen to discuss the important issues now facing them. Seven powerful vampires sat around the long, polished table set in a plush rear office on the fourth floor of a new downtown office building. Located on the corner of Jackson and Montgomery, the building was only the most recent in a spate of construction financed by Montelaine and his Tremere clan. The Mission Dolores, now surrounded by lower-middle-class neighborhoods of Irish immigrants and recently reconsecrated as a Catholic Church, was no longer used as a meeting place.

"I think we all know why we are here," Montelaine said.

No one assented, but the empty chair at the head of the table — the prince's traditional seat of honor — said it all. Delfonso had not been told of the meeting.

"It's time to get rid of the old man," Snake said, leaning forward in his chair, resting his elbows on the table. A large diamond ring sparkled on his hand. Snake controlled the lucrative southern waterfront, his South of Market domain now surpassing Vannevar's in value and nearly rivaling Montelaine's downtown financial center territory. "We cannot allow him to control the city any longer. We've all seen what happens under his hand."

The city had been through hard times of late. A recession in 1853 — the result of the general playing-out of the gold fields — had nearly led to the city's financial collapse, a crisis further exacerbated when Mayor "Honest Harry" Meiggs — supposedly Delfonso's man — embezzled the City's entire treasury and sailed to South America. In 1856, the assassination of a popular newspaper editor by a corrupt city councilman had led to a Second Committee of Vigilance that, in a zealous efforts to clean up the city, had nearly uncovered the secret vampire society existing in its midst. Over and over Delfonso had shown himself incapable of controlling the city he supposedly ruled.

But despite these setbacks the city had continued to grow, and the current population now numbered over 50,000. The recent discovery of the Comstock Lode in the Sierra Nevada Mountains promised huge amounts of silver and subsequent economic recovery, but the country now stood poised on the brink of civil war and no one was sure which way the state of California would fall. The majority of the citizens professed allegiance to the Union, but a powerful faction supported the Southern states' right to secession. Just a few weeks earlier the Chief Justice of California's Supreme Court — an ardent Southerner — had killed the U.S. Senator from California in a public duel over this very issue. Soon, California would have to take its stand. The Kindred of the cities of San Francisco and Sacramento — the state's capital — were in a position to tilt the balance. With Delfonso or Montelaine on the throne, the city, and ultimately the state, would side with the Union. If Snake Whitcomb took control he would do everything in his power to drive the state to support secession.

"We all know Delfonso is incapable of making the decision," Montelaine said. "We've all seen it again and again. He must be removed."

It was actually worse than that. Delfonso's mind seemed to be slipping; they had all noticed it at one time or another.

Whether it was due to the pressures of responsibility or some inexplicable effect of his unknown bloodline, none could guess. But they now all agreed he would have to go.

Montelaine said nothing about who might replace the prince. All knew that both he and Snake vied for the position, and that only one of them could assume it. The council was split evenly in its support, three for Montelaine and three for Snake Whitcomb, with Sergei abstaining.

"It would seem to me," said the small vampiress seated next to Vannevar, "that he is a reasonable man, and should understand why we would request this thing."

Marie Richaud was the Toreador primogen. Born and raised in Paris, she was a tiny, delicate woman, no more than an inch or two above five feet, even in heels. She was attractive and charming, though her features were a bit too sharp to be judged beautiful. At home in France she had been a stage and costume designer for the Paris Opera. She had arrived in San Francisco in 1851, shortly after the destruction of the Sydney Ducks, and now resided in a large house on Russian Hill on the city's northwest side. She was the gracious hostess of a regular salon that attracted some of the city's best writers, poets, and painters, and the steep hill was already gaining a reputation as the city's official bohemian retreat.

"And what if he says no?" Snake asked. "Then what do we do?"

Marie could only shrug. Delfonso would probably refuse to step down, which would lead to an all-out war among the vampires, a thing none of them wanted. Nonetheless, Marie hesitated to side with Snake on any issue. She was opposed to the Brujah both philosophically and politically, and candidly voiced her support for her fellow countryman, Montelaine, in the unannounced race for Delfonso's throne.

Joachim, the dark-eyed Gangrel sitting near the end of the table on Snake's side, had suggested simple assassination, but the primogen quickly overruled the idea, leaving it only as a last resort. Joachim was a supporter of Snake's politics. Of mixed Canadian blood, he had been discovered by Snake running with the Lupine tribes of Marin County to the north, disguised as one of the werewolves. Snake had invited him into the city, providing him with territory and protection. Joachim now roamed the western reaches of the peninsula, an area of rolling sand dunes, dusty winds, and a few scrub oaks. He had little in the way of political beliefs but could be counted on to support Snake and any motions he put before the council.

The latest member of the council was a member of the lunatic Malkavian clan, a man calling himself "the Commodore." Dressed in a rich blue naval officer's uniform resplendent with gold braid, he posed as an eccentric, roaming the nighttime waterfront, pretending privilege in all things regarding the harbor, the port, and the ships docked there. San Francisco had a habit of embracing such colorful characters, and the Commodore was allowed to continue his charade, coming and going as he pleased with the greatest deference shown to him at all times. All the sailors, captains, and dock workers knew him well, and when he visited their ships on his regular inspection tours, no one thought to challenge his make-believe authority.

The Commodore currently slouched in his chair, eyes intent on his steepled hands, apparently oblivious to the discussion going on. But Vannevar knew well enough that when called upon the Commodore would cast his vote for Snake. Not out of any devotion to Snake's cause, or even out of blind loyalty, but simply to make sure the council remained split and deadlocked. The Commodore had exasperated all of the council members at one time or another — and was proud of it. Vannevar despised him for it. The Commodore claimed he was insane, but Vannevar saw only pointless anarchy and gleeful obstructionism.

Vannevar had changed little in the intervening years — though those who knew him best said he had grown darker and more cynical since the attack on Doña. His domain had grown wealthier and, following the fall of the Ducks, he had annexed the territory once called Sydneytown to his own. He remained consistent in his support of Montelaine for the throne. Approached several times by Snake seeking support, he always turned down the Brujah's offers of territory in exchange for Vannevar's support.

He now stood up and addressed the primogen.

"I think this has gone on long enough," he told the council, still deadlocked in argument. He addressed Snake. "Please tell us of the plan to eliminate Delfonso you've been boasting about. It is obvious that we can reach no decision on this matter. Let us hear what you have to say."

Snake smiled slowly. His moment had come. He stood up.

"As most of you know by now, I have had some contact with the family of Chinese Kindred on Dupont Street. Despite their unwillingness to join our council, they wish to maintain a peaceful, friendly coexistence with us. They know the problem facing us and have offered their aid. They recognize that many of our goals are similar to theirs, despite whatever other differences we maintain."

The mysterious Chinese vampires calling themselves "the Family" had nearly taken over Chinatown, a neighborhood of only a few square blocks but one that contained perhaps ten thousand Chinese, almost all of them male. The few hundred Chinese women living here were, with few exceptions, imported whores.

The Irishman Sullivan was the newest member of their brood and the only non-Asian in the Family. Vannevar had met some of the others: a youthful vampire named Loo, and an elderly ghoul named Chi. There was also a woman, seen only briefly now and then. The one known as the Grandfather was a mysterious figure never seen above ground. The patriarch of the Family, he dwelled in a cellar somewhere below Chinatown, tended to by the others. The primogen had twice extended invitations to the

Grandfather, asking him to attend their meetings, but the offers had been politely declined. Reciprocal invitations had been sent to the primogen, inviting them to visit the Grandfather in his underground lair. As yet, none had dared to take him up on the offer.

The Family had so far posed no problems for the primogen, but as Chinatown continued to expand, so did their influence.

Snake continued. "We have all at one time or another expressed concern over the aims of the Family, but I have been personally assured that they offer us no threat," Snake went on. "And in this situation they can be of definite benefit to us."

Snake had made tentative arrangements with the Family to escort the prince to a private meeting in the Grandfather's chambers. It was a breach of protocol for the prince to call on one of his subjects. By rights, the prince should demand that his subjects pay court to him, but Snake was sure that with the backing of the rest of the primogen, Delfonso could be convinced to make the visit. Snake had lately taken great advantage of the prince's failing faculties to wheedle his way into Delfonso's good graces. Nonetheless, he needed the help of the other primogen to convince him.

There was a long discussion of the matter and much dissent. Vannevar, among others, objected to what seemed a dishonorable action — setting the prince up to be murdered.

"Don't misunderstand me," Snake pleaded. "The prince will not be harmed. The Family have given me their word on this, and if you know anything about their people, you know their word will not be broken. No, my friends, the prince will simply be convinced by them to abdicate. They have their ways, you know."

Vannevar remained skeptical of the Brujah and his plan, but sided with the rest of the council when they unanimously voted to accept Snake's proposal.

The proposed meeting was set for the following night. Snake would contact Delfonso and convince him of the need, then escort him to the Grandfather's lair. The meeting would take place an hour past midnight.

Following the council session Vannevar caught up with Sergei outside, before the Nosferatu managed to slip away.

"Sergei," he said. "Won't you reconsider your position regarding the election of a new prince?" he asked. "The Council is split on the issue. If you side with Montelaine, he will rule. I can't believe you'd sit by and allow Snake to take the throne."

The old vampire sighed, then, sitting down on the edge of a horse trough, looked up into Vannevar's face.

"You must understand, Vannevar. It is my choice to make, and the choice must be *no* choice."

Sergei had explained before why he refused to get involved in this sort of power struggle, but Vannevar remained unconvinced.

"I must stay aloof from these desires," Sergei said. "The pursuit of power is right only for those who desire it, and I do not. By even aligning myself with one or the other I take part in the pursuit, and run the danger of losing sight of my own goals."

Vannevar was unmoved by the argument. How could Sergei not care? He knew very well what kind of person Snake was.

"It is best to let be what will be," Sergei tried to tell him. "I feel assured it will all work out for the best, in the end."

Sergei said goodnight, leaving Vannevar alone and dissatisfied.

■

The following evening Vannevar went to visit Doña on Telegraph Hill. In the years following her attack she had grown steadily worse. At first Vannevar had visited her several times a week, sitting for hours at her bedside, watching as she slept, waiting for the day her sight — and her mind — would finally return. But Doña's condition steadily deteriorated. Not only did she remain blind but as time passed she became more childlike, helpless and demanding, continually cared for by her aging father.

Many nights Vannevar had sat weeping softly beside her, crying tears stained red with blood, but in the last few years his visits became less frequent. Doña's father feared and detested Vannevar, hating him for what he suspected Vannevar was; now, growing senile, he held Vannevar responsible for what had happened to his daughter.

Vannevar still stopped by at least once a week, silently entering the house to spend a few hours by his lost love's bedside before stealing away again. He left money on these visits, more than enough to support the old man and pay for the care of his invalid daughter, but Ferdinand remained aloof. Vannevar often worried what would become of Doña if and when the old man died. Who would care for her?

The house on the hill was dimly lit tonight. The front door was open. Vannevar, not bothering to knock, entered quietly. The old man and the local priest were there and they turned to look at Vannevar when he stepped inside.

No words were exchanged; the priest watched the vampire fearfully as Vannevar went down the hall to Doña's room, while the old man, as always, carefully crossed himself as Vannevar passed.

Doña lay on the bed, her dark hair spread over the pillows like a wreath. Pale and thin, her face drawn and etched with lines, she nonetheless remained beautiful.

Quietly, Vannevar sat down in the chair next to her bed and waited — for what, he didn't know. She rarely woke anymore, sleeping most of the day and night. During her short periods of wakefulness she was incoherent, often raving. The doctor said there was no longer any hope. Still, Vannevar remained faithful to the woman he had loved. The house was silent except for the rhythmic ticking of the clock on the living-room mantel.

At ten, Doña's father went to bed. Vannevar remained until after midnight, then quietly rose from his chair and, leaving five ten-dollar gold pieces on the mantel next to the clock, slipped out of the house.

Vannevar made his way down the fog-shrouded hill and through the roaring Barbary Coast on his way to Chinatown. The Barbary Coast reveled in its reputation as the city's premiere den of iniquity. Its saloons, brothels, and gambling halls were open seven days a week, twenty-four hours a day, and business was never slow.

With the annexation of Choker Barnes' territory, Vannevar had brought under his control much of the northern waterfront and part of the city's downtown, including a string of wharves, several banks, the U.S. Custom House, and many other valuable pieces of property. Vannevar had invested wisely and managed to parley his initial funds into a sizable empire. His name was on none of the papers. All investments had been made through dummy companies, many of them operated by Davey Foster. Davey now served as a front for Vannevar, though the man did not know it. Investment instructions and cash transactions were all handled through Riley, who had remained in contact with Davey throughout the years.

Vannevar met Montelaine on the corner of Kearney Street, at the edge of Chinatown. The district had expanded over the years, spreading up the slope of Nob Hill to Stockton Street and as far north as Broadway. The rowdy denizens of the Coast kept the Asians from spreading any farther east.

Montelaine looked anxious tonight. He seemed quieted than usual.

"Are you ready?" he asked Vannevar, when the latter appeared silently out of the fog.

Vannevar nodded and together they walked toward Chinatown.

The meeting was set for one in the morning. Snake would accompany the prince into the labyrinthine tunnels and cellars below Chinatown, personally guaranteeing the prince's safety. Other members of the primogen were to be allowed in the area, to keep watch, but none other than Snake and Delfonso would actually meet the Grandfather.

There were many rumors about the Grandfather. He was said to be incredibly ancient and very wise. Some said he was a huge and monstrous being, no longer human. The fact was that no one had ever seen the creature — at least, no one still alive.

The pair caught up with Delfonso and Snake on Dupont Street, a mere block from the Grandfather's lair. They were now accompanied by Joachim, the dark-eyed Gangrel, who had joined them to watch and wait. The streets of Chinatown were dark and nearly deserted. Only the secret fan-tan parlors, opium dens, and brothels were open for business this time of night, and these did not advertise.

Delfonso, though outwardly bright and smiling, seemed distracted. It was apparent to Vannevar that he was anxious about tonight's meeting. Once in the secret passages underneath the town, he would be at the mercy of the Family, vulnerable to attack. Only the constant reassurances of Snake kept him convinced this was the best course to take. Snake, for his own part, looked gay and cheerful.

"This will be it tonight, boys," he told the two primogen when he saw them. "If the meeting goes well, all our worries should be over."

Delfonso paid little attention to what was being said, assuming Snake referred to the undefined threat of the Family's presence in town. He did not see the wink Snake gave Vannevar and Montelaine after he'd spoken. Still, the prince was unsure. He spoke to Vannevar directly.

"My son," he said, smiling at Vannevar. "We have always trusted one another, ever since the first night we met. Tell me — you agree with this, don't you? You think it is right thing to do." Despite the influence Snake had gained over the prince, Delfonso had never lost respect for Vannevar, whom he counted his oldest, most trusted friend. "This visit is not beneath my dignity as a prince, is it?"

Vannevar lied and told him it was not, but he stopped short of saying Snake could be trusted. Although Vannevar had agreed to press for this meeting and had been repeatedly assured by Snake the prince would suffer no harm, he couldn't help but feel he was betraying a friend who asked his advice.

"Then I am ready," Delfonso said, turning around to face the alley across the street where his escorts were due to appear. He straightened his short coat, adjusted his tie, then smoothed the tips of his mustache with his fingertips. "Where are they?"

As if on command the escort appeared in the mouth of the alley across the street. It comprised the two Vannevar had met that night in Chinatown in 1851, when he discovered that Sullivan had been lost: the tall, cadaverous ghoul named Chi; and Loo, the small young vampire. Both were dressed in the black silk pajamas worn by the majority of Chinatown's residents. Behind them Vannevar could see other shapes moving about in the dark alley. He prayed he had not helped lead Delfonso into a trap.

The Chinese ghoul and the vampire approached to the center of narrow Dupont Street and stood in wait.

"Let's go," Snake said. Taking Delfonso by the arm, he led the prince down off the wooden sidewalk into the street. The other three primogen remained in the shadows, watching, waiting.

The two groups met in the middle of Dupont. Chi and

Loo bowed respectfully when introduced to the prince. Chi then spoke, his English nearly perfect and without accent, a far cry from the pidgin English he'd spoken the night Vannevar had first encountered him. Chi, Vannevar had learned, was extremely old and said to be remarkably wise and educated. Vannevar noticed that Chi did all the talking while the young vampire stayed respectfully silent.

"Blessed is the son who has a father," Chi said to Delfonso, bowing once more. Then, turning, he led the group back toward the alley across the street.

Near the alley's entrance Loo detached himself from the group and took up a sentinel position by the wall. A shadow in the alley suddenly detached itself from the wall and Vannevar saw someone join Chi, Snake, and Delfonso to fall in step beside them. It was a woman, her features hidden by the darkness.

As the four passed from sight, turning the corner at the back of the alley, Vannevar spied yet another figure standing watch over the proceedings. It was Sullivan, leaning against the wall watching the quartet as it passed.

Delfonso, visibly nervous, walked down the alley and through a doorway that led to a subterranean alcove. Here he passed through a series of narrow tunnels and dark chambers before finally reaching the quarters of the Grandfather. The air here was thick with smoke and incense, and the feeble oil lamps guttering in the fetid air provided little illumination. Beneath the odor of incense lurked another smell — one of rot and decay.

The Grandfather waited for him, a huge bulking creature swathed in silk robes, its face hidden by a black mask carved of wood.

"Welcome to my home," the monstrous creature said. "I...am glad you have chosen...to come this night." Unlike the vampiric Family, the creature breathed, slowly and raspily.

"It is my pleasure," Delfonso said, bowing slightly.

Then, without warning, two of the Family leapt upon the unsuspecting Snake, dragging him to the ground and garroting him with a wire before either he or Delfonso could react. Delfonso tried to flee but found himself unable to move, held fast by magicks.

"Wait..." the Grandfather told Delfonso. "There is something...we wish you to see."

Delfonso watched in horror as the dead Snake Whitcomb was decapitated and his head placed upon a hot brazier in the center of the room. Gestures and chants were performed over the head and the coals blown hotter with a bellows. Then, to Delfonso's horror, the head spoke, screaming in pain and fear while clouds of smoke roiled around it, taking the form of moving shapes, portents of a future to come.

Again Delfonso tried to escape but, still restrained, was forced to listen to the oracle of dead Snake's head as interpreted by the Family, promises of a future time when madness and death would rule, of a night when things would rise from the grave and destroy all the Kindred of the city, leaving the Family to rule.

Delfonso screamed in fear, but worse was to come. The smoldering head of Whitcomb spoke further, of Delfonso's own dark future, of a fate awaiting him identical to the one Snake Whitcomb suffered.

Delfonso passed out, collapsing on the floor.

Vannevar and Montelaine waited hours for Delfonso's return, frequently pulling out their watches to check the time. Joachim squatted on his haunches, occasionally sniffing the air. Across the street Loo also waited patiently, rarely moving, never taking his eyes off the three primogen standing across the street. Vannevar could see an occasional silver glint from the hatchet Loo kept concealed in the loose sleeve of his coat. At the rear of the alley Sullivan paced, then sat, then stood up again and leaned against the wall, seemingly bored and restless.

It was nearing five o'clock in the morning when Delfonso and his escorts emerged from the alley. Vannevar grew worried seeing that there were only three now.

The group reached the end of the alley, and Vannevar felt a wave of relief when he saw that Delfonso was among them. Something had gone wrong with Snake's plan, that much was obvious. But what? All Vannevar knew was that Delfonso was still alive, and that he was not, as he'd feared, responsible for the prince's death. He glanced at Montelaine and saw a look of relief on the Tremere's face as well. Vannevar wondered how much Montelaine knew about this, wondering if the Tremere wizard had secretly made his own deal with the mysterious Family.

Vannevar caught a fleeting glimpse of the woman walking with the group, a view of a porcelain-perfect face set with distinctive green eyes. Then she was gone, slipping back into the alley as Loo stepped forward to help Chi escort Delfonso back to the middle of the street.

The escorts left Delfonso standing there, obviously distraught, turning this way and that, not sure which direction he should go. The three primogen hurried down off the sidewalk, joining him in the street. Vannevar took the old prince by the arm and felt him tremble at the touch.

"What happened down there?" Vannevar asked him. "Where's Snake?"

Delfonso could barely answer. "Snake is no more," he finally said, shaking his head in disbelief.

The Family had honored its promise and had not harmed the prince. Unfortunately, Snake had failed to extract the same promise regarding himself. Vannevar pressed Delfonso for details, but the old vampire could not bring himself to describe what he'd seen.

"I must return home," he said, looking toward the sky.

"The sun rises." It was true. It was nearly dawn; pale gray light was breaking over the line of hills across the bay.

They escorted the shaken prince to the end of the street, where his carriage waited to take him back to the Mission District. Seeing him off, Montelaine and Vannevar hurried away on foot, back to their own havens while the Gangrel Joachim, assuming the form of a large bat, winged his way over the rooftops toward the western headlands and the small cave he called home.

Delfonso never spoke of what had happened, and the other primogen learned little about the actual demise of Snake Whitcomb. But whatever the prince had witnessed that night in the Family's underground chambers left its mark upon his mind. Two days after the event he announced his abdication from the throne, and Montelaine, unopposed, assumed the title of Prince. Soon after, California voted to remain with the Union.

∎

Three days later Vannevar wandered up the slope of Nob Hill, past Chinatown, into a neighborhood of nicer homes near the top of the hill. It was November, and although the temperature varied little year round in San Francisco, it was now the beginning of the rainy season. A drizzle had begun, spattering his cape and soaking his hat until the rain dripped steadily from its brim.

He was heading for Sacramento Street, where Davey Foster, now twenty-seven, lived with his wife and two children. Davey had done well by himself the last ten years. Vannevar had seen to it that he received additional money after recovering from his gunshot wound, and the young man, following Vannevar's own investments, had used it wisely. He now owned parts of several ships sailing in and out of San Francisco, as well as a handful of properties that paid him rent. In 1854, he had married a young woman

named Bess who'd come to California from the East with
her family. They now had two children: a four-year-old boy
and an infant daughter. Riley had told Vannevar that they
seemed happy together and the family was doing fine.

Davey had never met Vannevar and knew nothing about
him. Davey believed he was investing the money for Riley
and his partners, who had found themselves unwelcome
among the city's exclusively white financial circles. Davey
was paid a substantial cut of the profits for his services as
well as receiving tips on how to invest his own capital. The
partnership had proved a good one, and Riley and Davey
had become close friends over the years.

Riley was supposed to visit the family tonight, bringing
with him more cash and investment information, and
Vannevar had thought he would stop by to look in on them.

The Fosters' large, two-story house stood at the corner of
Powell Street, near the top of the hill, and when Vannevar
arrived it was aglow with lights. A fire burned in the
fireplace, driving the damp chill away. He stayed outside,
hidden in the shadows, watching through the window as
Riley and Davey, seated on a print couch, talked and laughed
together. Bess came in, bearing a tray with coffee while four-
year-old Samuel capered about the room.

Vannevar felt envy as he watched the gathering, noting
the warmth between Davey and Bess, and between the
family and Riley. Bess left the room, then reappeared,
carrying the new infant in her arms. She handed the baby
to Riley who, still sitting on the couch, poked and tickled
the child, making faces for its delight. Samuel, meanwhile,
tugged incessantly at Riley's knee, demanding the attention
he felt was rightfully his. Remembering better times with
Doña, Vannevar found the happy scene almost more than
he could bear.

Vannevar had his own family now: a young man named
Swede, chosen and taken by Vannevar not long after he'd
lost Sullivan; and a recent addition to the fold, a young

woman named Margaret. Embraced only a few days ago, she now rested at Vannevar's haven, regaining her strength.

Vannevar heard someone approaching from behind. He turned and saw Swede.

Vannevar's childe was a young man, blond with pale blue eyes. He stood several inches taller than Vannevar, with broad shoulders and a thick, bull-like neck. He'd proved a good man — honest and strong — and much to Vannevar's liking. He had so far served the older vampire well. Stopping in front of Vannevar, he waited for the elder vampire to speak.

"What is it, Swede?" Vannevar asked the man. Swede's face bore a look of concern; Vannevar noticed it immediately. "Is something wrong?"

"Choker's been seen," he told Vannevar.

"Where?" Vannevar asked him.

A rumor had gone around that the Duck had somehow slipped back into San Francisco and was once again on the prowl. He'd long ago sworn revenge against Vannevar, threatening to return someday and reclaim the domain he felt was rightfully his.

"Up on Pacific Street," Swede told him. "He was in Donovan's boasting about how he planned to take care of you."

"Go back home," Vannevar told him. "Stay with Margaret and make sure she's safe."

For some reason Vannevar's new childe had reacted badly to the change. She was still weak and in need of sustenance and protection. Vannevar and his family still dwelled in the Braxton House and he feared that Choker might come there looking for him.

"Here," Swede said before leaving. "I brought you this." He handed Vannevar his old saber.

"Thank you," Vannevar said, buckling it on. Then Swede was off and down the hill, back to the hotel. Vannevar quickly headed down to the Coast, in the direction of

Telegraph Hill and Doña's house. He was sure Choker would show up there.

When he reached Doña's house he was surprised to find it dark and silent, despite the early evening hour. The old man usually did not retire before ten o'clock, and Vannevar was concerned to see no signs of life about the place. He stepped up on the porch and, as was his custom, entered without knocking.

Inside, the smell of warm blood immediately assailed his nostrils; the house reeked of it. The urge to feed rose strong within him, but he suppressed it, forcing it back down.

The house was dark. There was no sound of movement.

"Doña?" he whispered. "Ferdinand?"

No answer, but a rustling sound came from the next room. Vannevar stepped through the doorway.

On the other side of the room something crouched in the shadows beneath the window, its back to Vannevar. It wore a white gown.

"Doña?" Vannevar asked, tentatively, taking another step into the room.

The figure near the window turned, still crouching. Its bloody face glowed a ghastly sheen in the pale light from outside. It straddled a lifeless corpse sprawled across the floor.

"Doña!" Vannevar gasped.

Her face was that of a madwoman, her hair hanging in wet strings clotted with the gore of her victim. She hissed at Vannevar — like an enraged cat — revealing long fangs.

The mangled body on the floor was Doña's father. Old Ferdinand lay dead, the flesh of his throat torn open, his shirt and the bare wood floor beneath him soaked with the man's congealing blood.

It was only then Vannevar realized that Doña could see.

He took a step toward her, extending his hand, but she only hissed again, drawing back fearfully, pressing herself against the wall.

" 'Fraid you're a bit too late, mate," said a voice from behind him.

Vannevar turned to face the intruder, automatically drawing his saber. Choker Barnes stepped through the doorway.

"She's with me now," the Australian grinned at Vannevar. "I'm back and I plan to take what's rightfully mine — starting with her."

Choker caught sight of Vannevar's blade for the first time.

"Whoa, what's that?" he said, betraying his fear, taking a step back. "Now you ain't plannin' to poke me with that pig-sticker, are you?"

Choker wore a huge knife sheathed on his hip, but Vannevar never gave him a chance to draw it. Vannevar's first slash opened a terrible wound across Choker's chest. The vampire screamed in pain and fear, and tried to run, but Vannevar brought the sword down on him from behind, burying it deep in Choker's shoulder. Stumbling, Choker spun and fell to his knees in front of Vannevar, blood spurting from his wounds. Choker tried to look up at his attacker, perhaps to beg Vannevar's mercy, but Vannevar brought the blade down again and Choker's severed head bounced across the floor. The beheaded corpse rolled over on its back, limbs thrashing wildly while the head, rolling to a stop, grimaced and hissed, teeth gnashing its own tongue.

Doña screamed, her eyes darting madly back and forth between the head of her slain master and the dark form of Vannevar now standing before her, bloody blade in hand. Vannevar looked into the eyes of the woman he loved and saw only hopeless madness.

She screamed again when she saw him raise the sword; then he brought the blade down, choking off the scream as he struck her head from her body.

Turning his back on the scene of the carnage, he went outside and calmly set fire to the house, pitching rocks through the neighbors' windows to alert them of the danger before fleeing the hill and losing himself in the darkness.

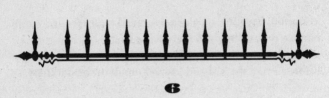

6

1877: Bonanza Kings

"Someday a railroad…"

The words still rang in Vannevar's head, stinging him.

He stood in front of a gilt-framed full-length mirror, squinting at the image before him, trying to put the finishing touches on the knot of his white satin tie. Satisfied it was finally straight, he fastened the cuffs of his white shirt with the oversized pair of diamond links he took from the dresser.

"How do I look?" he asked, turning as he again checked his appearance in the mirror. He was in his bedroom on the third floor of the Pacific Hotel on Clay Street. Vannevar had moved his brood out of the Braxton House several years ago, installing his family in this newer hotel. The rooms here were spacious, the ceilings high. The walls were wainscotted with polished oak, their upper halves covered in dark-green print wallpaper. The gas lights in Vannevar's room were turned up bright, emitting a soft hiss.

"Very dashing," said Margaret, seated on the bed. She wore a long skirt of brown material and a crisply starched white shirtwaist. Unlike Vannevar, she would not be attending the ball at the Crocker Mansion tonight. Margaret was not yet a recognized member of San Francisco's high society.

"I still wish I could go," she complained idly, staring down at the bedcover, picking absently at a loose thread.

Vannevar smiled to himself in the mirror. She was only

nineteen, or so she appeared. He could see her reflection in the mirror, sulking back at him.

"Maybe next time," Vannevar told her. He promised himself he would try to wangle her an invitation for the next affair. She had proved a difficult childe at times and Vannevar knew it was in his own best interest to placate her when he could.

Formal get-togethers were regular affairs these days. Big money had come to the city in the last few years — money from silver and, even more importantly, from the railroad, though precious little of it had found its way into Vannevar's pockets.

Tonight he was attending a fete celebrating the completion of the new Crocker Mansion atop Nob Hill. Completed just a month ago, it was only the latest in a series of opulent palaces constructed by San Francisco's leading citizens — the Bonanza kings and the rail barons.

The Comstock Lode, discovered in 1859, had proved a boon, but unlike the gold rush, during which the lone prospector actually stood a chance of striking it rich, the blue clay containing the precious silver ore required special machinery, financing, and organization. The profits had gone to the few men who managed to obtain control of the mines; the miners themselves worked for pitiful wages.

Most of the money from silver had fallen into the hands of four Irishmen: James Fair, James Flood, John Mackay, and William O'Brien. The other nabobs of the hill were the railroad men, sometimes called the Big Four, or the four tentacles of "The Octopus," as the Central Pacific Railroad was often called. Charles Crocker, Mark Hopkins, Leland Stanford, and Collis Huntington — former Sacramento grocers and shopkeepers — had become rich beyond imagination.

The mansion-building contest had begun in the early 1870s when Bank of California partner William Sharon built the first huge Victorian on Taylor Street near the summit of the hill, overlooking the city from a height of more than three hundred feet. Others, including Crocker, soon followed. Mark Hopkins built the most fabulous place, a seven-story Gothic Revival monstrosity that stood on the corner of California and Mason Streets. The house reportedly cost him more than three million dollars.

The city had grown tremendously during recent years, spreading west over the sand dunes and nearly into the Pacific Ocean, and south to the base of the San Bruno Mountains. The population would soon reach a quarter million. San Francisco was now a major American city and even boasted a U.S. Mint. Construction projects abounded, the most fabulous of which was the massive Palace Hotel. The Palace, occupying an entire block on downtown Market Street, stood seven stories tall. Costing more than five million dollars, when finished it would be the largest hotel in the world. Its creator, William Ralston, founder of the Bank of California, had spared no expense. Among other amenities, the hotel boasted a hundred-place dining set made of solid gold. Factories had been built on the West Coast just to provide the Palace with windows and furniture, offering Ralston and his associates additional fields of investment. As the final touch, Ralston hired away the chef of New York's famed Delmonico restaurant, placing him in command of the Palace's kitchens.

Despite all this, much of the city suffered economic woes. The transcontinental railroad, begun in 1863 and completed in 1869, had promised a new era of prosperity, but when the rail line suddenly stopped short of San Francisco, terminating in Sacramento eighty miles inland, the city was left high and dry. Not only did it suffer from loss of the rail terminus but, with goods now shipped quickly and efficiently cross-country, the city's once vital shipping industry saw its business cut in half. The only ones who survived the financial crisis were those who'd invested in the railroad and drew from the profits of its success. Vannevar, unfortunately, was not among these.

Vannevar had originally invested heavily in the project, but when the dispute over the line's terminus erupted he had withdrawn his investment, believing that if enough of the city's investors pulled out, they could force the rail line to come to San Francisco. The idea had been the plan of a new Brujah primogen, an Irishman named Dugan, and Vannevar and Montelaine in particular had been drawn into it. As it turned out, there had been more than enough outside investors to finance the completion of the project, and the two vampires had ended up being left out in the cold.

A major recession had followed completion of the line and a few years later the collapse of Ralston's Bank of California had spelled further losses for the two. The day after the bank's collapse Ralston drowned while enjoying his daily swim off Meigg's Wharf. The official cause of death was listed as heart failure, though many suspected suicide. Vannevar was one of the few who knew Ralston's death had been the result of supernatural revenge on the part of Prince Montelaine.

Neither Vannevar nor Montelaine was destitute, but they had seen the value of their properties plummet, and both had been forced to liquidate holdings in an effort to gather capital. As Vannevar lost control of property he also lost portions of his domain; other Kindred immediately began encroaching on the borders whenever they felt they could get away with it. Despite formal agreements among the primogen, competition between clans and individual vampires was fierce and any perceived weakness quickly exploited.

Vannevar was dressed and ready to leave when a knock came at the door.

"Come in," Vannevar said.

Riley opened the door and stepped inside.

"Hello, Riley," Vannevar said when he saw his old friend. "What brings you here?"

"Just thought I'd stop in and say hello. I'm on my way up to Davey's house tonight." He noticed Margaret sitting on the bed. "Hi," he smiled at her.

She smiled back. "Hello," she said.

"There's a carriage waiting downstairs," Riley told Vannevar. "That yours?"

"Uh-huh," Vannevar said, slipping into his black cutaway coat with tails. He had told Swede to send the carriage over at ten. "They're early," Vannevar said, pulling out his watch to check the time. Then he changed the subject. "How's Davey doing these days?"

"Not bad," Riley said. "Pretty good, in fact."

Davey Foster's financial situation was stable. For once he had not followed Vannevar's lead and had kept his investment in the railroad. His holding was small, but still was enough to afford his growing family a comfortable lifestyle.

"He became a grandfather last week, you know," Riley reminded Vannevar.

"Of course," Vannevar said, picking up his overcoat and draping it over his arm. "Margaret, you sent the present, didn't you, dear?"

Margaret, now on her feet, turned Vannevar around to face the wall so she could retie the red ribbon that kept his queue in place.

"I certainly did," she said. "It was a beautiful christening outfit, all of white satin." She held Vannevar by the shoulders while she checked him to make sure the ribbon was straight, then released him.

"Thanks," he told her, turning around and giving her a fatherly kiss on the cheek. He checked his watch again. "Time to go," he said. Leaving Margaret alone in the room, Vannevar and Riley headed downstairs.

"Have you found out anything about Kearney?" Vannevar asked Riley once they were away from Margaret and out of earshot.

Dennis Kearney, an out-of-work teamster, had taken advantage of the economic recession to become the city's most persuasive sandlot orator and political agitator. Finding a strong following among the many unemployed Irish of the South of Market and Mission Districts, he had last summer whipped his followers into a frenzy and then led them on a march against Chinatown. Angered by the Chinese willingness to work for wages far lower than the Irish demanded, the mob invaded Chinatown, where they burned and looted stores and mercilessly beat any Chinese unfortunate enough to fall into their hands. Kearney had made use of his political influence to escape arrest and since then had been relatively quiet, but rumors of renewed political unrest were rife.

"He's been keeping close to home down in the Mission," Riley told him. "But you can bet he's up to something."

"You've found nothing connecting him to Dugan?"

Both Vannevar and Prince Montelaine suspected Kearney was being backed and encouraged by Dugan, but there was as yet no hard evidence.

"Nothing," Riley said.

In front of the Pacific Hotel, on Clay Street, Vannevar found his coach waiting for him. Lacquered black and trimmed with gold, it was drawn by a matched pair of black horses. The driver and footman were dressed in scarlet livery. As Vannevar emerged from the hotel, the footman jumped down and opened the carriage door, allowing Vannevar to step inside. Like the driver, the footman was a ghoul.

"I'll see you later," Riley said, heading up Clay Street on foot, toward the next block.

Vannevar waved to him from the window, then ordered the driver off.

Clay Street began at the waterfront. The first few blocks

were level, built upon the landfill that had been dumped in the old cove, but at the foot of Nob Hill the street began climbing steadily, rising for several torturous blocks before finally reaching the summit of the hill.

Vannevar's coach was laboring up the second block, not yet halfway to the top, the two horses straining against their harness, when the Clay St. cable car, bell ringing loudly, passed them on the left. Vannevar glanced over to see Riley, seated on an outside bench, smiling at Vannevar as the cable-drawn vehicle was pulled steadily up the hill, passing the coach and struggling horses effortlessly.

The Clay cable car ran all the way from the waterfront up and over Nob Hill, eventually ending at broad Van Ness Avenue, the city's early western limit. The first vehicle of its type, the cable car had quickly proved a success and shortly thereafter a second, similar line had been installed on Sutter Street, a few blocks south. Currently, Leland Stanford was building a California Street line that would run right past the front door of his house. Other lines were in the works as well, steadily replacing the horse-drawn omnibuses on not only the steep hills but on level thoroughfares like Market Street as well.

Continuing to ascend the hill, Vannevar's coach passed through ever-growing Chinatown, which now, spreading south and north, was nearly the size of Vannevar's own territory. The population of Chinatown had swelled dramatically the last few years as Chinese rail gangs, put out of work by the completion of the transcontinental rail line, had returned to San Francisco and taken up residence. The sudden growth of Chinatown and the resulting enhancement of the Grandfather's power had given Prince Montelaine and the rest of the primogen cause for concern. The aims and goals of the Grandfather were, as ever, mysterious and unknown. The Family was a dark shadow perching on the lower slopes of the hill, overlooking both Vannevar's and Montelaine's downtown territories.

The driver turned left, cutting across the side of the hill for several blocks, letting the horses catch their breath before turning right on California Street to make the final two-block climb to the top.

It was autumn and the summer fogs were in retreat. The sky was unusually clear and a bright collage of stars looked down on Vannevar as he alighted from his carriage in front of Crocker's massive Italianate mansion. The windows of the huge house glowed brightly, lit by gas jets. Charles Crocker was one of the richest men on the West Coast and had no qualms about advertising his wealth.

The affair was already well underway when Vannevar arrived. He found the spacious first-floor ballroom packed with guests, a sea of black velvet and white satin, bare shoulders and sparkling jewelry. A small string orchestra played at the back of the room, filling the air with music, keeping the dancers on their feet. A soft, golden light poured down from thousands of candles burning in the imported crystal chandeliers hanging overhead. San Francisco's finest and wealthiest were all in attendance. Others had come from as far away as the silver mines of Nevada and the redwood timberlands of Oregon.

Somewhere someone dropped a glass, shattering it on the floor. A drunken woman's shrieking laughter and a man's crude cursing reminded Vannevar that, despite appearances, San Francisco's high society was no more than a gang of newly rich ex-grocers, teamsters, and miners with the luck and perseverance to have hit it big.

Surveying the room, Vannevar spotted most of the Nob Hill crowd: financiers, bankers — and many Kindred as well. Delfonso stood on the far side of the room, looking elegant and continental in his jet-black tails. These days the ex-prince posed as a Spanish count, living in a huge suite atop the Palace Hotel. Tonight, as usual, he was in the company of the vivacious Emma Flood, the beautiful brunette niece of one of the Bonanza kings. Since stepping down from the throne he seemed to have recovered from the shock he'd suffered years ago in Chinatown, but there were questions regarding his behavior. Rumors of bizarre, clandestine doings in the chambers beneath Mission Dolores circulated among the Kindred.

Delfonso spent a lot of time these days with Marie Richaud and her ever-expanding clique of Toreador vampires and other artists. Marie was also here tonight, standing on the far side of the room in the company of a foppish young man with long dark hair, a talented oil painter whom Marie was currently promoting among the city's well-heeled and influential citizens.

And there were other Kindred as well, lesser members of the city's undead citizenry. Vannevar spotted Cyrano, Montelaine's Italian Tremere, his thin black hair combed carefully forward to cover his bald spot. Vannevar thought him a shifty sort, but Montelaine seemed to have confidence in him.

At first Vannevar could not find Montelaine, then saw him standing alone near the fireplace across the room. The Tremere prince wore a frown, as he often did these days. The pressures of the throne had proved a strain and the added woes of financial instability had only made his situation more difficult.

Vannevar was about to join him when someone took hold of his arm.

"I was wondering when you'd get here," a woman said, now grasping Vannevar's upper arm with both hands. "I'd thought you'd abandoned me."

The woman's hair was honey-blond, curled and decorated with freshly cut violets. Her gown, made for the occasion, was white satin, cut low over her breasts. She had deep blue eyes that seemed to sparkle whenever she talked or laughed. Her name was Claire, and she was the daughter of one of Stanford's co-investors, a former tanner from Nevada.

Vannevar and Claire had been flirting the past six months
and Vannevar felt quite close to her. She was bright and
cheerful, fun to be with, though Vannevar knew he felt no
real love for her. He had not loved since Doña.

"Come on," she said, tugging at his arm. "There's someone
here I want you to meet."

Vannevar found himself being dragged across the room,
away from Montelaine. The next hour he spent engaged in
conversation with a Sacramento banker and his wife,
extolling the virtues of the city while at the same time
gathering valuable information about current business
dealings in the state's capital.

He was curious about the controlling interests in
Sacramento. The city itself was firmly in the hands of the
Tremere clan, many of whom, Vannevar guessed, exercised
control over members of the California legislature. In recent
years too many votes had gone against San Francisco's
interests, more often than not resulting in some boon to
Sacramento. The decision to end the transcontinental line
eighty miles short of the coast had been the first overt move
against the city by the Sacramento group, but it had not
been the last. Since that time, Vannevar and Montelaine
had found their plans thwarted at nearly every turn.

Eventually Claire and the banker's wife left for the powder
room and Vannevar, having learned from the banker all he
thought likely, excused himself and wandered off to leave
the banker standing alone at the bar.

Vannevar saw Dugan standing near the edge of the dance
floor, surrounded by a group of admiring ladies. The Brujah
primogen had arrived but a few minutes ago but already he
was smiling and charming his way into the ladies' hearts.

Dugan had come to the city a few years ago, replacing the
dead Snake Whitcomb as the Brujah clan elder and
primogen. Red-haired, pug-nosed and pugnacious, he'd
fought against English rule in his Irish homeland before
emigrating to America. Vannevar found little to like about

Dugan, and was unsure of the man's motives. Montelaine was convinced Dugan had intentionally led him and Vannevar into the railroad fiasco, and consequently despised him. If he could obtain sufficient evidence, Montelaine had promised Vannevar, he would see to it that Dugan never bothered either one of them again.

Montelaine suddenly appeared at Vannevar's side. "We need to talk," he said. Montelaine held a glass of whiskey in his hand. He occasionally sipped at the glass but didn't actually drink, the level of the liquor remaining always the same.

Vannevar said nothing, merely cocking his ear.

"I've got hard information tying Dugan to Kearney," Montelaine whispered. "The two are definitely working together."

Vannevar asked Montelaine what evidence he'd obtained, but the Frenchman was elusive. Since becoming prince, the crafty Tremere had become increasingly close-mouthed with Vannevar, rarely willing to share all he knew with his long-time friend and supporter. Vannevar had followed Montelaine willingly all these years, but more and more had reason to doubt the wisdom of some of the prince's decisions. Lately Vannevar found himself more often than not disagreeing with Montelaine and the decisions he made. Still, Vannevar felt compelled to be loyal to his prince.

Vannevar was about to ask Montelaine what he intended to do about Dugan when Claire suddenly reappeared, once more gluing herself to Vannevar's arm.

"I'll talk to you about it later," Montelaine said, bowing to Claire, then moving away.

"Come on," Claire said, once again dragging Vannevar off. "My uncle wants to talk to you."

Claire's uncle was Leland Stanford, an able man and a wizard of finance and business. Vannevar had lately been doing his best to ingratiate himself with Stanford, hoping to learn something of the multimillionaire's future investment plans. Vannevar had even entertained the idea of bringing Stanford directly under his control, but discarded it when he realized the repercussions such a move might cause among the city's ruling Kindred. But, as Montelaine had suggested, none could fault him for simply cultivating a friend. Stanford, sensing something odd about the pale stranger courting his niece, remained cagey with Vannevar, but it was obvious he bore a certain respect for the dark, somewhat grim man who was Claire's current flame.

"Good evening, Vannevar," Stanford smiled at him when the couple joined them.

"It's a lovely party," Vannevar told Stanford. "Crocker's outdone himself this time."

Stanford agreed then, changing the subject, asked: "Have you given any more thought to the position I offered you?"

Stanford, recognizing Vannevar's talent for investment, had offered him an important post in one of him many enterprises.

"Yes," Vannevar smiled. "But I'm afraid I'll have to turn you down. My own businesses require my full attention right now — though I must say I found your offer most generous."

The remainder of the conversation with the Stanfords was light and chatty, Mrs. Stanford talking endlessly of the remodeling plans she had for the couple's plush mansion two blocks down California Street near Powell. Vannevar was listening to her describe a new shipment of recently arrived Oriental rugs when he felt a tug at his pant leg. He looked down and his gaze met the bright, smiling face of a boy around eight years of age, dressed in a suit of wine-colored velvet. It was Leland Jr., the Stanfords' only child and the apple of their eye, born to them after more than twenty years of marriage.

"Why, it's little Leland," Vannevar smiled, bending over to pat the boy on top of the head. He was very fond of the child. "What are you doing up so late tonight?"

"My dad let me," Leland Jr. piped up. "I want to stay up all night."

"Oh you do, do you?" Vannevar asked him, jokingly.

"Uh-huh," the boy answered. "Just like you, Uncle Vannevar."

They all laughed. Vannevar's penchant for working through the night while sleeping during the day was well known among the group — though only Claire knew the real reason for this odd habit.

A few minutes later the couple slipped away from the Stanfords. Claire led Vannevar out of the ballroom and up the great curving staircase to the second floor above.

In her bedroom Claire sat on the side of the canopied bed while Vannevar, boots off, knelt behind her, gently massaging her bare shoulders. A pale-white moonlight spilled through the curtained window behind them.

She placed her hands on his, holding them tightly. Her eyes were bright, but she didn't turn to look at him. "My father wants to know if your intentions regarding me are honorable," she said, coquettishly.

"Never," Vannevar said, reaching around her, bending over to sink his fangs into her smooth throat. Claire sighed as they lay back together on the bed.

An hour later they were still lying next to one another in the dark when they heard shouts from the street outside and the sound of breaking glass. Vannevar slid off the bed and was heading for the window when a rock flew through the glass, scattering shards across the rug.

"What is it?" Claire gasped, sitting up in bed. She had been dozing.

"There's a crowd outside," Vannevar said, standing beside the window looking out on the streets. "It looks like Kearney."

A mob numbering in the hundreds was gathered around the Crocker Mansion, nearly surrounding it. Some carried torches; others hoisted rakes and tools in the air, brandishing them like weapons.

"Come out, Crocker! You can't hide in there forever!" a man shouted at the house.

Vannevar saw Dennis Kearney standing in front of the crowd. Kearney shook his fist at the house and shouted again: "Come on out, you lily-livered bastard! And bring some of your millions with you to help us feed our children."

The crowd growled ominously. Another rock was thrown and somewhere another window broke.

"Come on," Vannevar said, slipping on his boots. "We'd better get downstairs."

They hurried down to the ballroom and found the crowd hushed, the orchestra silenced. Men looked out the tall windows while most of the women huddled in the center of the floor. Vannevar and Claire joined Montelaine near one of the large windows. The prince still carried his glass of whiskey, still untouched.

"It's Kearney," Vannevar said.

"I know," answered Montelaine.

"What's he trying to pull this time?"

"I couldn't guess," Montelaine commented soberly. "But look over there."

He pointed to the other end of the room where Dugan stood near a window, excitedly watching the frenzied mob outside. He seemed to be enjoying every minute of it.

"What did I tell you?" Montelaine said.

Vannevar watched Dugan another moment, then nodded his agreement.

Despite fears that the mob would storm the residence, the scene remained largely quiescent. The crowd milled about outside, unsure of what to do next, then the police arrived and began dispersing the protesters, convincing the men to go back home. Fearful of touching off a riot, they made no arrests. Even Dennis Kearney, responsible for open death threats made against Crocker during the course of the siege, was allowed to leave unmolested.

The party then started to break up, guests leaving as soon as they felt sure the streets were safe and the hilltop cleared of rowdies. Vannevar was on the front porch, saying goodnight to Claire, when Montelaine passed him on his way out of the house.

"I'll get in touch with you in a few days," Montelaine said as he passed them. Vannevar indicated he understood.

Vannevar arrived back at the Pacific Hotel a half-hour later, tired from the night's events, worried about Dugan and Kearney, and concerned about Montelaine's plans. He did not expect to find more problems waiting for him at home.

Riley was lying sprawled on his back on Vannevar's bed while Swede and Margaret tended his wounds. A deep, bloody gash marred his forehead, and several scrapes covered his face. His arm was broken and his hand smashed, the fingers swollen almost beyond recognition.

"What happened?" Vannevar asked, hurrying to the bed, gently moving Swede out of the way to get to Riley's side.

"I got caught up in some trouble with Kearney's boys," Riley said, wincing as Margaret dabbed at his forehead. "Some of them caught sight of me at Davey's house. I was in the backyard with Bess looking at the vegetable garden when they saw us. I guess they got the wrong idea."

"How bad are you hurt?" Vannevar asked him.

"Nothing that won't heal," Riley said.

Though Riley was not nearly so strong or resilient as a vampire, his ghoulish constitution would quickly mend whatever injuries he'd suffered tonight. Besides, Riley was buoyed by the knowledge that he'd dealt out far worse than he'd received. More than one sandlotter would think twice before challenging Riley again.

"I'm more worried about Davey and Bess," Riley told him.

"I heard some of Kearney's men making threats about coming back to burn the place."

"They wouldn't dare," Vannevar said.

"Normally, I'd agree with you," Riley told him. "But they're whipped up something wild over this. I wouldn't want to guarantee it."

Vannevar nodded he understood. If Dugan was behind Kearney and the mob, pushing them, there was no telling what they might do.

Riley spent the rest of the night at the Pacific, receiving regular doses of sustenance from Vannevar's own veins, and rapidly regained his strength. By morning he was feeling strong enough to get around by himself and left the hotel just as the sun was rising, returning to his own lair a few blocks away.

Vannevar retired for the day.

■

The next night, Vannevar, Swede, and Margaret took turns guarding Davey Foster's house. Vannevar took the last watch, showing up around two in the morning to relieve Swede. It had been quiet, Swede told him. No signs of trouble.

Vannevar stood in the shadows across the street, motionless, nearly invisible, watching over the darkened house and its sleeping inhabitants when he sensed someone approaching.

"Sergei?" he whispered, turning to face the bulky figure shambling up the street behind him. As ever, Sergei was as silent as a shadow.

"Good evening, my friend," Sergei said, reaching Vannevar's side. "I have come to say goodbye."

"Goodbye?"

"I am leaving tonight, but I wanted to make sure I saw you one last time."

"Where are you going?" Vannevar wanted to know. Sergei had mentioned nothing of this to him the last time they'd spoken.

"Away," Sergei smiled. "I don't know exactly where." The vampire's face, hideous as it was, seemed to glow with an inner radiance.

Vannevar noticed Sergei's emaciation. He had been fasting and had not tasted human blood in over a year. Sergei sought Golconda, a reputed state of bliss discovered by only a few of the Kindred in the all the millennia the race had existed. Many held Golconda to be a myth.

"Why must you go?"

"I have learned all I can learn here," was the only explanation Sergei would give. Then he asked: "I have heard the prince intends to reprimand Dugan for involving himself with the Kearney mob. Is this true?"

Vannevar told him he believed it to be so.

"Is it the right thing?" Sergei asked.

Vannevar explained about the supposed link between Dugan and Kearney. Sergei already knew of Dugan's involvement in the rail-investment disaster.

"You should be careful," Sergei advised.

"I am," Vannevar told him. "That is why we are watching this house tonight."

"More than that," Sergei said. "Be careful how you follow Montelaine. He is a good man but prone to hasty decisions. Following Montelaine, you risk becoming entangled in the Tremere clan's internal power struggles."

The Tremere clan, though bound tightly by oaths and pledges, and presenting the most united front of any of the clans, was infamous for its internal political struggles. Backstabbing and dirty tricks were the order of the day. Even assassination was an accepted practice.

Vannevar assured Sergei he knew what he was doing; then, realizing he had snubbed the advice of an old friend, apologized and promised him he would be careful.

"It is my wish that you should prosper," Sergei told him before taking his final leave. "May you gain everything you want, and want everything you gain."

And then he was gone.

Vannevar waited, watching over the house until nearly dawn before hurrying away back down the hill to his haven in the Pacific Hotel. There he found a message from Montelaine telling Vannevar to meet him the next night at an abandoned warehouse south of Market Street.

■

The following night Vannevar arrived at the South Side waterfront warehouse at the time indicated by Montelaine. As requested, he came on foot to avoid his well-known coach being spotted in the area. Formerly Brujah territory, the South of Market area had been taken over by Montelaine shortly after the death of Snake Whitcomb. Montelaine had evicted the Brujah residing here, forcing them to relocate in the primarily residential neighborhoods of the city's newly developed Western Addition. The South of Market area had once been lucrative, filled with warehouses and other shipping interests, but with the recession it had fallen on hard times. Most of the warehouses now stood empty, the streets dark and deserted. It was easy to see why Montelaine had chosen this section of town for tonight's deed.

Vannevar knocked at the rusted steel door. It opened with a squeak, revealing the face of Cyrano, Montelaine's second-in-command.

"Come in," Cyrano said, looking worried. Evidently tonight's event disturbed Cyrano as much as it did Vannevar.

He followed Cyrano down the hall and into a dirty, empty storage area. Here Montelaine stood facing his prisoner, Dugan, who was chained sturdily to an iron column. The

Brujah was stripped to the waist, his head hanging down on his chest. Montelaine had his coat off and his sleeves rolled up.

"Good evening, Vannevar," Montelaine said softly, when he saw his friend. "Thank you for coming tonight."

Vannevar smiled a tight smile, looking back again to the prisoner.

"Has he confessed to anything?" Vannevar asked.

"No," Montelaine admitted. "He maintains that he's had nothing to do with Kearney — but I know better." His face was taut. Montelaine was not enjoying this anymore than Vannevar or Cyrano.

Vannevar walked over to the prisoner, took him by the hair and lifted up his face so he could see it.

"What do you have to say for yourself, Dugan?" Vannevar asked him. "Tell us the truth. Tell us what you know — about Kearney, about the Sacramento group. Everything. We have no reason to make you suffer. We only want the truth."

The tortured vampire looked up at his tormentor, his blurry eyes searching Vannevar's face a moment before finally recognizing him. "Vannevar!" he said, desperately, his voice harsh and broken. "I didn't have anything to do with it, honestly. I know the railroad thing was my fault. I shouldn't have promoted the idea. I took some bad advice, that's all. I'm sorry — you know that. I lost out too, you know. But Kearney's not mine. I don't even know him."

"You seemed to be enjoying it enough last night," Vannevar told him. He was thinking about what had happened to Riley, and the threats against the Foster house. His anger burned. "Come on. Tell us the truth." He shook Dugan's head.

Dugan only moaned. Vannevar let go of the Brujah, letting his head fall back on his chest. Vannevar turned to Montelaine and shrugged. There seemed nothing he could do to make Dugan talk.

Montelaine said nothing for a moment, simply staring at

the prisoner, wringing his hands.

"That's it," he finally said, as though making up his mind. "We must kill him."

Vannevar was shocked. He pulled Montelaine aside, whispering out of range of Dugan's hearing.

"Are you sure," he asked the Frenchman. "I'm not even convinced he did it," Vannevar told him.

"I'm convinced," Montelaine said firmly. "And there are other things, too," he added. "Things I haven't told you about, Vannevar. There has long been a lurking threat to my throne and I'm sure the Brujah clan is behind it."

Vannevar glanced back at their captive hanging in his chains, then back to Montelaine. "There will be repercussions," Vannevar warned him. "Dugan's demise will not go unnoticed."

"Undoubtedly you are right," Montelaine agreed. "But we must be prepared to withstand them. Our very future is at stake."

Montelaine, standing before the prisoner, took a stick of smoldering incense from his assistant's hands. Then, describing a series of circles in the air with the smoking brand, he began mumbling the words of enchantment he intended to cast on his victim, his eyes focusing hard on the slumping Dugan. As Montelaine increased the tempo of the chant, Dugan's body began to pulse and twitch in response. Dugan awoke, lifting his head to look upon his captors. He opened his mouth, trying to speak, but no words came out, only a sickening, wet sound. He groaned in pain.

His eyes were now distended, his mouth open and tongue fluttering. His chest throbbed in time with Montelaine's chant, swelling and shrinking rhythmically as the Brujah's heart began beating madly out of control. Dugan groaned again and there was a rending sound as his chest broke open and his madly pulsating heart slithered out and fell on the dirty concrete floor in a torrent of dark, steaming blood. Dugan collapsed, dead.

Montelaine, nearly exhausted, sat down, wiping his brow on his shirtsleeve; the episode had left him badly shaken. Vannevar said goodnight to Montelaine and left while Cyrano went about the tasks of cleaning up the warehouse and disposing of the evidence.

All the way home Vannevar was remembering the last advice given him by Sergei on the night he departed the city. Vannevar could not shake the feeling they'd made a grave mistake killing Dugan. Vannevar had no love for the Brujah, considering him a fractious troublemaker, but he'd not enjoyed watching the man suffer. He would continue to stand by Montelaine, but feared they may have overstepped their bounds.

■

The next night Vannevar and Montelaine invaded the Brujah clan's Western Addition domain, leading their followers in a series of swift raids that quickly quelled any revolt that may have been brewing. Dugan's two known childer both swore allegiance to the prince, formally accepting the execution of their elder. As suspected, they discovered other Brujah vampires in the area, illegitimate offspring of Dugan unknown to and unapproved by the prince. As a lessons to future malefactors, these Kindred were destroyed.

Once the territory was pacified, Vannevar and Montelaine split it between them, bringing its income and hunting grounds into their own domains. The Brujah clan members dwelling there would be allowed to hunt as before, but would be ultimately responsible to their two new lords, Vannevar and Montelaine. Vannevar took the southern half of the territory and assigned Riley to watch over it for him, fixing him up with a haven in the Fillmore District near City Hall. Montelaine's northern portion was given to Cyrano to administer.

With the Western Addition secured, Vannevar went looking for Kearney, seeking revenge. But his efforts were of no avail. Kearney, somehow learning of the convulsions taking place among the city's secret society, had taken the opportunity to leave San Francisco. For a time he toured the country as a labor agitator and paid speaker, but later settled down in Sacramento.

Dugan was replaced on the council by the current leading member of the Brujah clan, a dusky prostitute from the Fillmore area named Sarah. A tall, lean woman, with a taste for brightly colored, flashy clothes, she seemed satisfied with the promotion.

Several months later everything seem settled and quiet. The city's undead power-brokers felt sure that the situation had stabilized. Then the stranger came to town. No one knew of his coming or his presence until they were paid a visit. Montelaine was first on the stranger's list; Vannevar's visit came the following night.

The sun was down and Vannevar was awake. As always, after rising he went to the window and drew the curtains, checking the street below. When he turned back around he was startled to find the stranger in his room, sitting in his chair.

"Who are you?" Vannevar demanded, blood rising in response to the sudden, unexpected intrusion. His voice hissed with menace.

The stranger was a vision from the Orient, dressed in loose-fitting red silk pants and yellow shirt. A black sash was tied around his waist, and from it hung a deadly-looking scimitar. The man's ears were pierced, hung with loops of gold, while two smaller rings pierced his left nostril. His long, untrimmed curling hair was glossy black, his skin darkly olive. His dark eyes pierced Vannevar with a cool and steady gaze. He saw the angry look in Vannevar's eyes.

"Do not think of it," the stranger said, his voice unearthly, deep and hollow, as if echoing up from an abyss. His accent was guttural, foreign to Vannevar's ear.

Vannevar thought of his saber, hidden behind the mahogany bureau next to him. The strange man somehow read his thoughts.

"Do not even try it." The man now stood up, slowly. "You are a source of displeasure," he told Vannevar coldly, his voice like ice. "You have offended."

It was Karsh, Vannevar realized, finally recognizing the powerful vampire. His heart sank at the realization. A Turk, Karsh was the European Camarilla's deadliest agent. From what Vannevar had been told, Karsh was capable of destroying a vampire of Vannevar's stature with little more than a glance.

"I have journeyed long and far to avenge the wrongs done here — in this part of the world," Karsh told him. His eyes narrowed as he stared at Vannevar.

Vannevar was sure he was about to die. Dugan had been a favorite of an Irish Brujah close to the highest Camarilla powers in Europe. His execution had been a matter of grave offense in some quarters and retribution was demanded. Vannevar thought briefly of begging for his life, but knew it would have been useless. He couldn't have done it anyway; he would rather die on his feet.

"Montelaine has already been attended to," Karsh said, his teeth glinting wickedly in the darkness. "I have come here to deliver a warning."

Karsh told Vannevar that Montelaine had been paralyzed by a stake through the heart and, sealed in a coffin, was already aboard a ship due to sail for Europe, where he would have to face the ruling powers of the Camarilla. Vannevar, however, would be let off easier. The facts behind Dugan's murder were known, and Vannevar was not being held fully responsible for what had happened. Apparently, influential voices in Texas had campaigned on his behalf. But Karsh warned him he would be watched closely from now on.

Vannevar bowed respectfully to the powerful vampire, asking him to convey his deepest thanks to the Camarilla elders for their consideration and forgiveness. Then the scowling Karsh disappeared in a twinkling of tiny lights, leaving Vannevar standing alone in the room.

However, Vannevar did not escape punishment completely. Cyrano quickly assumed the throne and, once in power, began exercising it with a vengeance. His first move was to return the Western Addition to the Brujah clan, putting it back in the hands of the new primogen, Sarah. He then stripped Vannevar of much of his old territory, offering some to the Family as a gift but keeping the lion's share for himself. By the time Cyrano was through with him, Vannevar found himself left with little more than the old Barbary Coast and the few low-rent blocks immediately to the south. Cyrano had taken all his most valuable property: banks, government offices, and the ever-important wharves and shipping industry they serviced.

In the following months Vannevar discovered that the oily Cyrano had been behind Montelaine's downfall from the very beginning. Allied with the Sacramento Tremere, he had fed Dugan the false information about the rail financing and, through intermediaries, had been the influencing hand behind Dennis Kearney and his mob. Dugan, though destroyed, was exonerated, and Cyrano expressed great sympathy among the other Brujah, despite his complicity in the vampire's death. He let it be known he was disappointed the Camarilla had not removed Vannevar at the same time Montelaine was ousted.

Vannevar remained Ventrue primogen and retained his seat on the council but now, with little territory, finances, or support on the council, his influence was nil. Only the Toreador, Marie Richaud, openly remained his friend.

Financially strapped, Vannevar was soon forced to move his family to humbler quarters.

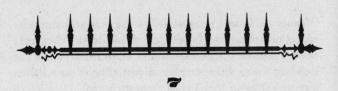

7

1884: Tong Wars

Vannevar ran headlong down a dark, narrow alley, flanked on both sides by towering Victorian row houses built side to side. An enraged mob howled close at his heels. At an intersection in the rear of the alley he turned right — only to find a dead end. The shouting sounds behind him closed in rapidly.

He was in Chinatown and lost among the maze of narrow streets and dirty alleys. Redwood Victorian row buildings two and three stories high hemmed him in like the walls of a deep canyon.

The mob appeared around the corner and, spying him, skidded to a stop. Nearly a dozen highbinders — Chinatown gangsters dressed in black silk pajamas, wearing broad-brimmed hats and armed with cut-down hatchets and revolvers — now began walking slowly toward him.

Vannevar snarled at the crowd, baring his fangs, and the gang slowed, their resolve wavering; but then one of their number shouted something in Chinese and, waving his hand in the air, led them forward again.

Vannevar sprang at them hissing, his eyes glowing angry red. The highbinders fell back, frightened by the vampire's unexpected lunge. Taking advantage of their momentary panic, Vannevar spun back around and leaped high into the air, landing on the rough wall of the nearest building, clawing and scrabbling his way toward the roof. The highbinders shouted and surged after him, but he was already up and out of their reach. One of them fired a shot, the bullet burying itself in the side of the house next to Vannevar's head. A hatchet embedded itself in the wall beside him and another clipped his leg, but then he was up and over the top, safe on the roof while the shouting highbinders below cursed after him.

Safe for the moment, Vannevar got to his feet and scanned across the dark rooftops of Chinatown, getting his bearings, wondering how Swede and Margaret were getting along.

Tong wars had racked Chinatown for several years, but had recently reached a new apex of violence. Powerful Kindred now backed the feuding tongs, providing them with weapons and money and provoking them into acts of terrorism, kidnapping and murder. The war was waged in broad daylight, and open murder contracts were publicly posted in alleys and shops. Although the newspapers waged periodic campaigns against Chinatown's numerous opium dens, fan-tan parlors, bordellos, and reputed slave-trading activities, the city police were usually bribed and business in Chinatown went on as always.

Chinatown was now ruled by two feuding Kindred: the ancient Grandfather, who had dwelled there for more than three decades; and a relative newcomer, a woman called the Dowager. The two were engaged in a deadly war to see who would ultimately rule the territory, using the local tongs as pawns in their deadly struggle for power. Vannevar and his small family had been sucked into the conflict, against Vannevar's will.

The Dowager had come from China at the behest of Prince Cyrano, who hoped another Asian vampire in Chinatown would force the Grandfather out. Vannevar had questioned the wisdom of the move, but Cyrano had insisted. The Dowager had arrived a few years ago, aboard a ship from the Far East, accompanied by a member of the Tremere clan, a Spanish ex-missionary named Don Benedict.

The prince had requested Vannevar to aid the Dowager in her war, and though Vannevar found it onerous, he had little choice. His territory decimated, his political influence at an all-time low, he had to cooperate or risk invoking the wrath of Cyrano and possibly the Camarilla. A letter from Texas had warned him that since the murder of Dugan he was being closely watched, and that resisting the prince's demands was unwise. He was forced by Cyrano to follow the wishes of the Dowager, his role little better than a lieutenant required to follow her commands.

Vannevar, still on the roof, crossed to the other side and looked toward a distant intersection, his ears trained for sounds, ignoring the clamor still going on below as the awed highbinders loudly discussed the supernatural escape they had just witnessed. Vannevar knew Margaret and Swede were out there somewhere.

Five blocks away he heard the distant clash of arms and the shouts of men, and guessed that Swede and Margaret were in trouble. He dashed across the rooftops, down the row of buildings, the pain in his wounded leg barely slowing him. Bounding leaps carried him over the streets three stories below, his dark cape billowing out behind him.

Following the noise of the battle, he finally found his two childer trapped in an alley, a gang of the Grandfather's highbinders closing in on them from two sides. And not all these highbinders were human. There were several ghouls among them.

Swede and Margaret were aided by a few of the Dowager's men, but theirs was a hopeless defense; several of the Dowager's men already lay dead on the ground. Vannevar vaulted over the edge of the building, dropping three stories and landing directly in the midst of the Grandfather's attacking hatchet-men.

Vannevar tore among them, raging, scattering them amidst shouts and screams, allowing Margaret and Swede to break out of the trap and flee the alley. Vannevar followed after them, leaving the Dowager's men to face their remaining attackers alone. Running swiftly, the three vampires fled Chinatown, back down the hill toward the Barbary Coast and the safety of home.

"Take yourselves back to the hotel," Vannevar ordered as they cleared the Chinatown border. "Get cleaned up and see to Swede's wound. I've got other business to attend to."

Swede had a gash over his forehead, the result of an earlier tangle with the Grandfather's feared henchmen, Sullivan.

"You're hurt, too," Margaret said to Vannevar, pointing to the bloody pant leg where he'd been shot.

"Nothing serious," he said. "Just get back home and stay put. I have to go back and see the Dowager."

Cyrano no longer trusted his Tremere confederate, Don Benedict, to help him manage the Dowager and had ordered Vannevar to serve as his personal ambassador to her. In truth, Vannevar was little more than a messenger boy. Cyrano had missed few opportunities in the last years to denigrate Vannevar, making it obvious to the other vampires of the city that Cyrano had little respect for the Ventrue primogen.

Vannevar headed back toward Chinatown, but this time by way of California Street, a route that would safely take him around the scene of battle. Turning up Dupont, he found the door marked "The Six Companies" and entered the Dowager's lair.

The Dowager received him in her private chambers, where she sat upon a thronelike chair atop a low dais. Tonight she dressed in splendid silk robes of red and purple, embroidered with gold. A broad rice-paper fan fluttered in her hand, concealing her face.

"I've come to report the night's confrontation," Vannevar told her after entering and giving her a perfunctory bow.

"Very good," the Dowager said, fluttering her fan. "How have we done tonight?"

"Not so well," Vannevar told her. "We lost several men."

"But how many did the Grandfather lose?" she wanted to know.

"He lost at least as many as we did," Vannevar told her.

The Dowager dropped her fan, revealing a grotesque face. She was Nosferatu, her misshapen head set with two beady, piglike eyes over a pair of flared nostrils and a mouth twisted inhumanly by the curving fangs that filled her mouth.

"Good," the Dowager cooed. "Soon we shall have the Grandfather where we want him. Then we shall crush him."

"You look radiant this evening," Vannevar told the woman.

The Dowager, reputedly once a great beauty, remained vain of her looks and Vannevar had learned flattery was the surest way to stay on her good side. A complaint from her to Cyrano might lead to further troubles.

"Thank you," she giggled, once again concealing her face behind the fluttering fan.

She rose from her throne and Vannevar offered his hand to help her from the dais. In the old tradition, the Dowager's feet were cruelly bound. Strapped into high platform shoes, her feet looked like ugly little pigs, toes pressed nearly flat and with yellow, badly ingrown nails.

"Thank you again," she smiled to him as she stepped carefully down to the floor. "Come," she said. "I have something to show you."

Vannevar followed her down a back stairway to the floor below, the Dowager mincing along in the tiny steps her misshapen feet required.

"We have taken a prisoner and are presently interrogating him," she told him.

She led him to a small chamber hidden away in the back of the building. There were no windows in this room and the walls were soundproofed with thick cotton mats.

Strapped to a large table in the center of the room was one of the Grandfather's ghouls. Above the ghoul's head hung a water tank fixed with a metering device. Every five seconds the tank released another drop of water to splash on the ghoul's forehead, eliciting a mad howl from the helpless creature.

"He has been here several days," the Dowager said, whispering to Vannevar. "He will talk soon."

Vannevar noticed the ghoul's bloody fingertips and realized that his fingernails had been pulled out. As they regrew, the Dowager would pull them out again.

"Very good," Vannevar smiled at her, though sickened by the sight.

Vannevar had long ago decided the Dowager was quite mad. Many of the Nosferatu were, he'd discovered. But there was no telling what effect the clan's curse would have on its victim. Some, like Sergei, turned inward, searching for truth; others, like the Dowager, were driven to the edge of insanity, and sometimes beyond. The Dowager took great delight in others' pain and suffering; Vannevar sometimes believed she did not so much want to win the war with the Grandfather, but merely to go on battling in the streets, bringing more death and pain to the community. The tongs, it was true, had been in existence long before the war between the two Kindred, but now, under the influence of the two vampires, the violence and killing had escalated. The residents of Chinatown lived in fear, afraid to set foot outside of their doors after nightfall. Tonight, Vannevar had almost lost both his childer to the senseless conflict.

He had argued with Cyrano to push for a peace treaty, but the stubborn Tremere, though realizing he'd perhaps made a mistake by encouraging the Dowager and escalating the war, would not back down. Rather than treat for peace, Cyrano continued to press the conflict, hoping for a decisive victory over the Grandfather. Vannevar, however, knew there was little chance of a resolution anytime soon. The

Grandfather, no matter what kind of losses he suffered, seemed to enjoy an endless supply of replacement forces.

After discussing future battle plans with the Dowager, Vannevar took his leave and returned home to the Coast. It was nearly three o'clock in the morning.

Vannevar and his family now dwelt in the Occidental Hotel, a small place on Jackson Street near the Barbary Coast. It was not nearly so luxurious as their former quarters; they had been forced into this area by Cyrano's unceasing absorption of Vannevar's domain.

As Vannevar approached the hotel's back entrance, a tall, very thin man stepped out of the dark.

"What are you doing here?" Vannevar said when he recognized the man.

It was Chi, the Family's ancient ghoul. "I have come to ask your help," he said. He was violating Vannevar's territory by coming here. "Times are desperate," he explained.

Vannevar, fearing a trap, went no closer, remaining six feet away from the ghoul. He was angered by his enemy's temerity, and fearful as well. He had been unaware the Grandfather and the Family knew the whereabouts of his haven. Involuntarily, his eyes flickered up to the third-floor windows where Margaret and Swede should be.

"Have no fear," the ghoul said, realizing what Vannevar was thinking. "I am alone. I have come not for war, but for peace."

Chi explained that he represented Kwon, a member of the Family, the beautiful green-eyed woman Vannevar had briefly glimpsed in a dark alley the night Snake Whitcomb was killed.

"What does your mistress want?" Vannevar asked him.

"She would speak with you tonight."

Chi was a wily old ghoul, Vannevar knew that, but listening to his words, he felt that he could be trusted — at least tonight.

"I am honor-bound not to harm you," Chi said, as though reading Vannevar's thoughts.

"Take me to her," Vannevar told him.

The meeting was in Portsmouth Square, the old city center, now a small, pleasant park with trees and benches, situated on the border between Chinatown and the Barbary Coast. When Vannevar and Chi arrived they found Kwon alone, sitting on a wooden bench in the darkest corner of the square. Chi pointed her out to Vannevar, then retired a few feet away, allowing them some privacy while still keeping a watch on them.

"Hello," Kwon said softly when Vannevar approached. She did not rise from the bench but turned her head up, gazing at him with those startling green eyes. Her voice was pure, musical, still tinged with the accent of her native China. Kwon spent little time among the outer world and her English was not nearly so polished as that of some other members of the Family.

"I was told you wished to see me," Vannevar said, standing before her. As before, he was struck by her beauty and quiet grace, but he tried not to let it show.

"Yes. A matter of greatest urgency. Please sit down."

It was an invitation, not an order. Vannevar sat down on another bench, facing the one on which Kwon sat. She began speaking immediately.

"We must bring peace to Chinatown," she said abruptly.

"It is the Grandfather — your elder — who chooses to fight," Vannevar countered.

"That is not true," Kwon refuted. "The Dowager brings the violence, the killing, and the death. She presses for war."

It was the truth and Vannevar knew it. The Grandfather was only fighting to keep what was his.

"What do you expect me to do about it?" he asked. He was sure that the Family knew his current status among the city's Kindred.

"You can pull out," she said. "Remove yourself and your family from the conflict. Without your aid the war will eventually be fought to a draw and then a treaty of peace can be concluded."

"And if I don't?" Vannevar asked her.

"Then," she said, "the Dowager will win, but only at first. The Grandfather has great resources and his retaliation will be terrible."

"Why are you telling me this?" Vannevar asked. "Do you betray your loyalty to the Grandfather."

She dropped her eyes.

"Never would I do that," she said, looking at her small white hands, which were folded in her lap.

"What are your master's intentions?" Vannevar asked, pressing her to reveal the plans of the Family. He was sure the Grandfather had future plans for the city. Though he spoke little about it, Vannevar still suffered from recurring dreams of a great dark beast with glowing red eyes. He felt sure the dreams were somehow prophetic, predicting a future time when the Grandfather would finally make his move.

"That I may not say," she told him, still staring down at her lap. "I cannot betray the Grandfather."

Vannevar remained silent.

Kwon looked back up at him. "The final and deciding conflict will not occur for years," she told him. "It cannot be decided now. Chi has seen this and told me."

Vannevar looked over to where the ghoul stood in the shadows, waiting. He knew Chi's sharp ears picked up every word spoken, regardless of their whispers.

"I would not lie to you, Vannevar," she said.

He looked into her eyes and was sure she spoke the truth.

"Why me?" he asked. "Why not take this offer to the prince?"

"Because," she explained, "you are a noble man, a man of honor. I recognized that the first night I saw you, the night Delfonso visited the Grandfather."

"That was the night I betrayed Delfonso," Vannevar said bitterly. "He asked my counsel and I answered falsely."

"You did what you believed was best for the city, Vannevar, even at the cost of betraying a friend. Much good was done after Delfonso stepped down."

Vannevar listened. He had told himself the same thing before, but to no avail. He did not feel absolved.

"You did what you believed was best then. Will you do that now?" she implored.

Vannevar had no answer. To break his alliance with the Dowager was to slap the face of the prince. Cyrano would not allow such a betrayal to go unanswered.

"I fear risking it," Vannevar finally said. "I don't know." Now he looked away, averting his eyes from Kwon's steady gaze.

Chi joined them, slipping up beside Kwon silently.

"We must go now," he told her. "Before we are missed."

Vannevar looked up, a question on his face.

"The Grandfather does not know you have come to speak with me?" he asked, surprised.

"No," Kwon said, rising from the bench. "Chi and I have chosen to act alone in this matter."

Vannevar remained sitting on the bench, watching as the two melted into the darkness.

■

The next evening Vannevar took Margaret to visit the salon of the Toreador primogen, Marie Richaud, atop Russian Hill. The petite Frenchwoman currently reigned as San Francisco's leading patron of the arts. Many galleries and theaters owed their existence to Marie's fundraising abilities, and it was generally recognized that no one in the city had done more than Marie to foster San Francisco's artistic and cultural growth during the last two decades.

Twice weekly Marie opened her home to guests, among

whom were many artists, writers, and other lively bohemians. Oscar Wilde, during his visit of 1882, had avidly attended the affairs, as had many others passing their way through the city over the years. Her guests were always interesting and the discussions lively. Margaret, who frequently complained that Vannevar kept her too close to home, had looked forward to the evening with anticipation.

Marie's spacious house stood near the top of Russian Hill's steep north slope, enjoying a sweeping view of San Francisco Bay, including Fishermen's Wharf and Alcatraz Island, currently an army post. Russian Hill was now a popular residential area and, like Nob Hill and Telegraph Hill, completely covered with houses and apartment buildings.

Vannevar and Margaret arrived near midnight. Despite the late hour, they found the house still lively with guests. Marie's maid met them at the door and took their wraps. Vannevar showed Margaret into the main sitting room and then turned her loose to amuse herself among the guests. She was a headstrong girl, always hungry for society and conversation, and Vannevar had learned it was usually in his best interests to let her have her way.

He looked for his hostess and found Marie huddled in the corner with Ned Greenway. Greenway was from Baltimore, an Easterner who'd come to San Francisco a few years ago as a salesman for Mumm's Champagne. Finding the city and its climate to his liking, he had stayed on but, soon discovering San Francisco deplorably lacking in the social graces, had gone about remedying the situation, organizing expensive cotillions and writing a society column for the San Francisco Chronicle. Now social dictator of the city, his opinion was held in high regard among the so-called "400," the city's high society. Greenway was a frequent guest at Marie's and she feted him, making good use of his influence to attract funding for works of art, museums, galleries, and theaters.

Taking a glass of red wine from a passing waiter's tray, Vannevar joined the pair.

"Good evening, Mr. Thomas," Greenway smiled at Vannevar's approach. "It's good to see you again."

Vannevar returned the greeting, then complimented the hostess on the turnout tonight.

"It's very lively," she agreed, smiling. "Bierce sent a note saying he could not come, but otherwise most of the important guests are here." Ambrose Bierce, newspaper writer and intimate friend of Marie's, also lived on Russian Hill. Bierce worked at the competing Examiner; his boss was a fiery young publisher named William Randolph Hearst. The Examiner was currently running a campaign to oust Greenway as social arbiter of the city.

Greenway sniffed. "Just as well," he said.

"Did you hear about the Stanfords?" Marie asked Vannevar, trying to change the subject.

"I heard Leland Jr. was ill," Vannevar told her.

She nodded. "Yes, but it's gotten worse, or so Ned tells me."

Greenway confirmed it. The young man, now fifteen, had been stricken with typhoid. The doctors worried he would not pull through.

"I'm sorry to hear that," Vannevar said. He meant every word of it. He liked the lad and knew that his parents doted on him. He was the Stanfords' only child, and Vannevar knew the senior Stanford intended to pass his vast holdings onto his son as soon as he came of age.

"It's very sad," Greenway said, then excused himself from their company, spotting someone across the room he wished to have a word with.

"We'll catch up later," he told them.

Vannevar and Marie smiled after him.

"Any news?" Vannevar asked Marie as soon as Greenway was out of earshot. She was his last ally, his only friend among the primogen, and he counted on her for information that would otherwise be kept secret from him.

Marie shook her head. "Nothing of interest," she said.

"I've been approached regarding a possible peace in Chinatown," he said.

Marie had long advocated a peaceful settlement to the Chinatown war.

"I've found no support for that," Marie said.

Most of the primogen sided with Cyrano, for one reason or another. The Dowager, of course, was hand-picked, and the new Brujah primogen, Sarah, also supported him, fearing the loss of her Western Addition territories if she balked Cyrano's demands. The Commodore, still a well-known fixture along the Embarcadero waterfront, usually supported Cyrano, and the latest Gangrel primogen, newly elevated to the post, was not expected to stand in Cyrano's way. Delfonso no longer attended council meetings.

"I'm afraid I can offer you little in the way of hope," Marie told him. "Cyrano's control seems absolute."

"Who's that?" Vannevar asked, changing the subject, his attention now drawn to a tall, thin male vampire across the room, flirting with Margaret.

"A new childe of Sarah's," Marie told him. "You should probably warn Margaret."

"I will," Vannevar told her.

"Come on," Marie said, spying one of her guests coming down the stairs. "There's a man here I want you to meet."

Marie introduced Vannevar to a small man of Japanese descent named Iwo. Iwo, Marie claimed, was a fortuneteller of great ability. The little man only laughed at her claim. He looked to be fifty years old or more, with a wispy white beard growing from his chin. But when he laughed his face beamed like a child's.

"Marie is very good to say that," he told Vannevar. "But it is nothing special, I assure you."

"Oh, bosh," Marie said. "You know better than that, Iwo,"

she scolded the man. "Take Vannevar upstairs and tell his
fortune for him. He needs all the help he can get right now."
Marie was smiling but she sounded sincere. Iwo's eyebrows
went up when he heard her words.

"She is right, you know," Iwo smiled up at Vannevar,
suddenly changing his mind. "I think it would be of benefit,
perhaps. Who can tell? Please. Would you allow me?"

Vannevar grinned, feeling a little foolish, but went along
with it. He trusted Marie and knew she wouldn't do this
without good reason.

Vannevar followed the little man up the stairs and to a
back bedroom. Vannevar learned that Iwo had been reading
fortunes this evening for many of the guests.

"So, what brings you to America, Mr...?" Vannevar
realized he didn't know the man's full name.

"Call me Iwo," he said. "Simply Iwo."

"So what brings you here, Iwo?" Vannevar asked.

Japanese were rare in the city, still bound to their island
by a feudal, isolationist government. The first citizens of
Nippon had arrived in San Francisco in 1873, after their
fishing boat was blown far out to sea and subsequently picked
up by an American merchantman bound for California.

"Our government is gradually loosening its strings," Iwo
replied. "I have left our isle to experience some more of the
world. I am a curious man," he winked.

Vannevar sat down in a chair as instructed by Iwo.

"Make yourself comfortable," he said. "You have heard of
the I Ching?" he asked.

"No," Vannevar admitted.

"It is an old method," Iwo said, now rummaging through
a trunk on the floor, "long used by many people wishing to
know the future. We Japanese have adopted it from our
neighbors, the Chinese, but I believe the basic idea is even
older than they."

Vannevar, looking around the room, realized Iwo must be
staying here at Marie's house.

Iwo pulled something out of the trunk. "Ha!" he said, triumphantly. He held up a large bag made of velvet. It held something round and heavy. Smiling, Iwo carried it to the fireplace, where hot embers of an earlier fired still glowed red. Setting the bag down, he poked among the cinders, kindling a little flame.

"You see," Iwo said, "all things are one and the same with the greater, are they not?"

For the sake of conversation, Vannevar agreed, though to what, he was not sure.

"If one thing is tied to another and another and another, then there can be no effect on one thing that does not affect all the others. Right?"

The coals now glowed brightly. Iwo set down the poker and untied the strings sealing the bag.

"Usually with this kind of reading," Iwo said. "I make use of a tortoiseshell or the shoulder blade of a deer, but in your case we need something special."

He winked at Vannevar as he said it, then pulled from the bag a yellowed human skull, minus its jawbone. Vannevar showed surprise.

"Don't worry," Iwo told him. "The owner died a natural death, and I had paid him well for his skull many years before. His wife and children still grow fat on the money."

Carefully he placed the skull in the fireplace, arranging the coals to provide maximum heat while not quite touching or scorching the skull.

"Now we must wait," Iwo said, squatting in front of the fireplace, keeping an eye on the skull.

A moment later there was a popping sound as the skull cracked under the heat. Iwo immediately removed it, careful not to dislodge any of the broken pieces that had been fractured by the heat. It was these random cracks that he would study, and from them cast Vannevar's fortune.

Vannevar sat and watched curiously as the man placed the hot skull on a table and carefully studied it, turning it round, handling it gingerly so as not to burn his fingertips.

"Hmm, yes. Uh-huh," he said, sounding like a doctor checking a patient's throat.

"Yes, of course," he said, straightening back up. "I see now why Marie was so insistent on you having your fortune read. You are a very interesting fellow indeed."

Iwo spied something else on the skull that he had not noticed and bent back over to look at it.

"Yes, of course," he said, now satisfied he understood all the skull could tell him.

Vannevar waited, feeling impatient.

"So what is it?" he finally asked.

"You are faced with grave decisions, I see," Iwo said. "Decisions that could chart the destinies of many."

"Does it tell you what I should do?" Vannevar asked, growing curious whether the man really saw anything or was merely making it up.

"A wise man would choose the middle path when facing such difficulties," Iwo told him. "In that way you will eventually triumph, though I can see that great strife and suffering still lie in your way."

That was all Iwo would say.

Back downstairs Marie found Vannevar and asked him how the session had gone.

"All right, I suppose," he told her. "I'm not sure whether I'm supposed to believe it or not."

"Oh, you can believe Iwo, all right," Marie assured him. "Listen to what Iwo tells you. I trust him implicitly."

Vannevar and Margaret left the affair at three o'clock, Vannevar's coach arriving on the hill at its appointed time. On the way home Vannevar talked to Margaret about the young Brujah she'd spent most of the evening with, warning her about associating with their enemies.

"You just don't trust me," she said, petulantly.

Vannevar relented. "I'm not saying you can't see him,"

he explained. "I'm just asking you to be careful around him, that's all. We have to be careful all the time."

Margaret continued her pout. She hated being told what to do. Vannevar realized he was only making it worse and dropped the subject. It seemed that lately they argued more and more as Margaret continually found fault with nearly everything Vannevar said or did. They rode the rest of the way back home in silence.

Vannevar was alone in his room when a knock sounded at the door. It was the desk clerk, bearing a message that had been left late last night. Vannevar thanked the ghoul and closed the door. Opening the letter, he found it was from Stanford up on Nob Hill. He needed Vannevar right away. Vannevar burned the message in the fireplace and then, donning his cloak, left the hotel.

The coach had been sent away and Vannevar was forced to climb Nob Hill on foot. He reached the Stanford mansion fifteen minutes later and, hoping he was not too late, knocked at the door. It opened.

"I was worried," said the man standing on the other side. "I thought you'd hadn't got my message."

"I came as soon as I got word," Vannevar said. The sky was already showing gray as the dawn drew near.

Showing Vannevar in, the man shut the door behind him. The great mansion was quiet and still, the gas lights turned low.

"How is he?" Vannevar asked.

"The doctor said he won't last much longer. The boy is very weak."

The father's eyes were moist with tears.

"Are you sure you want to go through with this?" Vannevar asked him. "Do you realize all that it means?"

"I understand fully," the man said with assurance. "Provisions have already been made."

"Then I will do as you ask," Vannevar told him. "Which way is his room?"

The man pointed him upstairs. Vannevar went alone.

Less than an hour later he came back downstairs.

"It is finished," he told Stanford.

"Thank you," the man said gratefully, pressing Vannevar's hand in both of his own, squeezing it tightly. "I can never repay you for this."

"Let's only hope that Leland Jr. someday finds reason to thank me," Vannevar said, casting a baleful look back up the stairs.

Then Vannevar left the house of mourning. Black wreaths were already being hung in the windows and on the doors.

■

Vannevar asked for a meeting with Kwon the following night and she proved agreeable. They met near Fishermen's Wharf on the north side of town, at the foot of Russian Hill. This was Marie's territory, far from both Chinatown and the Barbary Coast. It was quiet here this time of night; the Italian fishermen had all returned home for the evening. Their boats lay quietly in their slips. Vannevar had informed Marie of the intended meeting and she had taken pains to make sure the neighborhood was free of possible spies. When he arrived Vannevar found Chi and Kwon already waiting for him.

"I'm glad you chose to come," Vannevar told Kwon.

"Peace is our wish," she said. Chi nodded from where he stood behind her.

The meeting was brief. Vannevar told her he would withdraw active support from the war, leaving the Dowager to face the Grandfather alone. In return Kwon gave him her word the Family would sue for peace at the earliest opportunity.

"Thank you, Vannevar," Kwon told him. "We know what risks you take denying the prince his due."

So did Vannevar. He only hoped he and his family would survive his anger.

The meeting concluded, he headed back toward the Coast on foot, not risking having his carriage seen on the streets. He was in North Beach, a few blocks from home, when he ran into Margaret. She looked frightened, worried.

"What is it?" Vannevar asked her, as soon as he saw her.

"It's Swede," she told him. "He went into Chinatown, looking for Sullivan."

Vannevar cursed under his breath. He'd left orders with Margaret and Swede to keep a watch on the border between Chinatown and the Coast, but had specifically told them not to engage in any violence unless absolutely necessary.

"He's out to get even with him," Margaret said. "He's sworn revenge." Sullivan had given Swede the gash across his forehead a few nights ago. It was only the latest incident in a long feud brewing between the two big men ever since Vannevar had become involved in the tong wars.

"I want you to go home and wait," Vannevar told Margaret. He would go find Swede and drag him home.

"I want to come too," she said.

"No," Vannevar ordered her. "I told you to go home where it's safe."

Angry, Margaret stamped her foot and glared at Vannevar, but he said nothing, simply waiting for her to comply. His silence only angered her further and she spun around and stalked off. Vannevar watched her for only a moment, then turned south and headed into Chinatown.

He went to the rooftops, running silently across them, leaping over the streets with ease, searching everywhere for some sign of the disobedient Swede. He finally spotted him, some distance away, sprinting lightly down a street before turning up a dark alley. Vannevar took a shortcut over the roofs, arriving on the scene just in time to see Swede as he ducked into a shadowy doorway.

A second or two later Sullivan loomed round the corner,

moving stealthily, following Swede's trail. Not suspecting the ambush set for him, the Irishman walked right past Swede's hiding spot. Vannevar had to intervene.

"Wait!" he called down.

At the sound, Sullivan spun around in surprise, inadvertently catching sight of Swede rushing out at him from the nearby doorway.

"Stop!" Vannevar shouted, leaping over the edge of the building, dropping to the alley below. But the two big men, intent on settling their scores, paid Vannevar no heed.

Swede was a big man, every bit the size of Sullivan, but he lacked the Irish sailor's ferocity and animal-like survival instincts. Swede might hesitate before smashing someone with his fist; Sullivan would never stop to think about it, neither before nor after.

Even as Vannevar's feet hit the pavement Sullivan had met Swede's charge and, twisting him around, lifted Swede off his feet and threw him to the ground. Landing on top of him, Sullivan mashed his knee into Swede's throat, at the same time drawing out the huge knife he always carried, its blade flashing in the dark. Vannevar shouted again, but the knife plunged down, into Swede's heart. A second powerful blow and Swede's head rolled from his body.

"Don't!" Vannevar shouted, running toward them.

Sullivan looked up and, recognizing Vannevar, hissed at him once before turning and fleeing the scene. Vannevar did not bother to pursue him, instead stopping to examine the fallen Swede.

He was dead. Impaled and decapitated, there was no way to return his life. Even as Vannevar watched, Swede's body began to corrupt and dissolve, falling to pieces before his eyes.

"You bastard!" someone yelled from a rooftop above. Vannevar looked up and saw Margaret, peering down from a rooftop above. She screamed at him. "You son of a bitch! I saw what you did. Traitor!" Before Vannevar could explain,

she ducked back from the roof's edge and disappeared from
sight, running back toward home.

He caught up with her at the hotel, but Margaret refused
to speak to him, his explanations falling on deaf ears.
Convinced Vannevar's interference had led to Swede's
death, she packed her bags and the following evening moved
out, taking up residence somewhere in the Western Addition
as a guest of the young Brujah she had met the other night
at Marie's house.

Word of Swede's demise got back to the primogen;
Cyrano, taking advantage of the situation to condemn
Vannevar publicly, called him "heartless and unworthy of
the respect of other Kindred." Privately, he began plotting
Vannevar's downfall.

But Vannevar fought no more in the tong wars, and soon,
as Kwon had promised, the Dowager and the Grandfather
struck a bargain to share the territory. The tong wars would
continue off and on for another thirty years, but never again
would they be backed by any member of the Kindred.

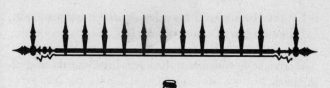

1894: The Midwinter Fair

San Francisco's Midwinter Fair opened in February of 1894 and ran for six months. The city's first world-class exposition, the fair was situated on two hundred acres at the eastern end of Golden Gate Park. The park itself was a half-mile wide, three-mile long stretch of green, reaching from the central city all the way to the Pacific Ocean. An area formerly nothing but rolling sand dunes, the land had been painstakingly reclaimed, then landscaped and planted with exotic flora collected from all over the world.

The fair itself featured pavilions from many different countries as well as from nearly every state in the Union. The centerpiece of the fair was the grand Tower of Electricity. Reaching several hundred feet into the air, it was mounted with a bright, rotating searchlight that could be seen for miles.

Vannevar was a frequent visitor to the fairgrounds. He enjoyed the crowds and scenery, the Egyptian- and East Indian-styled buildings, and in particular the Japanese Tea Garden. Most importantly, he felt safe while at the fair. The fair had been declared Elysium by the Kindred, allowing all to move about safely within its grounds without fear of suffering attack or reprisal from other vampires.

He was in the tea garden when he found Iwo. The small Japanese did not look a bit out of place amid the setting.

"You're visiting again," said Iwo, when he saw Vannevar.

"I like the place," Vannevar told him. He was developing a taste for the simple, Japanese style, so unlike the cluttered Victorian style common to San Francisco and the rest of America.

"I'm sorry about the tower," Vannevar told him.

The Tower of Electricity had been Iwo's design. He had hoped the city would see fit to keep it after the fair closed, but the decision had been made to tear it down after the fair, along with most of the rest of the attractions. Iwo had campaigned hard with the city, and Vannevar had tried his best with the primogen council, but to no avail. The tower would go.

"It's too bad," Vannevar added. The tower had been built to Iwo's specifications. The Japanese magician had told Vannevar that a great dragon dwelled somewhere below the city. A magical beast, Iwo's tower would allow it to "breathe." Without the tower, Iwo feared the dragon would have to find its own way to breathe. But Iwo took the defeat in good spirits. "What will be, will be," he smiled.

Vannevar knew better, though. He understood little of the bizarre metaphysics of the Japanese magician, but it was clear to him that Iwo had desperately wished the tower to stand. Vannevar worried that loss of the tower might lead to something terrible happening.

"I have been exploring the park," Iwo told Vannevar, changing the subject. "It is a very interesting place."

In the few years of its existence the park had been the scene of a number of odd occurrences. Some Kindred had reported seeing spirits moving through the woods at night; others claimed the park could be used as a gateway to other worlds. The park was administered to by a crusty Scotsman who Iwo claimed knew more than a little about magic and enchantments.

The two men became quiet for a moment, staring into the lily-laden pond, listening to the music of the water splashing over the rocks and into the pool, and watching the goldfish swimming lazily about. Iwo took a deep breath, then spoke.

"I have heard rumors," Iwo said. "Rumors about your well-being, Vannevar. I am afraid your enemies mean you harm."

Vannevar only shrugged. It was hard to imagine what anybody could do to hurt him these days. Since crossing swords with Cyrano over the tong wars, Vannevar had seen his territory slowly whittled away until he was at last squeezed into the smallest, seediest corner of the Barbary Coast. Swede was dead and Margaret had left him; he had no loyal retainers save Riley. He had created no more childer for himself and although he would occasionally employ lesser vampires, these usually remained with him only a short time. Most either left to serve another or were found slain shortly after involving themselves with Vannevar. Vannevar still retained his seat on the primogen council, and was still the nominal elder of San Francisco's Ventrue clan, but his power was waning and his influence nil. His finances were so meager that he had been forced to sell his carriage and team.

A group of noisy youngsters crossed the high wooden bridge arching up over the pond, disturbing his thoughts. His attention was drawn to a bright-faced, laughing boy of fifteen or sixteen, his arm around the waist of a pretty young girl about the same age. The boy looked just liked Davey Foster and, for a moment, Vannevar thought it *was* Davey. But then, recalling all the years that had passed, Vannevar realized the boy must be Davey's grandson. He would be about the right age, he guessed, and Riley had often commented on how much this young man resembled his grandfather. The grandson was named David, in honor of his grandfather.

The youngsters passed by, and after they'd gone, Vannevar again spoke to Iwo.

"I am to meet with Cyrano tomorrow," Vannevar said. "Do you have any advice for me?"

"Only that if you are to meet with Cyrano alone, be on your guard."

"We are to meet in the primogen chambers, at the Cliff House," Vannevar said. "I don't believe he would try anything there."

"You are probably right," Iwo said.

■

The Cliff House was an ornate, seven-story, Victorian mansion built atop a rocky bluff overlooking the Pacific Ocean. It was not the first such structure to occupy the spot, but it was by far the grandest. Constructed by multimillionaire Adolph Sutro, the spired mansion dwarfed the cliffs it stood upon; it featured downstairs dining rooms and restaurants, banquet rooms and bars, with private rooms above. Built to Cyrano's specifications, the top floor was reserved for the Kindred and contained the chambers of the primogen council.

The house was ideally located, overlooking the twin cones of Seal Rocks just south of the entrance to the harbor. The view from the windows was an inspiration to all who visited. Every ship that entered the bay had to pass by the Cliff House. Cyrano's personal haven was located in an office building in the heart of the financial district, but the Cliff House was continually occupied by his minions, who kept watch on the shipping traffic. Cyrano referred to the Cliff House as "his castle."

To reach the Cliff House from the Barbary Coast, Vannevar had to take the California cable car to the old Presidio and there transfer to the little steam train that ran through the dunes of the peninsula's western areas before it finally reached the coast. Even though the distance was little more than seven miles, Vannevar would normally have been fearful of exposing himself thusly if not for the fact he had been guaranteed safe passage by the prince's decree. There were many young vampires in the city looking to make their reputation, and slaying a vampire of Vannevar's status would be a feather in any cap.

Vannevar had avoided confrontation the last few years, staying within his own small territory. But on more than one occasion he'd had to defend himself against attacks from ill-advised and youthful vampires, once even being forced to kill his attacker.

Hopping on the California cable car, Vannevar rode it up and over the top of Nob Hill. The great mansions still stood atop the hill, but they were mostly empty now. All the great millionaires were gone, many having lost their fortunes and forced to sell out, others simply dying of old age. Leland Stanford had been the last of them, finally passing on in 1890. The Stanford house stood dark and silent as the cable car passed, and Vannevar remembered the night ten years ago when he had visited the ailing young boy upstairs and, at the father's urging, cursed the young man with vampiric immortality.

Stanford, lacking an heir, had willed his fortune to the construction of a great university down the coast on the peninsula. Stanford University had opened in 1891; Leland Jr. lived in a small chapel on the campus grounds.

As the car passed Jones Street and began the descent to Polk Gulch, Vannevar remembered those nights on the hill: the splendid parties, the beautiful women, the raucous businessmen and hustlers that were San Francisco's richest, most influential citizens. Vannevar himself had long wished to build atop the hill, but his plans had been foiled by failing finances and his waning power. Now the area stood deserted; the rich now built their grand homes along broad Van Ness Avenue and beyond, to Pacific Heights overlooking the northern bay.

Isolated and alone, the Cliff House gleamed brightly atop its rocky perch, a point of warmth in the dark night sky overlooking the icy black waters of the Pacific. The tide was coming in, the fog rolling inland while monstrous waves boomed against the cliffs, reverberating through the ground like distant claps of thunder.

Carriages cluttered the parking area in front of the Cliff House. The lower levels of the building were filled with weekend revelers; music blared and drinks splashed while waiters hurried about dressed in white jackets. The doorman recognized Vannevar and, unhooking the velvet rope that blocked a narrow, carpeted staircase, bowed slightly as Vannevar mounted the private stairs leading to the upper chambers of the council. Here, in a spacious, shadowy room, Vannevar found Cyrano waiting for him. Cyrano's pudgy apprentice lackey, Honerius, was in attendance, standing a step or two behind the prince.

"Good evening," Cyrano said when Vannevar walked in. "Please sit down." He invited Vannevar to take a seat at the long, polished mahogany table that served the primogen council. "Let's talk," he smiled.

Cyrano sat down in a large ornate chair positioned at the head of the table. Vannevar, instead of taking a seat close to Cyrano's hand, dragged one of the council chairs around and, placing it at the far end of the table, sat down directly across from the prince, a good ten feet away. Vannevar's pointed action was not lost on Cyrano.

The soft-spoken Honerius, afraid to seat himself at the table of the primogen, shuffled and fidgeted nervously, finally taking a spot standing behind Cyrano. Vannevar and Cyrano faced off against each other, their eyes points of red light in the darkened chamber.

"I'm going to come right to the point," Cyrano began. "I want you to leave San Francisco. I want you out of this city and out of the area."

Vannevar said nothing. He had expected something like this and had already decided upon his response.

"You must realize that your time has passed," Cyrano

persuaded, a smile now playing across his lips as he sat back in the tall, velvet-lined chair. "Your influence is gone. Not even the youngest, rawest vampire will work for you — at least not after they hear the story of poor Swede."

Cyrano's words cut Vannevar to the quick. The story of Swede's death had been told to all the Kindred, and blown all out of proportion. His lost childe, Margaret, had been his most ardent accuser.

Vannevar still said nothing.

"We won't send you away empty-handed, of course," Cyrano added. "We all recognize what you've done for this city, and I assure you your past efforts will not go unappreciated. I'm sure we can negotiate a cash settlement that will be agreeable — enough to provide you with a fresh start somewhere else."

Vannevar smiled inwardly. If Cyrano was making him this offer, it meant he still feared to challenge Vannevar directly.

Vannevar put his hand on the table and drummed his fingers, pretending to contemplate the offer. In the dark he sensed Cyrano's nervousness and knew the prince anxiously awaited his response.

"No," Vannevar finally said. "I don't think so." He stood up from the chair. "If that's all we have to talk about, I'll ask your Grace's permission to leave." He stood up.

Cyrano leaped up out his chair, kicking it back as he jumped to his feet, startling Honerius.

"Don't be foolish, Thomas!" he shouted at Vannevar. "I could crush you in a moment if I chose to do so. You know it."

"You might have the power, Cyrano, but you don't have the stomach for it," Vannevar told him coldly. "I still have a few friends in this town, and they won't make it easy for you. I know you can kill me — but I also know you don't dare try. You haven't the guts for it," Vannevar sneered.

Cyrano smashed the table with his fist, making the wood ring. "I could blast you now!" he swore through his teeth.

"Don't press your luck."

"You'd dare slay me in the council chambers?" he asked, laughing at the prince. "Then, my dear Cyrano, it will be you who is paid a visit by the Camarilla."

Cyrano's face clouded. Vannevar knew that Cyrano had manipulated Kearney and the mob, events that led to the execution of the Brujah, Dugan. He had also been behind the railroad fiasco, in league with the powerful Tremere faction in Sacramento. In short, he had sold the city out to satisfy his own clan's interests. Vannevar could not prove it, but fear of exposure kept Cyrano in check.

"You'd better watch out," Vannevar warned him. "Fat little Honerius standing behind you may be this very minute planning to do you in as you did in Montelaine."

Cyrano instinctively looked over his shoulder at Honerius standing behind him. Honerius, frightened the conversation had suddenly turned toward him, shook his head at Cyrano, desperate to deny any wrongdoing. Cyrano, angered by Vannevar's trick, turned back to his enemy.

"Mark my words," Cyrano hissed at Vannevar, who was already turning his back on the prince and striding out of the chamber. "You'll regret this evening, Vannevar. You certainly will."

Six weeks later Vannevar awoke in his cramped room in the Occidental to find a knife thrust into the pillow next to his head. It was the assassin's traditional warning, and Vannevar knew it meant he should leave the city immediately or face death.

■

"I'd rather stay here with you," Riley said. "You're gonna need some help."

"I can't let you risk it," Vannevar told him, watching Riley as the ghoul packed up his few belongings. "You'll be safer across the bay."

Riley was heading for Oakland. Vannevar had judged the situation in the city too dangerous for Riley to risk staying any longer. A paid assassin was stalking Vannevar — a member of the Assamite clan. The dagger thrust in his pillow had been a warning; the next blow would be aimed at his heart. Whether hired by Cyrano or the Camarilla, Vannevar did not know. Communications with Texas were sporadic lately, and Vannevar had no way of finding out who had sent the killer vampire. If the Assamite had been sent by the Camarilla, Vannevar knew that nothing he could do would save him, short of leaving the city, and he'd already decided that was an action he would never take. San Francisco was his home and in some ways he felt it belonged to him. If he could not live here, he'd decided, then he would die here.

"Okay," Riley said, strapping his bag shut and lifting it to his shoulder. "Take care." He and Vannevar shook hands and then Riley left, heading out the door and down to the Ferry Building to catch the last boat across the bay. Vannevar was left alone.

Vannevar finished packing what few belongings he needed and then left the Occidental himself. He had to find another haven, a place unknown to any other Kindred.

The Assamites were a small clan of vampires. Springing from somewhere in the Orient, they were rarely seen in this part of the world. Trained in secret methods of murder and nearly fearless, they were silent hunters who almost never failed their missions. Though not actually members of the Camarilla, they were often hired as contract killers by the elders of the Camarilla.

Vannevar, in need of a safe haven, had made arrangements to stay in a cheap sailor's boarding house just off Pacific Street, taking an upstairs room with a single small window. He was on his way to the boarding house when he ran into a group of drunken sailors. Luring one of them away from the others, he met the man in the alley a few minutes later and, after satisfying his hunger, left the sailor snoring peacefully, propped up against a wall.

The sailor had been quite intoxicated and Vannevar, on the way to his new home, felt the alcohol coursing through his veins, its familiar warmth relaxing him. He slept soundly that day, awakened only occasionally by the sounds of sailors tramping up and down the stairs and halls.

The next day Vannevar was awakened near sunset by soft footsteps outside his door. His eyes flew open at the sound, ears attuning themselves to the unfamiliar noise. There had been a creak from the stairway outside the door.

He listened, but heard nothing. The house was silent, lacking even the usual noises of the boarding sailors.

The top door panel suddenly splintered inward. Vannevar caught sight of a broad blade crashing through the wood. Then another blow was struck and the panel was knocked clean out of its frame.

Vannevar was already out of bed, on his feet and scrabbling behind the bureau for his saber. He found it and, pulling it out, yanked the blade free of the scabbard even as a third blow shattered parts of the door frame. Someone kicked the door, knocking it loose from it hinges. Then a man stepped through the rubble and into Vannevar's room.

The Assamite was an inch or two taller than Vannevar and strongly built, his thick muscles rippling under dark, oiled skin. He was stripped to the waist and barefoot, his long black hair tied up in a knot at the back of his head. He held a scimitar in his left hand.

The Assamite's eyes burned like red fires as he stared at Vannevar, his thin lips twisting into an evil smile as he slashed the broad blade back and forth. Vannevar saw a long dagger stuck in the orange sash encircling the Assamite's waist.

The Assamite took a step forward, spinning the scimitar

once in his hand. Vannevar stepped back, around the edge of the bed that nearly filled his tiny, cramped room. He hated to give ground but knew he would be no match for a skilled swordsman like the Assamite.

But he had no place to go. With a step or two the assassin would be upon him. Vannevar, trapped in the corner, would stand no chance against him. The assassin continued to smile as he pressed his advantage.

Vannevar made a sudden feint toward the assassin, catching him off guard. Then, before the Assamite could recover, Vannevar hurled himself backward through the small window near the bed, breaking out the glass and frame, falling three stories and crashing in a heap on the cobblestoned alley below.

Vannevar instantly bounded to his feet and, looking up, saw the Assamite glaring down at him from the shattered window. With a snarl, the assassin crawled out after him and leaped to the ground, landing on his bare feet like a cat.

But Vannevar was already gone, fleeing madly through the streets and alleys of the early evening Barbary Coast, his face cut and bleeding from the crash and fall, his queue untied, his long chestnut hair steaming out behind him. He eluded his attacker, disappearing into the night.

From that moment on, Vannevar spent no more than a day in any single place. Moving on night after night, always searching for a fresh haven, he knew that each place, once used, would be discovered by the relentless Assamite and would thereafter be of no use to him.

Vannevar finally awoke one evening in the dirty upper story of a burnt-out brewery, disgusted to find himself filthy with ash, dust, and dirt, his clothes crumpled and soiled. Then and there he decided he would no longer exist this way. He was not an animal to be pursued and run down. No longer would he stand to be the pursued quarry.

That night he abandoned the Barbary Coast to seek refuge elsewhere in the city. The Assamite would, of course, follow, but in the meantime Vannevar hoped he might find a way of defeating the killer.

He gathered up his few goods and left, slipping out the back window and stealing away from the Coast.

He went to Chinatown first, looking for Kwon. The two had continued meeting secretly the last few years and Vannevar felt the need to see her once again before abandoning this part of town. Their meetings had only been occasional, once or twice a year, and always with Chi in attendance, but Vannevar felt a great reverence — indeed, passion — for the woman. Kwon's words, always well chosen and spoken carefully, had done much to cool his anger over the wrongs done him by Cyrano. She had counseled him and he felt he owed her much. With the Assamite on his trail, he didn't know if he would ever see her again.

He found none of the Grandfather's people on the streets and it was with some frustration that Vannevar finally took up a post on the corner of Stockton and Washington, hiding in the shadows of the alley while he watched and waited.

A half-hour later he was still standing in the same spot when something flashed by the corner of his eye and a small hatchet buried itself in the wall of the building next to his head. He instinctively ducked, drawing out his saber from beneath his cape, looking around for his attacker.

He saw no one save a small Chinese highbinder barely five feet tall standing across the alley. The highbinder had a cigarette clamped in his lips and stared coldly at Vannevar. It was Loo, the Grandfather's childe.

"What are you doing here?" Loo asked, as he crossed the street to where Vannevar stood. Vannevar stepped aside as Loo pulled his axe out of the wall. "You're out of your territory," Loo told him. "I could kill you for this."

The threat was an empty one. One on one, Vannevar could have easily destroyed the smaller, less powerful vampire. Vannevar ignored the man's threat.

"I've come to see Kwon," Vannevar told him. "Where is she?"

Loo said nothing at first, ignoring Vannevar, looking up and down the street before finally responding. "What do you want her for?" he asked.

"I would speak to her a moment," Vannevar said. "That is all."

Vannevar knew Loo was jealous of his friendship with Kwon.

"I will take her your message," Loo told him, turning to leave.

"Thank you," Vannevar said after him.

Kwon showed up a few minutes later. At first Vannevar thought she was alone, but then he saw the cadaverous Chi lurking in the street behind her, as ever, keeping an eye on his charge.

"Good evening, Vannevar," she said, stopping a few feet away from him, standing straight, her arms folded in front of her waist, her delicate hands tucked inside the broad sleeves of her silken gown.

Once again Vannevar was struck by her flawless beauty, porcelain skin, and hypnotic green eyes.

"I'm going away for awhile," Vannevar told her.

"You are leaving the city?" Her voice was soft and flutelike.

She, like all the other Kindred, knew of Cyrano's threat to destroy Vannevar. He hesitated answering a moment, wondering if he should tell her the truth. He decided against it.

"Yes," he said. "But I hope to be back before long."

"I hope all will be well," she said, sincerely. "I hope we will meet again?" It was a question.

"I promise it," Vannevar told her.

Then she was gone. She had left with tears in her eyes, having already guessed the real reason for Vannevar's visit.

Vannevar headed north out of Chinatown, across

Broadway and into North Beach, now solidly populated by Italians. This was ostensibly the territory of Virgil, a Sicilian poet and Toreador who answered to Marie, but Cyrano held particular influence among certain members of the Italian community and Vannevar knew he could not be safe here. He skirted along the southern fringes of the territory, headed toward the steep slopes of Russian Hill.

He was looking for a one-night place of refuge. A week on the run had left his clothing soiled and torn, his body filthy. He needed to cleanse himself and perhaps find a change of clothes. It would be the greatest of favors to ask of a friend, for the Assamite would undoubtedly follow his trail to his host's residence, but Vannevar was prepared to ask that favor, and he was sure Iwo would not refuse him.

It was after midnight when he reached Iwo's strange little octagonal house, which was hidden away in a grove of trees near the top of the hill. He went straight to the front door and twisted the bell, watching carefully up and down the dark street while waiting for Iwo to answer the door.

"Vannevar!" Iwo said when he opened the door. "What brings you here this night?" Iwo saw the look of concern on Vannevar's face and quickly showed him in, shutting the door behind him and then locking it.

The interior of the house was bright and open, free of clutter, and sparsely decorated with some of Iwo's watercolors and a few carefully chosen objects placed in corners or on windowsills: a large, smoothly formed rock; a dead tree branch of particularly interesting form; and a few chunks of twisted driftwood. In the corner stood the strange stringed instrument upon which Iwo would occasionally play music in expert manner.

"I need a place to stay tonight," Vannevar told him. "But I must warn you there is a grave risk to anyone choosing to help me."

"I fear no risks," Iwo laughed. "You are welcome to stay as long as you like."

"Thank you, but that will not be necessary," Vannevar told him. "One night to rest and clean myself will be sufficient."

"As you wish," Iwo told him.

There was a noise from the back of the house. The odd, wedge-shaped rooms of the house were separated by sliding panels made of rice paper. As usual, they now stood open, turning the house into one large, open space. Vannevar tensed.

"You have company?" he asked Iwo.

"Yes," Iwo said. "As luck would have it, Don Benedict has also chosen to drop by tonight."

At the sound of Benedict's name Vannevar decided to leave. He did not want to be here with a Tremere. Iwo would be at risk if Cyrano were to learn that he had sheltered Vannevar in his home.

"No. Please stay," insisted Iwo. "Trust me when I say that you and Benedict have more in common than you realize."

Don Benedict had come to San Francisco from China, accompanying the Dowager on her long trip as requested by Cyrano. He had served as go-between for the Dowager and the prince before Cyrano had come to mistrust him and replaced him with Vannevar. Benedict had been expected to leave San Francisco but had chosen instead to stay on. Now that Vannevar was out of the picture, the prince had once again requested Benedict to represent him to the Dowager.

Vannevar had met Benedict only once or twice over the years. He'd found the man likable, but Vannevar had too much experience with the crafty Tremere and their vicious, Byzantine politics to trust any member of that clan. Cyrano himself had once appeared as no more than a meek underling until it was revealed that he'd spent years plotting Montelaine's downfall. Vannevar knew that Benedict and Cyrano were often at odds, but that alone was no reason to believe the Franciscan monk turned mage and vampire should be trusted.

But Vannevar trusted Iwo and, after taking off his shoes and replacing them with the odd *tabi* socks Iwo handed him, he followed his host to the rear of the house. Here he found Don Benedict waiting for them, sitting cross-legged on the floor at a low table.

Iwo was preparing tea and he beckoned Vannevar to take a seat at the table. While Vannevar took his spot, uncomfortably folding his legs on the pad in front of the table, Iwo brought him a cup of tea. Handing it to Vannevar, Iwo sat down as well, taking a spot between the two vampires who now faced each other over the table.

"Welcome, Vannevar," Benedict said, after the newcomer had made himself as comfortable as possible. "It is a pleasure to see you again." Benedict, like Iwo, sat comfortably on his legs and, unlike Vannevar, was not at all inconvenienced by the lack of chairs. He'd spent many years in Asia and was accustomed to Eastern ways. The two watched Iwo as he sipped the hot brew, each holding his own cup but unable to partake of the drink. Vannevar returned Benedict's greeting but said little more, feeling uncomfortable in the Tremere's presence.

"Vannevar has asked to stay here with me tonight," Iwo explained to Benedict.

Vannevar's eyebrows shot up when he heard Iwo speak. Didn't the man realize the chance he took? Could Iwo be so innocent he didn't know the danger of revealing such secrets to a Tremere?

Iwo noticed Vannevar's concern and tried to reassure him.

"Don't worry, my friend," he said, reaching out and taking hold of Vannevar's arm. "Nothing said here tonight goes beyond these walls. I promise you that."

"You can rely on that, Vannevar," Benedict added. "I would never betray Iwo — or you, for that matter."

Benedict sounded sincere but Vannevar could still not bring himself to trust him.

"I thank you for that," Vannevar said. "I would hate to

think that Iwo was at risk because he's agreed to do me a favor. I would consider it a grave insult, and one I could not let go unanswered."

Benedict understood the meaning. "Of course," he said, now looking into the black porcelain teacup he held in his hands.

Iwo conversed cheerfully, trying to brighten the mood of the room, attempting to bring the two men closer together. Vannevar was tight-lipped at first but it soon became apparent that Benedict already knew nearly everything regarding Vannevar's current situation. He was well aware that Vannevar was being tracked by a paid assassin.

"The thing is," Vannevar said, loosening up a little, "I'm not sure if he's been hired by Cyrano or the Camarilla."

"Oh, you can be sure this is Cyrano's doing," Benedict told him. "It is entirely his doing."

Vannevar felt a small glimmer of hope. If it had been the Camarilla, there was no way he could avoid the sect's vengeance. Its agents would pursue him no matter where he went, stopping at nothing to extract vengeance. If it was Cyrano's doing, Vannevar felt he might be able to survive and eventually turn the tables. Vannevar was impressed that Benedict would so openly defy the blind loyalty and secretive nature demanded of his clan. Under no circumstances should he have revealed his elder's plan. Unless, Vannevar told himself, it was part of an effort to gain his trust and thereby find a way to destroy him.

"I could end this quickly by killing Cyrano," Vannevar said flatly, without caution. "That is," he added, "if you would be willing to help me, Don Benedict. If I were on the throne I could see to it that you sat on the primogen council as representative of your clan."

Iwo was shocked by Vannevar's blunt proposal. Benedict immediately refused.

"I'm sorry," he told Vannevar. "But that I could not do. It

would violate all of my clan's traditions. Please do not ask such a thing of me again."

Vannevar was only testing Benedict. If the man had agreed too readily to the plan, Vannevar would have reason to suspect him. But Benedict's refusal showed that he still respected the traditions binding him. He was willing to extend the hand of friendship to Vannevar, but only so far.

"Please pardon me," Vannevar apologized. "I spoke hastily. I should not have presumed such a thing." The apology was sincere and was accepted by Benedict.

"Think no more of it," Benedict told him. "I understand completely."

They then discussed Vannevar's situation more openly, wondering what he could do.

"I don't suppose you'd consider leaving the city," Benedict asked.

Vannevar refused to think of it. "San Francisco is my home," he said. "Besides, I can't bring myself to run from a man like Cyrano."

Benedict understood his feelings. "Cyrano cares little for me either, I'm afraid. Unfortunately, I'm his only reliable connection to the Dowager these days." Once Cyrano's hoped-for solution to the Chinatown problem, the inscrutable Nosferatu had proved to be more trouble for Cyrano than she had been worth.

"Cyrano distrusts Benedict's fondness for Eastern ways," Iwo said with a chuckle. "He distrusts our magic and our philosophy, and dislikes the fact Don Benedict rejects his own Western heritage in favor of ours." Cyrano did not like foreign methods, feeling they somehow violated the magical precepts of his clan.

"He would have ordered me out of the city long ago," Benedict said, "if not for the fact he needed me to work with the Dowager."

An hour or two later the discussion broke up. After Benedict left the house, Vannevar was shown to his room.

Iwo heated water for a bath, and Vannevar, after carefully cleansing himself outside the tub as instructed by his host, spent an hour or more soaking in the hot water before finally turning into bed.

Vannevar got ready to leave Iwo's house the next evening as soon as the sun went down. Before going, he warned his host about the Assamite and his methods.

"Do not fear for me," Iwo said, apparently confident in his abilities. "Few would dare to invade my privacy," he grinned. "You know I protect myself well." Iwo's magic was potent.

Vannevar thanked him again for his generosity and then left.

He headed west, thinking he might find a spot somewhere in the sparsely populated avenues north of Golden Gate Park. The area was not yet strictly organized by the Kindred; Vannevar might clandestinely pass a few nights here, moving daily to different havens in and around the park, eluding the Assamite as long as he could. Beyond that, he had no plans.

Vannevar was riding on the Geary omnibus when he sensed a presence aboard the car. He scanned the faces of the passengers. All looked normal until his eyes fell on a middle-aged man in a suit, who was sitting and reading a newspaper. The man looked up at Vannevar, an evil smirk crossing his lips.

It was the Assamite killer, somehow disguised, and right on Vannevar's tail.

Vannevar got off at the next stop, jumping off the car at the last minute, hoping to catch his pursuer off-guard. He bolted down the street, heading south toward the fair. The Assamite, he knew, was right behind him.

He was trying to reach the Midwinter Fair and the safety of Elysium. He had doubts the assassin would feel bound by the Camarilla's declaration of sanctity, but Vannevar felt the crowds might at least offer him some protection. Neither the Assamite nor his employer would want a thousand witnesses to Vannevar's murder.

He reached the fairgrounds at a dead run, skipping the entrance booths and ticket salesman, scaling the fence, jumping down on the other side and disappearing into the crowd. Moving through the milling hordes of people, among the flashing lights and bright music, he felt the Assamite still following close behind. Vannevar did not linger, instead plunging forward into the thickest parts of the crowd, pushing his way by when necessary, casting furtive glances over his shoulder. The Assamite followed, still disguised as an innocuous, sandy-haired businessman apparently enjoying an hour or two at the fair before heading home.

Vannevar soon realized his attempts to lose himself in the crowd were futile. The Assamite tracked him like a bloodhound, rarely falling more than twenty feet behind. Vannevar might be safe among the crowds, but for how long? The fair would close in less than an hour and then he would be left alone with the killer. Reaching the large building that housed the sideshows, Vannevar suddenly ducked around the corner and fled the area, leaving the fair behind and disappearing into the wilds of Golden Gate Park.

Running as fast as he could, he raced through the back hills of the park, dodging among fantastic palm trees imported from the Canary Islands and the towering tree ferns of Malaysia. He tried every trick he knew, but still the Assamite clung to his trail, never wavering from his pursuit.

Vannevar was growing tired, nearing the end of his strength, when he realized that he had covered nearly the length of the park. He was nearing the Pacific Ocean now and the evening fog was rolling in, winding its way through the trees and over the foliage, turning the landscape into a mystical and mysterious garden.

That's when he thought he spotted Don Benedict.

"Benedict?" he whispered. He stopped running, despite his

certainty that the Assamite drew closer every second.

A milky form appeared before him, the outline human, the wispy features of its face barely recognizable.

"Vannevar," said the ghostly form, its voice sounding as though coming from some great distance. "Choose the path beyond the windmill," the ghost said.

"Benedict?" Vannevar asked, unsure of what he was seeing. He reached out his hand to touch the wavering form and found it insubstantial. His hand passed right through it. It was some kind of magical projection.

"I cannot stay," the ghostly form of Benedict said. "I cannot maintain this form overlong. Choose the path by the windmill. It is your only salvation."

The misty apparition then dissolved.

Vannevar fled the spot, heading toward the large windmill that stood at the western edge of the park. Though still unsure of Benedict's intentions, Vannevar felt he had little choice but to follow the advice. He had run out of options.

Vannevar found the path next to the windmill, a narrow trail beaten into the earth. It was nearly covered in a fog that swirled about oddly, blown by the cold offshore winds. Vannevar did not hesitate, but headed straight up the trail.

The fog swirled in such strange patterns that soon all sense of direction left him; he turned this way and that, unsure of where he was. He could no longer sense the assassin tailing him, but now there was something else — a sound in the air, a rhythmic throbbing, the beating of a distant drum. He followed the sound to its source.

He found the drummer in a small clearing surrounded by the swirling fog. A squat, powerful man, with copper-colored skin and straight, black hair, he was dressed in a jaguarskin cloak. A mounted jaguar head, feathered with plumes, sat atop his head; heavy rings of gold and jade hung from his ears. Under his arm he held a small drum upon which he beat with a stick.

Vannevar stood and looked at the man. He seemed an

unfamiliar type, decidedly different from the Indians he'd seen around this part of coast. Thinking back to books he'd read, he was reminded of the Aztecs conquered by Cortez centuries ago — and he remembered their mad human sacrifices.

"You are correct," the Indian said, ceasing his drumming and setting the instrument down on a nearby rock. His voice was deep, authoritative. "I am Aztec," he told Vannevar. He had somehow read Vannevar's mind. "I am called Hortator, high priest and subject of Moctezuma."

The Aztec leader Moctezuma had handed over his entire empire and all its riches to the invading Spaniards. His wise men had foretold the coming of a "white god" and Cortez had been accepted as the manifestation of the prophecy. Only too late did the Aztecs realize their error. It had proved their downfall.

"I was that seer," Hortator said. "The one who convinced Moctezuma to trust the Spanish."

Vannevar wondered why the stranger was telling him this. He then remembered the Assamite still pursuing him and, listening, sensed nothing.

"Have no fear," said the Indian. "You are quite safe here, at least for now. I'm glad you've come. Benedict has told me a lot about you."

"Benedict?" Vannevar said, this time speaking out loud, recalling the encounter with the phantom Benedict in the woods.

"Yes," the Indian said. "I suspect he had something to do with you finding me."

"He pointed the way," Vannevar told him. "Or at least his spirit did."

Hortator nodded. "That's the most he would dare to do, I'm sure. He must be careful to avoid offending Cyrano."

"Why am I here?" Vannevar asked, beginning to realize this encounter was no accident.

"I'm looking for the new White God," Hortator told him.

Vannevar was puzzled by the remark. "What do you mean?" he said, wondering what the savage was talking about.

"Oh, I'm sorry," Hortator apologized. "I shouldn't have used the term. It's 'old form,' not really appropriate for this day and age." Hortator's manner relaxed. His accent disappeared, along with the formal terms. "It's really just a figure of speech, you know."

Hortator sat down on the rock next to his drum, motioning Vannevar to take seat on another rock nearby.

"Look," he said, after Vannevar sat down. "I'll get right to the point. I set up this meeting. We need to talk."

Vannevar nodded. "Benedict was in on it? And Iwo?"

"Benedict helped," Hortator told him. "Iwo, not really. He's more of an observer. Not one to get involved, if you know what I mean."

Hortator went on while Vannevar listened.

"There are big changes in the wind," he said. "And I believe your own destiny is tied up with them. Is it true that there is some Indian blood in your family?"

Vannevar admitted to it. "I'm one-eighth Powhatan," he told Hortator. "On my mother's side."

"I thought so," the Aztec commented. "It shows a little bit."

"So why am I here?" Vannevar asked him.

"Centuries ago I divined the coming of the white man — and others — to this country. It was clear to me that the people then occupying this land — my people — stood no chance once your kind 'discovered' us. It was as obvious as two and two, really."

Vannevar nodded his understanding. He was familiar with the history of his country's native population. Like most, Vannevar felt the coming of the white man to the New World to be a blessing bestowed on a savage land, but at the same time he felt a certain tinge of guilt. The natives were now dispossessed of most of their lands, their cultures destroyed, living miserable existences on reservations. Vannevar was not without sympathy for the plight of the Indian.

"I felt tremendous concern when I first figured it out," Hortator said. "But it was obvious it couldn't be avoided. And let's face it," Hortator continued, "my people fell right into the trap, wanting horses, whiskey, guns. They proved just as susceptible to the European toys and vices as the Europeans themselves. I'm afraid most of my kind were just as willing to give up their culture as the Europeans were to extinguish it. By the time any of us realized what was happening, it was too late. *C'est la vie*, as they say." He gestured with his hand, the French rolling off his tongue with a smart Parisian accent — but there was a wistful look in his eyes and a sad tone to his voice. The Aztec obviously missed the times that had once been. Hearing the French spoken so easily, Vannevar wondered where this Indian had been spending his time all these years.

"I've been around," Hortator winked at him, again one step ahead of the conversation. "Look," he said, changing the subject, "let's forget this White God business. I'm sorry I even tried that tired old line. The term has absolutely no currency these days. The point is that I long ago saw two forces pressing down on this continent, one from the West and one from the East. I thought about it a great while and, realizing that my people would be crushed in any event, I weighed one against the other until I finally decided that the forces of the West were marginally better than those of the East. Or at least that was my best guess."

"You mean you decided to back the European Kindred rather than the Chinese?" Vannevar asked.

"Oh, no, no, no," Hortator protested. "It's not so simple as that. It's really all part of something much bigger and much older than the present races of mankind. The Chinese working for the Grandfather are only tools in the hands of greater powers. No," he said, "I'm afraid it's much more complicated than that." He did not elaborate, alluding only to the fact that the Eastern powers dwelt somewhere deep in Asia, in a high mountain fastness. "They have been held in check for many years, but they will soon try to penetrate the West — and when they do," Hortator told him, "San Francisco and the Golden Gate will be the first to fall."

Vannevar pressed him for details but Hortator had no more information to give. "Much of the future is cloudy, or even invisible," he said.

But Hortator — or fate, as Hortator claimed — had chosen Vannevar to represent the forces in this struggle.

"What about Cyrano?" Vannevar asked.

The Aztec priest only made a face. "Hopeless," was how he characterized the Tremere prince. "He's good for nothing."

"Well," Vannevar said. "How do you know I'm the one?"

"The *one*?" Hortator replied with a grin. "No. You misunderstand. There is no *one*."

Vannevar didn't understand.

"Look," Hortator explained. "Certain things are almost bound to happen, and almost certainly people emerge to play roles in these events, but don't think that anything happens the way it does simply because of the efforts of any one individual. It's not so simple as that. There are others who might play the part I'm asking of you. It's just that I think you the best-suited. I actually had Delfonso in mind originally. I Embraced him centuries ago, having gotten the idea that a mix of European blood and Aztec vampirism would result in some kind of superior breed. But I'm afraid the experiment was a failure," he frowned. "Delfonso has not become what I hoped for."

In fact, Delfonso had become exactly the opposite. Instead of an elevated and competent leader and visionary, he had become increasingly detached from reality, petty, and almost senile.

"I think that you are the man we need in the spot,"

Hortator told him. "Have you ever entertained thoughts of ruling the city?"

In fact, Vannevar had long thought about the possibility, but had hesitated to become involved in the power struggles between Delfonso, Montelaine, and Cyrano, instead choosing to back the vampires he felt best. But he had come to realize that he himself was as suited to rule as any of them. Their mistakes and errors were obvious to Vannevar, and he'd felt sure he could do a better job.

"Of course," he answered honestly.

Hortator smiled.

"Your chance will come and when it does I think you will fight your battle well."

"You will help me to gain the throne, then?" Vannevar asked.

"No," Hortator told him. "I cannot aid you in that. You must do that for yourself. Await your opportunity, and when it comes, seize the moment."

Vannevar said he would heed these words.

"Now," Hortator said, reaching behind the big rock and pulling out a buckskin sack. "Your first problem is dealing with the Assamite. Fortunately, that's a problem I _can_ help you with."

He pulled out a short spear from the bag. It was barely four feet long, of carved wood, but its tip was set with wicked-looking, razor-sharp flakes of obsidian.

"Here," he said, handing the weapon to Vannevar. "This should be enough to put a stop to our Assamite friend."

Vannevar hefted the stout spear in his hand. He had never thrown such a weapon before.

"Don't worry about that," Hortator told him. "This weapon takes care of itself. Just heave it at the Assamite as soon as you see him — the spear will do the rest."

Vannevar, nodding his understanding, juggled the spear in his hand, finding the balance point.

"If you're ready," Hortator said, standing up. "I'll take my leave and you can finish your business." Hortator stood up, picking up the drum and his buckskin sack. "All set?" he asked. "The Assamite will come from that direction." He pointed down the path. "He was close on your tail, so be ready to act as soon as the mist clears."

"I understand," Vannevar said over his shoulder, standing at ready with the spear over his shoulder, ready to cast.

"Good luck," Hortator said. Then he hiked up the slope and silently disappeared into the fog.

The air began clearing, the fog dropping away, and once again Vannevar could sense the proximity of the Assamite stalker. As the Aztec foretold, the assassin suddenly appeared from out of the mist, racing down on Vannevar, wheeling the gleaming scimitar in slow circles over his head.

Vannevar launched the spear with all his might and watched it as it flew unerringly toward the assassin's heart, burying itself deeply in the vampire's chest.

On contact the spear glowed a deep red and the assassin fell over backward, screaming, clutching at the spear protruding from his body. As the shaft continued to glow and pulse, the Assamite writhed his last on the bloodstained grass, giving a final kick before dying.

Vannevar approached the body as the spear dissolved, disappearing to leave a ragged hole in the vampire's chest where it had devoured the Assamite's living heart. Vannevar took up the assassin's fallen scimitar and finished the deed.

An hour later Vannevar sat on the empty steps of the Coliseum amid the darkened fairgrounds. The place was empty now, closed for the night, the crowds long gone. Between his feet lay the severed head of the assassin, gazing up at him with dead, clouded eyes. Having destroyed this threat, Vannevar knew he would evermore be safe from the deadly Assamite clan. Any victim who managed to destroy an assassin sent against him gained the respect of the clan and never again would they threaten his life. But Cyrano still remained. The death of the Assamite was only a reprieve. The prince would continue to harass Vannevar by any means available, trying to force him from the city.

He mulled over Hortator's words, remembering also the cryptic reading of the skull performed by Iwo years ago. And he recalled old Sergei's words as well: "The pursuit of power is right only for those who desire it." Did he truly desire it?

The problem with the Tremere princes had been their inherent dishonesty, he felt. The constant plotting and playing off of one Kindred against another, keeping their political enemies off balance, fostering distrust, anger, and thoughts of revenge. The city needed a prince that could be trusted and would naturally attract the loyalty others tried to gain by fear and intimidation.

He got up from his seat on the steps and paced the ground in front of the Coliseum, further designing the rule he would put in place, were he to be given the chance.

An hour later he'd made his decision. As advised by Hortator, he would be patient and wait his chance, but in the meantime he would send a message to Cyrano, letting the prince know the struggle was not yet over. He bundled the head back up and left the fairgrounds.

■

Cyrano was gravely shocked the following evening when, upon entering the primogen council chambers, he found the bloody head of the slain Assamite sitting atop the council table in a pool of clotted gore, facing the prince's throne. Vannevar's message was abundantly clear.

9

1906: The Dragon Breathes

With the destruction of the Assamite and the warning sent to Cyrano, Vannevar returned to his haven in the Occidental Hotel near the Barbary Coast. Riley came back from Oakland — Vannevar spreading the word that should any harm befall him there would be the devil to pay.

Vannevar remained primogen but he no longer attended the council sessions. His seat remained vacant, for none of the city's other Ventrue felt daring enough to assume the position. He remained a grim and lonely figure, stalking the old Barbary Coast by night, his active presence in the city a constant and irritating reminder to Cyrano that he had failed to oust his rival.

Vannevar feared little anymore. A few younger vampires, trying to make their mark, had challenged him, but he had destroyed them all — ruthlessly — making examples of their folly. Cyrano was too fearful to challenge him directly.

Vannevar rekindled his chaste romance with Kwon, much to the anger of Loo who, as Vannevar had learned, also felt passion for the green-eyed beauty. Kwon treated Loo like a little brother, though, never responding to his clumsy overtures. She had made it clear to Vannevar that he was the only one she cared for. He knew little of the clan from which she descended, other than its members were some type of shapeshifters. She often appeared at their meeting in the form of a white dove that fluttered down from out of the sky. They met often in Portsmouth Square, always monitored by her protector, Chi, sitting across from one another on opposite benches, never touching, forever separated by race, culture, and clan.

Meanwhile Vannevar waited patiently for his opportunity to seize the throne.

Vannevar awoke on the evening of April 17 to the sound of the telephone ringing. He got up and crossed the room, lifting the earpiece from the wooden box mounted on the wall.

"Hello?"

Riley was on the line. "Hi, boss," he said. "I'm on the other side of town."

"What's going on?" Vannevar asked.

"Just takin' care of a little business," he said. "I'll catch up with you later, all right?"

"That'll be fine," Vannevar said, and rang off, hanging the earpiece back on the phone.

Vannevar went out alone that night.

It had been an unusually warm day and the night was strangely quiet. No breezes stirred the air.

Hungry, Vannevar wandered north, toward Pacific Street, looking for food. The hunting was successful and Vannevar fed well that night.

Around midnight Vannevar noticed a flock of birds that suddenly awoke and, taking flight, circled twice over the downtown area before wheeling in formation and winging their way across the bay to Oakland. At two o'clock in the morning the city's dogs set up a howling that lasted nearly thirty minutes. Vannevar could determine no cause for these strange occurrences.

Returning to the Occidental, still puzzling over the night's bizarre events, Vannevar encountered Riley, pulling up to the curb in a shiny new Oldsmobile. Parking the automobile, he shut the engine off and hopped out. He was grinning proudly.

"Well?" he asked Vannevar. "What do you think of her?"

"Where'd you pick that up?" Vannevar asked him. He was cautious of the new machines. In fact, Vannevar had yet to ride in one. He didn't think much of the smoke and noise they made.

"Bought it from a friend," Riley answered. "What do you think?" he asked again.

"I'll stick with our four-footed friends, if you don't mind," he said, kidding Riley. But he had to admit the auto looked pretty sharp under the gaslights. It had a shiny brass horn with a rubber bulb.

"It's the coming thing," Riley told him. "We've got to make an effort to stay up with the times."

Vannevar grudgingly admitted that Riley was probably right.

It was nearing dawn and, after a few minutes spent admiring Riley's new acquisition, Vannevar bade him goodnight and retired to his room in the hotel.

At 5:12 A.M., the earthquake struck. Vannevar was sitting on the edge of his bed, about to retire, when he heard — or felt — a roaring from deep below the surface of the ground. Then the room began to shift back and forth, small objects toppling over and rolling off shelves and bureau tops to fall to the floor. Vannevar tried to stand up and save some of the more delicate pieces but the shaking grew too powerful and soon it was all he could to hold himself erect, grasping desperately to the bedpost. Outside, he heard the sounds of breaking glass and several loud booms as brick building facades fell away and crashed into the streets.

He knew then the earthquake was a big one. He'd felt hundreds in the years he'd lived here, the last real tremblor back in 1868, but this one was bigger than any he'd yet experienced.

After nearly a minute the oscillations slowly faded away. Vannevar bent to the floor to retrieve some of the fallen items; then the second quake hit, forcing him once again to steady himself against the bedpost. The second quake lasted only twenty seconds. As the last rumbles faded away, Vannevar heard voices shouting through the hotel. Outside, on the streets, more voices were raised.

Riley stuck his head in the bedroom door. "You all right?" he wanted to know.

"I'm fine," Vannevar told him. "How's it look outside?"

"I haven't checked," Riley said. "But it looks like there's a lot of damage out there. I'll go check. You get your rest," he told Vannevar. "The sun is coming up. If there's any danger I'll come and wake you."

Vannevar thanked Riley and then turned in for the day.

The recently discovered San Andreas fault had suddenly shifted, ripping along its length for several hundred miles up and down the coast. Although San Francisco, lying several miles west of the actual fault line, suffered less than San Jose to the south or Point Reyes to the north, the effect on the city was nonetheless devastating. Witnesses south of Market Street claimed to have seen the soft, sandy ground moving in undulating waves two and three feet high, rocking buildings, snapping power lines, gas and water mains, and twisting rail and trolley tracks out of their footings. But the major damage was north of Market Street, in the financial and business districts. Here, brick buildings and stone facades had collapsed, crumbling into the streets, burying residents and passersby alike. Much of the downtown area was built atop landfill used to reclaim the old cove; this soft and sandy ground was later held responsible for many major building collapses.

Riley was appalled by what he found when he stepped outside. Everywhere he looked he saw masonry buildings collapsed, bricks and stone shed from their steel skeletons, leaving the buildings' interiors exposed like cutaway doll houses. Others had tipped on their foundations and stood at cocked angles, ready to collapse at any moment. Few windows in the city remained intact and streets everywhere were covered with shards of sparkling glass. Power lines twisted on the ground, sparking and sputtering while the shouts, groans, and screams of trapped victims rose everywhere from the ruins.

The Occidental weathered the quake well but Riley's new Oldsmobile across the street lay crushed under thousands of pounds of bricks where an old warehouse had fallen into the street. Riley had only a few minutes to mourn the loss before he noticed the first plumes of smoke rising from down near the waterfront.

More than fifty fires had been touched off by the quake; furthermore, most of the city's firehouses, of brick construction, had collapsed, injuring firemen and destroying equipment. To make things worse, the aqueduct running up the peninsula — the city's sole source of water — had been snapped by the quake and the few firemen able to dig out their equipment and respond to calls found the hydrants dry, with no water to be had. Worst of all, the winds were blowing hot and dry from the west, in contrast to the usual cool fog-laden breezes from the ocean. These hot winds whipped the flames and soon the fires began to spread.

The worst blazes were along the waterfront, both north and south of Market Street. While the these fires began working their way inland, a third major fire burned out of control in Hayes Valley, near City Hall, the Public Library, and the Opera House.

The waterfront fires south of Market spread most quickly, joining together in a single conflagration that soon became a colossal firestorm blasting its way through the southern business district, destroying everything in its path.

North of Market, the shoreline wholesale district went up first as the easterly winds drove the flames higher, lifting sparks into the air and spreading flames through the main business areas. Already two major fires were burning within a block or two of the Occidental. The fires along the waterfront joined with one another to become a single wall of flame that marched west across the city, the smoke rising miles in the air, nearly blotting out the sun.

Riley knew that if he could not save the Occidental, Vannevar would have to flee. At midday, the vampire would be vulnerable to the sun.

Recruiting the few loyal followers he and Vannevar had in the area, and impressing several of the local residents, hotel occupants, and a squad of government employees from the nearby Appraiser's office, Riley began organizing crews to the fight the flames — a desperate attempt to keep the fires from reaching the Occidental.

Some men began clearing firebreaks in the rubble, while others mounted the roofs and from there began fighting the small fires that sprang up from falling sparks. An old cistern was uncovered and the greenish water hauled up in buckets and used to douse the flames.

The fire kept marching west, engulfing block after block of the financial district, all the time bearing down on the Occidental. But Riley's crew managed to halt the flames at Montgomery Street, just across the street from the stone Appraiser's office. Over the next few hours the flames burned all around the area of the hotel, eventually passing it on either side but leaving the territory defended by Riley and his tireless crew untouched.

North of the Occidental, the fires eventually were brought under control, saving the North Beach area, but not until after Pacific Street and the Barbary Coast were totally immolated. The southern wall of flame, however, passed by unchecked and soon it was advancing up the slope toward Chinatown and Nob Hill above.

■

Delfonso had retired to bed in his Palace Hotel suite just minutes before the earthquake struck. He'd spent a wonderful evening the night before: attending the opera, applauding Caruso in *Carmen*, followed by a late-night dinner in the famous singer's room at the Palace. It had been a splendid event, Delfonso told himself as he fell asleep.

He was jarred awake by the shaking of the bed and the shattering of windows in his room.

"Adolpho!" he screamed in panic, suddenly awake. He had been in the midst of the one of the strange dreams lately plaguing him and awoke unsure of what was his dream and what was real. "Adolpho! Please!"

Adolpho, a slim, genteel Mexican that served Delfonso as his valet, appeared in the doorway, holding on tightly as the Palace swayed and rocked, the hanging light fixture overhead dancing madly on its chain while trickles of plaster dust spilled down from a cracking ceiling.

"It is an earthquake, sir," Adolpho told him, desperately clutching the door frame as he was tossed him back and forth.

He could see his master was in a panic; Delfonso's face was drawn with terror. He had seen Delfonso this upset several times before, always when awakened from one of his terrible nightmares.

"Do not be alarmed, sir. It will soon stop."

As if by command the tremors resided, the rocking building coming to a slow, creaking stop.

Delfonso scrambled from his bed. "We have to flee!" he told Adolpho, taking the man by the shoulders and shouting into his face.

"No, sir. Please, go back to bed. It is daylight. You can't go out there just now."

Delfonso, finally understanding his valet's advice, let Adolpho lead him back to his bed.

"The hotel is safe, I'm sure," Adolpho reassured him. "I

am told that it was specially built to withstand earthquakes such as this."

And it was. Ralston had spared no expense making sure his grand dream could weather any disaster. Seven huge water tanks stood atop the roof, always ready to fight fire.

"Please rest," Adolpho said, pushing Delfonso back into the bed. "If there's any problem, I'll be sure to wake you."

Delfonso, mumbling, still wild-eyed, allowed the ghoul to tuck him back in, thanking his faithful servant for his care and concern.

The fires south of Market Street spread rapidly, burning their way inland from the wharfs, destroying the great office buildings lining Market Street and rapidly turning the flatlands south of Market into an inferno. By ten-thirty in the morning the landmark office building of the San Francisco *Call* just a few blocks away was ablaze, and the Palace now obviously endangered.

The staff of the hotel fought valiantly to save the great edifice, spraying water from the roof, keeping buildings surrounding the hotel wet and free of flames, but by one o'clock in the afternoon the great water tanks had run dry. There was nothing left to fight the fires.

"Quickly, sir. You must rise," Adolpho said, shaking the sleeping Delfonso by his shoulders. "We must flee. The fires draw near."

Delfonso's eyes suddenly shot open. The terror had not left him. He quickly grasped Adolpho's arms and looked into his eyes.

"I will die," he said, frightened beyond reason. "I will be consumed in the flames of hell as the dreams and the Grandfather have foretold."

Worried by his master's words and the look of madness in his eyes, Adolpho tried to remain calm.

"It will be all right, sir," he reassured the aged vampire. "I have made arrangements to get us out of here safely."

He helped Delfonso out of bed and into his clothes.

"Hurry," Adolpho said. "There is a wagon waiting for us below. But we must leave quickly." The last of the hotel's staff was already fleeing the building, abandoning the hotel to its fate.

Adolpho pushed the staggering Delfonso out of the suite and down a back flight of stairs to the ground-floor court. Waiting outside, on a back street away from the advancing flames, was a wagon and driver. Wrapping Delfonso's face in heavy cloth to protect him from the little sunlight able to penetrate the pall of smoke, Adolpho led him out the door and into the alley where an open coffin on the back of the wagon awaited him. Delfonso's eyes grew large at the sight of the polished casket and he began to falter.

"Hurry sir," Adolpho urged him. "There is little time left."

But the sight of the coffin terrified Delfonso.

"I'm not sure..." he said, suddenly refusing to budge.

But Adolpho gently coaxed his master into the coffin.

"Are you sure?" Delfonso asked, imploringly, as he settled into the casket and Adolpho began to close the lid.

"It is the only way, sir. No other method of transport could be found on such short notice."

Delfonso closed his eyes tight as Adolpho closed the lid and screwed it down.

Adolpho climbed up on the wagon next to the driver and they turned around, leaving the area, heading west and south away from the flames, to the refuge of an old house down in the Mission District located behind the old Mission itself.

■

Deep underground, beneath Chinatown, the members of the Family were sleeping in their communal crypt when they were awakened by the shaking and rumbling of the earthquake.

Chi, after making sure everything was secure, visited each of them in their individual alcoves, assuring them that all was safe and that he would be keeping an eye on the situation on the surface.

All day Chi watched from the lower slope of Nob Hill as the wall of fire marched steadily, inexorably up from the waterfront, across the financial district and toward the hill. By late afternoon the city's *ad hoc* fire-fighting teams, deciding they could not stop the fire's march by conventional means, attempted to create a firebreak by dynamiting entire blocks of buildings in a broad swath across the path of the flames.

At six-thirty that evening, with the sun still setting in the west, the dynamite was in place and soon after the explosions began. Unfortunately, the demolition crews were far from experienced. The explosions blasted bits of flaming debris high into the air; these then settled down in advance of the fire, quickly setting all of Chinatown ablaze. Within minutes the whole of Dupont Street broke out in flames while the main fire leaped over the badly executed firebreak and raged forward, unchecked.

Chi realized he had to move fast. Everything was already in place for an emergency evacuation, but he would have to wake the Family. Heading back underground, he moved quickly among the sleeping Kindred, raising the Grandfather, Loo, and Sullivan, preparing them for the trial to come. Kwon had already left the communal crypt to dispatch orders to a boat waiting at Meigg's Wharf to the north. Assuming the shape of a white bull, she was able to move safely about in even the strongest sunlight. She had assured Chi she would return soon.

All three vampires were groggy, at first wondering why they were awakened so early. They could see shafts of sunlight still streaming down the broad stairs that led to the alley above. But then they saw the smoke, dust, and ash dancing in the bright beams and understood.

Helping the huge, stumbling Grandfather to his feet, Loo and Sullivan guided him forward, helping him into the antique red-and-gold litter in which they would carry him to safety.

Chi then provided Loo and Sullivan with broad lengths of black silk, instructing them to wrap their faces and hands to protect themselves from the sun. The two lesser vampires, along with Chi and another ghoul, would carry the Grandfather's litter through Chinatown, all the way up Dupont, through North Beach, to Meigg's wharf where a boat awaited to carry them to safety. Chinatown, Chi knew, would soon be nothing but ashes.

"Where's Kwon?" Sullivan asked as he wrapped his face and hands.

"She has gone ahead to the wharf in the guise of a bull," Chi told them. "She will make sure all is ready, then she will meet us back here."

Grasping the poles of the litter, the four men bent their backs and, grunting under the strain, lifted the Grandfather's sedan to their shoulders. The four staggered under the weight as they ascended the stairs to the smoky alley above.

On the surface they made their way through the crowds thronging narrow Dupont Street, keeping to the western side, using the shadows of the buildings to protect them from the setting sun. Their progress was slow and tedious, Sullivan kicking out at the mobs of Chinese, cursing at them as they fled the neighborhood, belongings strapped to their backs and piled in wheelbarrows. Crossing streets momentarily exposed them to the rays of the setting sun, causing Loo and Sullivan acute pain, but they carried on, unflagging, plodding north toward the wharf and eventual safety.

Kwon had not yet caught up with them and they were all beginning to worry when Chi suddenly spotted her coming toward them, down the center of the street, still in her guise of a pure white bull.

"There she is," Chi said, excitedly pointing her out. And then he saw the mob that pursued her.

Brandishing knives, axes, and clubs, a crowd of howling

Chinese harried her as she ran, beating her with their clubs, opening great gashes in her flanks with their knives and axes. In the panic, the crowd mistook her for one of the Great Bulls the Chinese believed supported the world upon their backs. Thinking Kwon one of the bulls who had deserted its post, causing the earthquake, they now attempted to drive it back.

Chi and the rest of the Family watched with horror as the bull that was Kwon, now hamstrung by her attackers, fell beneath a flurry of flashing blades, collapsing first to her knees, then falling over on her side as her life's blood gushed forth, running into the filthy gutters. The crowd fell back with a gasp as the form of the bull wavered, changing back briefly to that of Kwon before she crumbled to dust in the golden light of the setting sun.

The Family could not afford to mourn or hesitate.

"Forward," Chi kept commanding them, kicking at the crowds blocking his way. "We must move forward."

An hour later they safely reached the pier and here boarded the boat upon which they would live for the next few months.

■

When Vannevar awoke early the next evening, the fire had already passed safely by the Occidental Hotel and was now in the process of devouring Chinatown on its relentless march through the city. Climbing to the roof of the hotel, accompanied by Riley, it was with a sense of awe and wonder that Vannevar surveyed the devastation that lay south of his haven. Block after block, east to the waterfront and south beyond Market Street, nothing could be seen but burned ruins, a sea of glowing embers, the exposed and twisted steel skeletons of buildings still glowing red-hot in the deepening twilight. There was simply nothing left.

Behind them the wall of fire raged on, a hundred feet high,

casting its wavering orange light over the plain of ruins surrounding the hotel. Within hours it would crest Nob Hill, destroying the great deserted mansions on its summit, then continue on down the other side.

Scanning the scorched wastelands of the financial district, Vannevar tried to spot the domed Tower Office Building that had once served Cyrano as his haven, but he could not spot the familiar outline against the dark sky. It appeared that the building had been destroyed along with the rest.

Leaving Riley to keep an eye on things around the hotel, Vannevar left the Occidental and plunged into the ruins.

It was slow going. The pitch-black streets were strewn with rubble, occasionally blocked by live electrical wires dancing and twisting in the darkness. Ruptured gas mains burned brightly, lighting parts of the ruins with a pale, ghostly light. Odd pops and bangs sounded from the scorched ruins as metal cooled in the night air.

Vannevar moved carefully, staying out of sight. Soldiers were already patrolling the streets and there were rumors that looters had been summarily shot.

It took him the better part of an hour to pick a safe path through the seven blocks of rubble separating him from the ruin of Cyrano's lair. Finally reaching the spot, Vannevar was gratified to find that nothing remained of Cyrano's once-proud structure. It looked as though the building had collapsed during the first moment of the quake, folding in upon itself and crashing into its own basement. What had not been destroyed in the collapse had been incinerated by the wall of fire that had passed over it a few hours later.

Vannevar carefully entered the ruins and began exploring what was left. As he sifted through the rubble with a piece of wood, he heard a moan from somewhere below. Following the sound, he discovered Cyrano in the ruined building's second basement, deep below the surface, trapped by an iron beam fallen across his legs. He had fallen from the upper stories, rubble crashing down on top of him to pin him in the ruins. Hidden from the sunlight by the wreckage that trapped him, he had remained caught while the fire passed over him, leaving him grievously burned. Most of his skin was peeled away and his face partially consumed. Yellowed, scorched bone showed through his charred cheeks and scalp. Semi-delirious from the pain, it was a moment before Cyrano recognized Vannevar, now standing over him.

"Vannevar," he croaked. "Help me out of here," he pleaded. Although Cyrano's injuries were grave, if freed he would, in time, recover.

Vannevar looked down at him, not answering, considering the situation. Hortator had told him to be ready to recognize the opportunity when it came, and he saw it now. He dislodged one of the heavy stones crushing Cyrano's ruined legs.

"Thank you," Cyrano gasped, but then grew fearful when he saw Vannevar raising the jagged stone over his head, looking down on him, coldly.

"Don't!" Cyrano protested. "Please don't—"

But Vannevar brought the stone down, crushing Cyrano's head, destroying him forever.

A few minutes later he crawled back out of the smoldering ruins, brushing soot and dust from his clothing. He straightened up and once more surveyed the ruins. His eyes were bright, highlighted in the glow of the scattered fires, but distant. The lines of his jaw were set firm. He left the scene, his heart now grown colder, his feelings numbed.

The fire raged on for two more days, the following morning burning down the slope of Nob Hill all the way to broad Van Ness Avenue. Here, using dynamite and field guns, the army destroyed many of the great mansions lining the broad boulevard, attempting once again to halt the flames by means of a firebreak. But about the same time the wind suddenly changed direction, now prevailing from the west, and the fire turned north and east, by nightfall reaching the foot of Russian Hill, still burning out of control.

Meanwhile, in the south of town, the fires below Market Street, after consuming the Palace, continued on south and west, advancing down Mission Street before finally being put out the following day just as they reached the old Mission Dolores itself. The old adobe church was left untouched by the flames, as were many of the cheap frame houses in the surrounding neighborhood. In one of these houses, Delfonso cowered in fear.

During the second night of the fire the flames tried to cover Russian Hill but Iwo, by use of secret magicks, managed to stave them off. The fire burned its way around the hill instead, north to Fishermen's Wharf and the waterfront, then turning due east and marching through the flatlands of North Beach. By the time the conflagration was finally put out the following day, the fires had destroyed all the area north of Vannevar's territory — save the very top of Telegraph Hill — leaving only the few blocks surrounding the Occidental Hotel, a veritable island amidst a sea of ash.

As advised by Hortator, Vannevar had seized his opportunity when he saw it, and though the city was now destroyed, he vowed that, like a phoenix, San Francisco would rise from its own ashes. The kingdom would be his.

10

1916: A New Beginning

"Here. Sign these too."

A tall, strongly built man with a shaved bald head handed a sheaf of contracts and other papers to Vannevar. Vannevar, seated at a small, round table covered with a heavy black velvet tablecloth, smiled ruefully as he took the papers from the man's hands and placed them on the table next to the stack already signed.

"What are these for, Nickolai?" he asked the well-dressed Russian seated across from him.

"Just more of the same," Nickolai told him. "Contracts, insurance, the usual."

This tall, aristocratic Russian had come to San Francisco only a few months before, but Vannevar already trusted him implicitly. Driven out his home country by the brewing Bolshevik Revolution, he'd fled to San Francisco in search of refuge. Vannevar had quickly taken him in. Without contacts or friends in this country, Nickolai depended on Vannevar for everything and therefore, Vannevar reasoned, would be loyal to the man who befriended him in his hour of need. Nickolai was a Ventrue, a former advisor to Tsar Nicholas II, and had already proved his usefulness to Vannevar in many ways. He now sat on the primogen council as the Ventrue elder.

It had been more than ten years since the great earthquake

and fire, and while many had predicted that San Francisco would never recover, Vannevar had proved them wrong. Some had estimated that clearing the rubble alone would take years, but Vannevar had seen it completed in little more than three months. He had even ordered the wreckage used as landfill along the edges of the bay, thereby creating new and valuable real estate for Vannevar and the city. With most of the city's real estate already developed, this new, fresh acreage along the waterfront would command premium rents.

The city had celebrated its recovery and rebirth in 1915 with the Pan-Pacific Exposition, the city's second world's fair, staged in honor of the opening of the Panama Canal. The fair had been Vannevar's triumph, showing the world that the city of San Francisco had recovered from the devastation of the quake and demonstrating to the Camarilla elders that Vannevar was a competent and capable ruler. The fair had stood on the north shore of the city, at the edge of the bay, built atop earthquake rubble used to fill these former marshlands. The 432-foot Tower of Jewels, Iwo's latest creation, had been the fair's central attraction and landmark. It had been encrusted with thousands upon thousands of pieces of colored glass; bright searchlights played over it at night, creating a dazzling effect.

After a successful run of several months, the fair had closed, the tower and most of the exhibition halls had been torn down and the real estate sold off, bringing Vannevar a pretty penny. Homes had since been built in the area, now known as the Marina District.

Vannevar signed his way through the papers and handed them back to Nickolai.

"Thank you," Nickolai said, shuffling through the stack to make sure Vannevar had not missed any. Vannevar had signed using the numerous aliases and different signatures he had developed over the years in order to cover his business practices. "I think this should take care of the last

of the legalities," Nickolai told him, and hurried off to file
Vannevar's copies before giving the rest to a messenger.

The papers were the last to be signed before the opening
of Vannevar's newest venture, a nightclub some were already
calling "The Vampire Club."

Vannevar currently sat in the club's darkened main salon,
located one level below ground. The grand opening was
scheduled for tomorrow night and all around him workmen
were putting the finishing touches on the place.

The club was actually a steel-hulled yacht that formerly
belonged to an eccentric English millionaire. Dubbed the
Royal Phoenix, the yacht had been washed ashore during the
earthquake and left beached on the mud flats. Left in place,
half-buried in muck, and further buried by the landfill
project, the ship had served as a foundation for one of the
smaller exhibition halls constructed for the 1915 fair. It had
been scheduled for demolition after the fair's conclusion, but
one of the city's Kindred had suggested that the structure
be saved and put to another use.

After some thought Vannevar had agreed and since then
the aboveground exhibition hall had been redecorated and
named the Alexandrian Room, in honor of Vannevar's
birthplace. Below ground, the ship's decks had been gutted
of engines and machinery and remodeled into a special
nightclub that would cater to only the most select guests.
The lower levels would entertain vampires and ghouls only;
the upper floors would be reserved for their human retainers
and others. The club would be managed by the man whose
idea it all was, Sebastian Melmoth.

"Vannevar!"

Vannevar turned toward the sound of the voice calling
him. Speak of the devil...

"Vannevar," Sebastian repeated, hurrying across the salon
toward the prince. He looked concerned. All manner of last-
minute problems had cropped up, threatening to disturb
Melmoth's carefully laid plans for the club's opening.

"The glasses haven't arrived yet," he said in a huff, sitting down at the table next to Vannevar. "The opening's tomorrow night and I have a nightclub and a restaurant without a single glass on the premises."

Vannevar smiled at the man. Melmoth, usually casual, witty, and charming, was starting to show signs of strain. As the date of opening drew near, more and more problems had arisen, nearly driving Melmoth to distraction. He had solved them all, but with each new problem the pressure increased. And so did Melmoth's fear of failure. A replacement shipment of glasses had been ordered several days ago after the first shipment had arrived, in shards, aboard a truck.

"Someone's out to get me," Melmoth told him, holding his head in his hands, staring at the black velvet tablecloth. "They're trying to make me look a fool. I know it."

Vannevar wanted to laugh, but didn't. He'd never seen Melmoth in such a tizzy.

The vampire Sebastian Melmoth had come to San Francisco in 1908, the childe of a British Toreador named Endymion. They had stayed in the city a few months but when Endymion was ready to return home Melmoth told him he wished to remain in San Francisco. With his elder's blessing and the permission of Prince Vannevar, he had taken up permanent residence in the city.

Melmoth had visited the city once before, in 1882, when he was still human and still called himself Oscar Wilde. Vannevar had met him several times while attending Marie's salons. Vannevar had always liked the young man, and Melmoth had wisely refrained from ever stinging the prince with his barbed wit.

"Relax, Sebastian," Vannevar told him. "I'm sure the glassware will show up in time, and if it doesn't we can always commandeer some from somewhere else." Vannevar's holdings in the city were vast. Some whispered that since the earthquake the prince had managed to acquire as much as fifty percent of the city's businesses. That figure was a gross exaggeration, but it was true that Vannevar's influence now seemed to extend everywhere.

"But our glasses are monogrammed," Melmoth insisted. "I had them designed and made special."

"The problem will be solved," Vannevar assured him. "I have great faith in you." He couldn't resist teasing Melmoth in his moment of frustration.

Melmoth lifted his head from his hands and looked up, past Vannevar, to where three workmen were busy mounting a large oil painting on the wall.

"No, no, no, no!" he said, getting up from the table and striding across the club, berating the workman all the way. "Not *there!*" he insisted. "*There!*" he said, pointing at a wall the other end of the club.

Vannevar, deciding to leave, checked his wristwatch. It was nearly two o'clock in the morning. He had an appointment at two-thirty. He got up from the table and, scooping a few papers back into his black leather briefcase, headed upstairs.

He found the Alexandrian Room quieter; the work here had been finished long ago. Nickolai stood in the far corner, talking with the ghoul that would serve as the club's day manager. Vannevar waved the pair a goodnight, then went out the front door, where his long black Lincoln limousine awaited him. A liveried chauffeur got out of the driver's seat when he saw Vannevar emerge from the club and opened the back door for the prince to climb in. The ghoul then got back in behind the wheel and the pair drove off down the drive, past the guarded gate, and out into the city.

"Take us to the south waterfront," Vannevar told his driver. "Pier 10, please."

"Yes, sir," he answered.

Vannevar sat back in the seat, enjoying the view of the sparkling nighttime city he had done so much to re-create. New construction was still proceeding, but most of the business and downtown areas had been rebuilt, the ruins replaced by new and even grander buildings than had graced the streets before. Following the earthquake many people had predicted the city's doom, and little help had been forthcoming from the Tremere in Sacramento, but San Francisco — and Vannevar — had prevailed.

Though he had earlier laughed at Melmoth's near-comic distress, Vannevar also felt the pressures of opening night. The Vampire Club was a radical idea, never before tried in a city of this size, or in this age. The club would be an Elysium where the city's Kindred could meet and mingle without fear of hostility. Many new Kindred had flocked to the city in the wake of the earthquake and fire, and many more passed through on their way to other places — or came simply to visit. Vannevar hoped the club would become a place where ideas could be exchanged and problems solved. More communication among the Kindred, he believed, would lead to better relations. The community as a whole stood to benefit.

He also hoped the club would serve him as another set of eyes and ears. Rumors and information would pass through regularly, to be noted by Vannevar's people and passed back to him through discreet channels. New Kindred in town would be noted, plots discovered, and secret alliances revealed. All would be relayed to Vannevar.

But first the club would have to prove itself a success. Vannevar had left the details of decorating, entertainment, and atmosphere to Melmoth, the club's host, trusting him to provide a place that would flatter and cater to the city's Kindred. It was up to Vannevar to convince the Camarilla that the club was a good idea.

Invitations had been sent across the country and even around the world. Some of the Camarilla's most powerful Kindred had been asked to attend the club's grand opening. The response had been surprisingly positive and several major figures had agreed to attend. Some were already in town. Their approval was important, Vannevar knew. If they chose to, they could force Vannevar to close the place — forever. He still had enemies among the Sacramento Tremere and he knew they continually worked to discredit him. Additionally, anarchs — vampires lacking ties to any clan or the Camarilla — had lately shown up in the city. They ranged up and down the West Coast, stirring up trouble wherever they went.

Many of the more conservative Camarilla elders had been opposed to Vannevar's club, citing it as just another example of dangerous liberal trends. Vannevar was out to convince them otherwise.

Vannevar arrived at the deserted pier at exactly 2:28, two minutes early for his appointment. There was no sign of the party he intended to meet, and the driver parked the limousine in a shadowy corner out of sight. Vannevar waited.

A few minutes later Vannevar checked his watch and found it was now 2:36. The man he was supposed to meet was late. He grew increasingly impatient.

Vannevar was about to order the driver to leave when a pair of figures came walking around the corner. The pair sauntered along casually, the woman hanging on the young man's arm, laughing loudly as he joked and teased with her. The man spotted Vannevar's parked limousine and told the young woman to wait, leaving her to walk across the street toward the limo and his appointment. Despite the fact he was late, he seemed in no hurry, walking at a moderate pace, hands shoved in his pockets, whistling tunelessly. He wore a cheap suit coat over a brown workshirt open at the collar. A crumpled fedora sat jauntily on the back of his head.

The young vampire's name was Dirk, an anarch from somewhere back east. He was Caitiff, a clanless castoff, a vampire who'd been Embraced and left to fend for himself. He owed allegiance to no one.

Dirk had shown up in town a few years ago, taking up

residence in various places up and down the waterfront. He was actively involved with many of the city's unions, and Vannevar knew he was responsible for the recent plague of wildcat strikes, work place sabotages, and other labor problems the city's shipping industry was currently suffering. For a time Dirk and Sullivan had hooked up, the two of them running wild all up and down the Embarcadero, wreaking havoc with shipping, sailors and harbor security. A word from Vannevar to the Grandfather had put a stop to Sullivan, who was ordered to remain in his Tenderloin territory, but Dirk continued his activities unabated. The port of Oakland across the bay was benefiting greatly from the ship owners' fears, and dockings in San Francisco were on the decline. Its reputation as a troublesome port was growing, and Vannevar wanted it stopped. Nickolai feared the unions had been infiltrated by Communists and political anarchists. Vannevar knew that, to some extent, this was true.

Worse yet, Dirk had never presented himself to the prince. It was Tradition that any vampire entering another's domain had to call upon and pay tribute to the ruling prince. Dirk had never done this, despite repeated requests sent to him through channels. Vannevar had tolerated the snub so far, but it had gone on far too long. Many powerful and influential figures were in town and Vannevar knew he was being carefully watched, his rule scrutinized. He needed no trouble from Dirk the next few days. He had even gone so far as to initiate tonight's meeting, agreeing to a neutral location instead of requiring Dirk to appear before him, as demanded by convention. Vannevar had kept the meeting a secret. Only a few of his most trusted friends knew anything about it.

Watching Dirk draw near, Vannevar was amazed at the casual attitude the young anarch displayed. He seemed without a care in the world, even though he was meeting his prince, a vampire Dirk knew could destroy him almost as easily as look at him. Despite the insults he'd offered Vannevar, Dirk somehow seemed convinced the prince would not violate his trust.

Dirk reached the car and peered in the rear window at Vannevar.

"Hi. Am I in the right place?" he smiled.

"You're late," Vannevar said. "Get in."

"Sorry," Dirk told him. He opened the door and stepped in, taking a second to wave to the young woman waiting for him across the street. She raised her hand in response, then turned on her heel to face away from the parked limousine. Vannevar saw her light a cigarette.

"I got held up at a union meeting," Dirk explained.

Vannevar took a moment to look Dirk over, noting his scuffed shoes and patched trousers. The sole of one shoe had a hole in it.

Dirk took his hat off and ran his fingers through his untrimmed hair, combing it back before replacing the fedora on his head.

"So," he said, turning to face Vannevar. "What did you want to talk about?"

Vannevar just stared at him a moment, bewildered by the man's callow attitude. He chose to remain calm.

"As you may or may not know," Vannevar began. "this week is very important to me."

"I've heard about the club you're opening," Dirk interrupted him.

Vannevar guessed that Dirk was somehow responsible for the damaged shipment of glasses. He didn't bring it up.

"It's more than that," Vannevar continued. "There are many important figures visiting the city right now and I'm sure you can see it's in both our best interests that they find San Francisco an orderly and properly governed city." He said nothing about Dirk's labor connections but the young anarch couldn't resist responding to the unspoken accusation.

"Hey, look," he told the prince. "Don't go blaming me because working men are getting fed up and feel forced to take the future into their own hands. The price of freedom demands—"

"Don't," Vannevar warned him, cutting off his speech, holding up his hand. "I really don't want to hear all this."

Dirk fell quiet.

"I've got a letter of intent here I want you to sign." Vannevar said. He pulled a pair of typed documents out of his briefcase and handed them to Dirk, along with a pen.

"What?" Dirk protested, wrinkling his brow, not taking the documents from Vannevar's hand.

"Just sign them," Vannevar ordered him, glowering, his voice growing angry. He shoved the papers at Dirk.

Dirk snatched the papers from the prince's hand and, taking the pen, scrawled his signature on both copies before handing them back to Vannevar. Vannevar took them and, separating the two copies, tried to hand one back to Dirk.

"This is yours," he said.

"Keep it," Dirk told him. "What good is something like that anyway?" he scoffed.

"Simply put," Vannevar told him calmly, now putting both papers away and closing the briefcase, "it says that if you fail to behave during this period of time you give me complete permission to kill you — and make an example of your death as a warning to others. Any questions?"

Dirk glared at the prince but said nothing.

"We just like to have these things on record," Vannevar told him. "In case there are any questions later."

"Can I go now?" Dirk asked him, a sneer in his voice.

"One thing more," Vannevar said, taking Dirk's arm, his tone now more conciliatory. "I wanted to ask you how Margaret is doing."

Margaret still stood across the street, waiting for Dirk to return. He had invited her to join the meeting with the prince, but she had declined. She would have nothing to do with Vannevar.

"What do you care?" Dirk sneered at him. "She's told me all about how you take care of your childer."

The words were like a cold knife in Vannevar's heart. Obviously, she had still not forgiven him Swede's death. Dirk tried to pull his arm away but Vannevar's iron grip held him fast. Vannevar, suddenly realizing he still had hold of Dirk, released him.

"Thanks," Dirk told him sarcastically, pulling his arm free and straightening the rumpled sleeve of his coat. "See ya later." He got out of the car and was gone.

Vannevar ordered the driver to take him home.

■

The following night, Vannevar arrived at the club's opening at eleven-thirty, dressed in white silk tie and tails. Melmoth met him at the door, looking nearly as bedraggled as the night before. But he was lively and full of energy.

"Come in, come in," he welcomed the prince. Everybody's here — or almost."

The invitations had been carefully scheduled: all the invited city's Kindred, including the primogen, were expected to be in place by eleven o'clock. The prince would arrive at eleven-thirty, followed by the first of the out-of-town guests of honor at midnight.

"Anyone missing?" Vannevar asked him.

"Just Delfonso and Serata," Melmoth told him. "I suspect they'll be fashionably late."

Vannevar shrugged. Delfonso had fallen in with a recently arrived Toreador named Allanyan Serata, a young woman the ruling Toreador, Marie Richaud, found unlikable. Serata had taken up residence on top of Telegraph Hill, surrounded by a bevy of posing sycophants. So far she had grudgingly obeyed the will of her elder, Marie, but the rivalry between the two had grown steadily, and their feud was common knowledge among the city's Kindred.

"I suppose they'll be here when they get here," Vannevar said, privately hoping they would at least have the good sense to show up before the guests of honor arrived.

Vannevar handed his wrap to a female ghoul in the upstairs cloakroom, then followed Melmoth through the dim and quiet Alexandrian Room to the stairs leading to the party below. The Alexandrian Room would not open until tomorrow night. This evening's celebration was for Kindred only.

Downstairs Vannevar was pleased to find the party in full swing, the crowd so loud and lively that Melmoth had to shout to announce the prince's arrival. There was a brief round of applause for the prince, then the guests turned back to their conversations. Marie Richaud made her way through the crowd toward the prince, the first to greet Vannevar in person.

"Good evening. Good to see you," she told Vannevar, taking his hand in hers. "I think the club will be a great success, don't you?" She looked around at the vampires seated at tables and leaning against walls, most of them animatedly conversing with one another. Marie wore a tight black velvet dress, accenting her tiny figure. A broad choker set with diamonds hugged her throat. Her short blond hair was cut in bangs low over her eyes.

Virgil, her Sicilian poet friend from North Beach, was with her. Like Marie, he was a Toreador.

"Congratulations, your Grace," Virgil told Vannevar, shaking his hand vigorously. "I'm very happy to say that this is a wonderful idea you've had."

Virgil, as usual, was not himself around the prince. Vannevar liked the man but resented his constant attempts to garner favor.

"It was Melmoth's idea," Vannevar told him. "He dreamed the whole thing up."

"Of course," Virgil said with the hint of a bow. "I understand. But it could not have happened without your guidance, I'm sure of that."

Vannevar thanked him, then found an excuse to leave the pair. "I'm sorry, but I see Nickolai over there. I really must speak with him. Excuse me, please."

Vannevar left the two, Virgil again wondering what he'd done to offend the prince.

"Nickolai," Vannevar said, reaching the man's side and putting a hand on his advisor's shoulder. "Can I talk to you a minute?"

"Certainly," the Russian told him, excusing himself from the young Brujah he was talking to. "I'll only be a minute or two, my dear," he promised her before stepping aside with the prince. Nickolai was dressed in perfectly tailored tails, his shaved head polished and gleaming. Like many Russians, his features were distinctly Asian. Nickolai, though heavier, closely resembled his hated nemesis, the revolutionary Communist, Lenin.

"Any word from Prince Lodin?" Vannevar asked Nickolai. He had been hoping for a last-minute response from the powerful Prince of Chicago. Lodin was an influential figure among America's Camarilla. It was said he ruled his city with an iron hand.

"Nothing," Nickolai shook his head, frowning. "Not a word since the last refusal."

Vannevar scowled, but really wasn't surprised. Lodin was the most powerful Kindred in the Midwest and his attendance at tonight's event would have signified his approval of the project. But Lodin, a reactionary conservative by nature, had disapproved the idea. He ruled his own city in a fashion Vannevar judged practically medieval.

"All right," Vannevar told Nickolai. "I was just hoping we'd get a last-minute wire."

"Sorry," Nickolai told him.

It didn't matter much, Vannevar felt. Both Prince Marissa from Washington, D.C., and Don Sebastian, ruler of the fast-growing city of Los Angeles to the south, had agreed to attend — as had two representatives of the European Camarilla. If things went well, Vannevar wouldn't need Lodin's support.

"Go back to your company," Vannevar told Nickolai, winking at him.

Vannevar turned to walk away and nearly bumped into Sarah, the dark-skinned Brujah primogen.

"Hi," she said, standing on her toes to give the prince a quick kiss and hug. Her vivid purple dress was a sequined Parisian copy, strapless, the hem slit on the left side nearly to her knee. Her matching pumps were fitted with silver caps on the toes and heels. Her dark skin contrasted well against the royal purple. Her eyes sparkled in anticipation of tonight's events.

Vannevar returned the hug, smiling. Sarah, since the death of Cyrano, had been one of Vannevar's staunchest allies. She had never liked Cyrano, it turned out, but had felt compelled to support him out of fear of losing her Western Addition territory. Since Vannevar's ascension to the throne, she'd backed him unwaveringly on all his plans and projects. But as of late she had a complaint.

"I hate to talk business tonight," she apologized. "But have you accomplished anything with the Grandfather?"

Following the rebuilding after the earthquake, the Family had made their one and only overt territorial grab in their entire history in the city, putting Sullivan in charge of a seedy neighborhood at the southern foot of Nob Hill known as the Tenderloin. Traditionally a part of the Brujah clan's domain, Sullivan had moved in and brutally taken over the whores, dope, and other illegal trades that somehow always thrived in the streets of this area, eventually driving out the lesser Brujah vampire Sarah had placed in charge there.

Unfortunately, relations between the primogen and the

Family were still undefined. Although Chi, Loo, and Sullivan had attended Vannevar's formal coronation ceremonies and there pledged the proper obedience to his rule, the Grandfather had, of course, not shown. He remained, as always, hidden away in his underground lair. Vannevar had already contacted the Family regarding the matter of the Tenderloin.

"I've sent a inquiry to the Grandfather," Vannevar told her. "I'm still waiting for a response."

Though Sarah didn't know it, Vannevar had already decided he would allow Sullivan to remain in the Tenderloin. Since the earthquake and the death of Kwon, Sullivan's relations with the Family had grown cooler, no doubt due in part to Sullivan's non-Asian background. Vannevar feared that if he forced Sullivan back into Chinatown the Grandfather would see fit to eliminate him.

"But don't hold your breath," Vannevar warned Sarah. "There's a chance I might not get it back." He reminded her that he had already recompensed her loss with additional and more prosperous territories further west.

"But it's still not right," she complained.

"Hush," Vannevar told her. "No more business tonight, all right. This is supposed to be a celebration."

Sarah shrugged her shoulders, smiling sheepishly. "Sorry," she told him. "Forget about it. I'm sorry I bothered you with it."

"Thank you," Vannevar said. "You're probably better off without it, anyway."

Vannevar made a point of greeting the rest of the primogen: dark-eyed Joachim; Honerius, the current Tremere elder who had replaced Cyrano; and even the Dowager of Chinatown, the hideous Nosferatu garbed in splendid silken robes and attended to by a bevy of her most loyal retainers. Vannevar even sought and shook the hand of Olaf Petersen, the new Malkavian elder who had taken the place of the Commodore, missing ever since the earthquake eleven years ago. The new Malkavian elder muttered something in reply to Vannevar's greeting before turning back to the upside-down magazine he seemed intent on reading.

As expected, Delfonso and Serata showed up late, just minutes before the scheduled arrival of the first of the guests of honor, making a great show of it as they traipsed down the staircase arm in arm. As the couple made their grand entrance, Vannevar saw Marie deliberately turn her back to the pair, pointedly ignoring them. Once close friends, Delfonso and Marie barely spoke to each other these days, ever since the old Spaniard had allowed himself to be lured away by the younger Toreador.

Delfonso, as always, exhibited great charm and manners while escorting Serata around the room on his arm. Serata looked her Bohemian best, with short hair cut European-fashion, topped by a sporty French beret.

Delfonso, eventually finding Vannevar among the crowd, greeted the prince warmly, as always treating him as a "son" that Delfonso had somehow helped raise to his current position. Vannevar had always made an effort to humor the old vampire and had honored Delfonso with special hunting privileges no other vampire in San Francisco enjoyed. But Vannevar was worried that the old Spaniard's mind was beginning to slip. Since his narrow escape from the burning Palace Hotel, he had moved out of the city, choosing to dwell in a humble frame house down in the Mission District. Rumor had it that he had taken to sleeping in a coffin, generally considered an ominous sign among the Kindred — an indicator that the vampire was beginning to think of himself as something more dead than alive.

At midnight sharp, Prince Don Sebastian, Lord of Los Angeles, made his arrival. Vannevar greeted him at the bottom of the stairs, welcoming him to his domain and making the usual formal promises of hospitality and safety.

Sebastian thanked Vannevar, then allowed himself to be introduced around the room. The Toreador Prince of Los

Angeles was the leader of a formerly small town that had
suddenly, almost overnight, grown by leaps and bounds.
Discovered by the movie industry as a place where outdoor
filming could be conducted year-round, the sleepy little town
was now the heart of a booming industry and boasted a
population of more than a million, surpassing that of San
Francisco. Many judged Don Sebastian's domain was growing
too fast for a prince who was accustomed to a lax rule. Word
was out that the city was fast becoming a haven for anarchs.
In meetings they'd held earlier this week Sebastian had
talked to Vannevar about some of the problems he faced
trying to maintain control of a city growing almost out of
control. Vannevar had dealt with similar problems in San
Francisco's early days but nothing like the problem that
faced this southern prince.

Ten minutes after Sebastian's appearance, the Prince of
Washington, D.C. arrived. Marissa was a tall, glowering
figure, more formal and less friendly than her Los Angeles
counterpart. A Tremere, she had sat on the throne of the
nation's capital for many years. But despite their differences,
Vannevar and Marissa had found they liked one another.
Marissa was particularly impressed by how fast Vannevar had
restored his once-devastated city and, as it turned out,
neither of them had much use for the upstart Prince Lodin
of Chicago. Vannevar began to feel he might be able to ask
Marissa for support on future projects.

The two representatives of the European Camarilla arrived
fifteen minutes later. Both were Ventrue, but the elder, Lord
Kelvin, was the dominant half of the pair. He hailed from
London. His associate, Josef Bar, was a Prussian Jew currently
living in Zurich. These two powerful vampires represented
the highest-ranking Ventrue of the European Camarilla and
had traveled to San Francisco to witness Vannevar's
achievements and to seek his support.

The Ventrue clan was currently locked in a struggle with
members of some of the other Camarilla clans, a deadly affair

that had already spilled over into the world of humans, resulting in the Great War now ravaging Europe. The two Venture had been touring America, visiting influential clan members in different cities, trying to enlist their support and thereby draw America into the war. It was generally believed that if America joined the struggle, the balance would tip and the conflict would be quickly resolved. Of the actual issues at stake behind the scenes, Vannevar knew little, but he did know that the Tremere clan maintained its traditional headquarters in Vienna, the capital city of the Axis member Austria-Hungary.

War fever was sweeping America in the wake of the elders' visit and Vannevar had fallen in step, promising them a Preparedness Day March that had been scheduled for tomorrow — an exhibition of the city's support for the war effort.

As the arrival of the two elders was announced, Vannevar noticed the party quieting down. Lord Kelvin and Josef Bar were both powerful and ancient creatures, their voices deep and hollow, their physical presence nearly overwhelming. He noticed the rest of the Kindred growing uncomfortable in their presence. Vannevar even felt it himself.

The two elders were introduced around the room, each of the Kindred showing them deep signs of respect. Kelvin and Bar tried to be warm and friendly, but were not convincing. After the introductions, Kelvin drew Vannevar aside to speak with him privately.

"The parade is still on for tomorrow?" Kelvin asked him.

"Most assuredly," Vannevar told him.

"Nice touch, I must say," Kelvin congratulated him. "I think it will show you in favorable light, back in Europe."

"Thank you, milord," Vannevar told him, grateful to hear his efforts had not gone unappreciated. "I think I can promise you that San Francisco will fully support your efforts to put an end to this terrible war."

"And we thank you, sir," Kelvin told him. "Your aid and

assistance will not go unrewarded, I promise you. We shall be grateful."

Kelvin and Bar left a short time later, their visit to the club scheduled to last but a scant half-hour. With their departure the mood of the party once again lifted, the revelers' voices growing louder. Looking round at the gathered Kindred, some of them meeting each other for the very first time, Vannevar had to smile. It looked like the thing would be a success after all.

A few minutes later Prince Marissa and Prince Sebastian also prepared to leave. They were to commence their journeys home tomorrow night, both traveling by private rail car to their respective cities. Vannevar saw the two upstairs and walked outside with them to their waiting limousines. He wished them both a goodnight and a safe journey home.

"Good luck with the parade tomorrow," Marissa told him before she left. Washington had already staged its own successful parade, as had a number of other cities across the nation.

Vannevar thanked her, then watched as the two cars drove off. He went back inside, intending to return to the party, but at the top of the stairs noticed that the party had grown another notch livelier since he and the other two princes had left. He hesitated at the top of the stairs; then, not wishing to be a damper on the proceedings, left the club. At the cloakroom he picked up his wrap and had the woman call for his car.

A few minutes later the chauffeur dropped him off at the front door of his haven, the new, fourteen-story Breakstone Hotel built directly over the ruins of Cyrano's old Tower Building. Vannevar did not go in immediately, instead engaging the doorman in a chat until his chauffeur had driven the limousine out of sight. Then, wishing the doorman goodnight, the prince turned and walked up the street, north toward old Portsmouth Square.

Vannevar was a frequent visitor to the old square, coming here late at night to sit alone for hours, remembering earlier days in the city. He recalled Richardson's old adobe house that once stood here, and the hangings of the Sydney Ducks, but most of all, he remembered the late-night meetings he had once enjoyed with Kwon.

The square was near Pacific Street, and the neighborhood bordered on the old Barbary Coast. But it was a quieter area these days. The earthquake and fire had leveled all the old Pacific Street dives, and while some had rebuilt and tried to get business going again, it never was the same. In 1914 the Tremere-controlled California legislature had passed the red-light abatement act, putting an end to the city's open bordellos — a last, nearly pathetic attempt on their part to avenge themselves against Vannevar's assumption of the San Francisco throne. In any event, the law had effectively put an end to the Barbary Coast.

The murder of Cyrano still weighed heavy on Vannevar's mind. True, he had never felt any respect for the man, nor did he feel that Cyrano deserved any better than he got; but in killing him the way he did, Vannevar felt he had compromised his values. The city was better for Cyrano's death — of this he was sure, but it still haunted him sometimes.

And he now found himself alone. Kindred he had once known well and counted among his closest friends now treated him with deference. And the terrible death of Kwon during the earthquake had left him without the will to pursue another romance. Except for Riley, Vannevar had no one in whom to confide.

Looking around the city from the square's vantage point, he had to marvel at how much he had been able to accomplish in such a short time, but still he felt something missing inside.

It was nearly daybreak when Vannevar finally left his seat on the bench and walked home.

■

Vannevar was awakened at sunset by the phone ringing. It was the hotel desk.

"There's a telephone call for you, sir. Shall I put it through?"

"Yes," Vannevar said, wondering who would call so early. It was Nickolai.

"There's been an accident," the Russian told him. "Have you heard?"

"No," Vannevar answered, his anxiety rising. Today had been the Preparedness Day Parade, kicked off at two P.M. and led by Governor Hiram Johnson and the city's popular mayor, "Sunny Jim" Rolph.

"Somebody threw a bomb at the parade. Ten people were killed."

Vannevar was shocked. He'd not expected anything like this. There had been counterdemonstrations at similar parades around the country, but nothing this violent. At first at a loss for words, he finally asked: "Who was hurt?"

"Some of the marchers," Nickolai said. "The mayor and the rest had already passed by."

"Who do we think's behind it?" Vannevar demanded.

"Dirk's the prime suspect, of course," Nickolai told him. "But we don't have anything solid yet. We're working on it."

Vannevar hung up the phone.

Dirk was walking up the Embarcadero, near Pier 22, in the company of a pair of union officials when Vannevar suddenly appeared in front of them, coalescing out of thin air. Dressed all in black, he blocked their path; his pale face, burning with wrath, was terrible to behold.

Dirk's companions started, one of them fumbling for a loaded revolver stuck in the back pocket of his pants.

"No," Dirk warned the man, restraining him with his arm but keeping his eyes on the silent figure before them. "Don't do it, Henry. I'll take care of this. You two just get out of here. Leave me alone for a minute."

"Are you sure?" the other man said. "We don't wanna run out on you if there's trouble."

"There's no trouble," Dirk insisted. "I just got some business to discuss. Don't worry about it. I'll meet you back at Cogan's Grill later on."

Vannevar remained silent, waiting until the two men finally rounded a corner and disappeared from sight. Dirk stood facing the prince, waiting for him to say something. He wore a defiant look on his face but he grew nervous waiting for the prince to speak. He finally spoke up himself.

"What's cookin', Pops?" he asked.

Vannevar exploded. With a roar, he leaped at the anarch and, grabbing him by the shoulders, dragged him around and threw him against the side of a freighter moored at the pier. The hull rang as Dirk's head bounced off the steel plate.

"Bastard!" Vannevar shouted; then he backhanded Dirk, knocking him to the asphalt. "Do you know what you've done?"

Dirk tried to get back up but had trouble finding his feet. "I didn't do it," he mumbled at Vannevar, spitting out blood and pieces of a broken tooth. He wasn't pleading. He said it as though stating a fact. "It wasn't me, goddammit!"

"Get up," Vannevar hissed at him.

Dirk hesitated and Vannevar, grabbing him again, lifted him off his feet and once more slammed him against the ship's hull, this time pinning him against it by the shoulders. Again the hull rang as Dirk's head bounced hard.

"Why did you do it?" Vannevar demanded, his booming voice echoing up and down the waterfront. "Why?" He banged Dirk's head again, this time eliciting a groan from the anarch.

"Go ahead," Dirk said weakly, still challenging him. "Kill

me. That's what you want, right? It doesn't make any difference to you if I really did it or not. You just don't like me being around reminding you that you don't run the whole show. You know there's still a few of us out here with minds of our own, and you don't like it." Dirk turned his head away to spit out more blood, coughing.

Vannevar snarled, but then Margaret appeared as if from nowhere. She grabbed Vannevar's arm, trying to pull him away from Dirk.

"Leave him alone!" she screamed, for all her pulling accomplishing nothing. Vannevar was far too strong. "He didn't do it, you sonofabitch!"

Vannevar let go of Dirk who, once released, slid down to the ground. Margaret's face was livid, her blue eyes angry, burning bright.

"He didn't have anything to do with it," she told Vannevar, hotly. "I know that for a fact."

Vannevar said nothing, waiting for more.

Finally she said, "I wouldn't lie to you about something like that. You know I wouldn't."

Vannevar turned and looked down at Dirk, still sitting on the pier, then looked back at Margaret. He said nothing. Then he vanished, disappearing in a cloud of black mist.

11

1928: The High Tower

Vannevar sat alone in a chair in a darkened spacious room, his eyes glued to the huge lighted aquarium in front of him. Beyond the aquarium, on the far wall, a tall, broad window offered a vista of the city below: its electric lights sparkling, its hills wreathed in fog. Vannevar's new penthouse suite overlooked San Francisco from four directions.

The new hotel was built atop Nob Hill on the former site of one of the great railroad barons' mansions. The hotel stood at the summit of the hill, the penthouse at the very top of the twenty-eight-story structure, towering grandly over the surrounding establishments. Vannevar had finally achieved a dream: a haven worthy of his position and achievements.

But he wasn't interested in the view. He was watching the fish in the tank — silvery things, some of them nearly six inches long, hiding in the weeds, peering out fearfully. Like all his fish, they stayed awake at night; Vannevar used electric lights to reverse their natural day/night cycles to match those of his own. These fish were piranha, specially shipped here from South America at Vannevar's request. Among all the aquariums and fish he now kept, these had become his favorites. Not because they were the most beautiful, or the most intelligent, but simply because they reminded him the most of himself and the rest of the

Kindred. Vicious and carnivorous, but at the same time cowardly and fearful, they spent most of their time hiding in their lairs, peering out fearfully, somehow convinced that the rest of the world was every bit as savage and dangerous as they. They trusted no one, not even their own kind. If not fed properly, Vannevar knew, they would quickly turn on one another. The parallels between the fish and the Kindred were endless, he reasoned.

The fish had originally been Iwo's idea; he thought Vannevar needed a hobby. Iwo had several goldfish of his own. Vannevar had taken Iwo's suggestion and, finding the pursuit to his liking, had indulged heavily. His penthouse now featured more than a half-dozen specially built aquariums in a variety of sizes and shapes, and the apartment was filled by the soothing sound of trickling water circulated by the pumps and filters. Vannevar had made a point of collecting several different species, but had found the South American killers the most interesting.

Vannevar had lived atop the hotel for more than three months now, while workman finished up the lower floors of the building in preparation for hotel's grand opening. Already many of the upper floors housed permanent, resident tenants, and last week the hotel had begun accepting its first overnight guests. But tonight marked the official opening with a reception held in the hotel's downstairs ballroom to mark the event.

Vannevar planned to put in an appearance at tonight's event, though he would keep a low profile. Only a very few of those involved in the construction of the hotel had personally met Vannevar and even they believed him no more than a minor investor and well-heeled tenant. Vannevar's controlling interest in the property was hidden behind a screen of paperwork and company fronts.

The hotel atop Nob Hill had been his crowning achievement, marking the completion of the first phase of his reign as prince. He had taken the throne, gained control of the primogen, and overseen the rebuilding of his once-destroyed city. His occupation of the high penthouse apartment was a symbol of his success.

Now he had to find a way to ensure that the city would survive. Great rumblings were being heard among the international society of Kindred. The growing number of anarchs in Los Angeles and other parts of America now appeared to pose a serious threat. Vannevar had lately been under pressure to eliminate undesirables like Dirk but, thus far, had resisted these demands, maintaining that Dirk and the anarchs, though still capable of fomenting trouble along the waterfront, were more or less under his control. Nickolai's investigation into the Preparedness Day bombing had exonerated the anarchs, and Dirk, as Margaret had insisted, was found innocent of any wrongdoing. The bombing had turned out to be the work of the Sabbat, which Vannevar felt posed an even greater danger to San Francisco than the anarchs did.

The Sabbat was a dark and deadly cult of vampires, secretive, and in most ways opposed to the aims of the Camarilla. Its members were said to practice blood magic and indulge in the worship of dark deities. All manner of stories were told about them, though Vannevar doubted all could be true. One thing was known for sure: the Sabbat had long ago achieved a stranglehold on Mexico, one it held to this night.

Continual evidence of the Sabbat's presence in the city was being uncovered, most of it by Nickolai during his relentless surveillance of Dirk's and the other anarchs' activities. The Sabbat's ability to manipulate other vampires was well known and Nickolai harbored suspicions that Dirk might have connections to them. Vannevar doubted Dirk was under Sabbat influence, though it didn't keep him from having Dirk closely watched, anyway.

And still, Vannevar knew he had to face the unnamed threat from Asia, and the Family's continued presence in

Chinatown. Vannevar had lost his informal connection to the Family with the passing of Kwon; since then, all communications had been handled through formal channels. Vannevar had not spoken face-to-face with any member of the family — not even Chi — since that time.

Now Vannevar sensed a dramatic turn of events in store. Even Iwo, usually aloof from the details of this endless struggle, had warned Vannevar that he felt the situation was approaching a crisis point. And the dreams had returned: the great dark beast with glowing red eyes.

Vannevar had taken steps trying to discover the exact nature of the menace, hoping that when the time came he would be ready to respond appropriately.

The telephone on his desk rang, startling him back to the present.

He picked it up. "Hello?" he asked.

"It's almost midnight," a man's voice said. "It's about time you put in an appearance down here, don't you think?" It was David, Vannevar's aide.

"I'll be down in a moment," Vannevar said, stealing a glance at the clock on the mantel. "I'm already dressed."

He hung up and, grabbing his tuxedo jacket from the doorknob, left the apartment, riding the small private elevator down to the ground floor. The caller had been David Foster, one of Vannevar's finance fronts. Forty-nine years old, David was the grandson of Davey Foster, the young boatman who had piloted Vannevar and Riley down the river back in 1849. David Foster II had learned a lot from watching his grandfather and now worked directly for Vannevar. Unlike old Davey Foster, he knew Vannevar personally — even his secret.

Vannevar had found a need for normal humans in his organization, people who could move and mix with human society easily. But care had to be taken when choosing such aides. The risk of exposure was always a concern. Vannevar trusted David implicitly but nonetheless had taken steps to place hypnotic commands over the man's mind, making it impossible for him to reveal Vannevar's secret even if he wanted to.

When Vannevar arrived on the ground floor he was met by David at the elevator door.

"Good evening," David said. His blond hair, thinning on top, was marked by steaks of gray. Like Vannevar, he was dressed in a tuxedo.

"Good evening, David," Vannevar told him. "The reception is going well, I trust?"

"So far, everything's been fine," David told him. "But Delfonso showed up a few minutes ago and I thought you'd better get down here."

"Yes," Vannevar told him. "You were right to call me. Thanks."

Delfonso was becoming more of a risk all the time. Reports from Nickolai indicated the old Spaniard was becoming a danger to the Masquerade. He had broken off relations with the Toreador Serata, she having suddenly grown tired of the old man after her elder, Marie Richaud, had left town, freeing the Toreador primogen spot in the meantime. Marie, tired of continually bickering with Serata, had moved to Los Angeles, where she was now involved with the film industry. As a primogen, Vannevar had found Serata difficult to work with. She often opposed Vannevar's schemes — more out of contentiousness, he judged, than any real reason.

Delfonso had lately taken to running with some of the Hollywood clique who regularly visited San Francisco on weekends looking for parties and excitement. Los Angeles, still a growing community, lacked the theatres, restaurants, and hotels available in San Francisco. But the Hollywood crowd's wild behavior had done little to enamor them with the town. Following the Fatty Arbuckle scandal in 1923, many major hotels made it policy to refuse rooms to members of the film community. Additionally, Vannevar and Nickolai knew the Hollywood ranks were infiltrated by anarchs and, in some cases, possibly even controlled by them.

Vannevar entered the hotel's ballroom and found the reception buzzing, the hall nearly filled to capacity. Vannevar spotted the city's mayor and other local officials in attendance. Much of the city's upper crust were present as well. And the liquor was flowing. Nearly all the guests were drinking, despite the nation's ban on alcohol.

Prohibition had proved a windfall for Vannevar. The majority of Americans had chosen to continue indulging in alcohol despite the law, and Vannevar was making new fortunes bootlegging liquor into the country. The hundreds of miles of California coastline were impossible to patrol, and liquor poured in steadily from Canada, Mexico, and South America, the rumrunners landing in harbors and bays all up and down the coast. Vannevar's control currently extended all the way south to Monterey and north beyond the Oregon border. Vannevar smiled, knowing that every guest attending the reception was drinking his liquor.

He spotted Delfonso standing in the company of several Hollywood types: an older director and a well-known leading man Vannevar recognized right away. The third member of the troupe was a young woman — a flapper — that Vannevar guessed a young starlet hoping for her first big break.

Vannevar, standing across the room from the group, caught Delfonso's eye and nodded a silent "Good evening." The old Spaniard returned the greeting, then turned back to his companions to partake in whatever discussion they were holding. Vannevar wanted to make sure Delfonso was aware of his presence. He wanted the old Spaniard to know he was being watched. Vannevar still suspected the old vampire had something to do with the murder scandal involving Fatty Arbuckle several years ago.

David still stood by Vannevar's side.

"How do you think he looks," he asked the prince.

"Hard to say," Vannevar answered. "What do we know

about the people he's with?" David had taken the trouble to run standard background checks on them.

"Hollywood," David told him, as if the single word said it all. "They're up here on a weekend holiday. The three of them supposedly start shooting a new film sometime next week."

"And the young woman?"

"No one in particular," David told him. "A hopeful, looking for her break in films. They're all staying at the St. Francis."

The St. Francis was one of the city's best-known hotels, located several blocks downhill on Powell Street, situated across the street from Union Square, in the heart of downtown. Built shortly after the earthquake, it replaced an earlier St. Francis destroyed by the fire and was a favorite with visitors to the city. Vannevar owned it.

"Give Riley a call," Vannevar told him, "and tell him to keep a close eye on this bunch. I don't like their looks."

Riley currently managed the St. Francis, though from behind the scenes. The hotel's exclusively white clientele were reluctant to deal with a black hotel manager, forcing Riley to don the disguise of hotel doorman. The ploy had proved better than expected, the guests somehow more open and less cautious around service employees. And, working outside, Riley found he was able to keep an eye on busy Union Square and much of the rest of this important downtown neighborhood.

"Will do," David said, and left the ballroom to put the call in to Riley. Vannevar was left to mingle with the guests.

An hour later, just as Vannevar finished up a conversation with a visiting congressman, he heard someone call his name. The woman's voice sounded familiar but he at first couldn't place it. He turned around and found an older woman standing behind him. She was well-dressed, with a fox stole wrapped around her neck, and her silver-gray hair was arranged tastefully on her head. She looked to be in her late sixties. She wore diamond-encrusted earrings and a matching necklace. Vannevar tried to place the face but was at first baffled. Then it all came rushing back to him.

"Claire?" he asked, a broad smile spreading across his face.

"Hello, Vannevar," she smiled back. "How have you been, dear?"

Memories flooded back over him: the splendid balls and parties on Nob Hill, carriage rides through Golden Gate Park — golden years spent in the company of the young and vivacious Claire. Their romance had lasted barely two years, Claire eventually leaving the city to marry an East Coast banker. She had resided in New York ever since. The two had written each other for awhile but eventually the correspondence had stopped and they had fallen out of touch.

Vannevar, surprised beyond imagining, wanted to see and talk to Claire right away, and someplace away from the crowded ballroom. He escorted her out of the room to a small salon on the side where they could sit alone, sharing a small leather settee. He looked into her eyes, remembering the early days and what now seemed like better, easier times. Claire's face was lined, heavy with powder, and she had gained a few extra pounds over the years, but Vannevar hardly noticed. He kept seeing the young woman he had once so much enjoyed.

"What are you doing here?" Vannevar asked her, still not quite himself. He felt oddly nervous around his old flame.

"I had to come back to town for a few days and I thought I'd look you up," she told him. "Riley helped me track you down." Claire's husband had died several years ago. She still held title to several properties around the city and had returned to transfer them to her heirs. One of her daughters had accompanied her on the cross-country train trip. Claire had other children: another daughter and two sons. She showed their snapshots to Vannevar. He approved.

"They've all done rather well for themselves," she said, her maternal pride showing through.

"I'm very happy for you," Vannevar told him. "You've done very well for yourself. You have every right to be proud."

The old woman sitting next to him was gone from his mind now. Vannevar saw nothing but the young woman he'd known years and years ago.

Claire talked about how much the city had changed, complimenting Vannevar on the wonderful job he'd done rebuilding San Francisco from the ruin of the earthquake, but he wasn't listening. Finally he spoke up, interrupting her.

"Claire," he said. "Would you like to go upstairs to my apartment, where we can be alone?"

She giggled girlishly, her face blushing under the layer of powder. It was young Claire all over again.

"My dear," she said. "I thought you'd never ask."

Iwo came to the penthouse on the following night, invited by Vannevar to confer with him on the impending crisis they both believed the city to be facing. Recent signs from deep within the Asian continent were jointly viewed as a portent of impending conflict between the Asian powers and the Camarilla. Vannevar had been contacted by Hortator the Aztec several times in recent months; Hortator had warned the prince of ominous things he'd seen in dreams and visions. The Aztec could not elaborate, barely understanding the signs himself, but they both guessed a major confrontation was imminent. Vannevar was applying himself hard to the mystery.

Scholarly research into the matter was being conducted by the young vampire Leland Stanford, who lived in the small campus chapel at Stanford University. A hard-working and capable scholar, Leland had been tirelessly poring through the school's vast collection of tomes in search of clues about the mysterious past of the Kindred. The information was sparse and Leland had been able to learn little until the university managed to purchase an extremely rare Greek codex called *The Book of Nod*. Though often prolix and difficult to decipher, this nearly unknown text contained many clues about the clouded history of vampires.

Leland came across a passage that seemed to pertain to the problem facing them but, questioning his own attempts at translation, had sent a copy to Vannevar, asking for the prince's opinion. Looking at the copy, Vannevar was dismayed to find that what little Greek he'd once known had fled his mind completely. His efforts to decipher the original had come to no avail, causing Vannevar to wonder how many other things he'd forgotten during his nearly two centuries of existence. Baffled, he decided to ask Iwo for help.

Iwo approved heartily of Vannevar's mixture of methods, coupling ancient intuitive methods with modern, incisive rational thought. But Iwo declined to make himself an active part of Vannevar's efforts. Like old Sergei, Iwo described himself as an observer: interested in the dynamics of the conflict, but detached and indifferent to the actual end results. But Iwo was Vannevar's friend, and Vannevar knew that secretly the little Japanese wished him success in everything he tried. Vannevar had conferred with Iwo frequently about the crisis, knowing that if he posed a problem often enough to Iwo, the mage could not help but offer an occasional suggestion or two. This, in fact, had been Vannevar's purpose in inviting Iwo over tonight.

"This passage is the one that confuses us most," Vannevar said, seated at his desk across from Iwo. "Leland has effected two translations, but of widely varying meaning. It's left us stuck for the moment."

Iwo asked to see the translations.

"Do you want the Greek original too?" Vannevar asked, hopefully.

"No," Iwo told him. "Sorry, but I don't know the language."

Vannevar handed him the piece of paper containing the two variant translations. Iwo examined it, reading silently to himself.

"*The sons of Caine, eastern Nod and western [Nadod? (untranslatable)], will someday meet in struggle for [predominance? power?] but in a land both east and west, where the [dead? undead?] shall [walk? motivate?].*

The second variant was less explicit.

"*Children of Caine, eastern Nod and western [Nadod? (see above)] will someday join against the struggle for [see above] in a land both east and west. They are [dead? undead?] but shall [walk? motivate?].*"

"It's hard for me to say," Iwo apologized, handing the paper back. The difference is very subtle. Does the "dead, undead" translation refer to the Kindred?"

"That's the problem right now," Vannevar said. "We can't be sure exactly what the original means."

"But everything you've learned otherwise points toward some sort of invasion?"

"I'm afraid it does," Vannevar said. "I have little doubt."

Iwo nodded his approval. The danger grew greater with each passing year.

Vannevar questioned Iwo further, trying to draw him out, but the mage proved evasive this night, offering little insight to the problem. Growing exasperated with the mage's reluctance, Vannevar gave up and changed the subject.

"How's Don Benedict these days?" he asked Iwo.

Benedict still resided in the city, having petitioned his elders for the right to stay. Though affiliated with the local Tremere chantry headed by Honerius, he was not actually a member. Vannevar had supported Benedict's petition for residence, explaining that Benedict's close relationship with the Dowager made his continued presence in San Francisco of benefit to himself and the Camarilla.

And Vannevar had not exaggerated. He desperately needed Benedict's help keeping the Dowager under control. The old Nosferatu was frequently difficult to work with and Benedict seemed the only one capable of dealing with her. The longer Vannevar knew Benedict, the more the man gained his respect. He now counted him among the very few allies he felt worthy of his complete trust.

"Our friend Don Benedict is well," Iwo told him. "But, as always, less happy than we think he should be. He still spends too much of his time locked away, reading and studying books about Eastern philosophy and mysticism." Iwo often complained that although Don Benedict was a good student, he had to be continually cautioned against wholesale rejection of Western ways.

"I'm afraid that Don Benedict would throw the baby out with the bath water, so to speak," Iwo said. "He continues to turn his back on what he once was, insisting it is all worthless."

Benedict had been a Franciscan missionary but, after being Embraced, had rejected his religious and political views. Discovering Buddhist philosophy, he had sailed to the Orient, where he found and studied under a number of different teachers. While in China he had met and befriended the once-beautiful woman who was now the Dowager.

"I keep telling him to follow the middle path, over and over," Iwo lamented, though with a smile. "Still he refutes everything he once knew, convinced always that the secret of existence lies somewhere in the East. I tell him: 'Don Benedict! Look at me! Your teacher! I have left my home and traveled all the way to your land, just to study and learn your ways.' I tell him over and over: 'Truth is spoken everywhere — but only for the man who has ears.' "

Iwo took hold of his own ears and wiggled them back and forth in comic fashion, forcing Vannevar to laugh. Iwo laughed with him. He had once cautioned Vannevar with the very same statement.

The phone rang. Riley was on the other end.

"Big problems," he said. "You'd better get down to the St. Francis right away. Come by the back entrance. There are police all over the front."

Vannevar thanked him and hung up.

"Sorry, Iwo," he told his guest. "Something important's come up. I'm afraid I have to leave."

"No bother," Iwo told him, already up and ready to go. "I understand."

Vannevar's long, black, shiny Cadillac waited for him at the front door. The chauffeur drove him down the hill to the St. Francis, using the back entrance off Post Street. As they pulled in the alley, Vannevar noticed the rows of police cars parked out front on Powell Street, lights flashing. Riley met him at the back door; Nickolai was with him.

"This way," Riley said quietly, showing Vannevar to a back staircase. Police were swarming over the building and Riley didn't want to bump into any of them. "Downstairs."

They headed down to the second basement of the hotel.

"We've got a woman dead on the fourth floor," Nickolai told the prince. "Murdered. Tortured first. A couple of Hollywood people — a director and an actor. The police already have them under arrest. I was able to get to them before they were taken away. They won't reveal anything. We got Delfonso out of there before anyone spotted him."

The old Spaniard had taken part in the abomination and was now being held in the basement of the hotel.

Vannevar found Delfonso in a back furnace room, seated in an old wooden chair, bent over, face to the floor, head propped in his hands. His evening attire was soaked in blood.

He looked up as Vannevar entered and, seeing his old friend, tried to stand to greet him.

"Vannevar. I'm sorry," he pleaded. "I don't know what happened. I—"

Two of Nickolai's men standing behind Delfonso grabbed him by the shoulders and thrust him back down in the chair.

"Enough," Vannevar said to the men. "There's no need for that."

The woman's body had been found tied hand and foot to the bed, her heart cut out. It had all the earmarks of Delfonso's strange passions. The old Spaniard usually confined his abominable indulgences to the secret chambers under Mission Dolores, but this time he had brought them into the city, and into Vannevar's domain.

"Do you realize what you've done here tonight?" Vannevar asked him, glaring down at Delfonso. The Spaniard looked up at him, his eyes now wet with bloodstained tears. His mouth moved to say something, but no words came out.

"Take him out of here," Vannevar ordered the men. "Make sure he gets back home. I'll deal with it later."

The two men lifted Delfonso out of the chair and escorted him from the room. As he was hustled out, Delfonso turned to look back at Vannevar, but the prince ignored him.

"The other one's in the back," Nickolai told Vannevar. There had been a confederate involved — a Mexican female, Delfonso's childe.

Vannevar found the woman bound to an old furnace, held in place with thick chains. Three more of Nickolai's men stood by, heavy metal bars in their hands. The captive had been severely beaten.

She hissed when she saw the prince enter, displaying huge fangs. Her face was hideous: deeply sunken pits for eyes, hair straggling down her bestial face. Two small horns sprouted from her forehead, curling back tightly over her skull. Obviously Sabbat, she had kept her appearance disguised by magicks.

Streams of obscenities poured from her mouth as Vannevar approached; she spat at the prince. One of Nickolai's men stepped forward, silencing her with a blow from his iron bar.

"Sabbat?" Vannevar asked, turning to Nickolai. He'd never seen one before.

"Without doubt," Nickolai said. He was more familiar with the evil cult, having encountered it in Europe more than once. "She hasn't admitted to it yet, but I'm sure we'll make her talk."

"Carry on," Vannevar told Nickolai, turning on his heel and leaving the room.

■

Vannevar left his penthouse the next night, headed for the Ferry Building. Claire was leaving town tonight, taking the last boat across the bay to her train waiting in Oakland. Vannevar did not want her to get away without saying goodbye. She had told him this would probably be her last trip to the West Coast, and they both knew it was unlikely they would ever see each other again.

A new chauffeur was on duty tonight, temporarily replacing Vannevar's regular driver. Nickolai had advised Vannevar of the change, assuring him that the new man had been thoroughly checked out.

"Good evening, sir," the chauffeur said as he held the door open for the prince. The man's uniform was spotless, his tall boots gleaming like polished mirrors.

"Good evening," Vannevar smiled to him. "To the Ferry Building, please."

"Very good, sir." The man shut the door, then climbed in behind the wheel. The two drove off.

He found Claire waiting for him at the pier, accompanied by her middle-aged daughter. They spoke for a few moments, but Vannevar had to be careful around the daughter, who'd been told that Vannevar was the son of an old friend of Claire's. Her presence made the goodbye a bit uncomfortable; Vannevar was unable to say the things to Claire that he wished. But when the chance arose and the daughter was distracted, Vannevar managed to give her the kiss and hug he wanted.

"You'll take care of yourself, I hope," Claire told him, smiling, her eyes glistening with a trace of tears. "Promise me you'll stay out of trouble." Like Vannevar, she was sure this would be their last moment together.

"I will," he smiled, feeling vaguely empty as the time for departure drew near. "I wish you the best of luck."

He watched the two women go aboard the ferry and then they were gone. Vannevar stood on the pier for a few moments, watching the ferry disappearing into the foggy night as it chugged its way across the bay. He wondered what life would have been with Claire: if they would have raised children of their own, grown old together, and perhaps died still friends and lovers. He wondered what it would be like to be human again, to know that there would finally be an end to it all.

Then he returned to the limousine, picking up a late edition of the *Chronicle* from a sidewalk vendor along the way.

"Take us back home," Vannevar told the chauffeur after climbing into the back seat. Settling into the heavily padded seat, he opened the newspaper and began to read.

A few minutes later he chanced to look up and noticed they were heading south, along the waterfront.

"Where are you going?" Vannevar wanted to know. "You're heading in the wrong direction."

The driver said nothing, instead stepping on the gas and speeding up.

It was then that Vannevar realized he was in trouble.

He grabbed at the door, ready to step out of the moving vehicle, but the seat around him suddenly exploded. Clawed hands ripped through leather upholstery, clutching and clawing at Vannevar, holding him back, keeping him from escaping. The car's tires squealed as the chauffeur wheeled the big automobile around a sharp corner and into a dark alley, where he slammed on the brakes and killed the engine before diving over the seat to join the attack on the prince. The driver's face was now transfigured into a mask of horror, a thick, black forked tongue sliding in and out between his lips.

Meanwhile, the other Sabbat killers were tearing their way through the back seat, crawling from the car's trunk, where they'd lain hidden and waiting. They now swarmed over Vannevar, overpowering him with numbers, their filthy claws digging at his face and eyes while their fangs sought out his flesh and blood. The monstrous face of a degenerate-looking twelve-year-old girl flashed by his face, then ducked under his chin as the child sunk her fangs into his throat.

Vannevar kicked with both his legs, trying to break free while simultaneously grappling with the little girl. He threw himself backward against the car door, breaking the latch as the door flew open and Vannevar tumbled out onto the pavement. The Sabbat piled out on top of him, the child-monster still locked on his throat, greedily lapping at the blood spilling from Vannevar's wounds. Grabbing the child's chin, Vannevar yanked her head away. He heard her neck snap. He threw the quivering corpse aside, rolling over and shaking off a couple of the attackers, trying to gain his feet.

But then the three adult-sized Sabbat were back on him, one of them wielding a sharpened wooden stake, which he tried to plunge into the prince's heart.

Brakes screeched somewhere nearby and Vannevar heard the sound of car doors slamming open and shouts of men. Vannevar felt the Sabbat attackers being pulled off him, heard screams and more shouts, and the snarls of vampires fighting. Someone took him by the arm and pulled him to his feet, practically dragging him away from the fight. It was Nickolai.

"Are you all right?" the Russian asked him, steadying the prince with one hand while brushing off his dusty clothes.

"I'm okay," Vannevar told him, putting a hand to his throat, feeling the savage wounds already healing and closing.

Nickolai's men made short work of the Sabbat killers. In moments they were all dead.

"I'm very sorry about this, milord," Nickolai apologized. "We just discovered the chauffeur's body in a garbage bin a half-hour ago and immediately went looking for you. I'm glad we weren't too late."

Nickolai noticed the Sabbat child with the broken neck was still alive, twitching but unable to move or speak. He barked an order and one of his men dispatched it. Vannevar turned his face so as not to watch.

"This attack is a warning," Nickolai told Vannevar. "The Sabbat are trying to avenge the death of their friend." After being thoroughly questioned last night, the Sabbat woman had been put to death.

Vannevar nodded that he understood. "Take me home," was all he said.

Later, back in his apartment, Vannevar was again seated in front of the piranha tank when the phone rang.

"Yes," he said, picking it up.

The call was from Los Angeles, one of Prince Sebastian's men.

"Prince Don Sebastian asked me to call you, sir," the voice said. "I'm afraid I have bad news."

"Yes," Vannevar said, calmly.

"Marie Richaud is dead," the voice told him. "Killed by anarchs. They trapped her last night on one of the studio back lots. She was torn to bits."

Vannevar said nothing.

"Prince Sebastian just wanted you to know, sir," the voice said, hoping for some response.

Vannevar spoke this time. "Thank you," he said, then he gently set the receiver back in its cradle.

He turned his attention back to the piranhas. They were skittish tonight. They had not been fed in several days and the little carnivores were hungry.

"Are you hungry, my little dears?" Vannevar asked them, slowly rising to his feet. "Do you wish to be fed? Like all the rest?"

He plunged his hand into the water, closing his eyes, anticipating the pain as the hungry piranhas closed in. Soon the water was churned to bloody froth, but Vannevar did not remove his hand until his charges had devoured all the flesh of his hand and were gnawing at the very bones.

12

1936: The Plot Thwarted

A thick, cold blanket of fog shrouded San Francisco's Laurel Hill Cemetery, located just south of the Presidio at the bottom of 400-foot-tall Lone Mountain. The city's largest and most prestigious burying ground, Laurel Hill had long been home to more than 47,000 of the city's dead. Now it was nearly empty. Chilly, twisting tendrils of fog crept curiously into empty mausoleums, wrapped around stacked piles of broken headstones, and quietly explored the bottoms of emptied graves. Of the thousands of dead that once rested here, fewer than a hundred still remained, and these were scheduled to be exhumed and hauled away in the next few days.

San Francisco's citizens, hungry for real estate, had voted the city's cemeteries out of existence. Laurel Hill was the last to go, following such landmark burying grounds as the Masonic, the Calvary, and others. The dead were unearthed, loaded onto the backs of trucks, and carried south out of town, beyond the San Bruno Mountains to the little town of Colma, where they would be reinterred in new cemeteries built specifically for the purpose. By the time the project was finished, only the old military cemetery in the Presidio and the tiny burying ground beside Mission Dolores would remain.

The city, now expanded and developed to its limits,

looked forward to this additional real estate, hoping it would solve the housing shortage. Developers predicted great profits from this newly available land, much of it in prime locations and worth millions of dollars. The voters had passed the measure easily.

The Kindred knew the real reason. Removal of the cemeteries was part of an attempt to keep San Francisco free of Sabbat influence. The evil sect's habits were well known; graveyards were popular havens for the Sabbat.

One spot in the cemetery was free of the blanketing fog, a place where a small group of men stood around a freshly opened grave. Vannevar, accompanied by Nickolai, Don Benedict, and the Tremere primogen Honerius, were overseeing the removal of one of the last bodies from the cemetery.

"What do you think, Don Benedict?" Vannevar asked, watching as the Tremere, on hands and knees, flashlight in hand, peered down into the open grave, inspecting the cracked cover of the rotting coffin they'd uncovered.

"The marks are there," Benedict announced. "This is a good one." He stood back up, brushing dirt from the knees of his pants.

Vannevar nodded to Nickolai, who, with silent signals, ordered the ghouls and vampires standing nearby to pull the coffin out of the grave and load it onto the back of the parked truck nearby. Vannevar and the primogen planned to conduct an experiment on this particular corpse.

Vannevar had cracked the secret of the impending Asian invasion, discovering that special corpses had been buried all over the city, awaiting a day when animating spirits would bring them to life. The corpses would rise from their graves at night and then seek out and destroy all the Kindred of the city — except, of course, the Family. With the resident Kindred destroyed, the city would prove an easy invasion point for the enemy from the East.

The Family had, of course, been behind it all. For years they had been bribing and threatening the city's undertakers, forcing them to embalm certain corpses with a magical mixture of herbs and spices that would make these bodies suitable hosts for the animating spirits.

The actual locations of these special corpses were known only to the Family, and though the coffins were marked by secret and subtle symbols, Vannevar had chosen to remove all the bodies in the city rather than risk failing to discover even one of them.

The only thing left unknown to Vannevar was where and how the animating spirits would manifest themselves. He was sure that removal of the bodies would thwart the plan, but he could not rest until the means of introducing the spirits was known to him.

Vannevar watched as the ghouls loaded the coffin into the waiting truck.

"You can take care of it from here?" he asked the two Tremere, Benedict and Honerius.

"I think we have it under control," Benedict answered him. "We'll take the body directly to the chantry and prepare it tonight." Tests scheduled for the corpse would be conducted in the basement of the Pacific Heights mansion Honerius had inherited from the slain Cyrano.

"We'll see you there tomorrow evening, then," Vannevar told him. Accompanied by Nickolai, Vannevar left the scene, walking to his limousine parked a few yards away.

Nickolai waited until they were inside the car and the doors closed before speaking to the prince.

"I still don't think we should trust Honerius," Nickolai told him. He'd advised against the Tremere primogen's attendance tonight. "The less he knows about our plans, the better."

Despite the fact that the rotund Honerius had repeatedly sworn his allegiance to Vannevar, Nickolai's spies had established that the Tremere was in constant secret contact with his clan's chantry in Sacramento.

"We needed Honerius tonight," Vannevar told him. "And we need his expertise for the experiment tomorrow." Honerius had provided tonight's fog, screening their actions from any late-night passersby. "I don't deny your suspicions," he told Nickolai. "But he knows all our futures are at stake in this matter. I trust he will cooperate. At least for now."

Nickolai grunted an affirmative, though it made him unhappy. He raised no objection regarding Benedict's involvement. Time had shown Benedict to be a faithful, trustworthy supporter. But Nickolai shared Vannevar's deep-rooted distrust of the Tremere clan and its members' complex political machinations. He kept the local members of the clan under constant surveillance.

Vannevar had his driver drop off Nickolai near his home, then told the chauffeur to swing around and head for San Francisco General Hospital. Though it was 1:30 in the morning, he wanted to visit a sick friend.

In a darkened private hospital room Vannevar found a small group of people huddled around a bedside. The patient was a very old man. A few strands of gray hair covered his pate; his neck was thin and wattled, and his skin marked by liver spots. His eyes were closed, his breathing shallow, though even.

Vannevar silently joined the group at the bedside, taking a spot next to Riley, and looked down on the dying Davey Foster, a frail little figure so unlike the energetic teenager Vannevar had encountered nearly ninety years ago. Just two weeks ago the old man had celebrated his 104th birthday, an event commemorated in both the *Chronicle* and the *Examiner*. "San Francisco's Oldest Resident" they called him. There were pictures of old Davey, in bed, surrounded by dozens of his descendants, the mayor of the city, even the governor of California. Both newspapers published interviews wherein Davey recounted events of the city's earlier days: the gold rush, the Vigilantes, the great earthquake and fire. Davey claimed the only regret he had was that when his time finally came, he would not be allowed to be buried in the city in which he'd lived so long. The voter referendum removing all the cemeteries had made it impossible. Two weeks later he suffered the sudden stroke that had put him in the hospital. Today the doctors had informed the family that they believed the old man had but a short time left to live.

"Has he been conscious at all?" Vannevar asked David, his aide and Davey's grandson, standing on the other side of the bed.

"Off and on," the man answered him. "He's coherent occasionally, but then he slips away again."

David, himself now nearly sixty, was accompanied by two of his own middle-aged children, a daughter and a son. Both worked for Vannevar.

Riley watched Davey breathing. Unlike Vannevar, who had never met Davey face to face, Riley had known him well. Watching his old friend lying in bed, waiting for the time to come, Riley's eyes grew moist. He wiped a tear away with the edge of a hand, hoping none of the other visitors noticed.

"Is there anything we can do to help?" Vannevar asked David.

"Not much, I'm afraid," David told him. "The doctors said that all we could do was try to make him as comfortable as we can."

There was a catch in the sleeping man's breath and they all looked back down at him, suddenly worried. But then the breathing resumed, smooth and steady, and they relaxed.

"How much does he know about me?" Vannevar asked.

Vannevar's secret had never been revealed to the old man, though Riley had once told Vannevar that he thought Davey probably guessed more than he let on. Riley's failure to show any signs of aging had raised questions that Riley had never been able to answer satisfactorily. When Vannevar had first invited the younger David to work for him, the old man had asked his grandson about the secretive man employing him but, bound by the mental restraints implanted by Vannevar, David had not revealed the secret.

"Call us if there's any change," Vannevar told the trio standing the other side of the bed.

Vannevar and Riley slipped silently out of the hospital room.

After dropping Riley off at the St. Francis, Vannevar ordered his driver to take him home.

■

The next night Vannevar stood on the end of a windy pier that reached out into the bay from the city's eastern shore. Near him stood Nickolai and Don Benedict. The three of them watching as a crane slowly raised a cargo skid out of the freighter moored at the pier.

"Is that it?" Benedict asked the prince as the crane swung the load away from the ship, preparing to set it down on the dock.

"It should be," Vannevar told him. "Dirk said he had it marked by some of his people."

The crate's side displayed a big red "X" splashed across it. Some of Dirk's men had found it while unloading the ship. As soon as the anarch had learned of it, he had ordered the cargo kept aboard and then contacted the prince.

"I still don't trust Dirk," Nickolai said to the prince. "Why should he help us?"

"Because, like Honerius, he knows the entire city's welfare is at stake this time. It's in his own best interests to help us thwart the Grandfather's plans."

Vannevar had struck a deal with the anarch union leader, promising him and his unions numerous concessions in return for Dirk's promise of cooperation in certain important matters.

The crate being unloaded contained a shipment of earthenware jars, sent here from somewhere deep in Asia. Nickolai had thwarted the Family's plans, closing the area off to them and moving in with his own men to make sure the shipment did not fall into their hands. He had men posted all around the area, just in case the Family tried some desperate last-minute attempt to obtain the jars. Nearby, a truck waited to haul the shipment off and spirit it away to a secret location outside the city. Vannevar believed the earthenware jars contained the spirits intended to animate the special host corpses buried round the city, but he could not be sure until his minions had examined them and run some tests.

The crane gently lowered the crate to the pier. Longshoreman leaped forward as it settled gently down on the concrete. They unhooked the cargo net, pried off the crate's side and stepped out of the way. The three vampires approached the crate, almost cautiously, knowing already what it probably contained.

"Take a look, Benedict," Vannevar said. "Tell us what you think."

Benedict dug through the thick layers of excelsior padding the shipment, finally uncovering the jars, mounted in wooden racks. As suspected, there were exactly one hundred jars.

"Exactly the number of specially prepared corpses we've discovered," Benedict commented. The three smiled to themselves.

Benedict pulled out the nearest jar, cradling it carefully in his arms. The lid was sealed with a sticky, pitchlike substance. The lid itself was marked by Chinese characters.

"What does it say?" Vannevar asked anxiously.

Benedict squinted at the writing a moment. It was of very ancient style, and difficult to read. He frowned, then smiled.

"This is it," he said, a note of triumph in his voice. "I think we've beaten them."

Orders were given to unload the crate, the jars were carefully stored in the truck, and then they were carried away from the dock. Congratulating themselves, the three men got back in Vannevar's limousine and drove off, headed for the Tremere chantry in Pacific Heights, Benedict still cradling the one jar in his lap.

Arriving at Honerius' home they found everything in place and ready for the experiment. Honerius conducted his visitors to the deep basement below the turreted Queen Anne mansion. Here, in the underground chambers below the house, they would test their theory.

"Is everything ready?" Vannevar asked Honerius as they reached the lowest level below the house.

"All is prepared," Honerius told him. "Follow me."

Honerius led the group through a narrow passage that finally opened onto a small, stone chamber. A barred cell held a depraved-looking Sabbat vampire, who was chained by the wrists to one of the cell walls. The Sabbat hissed at them as they entered. He was a dark-skinned man, hair streaming wildly from his head, his mouth nothing more than a wide, ragged gash filled with razor-sharp teeth. He struggled at his bonds, but the chains held him fast. On the far side of the cell was a small pedestal table made of stone and, next to it, lying on the floor, the rotting coffin they had pulled out of the ground last night.

The lid of the coffin had been removed and set aside, exposing the withered remains of an aged and once-buried corpse. Little was left of it save brownish-yellow flesh, dried and stringy, barely enough to hold the bones together. The skull was hard and dry, the eyes mere sunken black pits.

Benedict carefully handed the jar to Honerius, who, in turn, gave it to his apprentice. Unlocking the barred door of the cell, the apprentice cautiously entered and, carefully

avoiding the clawing, snarling Sabbat, placed the jar atop
the table. With a stick of chalk, the apprentice next drew a
pattern of circles, loops, and other curvilinear designs around
the jar. Honerius and Benedict watched him carefully from
outside the cell, making sure the apprentice made no errors.
Finished, the apprentice hurried back out of the cell, again
avoiding the hissing, spitting monster in chains, and quickly
shut the door behind him.

Then they waited.

A few minutes later, trickles of smoke began to appear
around the jar, issuing from the sealed lid. Even from a
distance, the heat could be felt as something inside the jar
began reacting to the spell that had been placed upon it.
Then, with small popping sounds, the jar cracked, crumbled
a little, then fell apart, collapsing into fragments on the
table. A swirl of greenish smoke rose up from the shards,
twisting like a tiny, gentle whirlwind.

The Sabbat prisoner fell quiet, as entranced as the rest of
them by the movements of the dancing smoke.

Now nearly three feet high, the spinning column of smoke
began to curl over, reaching down toward the withered
corpse on the floor. The tip of the smoke gently touched
the face of the corpse, then oozed between the dried lips of
the corpse's mouth.

The corpse's eyelids sprang open and it sat creakingly
upright, the empty pits of its eyesockets now glowing green
and lambent. The withered thing struggled to its feet,
rocking back and forth, its eyeless sockets searching the cell.
Then, spying the bound Sabbat on the far wall, it sprang
forward. The Sabbat screamed, trying to push the thing away
with his chained arms, but the corpse was far stronger. It
pressed the Sabbat back against the wall, wrapping its
withered arms around the captive in a horrible embrace.
Burying its snapping, snarling head in the Sabbat's chest, it
gnawed viciously at the flesh and bone that stood between

it and the vampire's heart. The Sabbat screamed and kicked as the undead thing chewed into him. But the corpse clung to the Sabbat's chest like a demon, biting and chewing. Bits of the Sabbat's flesh and bone fell to the floor around the prisoner's feet.

Then the thing broke through the Sabbat's sternum and, finally reaching the vampire's heart, redoubled its efforts. Blood sprayed and the Sabbat's screams reached an impossibly high crescendo. The vampires outside the cell watched coldly, their expressions unchanging.

The chained vampire suddenly fell limp as the corpse tore the remains of the Sabbat's heart out of its chest and greedily devoured it, sucking and lapping noisily, though the thing was so rotten and unwhole that what it swallowed merely spilled on the floor through the rents and holes in its moldering body.

The vampires watched the thing at work, awed by its strength and deadliness, horrified to think what a hundred such monsters loosed on the city would have done to San Francisco's Kindred population. Undoubtedly they would have been all wiped out in a single night.

"How long do they live?" Vannevar asked Benedict, his eyes still on the gruesome sight, despite the revulsion he felt.

"Till sunup," Benedict told them. "Then, supposedly, the spirits flee and the corpse crumbles."

"I see," Vannevar said, still fascinated by the grisly scene.

Honerius' young apprentice crossed the room in front of them, walking a little too near the cell. With a single movement, the ravening corpse lunged at him, reaching through the bars and grappling the unsuspecting young vampire. The apprentice screamed, but the thing already had him. Yanking the apprentice against the bars, it buried its hideous face in the vampire's back, chewing its way into the back of its second, unintended victim.

Vannevar moved to help the apprentice, but Nickolai

grabbed the prince's arm and pulled him back. Honerius immediately stepped back out of the way, his hand flying to his mouth in fear.

Don Benedict had not panicked, but was already working a spell to dispel the creature's animating force. His hands described forms and figures in the air while he murmured the words of the magical chant. But Benedict was not fast enough to save the helpless apprentice. Even as the spell took effect, the bloodied, skull-like face of the animated corpse poked through a ragged, ever-widening hole in the dead Tremere's breast. Then Benedict's magic drove the spirit out of the body, leaving the withered corpse to collapse in a heap on the floor. The dead apprentice slid down the bars into a sitting position, a gaping hole in his chest, his clothing soaked with his own blood.

The four were left speechless. None had imagined anything quite like this.

They exchanged glances but said nothing. By the narrowest of margins they had escaped certain destruction. At least for the present.

■

Davey Foster died a few days later, his old heart finally giving out. Most of the family was at the bedside when he passed on.

Toward the end he briefly regained consciousness, once more lamenting the fact that after all these years he would not be buried in his own beloved city.

After receiving word of Davey's death, Vannevar made a few phone calls. A couple of bribes were paid, and late one night workmen appeared at Mission Dolores and did a little rearranging in the tiny, cramped burial ground beside the church, making just enough room for one more small grave. A tiny, nearly unnoticeable slab in a shady corner now marks Davey Foster's final resting place.

The special corpses were all reburied in the new Colma Cemeteries. Vannevar told the Kindred that the earthenware jars had all been destroyed. Secretly, however, Vannevar had them placed in an empty mausoleum specially constructed in one of the new cemeteries, awaiting a time when he might have need of them. The prince had a plan, one known only to him, Nickolai, and Don Benedict.

13

1946: The Palinate Treaty

World War II enveloped the globe for several years. America's war in the Pacific, facing off against the Japanese Imperial troops, was closely watched by the exposed coastal citizens of California. Nowhere in America was the fear of attack greater than in San Francisco. During the war the bay served as a staging area for troops and ships, and numerous naval bases were established around the area. The city also served as a depot for both the U.S. Army and Navy.

Finally the war ended, the Japanese forces were defeated, and their secret Asian manipulators forced to retreat. V-J day had been celebrated with great fervor in San Francisco, but Vannevar now faced his greatest challenge — a challenge mounted against him by his own supposed allies.

Vannevar sat in a back room of the Vampire Club, at the head of a long table. With him sat four other vampires, each one of them far more powerful than he. The Camarilla's representatives had come to San Francisco and now they wanted Vannevar to hand the city over to them. Prince Sebastian and Los Angeles had fallen to the anarchs in 1944 and the Camarilla feared Vannevar's liberal rule would lead to the same result in northern California.

Plans to oust Vannevar had been in the works for more than a decade, a secret uncovered by Nickolai in the course of his relentless investigations and constant spying. Nickolai, now commonly known as Vannevar's "Russian Wolfhound," had gained a reputation so fearsome that few of Vannevar's enemies could utter his name without at least a small shudder of fear. It seemed Nickolai knew something about everybody in the city — and he was absolutely loyal to the prince.

Vannevar had taken steps to counter the Camarilla's moves. Following the war, he had received an official demand to abdicate his throne. He had ignored it. Other demands followed, but Vannevar did not respond. Now the Camarilla had sent four representatives with orders to force Vannevar to abdicate. If he refused, they were to destroy him. Vannevar's Texas elders, unable to offer him any aid, monitored the developments anxiously, waiting to see how the crisis would resolve.

Vannevar sat at the head of the table, with Lord Kelvin and Joseph Bar on his right. On his left sat Karsh the Turk; next to him was the Tremere Pontifex Abraham Powell, overseer of the powerful Sacramento chantry — and Vannevar's long-time rival. A meeting earlier this week had been the first time Vannevar and Powell had met face to face. Today was the second occasion.

"I demand to know where Honerius is," Powell told the prince. "Produce him now."

Honerius had been ordered by his superiors to attend the meetings — probably in order to assume the throne once Vannevar had been deposed — but the Tremere primogen had suddenly disappeared. Powell suspected foul play on Vannevar's part but could prove nothing.

"Honerius does not respond to messages," Vannevar told him. "I can't imagine what's keeping him."

Honerius had been taken out of circulation. Staked and paralyzed, his body lay in Vannevar's apartment under the watchful eye of Nickolai. Vannevar needed a hostage during this crucial week. If anything happened to Vannevar,

Nickolai would make sure the Tremere primogen died as well.

Vannevar sat down in his chair, opened his briefcase, and took out a handful of papers.

"I took the liberty of having these contracts drawn up. You may read them over if you wish, but I assure you that you will find nothing aside from the conditions I outlined to you at the meeting two days ago."

Vannevar had caught the four off-guard by simply refusing their demands, countering with demands of his own. Vannevar was asking for no less than partial autonomy in the region, citing the hazards he had already seen the city safely through and the great dangers the city still faced. His demands had been met with flat refusals from all four. Vannevar had then resorted to threats. He had told the elders that if his demands were not met, he would turn loose a scourge upon the city that would leave every Kindred dead.

"We have spoken among ourselves," Lord Kelvin told him, "And I'm sorry to inform you that none of us takes your threat very seriously, Vannevar."

Kelvin had not turned out to be the ally Vannevar had hoped for when he'd last met Kelvin in 1916. It had turned out the ancient vampire still held Vannevar accountable for his support of the American rebels in 1776, even though Vannevar had been a mere mortal at the time.

Joseph Bar chimed in: "We do not think you would end the lives of yourself and all your friends in such a hopelessly self-destructive manner, Vannevar. We think we know you better than that."

Vannevar smiled. "Don't underestimate me, gentlemen," he told him. "If I do not telephone Nickolai within the next fifteen minutes and tell him you have complied with my demands, he will notify Don Benedict to unleash the spirits in Colma. Do not for a moment doubt that I would destroy all I have created before I let it fall into your hands."

Neither the magically embalmed corpses nor the

earthenware jars containing the spirits had been destroyed. Both were stored carefully away in Colma, in anticipation of a day when Vannevar would be required to wield just such a threat. If unleashed, the monsters would descend on the city, destroying all the resident Kindred. The four powerful Camarilla elders would likely escape — their powers were great — but with all the resident Kindred dead, the city would be left wide open, easy prey for Asian invaders, Sabbat intruders, or the ever-present bands of anarchs. If San Francisco fell into enemy hands, in all likelihood the Camarilla would never recover this valuable gateway to the North American continent.

"We don't believe you, Vannevar," Kelvin said. "We will wait."

They had called his bluff. But Vannevar had anticipated just such a move and prepared to play his trump card. Reaching into his briefcase, he pulled out four folders, each marked with the name of one of the four elders, each stuffed with dozens of papers. He stood up and, reading off the names of his guests one by one, handed each the proper folder.

"We have a few minutes left, gentlemen," he said as he passed the folders out. "Perhaps you'd like to do a little reading while we wait."

The four men picked up the folders, glancing at Vannevar as they carefully opened them and began perusing the pages they contained.

"Dossiers, gentlemen," Vannevar told them, sitting back down in his chair and leaning back a bit. "One for each of you, describing your personal activities over the last several hundred years. Go ahead and read them. I'm sure you'll find them very interesting."

The four vampires began flipping through the pages, stopping here and there whenever they found something of particular interest. Powell, finding one paper particularly distressing, swore out loud.

Each dossier contained information on the vampire it had been given to, outlining the schemes, double-dealings, and secret alliances each had conducted behind the others' backs. The information had been collected by Nickolai. It had taken him years.

"These are, of course, only copies of the original documents," Vannevar explained. "Other copies are tucked away in several secret locations around the country, you can rest assured."

"What is the meaning of this?" Joseph Bar exploded. Dark Karsh looked at Vannevar as though planning to kill him, but a signal from Kelvin warned him to hold his place.

Vannevar waited for them to calm down.

"The meaning is simply this," Vannevar told them. "If you don't sign the charter recognizing San Francisco and the surrounding territory as a free domain under my patronage, absolutely allied to the Camarilla but recognized as a free and independent state, I will expose every one of you for who you really are."

The four glanced nervously around the table, each wondering how much the others guessed about his own secret activities. Powell destroyed his own dossier, making it disappear in a puff of smoke and flame.

Vannevar then knew he had them.

Within an hour details of Vannevar's new domain — called the Palinate — were worked out and copies of the new charter signed all around. In another hour the four Camarilla elders had left the city, on their way back to their distant homes.

Nickolai swung by the vampire club, meeting the prince at the door. Vannevar was smiling broadly but, Nickolai noticed, his hands were trembling. His prince had brought all of them within a hair's breadth of losing the city, their lives, and everything.

14

1956: The Angry Young Men

"It was a nice evening," Vannevar told the young woman sitting next to him in the back seat of his limousine. He held her slim white hand in his own.

Margaret smiled up at him. "I had a good time," she told Vannevar.

Vannevar wore a tuxedo; Margaret was dressed in blue jeans and a black leather motorcycle jacket. They had spent the early part of the evening together in his apartment, celebrating her birthday, a regular affair they'd been enjoying for the past several years.

The two had made amends in the years just prior to World War II, helped in part by Vannevar's unexpected friendly approach to Dirk. The San Francisco docks were then still wracked by strikes, crippling the city's economy. Vannevar had offered Dirk's unions a package meeting almost all their demands, asking in return only Dirk's limited cooperation during the war years and those immediately following. The laborers had soon gone back to work.

Nickolai had cautioned Vannevar against it, but the prince's gamble with the anarch had paid off when Dirk informed the prince about the shipment of odd jars from Asia. The truce between the two led to further contact with Margaret and a gradual easing of the hostilities between them. They spent time together only once or twice a year, but Vannevar treasured these moments.

The limousine was parked near Pier 39 on Fisherman's Wharf, looking out over the northern bay, Alcatraz Island, and Marin County beyond. Crowds of tourists moved along the piers, visiting the many restaurants and souvenir stands that now populated the area.

Fisherman's Wharf was only one of several tourist stops in the city. In the years following the war, San Francisco had become a popular vacation spot. Vannevar had made great efforts to cultivate this reputation, realizing San Francisco's shipping trade would almost inevitably fall to competing ports in Oakland and other places around the bay.

Although, as promised, Dirk had cooperated in the years leading up to and through the war, he had not been bound by the agreement once the conflict was over. Dirk's last hurrah as a labor leader was a devastating waterfront strike, staged in 1955, that finally put an end to San Francisco's claim of being the West Coast's leading port. With the wharves tied up and silent for months, most of the shipping business had gone to Oakland. When the labor conflict was finally resolved, it was too late. The rival ports had moved in on the business and it was unlikely San Francisco would ever regain its preeminence.

Dirk, at last grown bored with union bureaucracy, meetings, boards, and the rest, had given it all up, bought a motorcycle and, with Margaret packed on behind him, taken up life as a freebooting "rebel without a cause."

Dirk stood nearby, across the street, waiting for Margaret. Dressed in black boots, zippered black leather jacket, and blue jeans, he casually lounged over the huge Harley-Davidson parked behind him. He wore sunglasses, despite the fact it was after ten o'clock at night.

"I'm sorry I couldn't stay longer," Margaret apologized. "But Dirk wanted to get out of town early. We're planning a ride through the Marin foothills tonight."

"Just be careful up there," Vannevar warned her. "The woods are full of Lupines."

The Lupines — werewolves — were found all over the bay area, bound into tribes and septs. By nature they were antagonistic to the Kindred.

"We will," she promised him, getting out of the car. "Thanks for everything." She leaned back in through the open door and gave him a kiss on the cheek.

"Take care," he told her, then she shut the door and was off to join Dirk.

Dirk, upon seeing her, straightened up and, after giving her a quick hug, mounted the motorcycle and kicked it to life. Margaret hopped on behind him and then they were gone.

Back in the penthouse, Vannevar took a few minutes to feed his fish before sitting down on the couch with the late edition of the *Chronicle*. A front-page story covered the latest developments regarding the State of California's attempts to convict San Francisco beatnik poet Allen Ginsberg on charges of obscenity. Ginsberg's published poem, "Howl," had raised hackles everywhere, and the state, undoubtedly instigated by Vannevar's Tremere enemies in Sacramento, was trying to make an example of him.

The beats had begun appearing in the city a few years after the close of the war, attracted by both the gentle climate and the sense of respect for personal freedom San Francisco seemed to exude. They congregated in the North Beach area — the flatlands between Russian Hill and Telegraph Hill — and by the middle of the decade the area was rife with bookstores, coffeehouses, and nightclubs. The growing reputation of the beatniks had even helped encourage the city's tourist trade; the bus tour companies regularly included this area on their lists of regular stops.

Vannevar thought the beats were not wholly without talent, though he admitted he failed to understand much of

their poetry. The Poseur Allanyan Serata moved among
them, he knew, but so did Sebastian Melmoth, a Toreador
for whom Vannevar had much more respect. Vannevar
recognized some of the Englishman's style in their works.
In all, Kerouac, Corso, Burroughs, and the rest seemed a
more sincere bunch than Serata's usual gang of bohemians,
despite sharing many similar depravities. The prince even
surreptitiously encouraged some of their often outrageous
behavior, enjoying the effect it had on more conservative
Camarilla vampires, while at the same time adding to his
well-earned reputation as a liberal ruler. Both he and the
city were enjoying the freedom the Palinate Treaty provided
them.

Vannevar, reading the latest details of the California
authorities' ongoing frustration over the affair, chuckled to
himself. Vannevar could just imagine the anger and
arguments the whole issue had raised in Sacramento. A
regular tempest in a teapot, he imagined it.

Noticing that it was nearing eleven o'clock, Vannevar rose
and turned on the television, giving it time to warm up
before the late news came on. When the picture finally
appeared, it was sharp and clear, thanks to the new broadcast
tower atop Mt. Sutro in the center of the city. Designed by
Iwo, this monstrous eight-hundred-foot iron structure stood
atop a nine-hundred-foot mountain in the middle of San
Francisco, transmitting radio and TV signals that could
reach to nearly every nook and cranny of this hilly town.

Vannevar sat back down, ignoring the show, continuing
to peruse the evening paper. Then he heard someone on the
television mention the name "Virgil." Setting the paper
aside, he turned his attention to the TV screen, watching
as an interviewer talked with a "local, hot new poet," who,
she claimed, had recently been published here in the city.
The poet was the Toreador Virgil. Dressed in tweed jacket
and turtleneck sweater, he stood in front of the camera,
smiling, preparing to read excerpts from his new book, *The*

Scarlet Letters. Vannevar noticed Allanyan Serata lurking in the background, dressed in an oversized sweatshirt and black leotards. She stood behind Virgil, a proud smile on her face.

"Dark night, dark fright,
Prince delight.
Life's blood, night's flood,
We drink, drink, drink."

Virgil's reading went on for nearly another minute, but Vannevar was already up and on the phone, his fingers spinning the dial.

"Nickolai!" he barked, after someone on the other end picked up. "Do you see what's on television?"

"I've got Channel 5 on," Nickolai said.

"Change to 4."

There was a moment while Nickolai left the phone to change channels. Then he was back. "I don't know what happened," Nickolai tried to explain. "Who gave him permission to appear on television?"

"No one, I imagine," Vannevar said, angrily. "Did you listen to the lyrics? What he was saying? Did you approve that tripe?" The text of the book had been presented to Nickolai for censorship just prior to publication. The Russian had okayed it.

"That's not the copy I read," Nickolai apologized. "They pulled a switch."

"I don't want excuses, Nickolai! It's your job to see that these things don't happen!"

Vannevar slammed the phone back down, angered almost beyond reason. Like a glass overfilled, his ongoing anxieties were ready to spill over at the slightest touch. Virgil's ill-chosen venture had opened the floodgates.

Virgil still declaimed from the television screen. Seeing him, Vannevar snatched up a paperweight from his desk and made to hurl it at the screen, but then, stopping himself, regained his control. Juggling the paperweight once or twice in his hand, he set it carefully back down.

■

Virgil was ordered to appear before the prince the following evening, but Vannevar was forced to cancel the appointment after a deadly event took place in Golden Gate Park. The city's Gangrel clan had been enjoying an impromptu gathering in the park's wooded western reaches when they were suddenly set upon by a pack of werewolves. Over half the Gangrel were slain before the remainder escaped. The current clan primogen, Alicia McGreb, suffered grievous, nearly fatal wounds. She was recovering now, but raving nearly out of her mind, angered over the deaths of her childer.

Evidence showed the attackers had come from Oakland across the bay. Nickolai identified a certain black Baptist minister as the most likely culprit. The man was known as the Reverend Hayes.

McGreb and some of the other Kindred were already calling for an all-out war, demanding that the prince mount an immediate attack on Oakland, ferret out the killer Lupines, and destroy them. Vannevar preferred other means, concerned what might result from rash actions.

Immediately following the war Vannevar had given the East Bay to Sarah, the Brujah primogen, to rule as she saw fit. The area was a fractious domain, beset by many rebellious vampires and inhabited by secret groups of Lupines as well. Immediately following the killings, Vannevar had contacted Sarah and had her put out feelers. Word on the street also pointed to Hayes, who was identified as the pack's leader. Through Sarah's connections, Vannevar requested a meeting with the werewolf.

Tonight's meeting with the Lupines was to be held in the

middle of the San Francisco-Oakland Bay Bridge, inside the yawning tunnel bored through rocky Yerba Buena Island where the two separate spans of the bridge are linked. The island, halfway between the two communities, was considered neutral ground.

The bridge was closed tonight for repairs, and the tunnel would conceal their activities from possible watchers stationed on either shore. The meeting would be held at midnight.

Vannevar arrived on time, in his limousine, accompanied by Nickolai and Riley. Hayes the werewolf was already there, his dusty black station wagon parked a hundred yards away, facing back toward Oakland. He stood outside the car, dressed in a suit and tie. He was tall and strongly built. A younger black man was with him, slimmer, and a couple inches shorter.

Vannevar got out of the back seat of his car and, accompanied by Riley, started walking toward the center of the tunnel, leaving Nickolai to stand next to the limo. Hayes and his companion, spying the prince, began walking toward them from the other direction, intending to meet the pair in the center of the tunnel.

Hayes was a strict Baptist, preaching fire and brimstone from his pulpit in one of Oakland's poorest black neighborhoods. He condemned San Francisco as a city of sin and depravity, and, privately, singled out the Kindred as the primary reason for San Francisco's fallen state. His attack on the city last night had been "holy retribution," the victims happenstance, merely the first Kindred he and his pack had chanced upon. Hayes deeply resented the second-class treatment blacks received from American society, resulting in a deep distrust of all white people. Vannevar had made a point of bringing Riley along, hoping his presence would put Hayes more at ease.

The four men stopped at the center of the tunnel, about six feet apart, Vannevar across from Hayes, Riley opposite the younger man. No pleasantries were exchanged. Hayes folded his arms over his broad chest and waited for Vannevar to speak.

"I must demand that you no longer enter the city," Vannevar told Hayes flatly. "It is for your own good. The Kindred are angry and demanding revenge. I don't wish it to come to that."

Hayes said nothing. He knew that if the Kindred came looking for him, he would probably be forced to flee Oakland or die; he could not possibly hope to win a war against the united Kindred of the entire city.

"I thought San Francisco was a 'free' city," he said to Vannevar. "Freedom for all." He looked the prince straight in the eyes, defiant.

The young man standing next to Hayes suddenly piped up, addressing Riley. "Hey, nigger? What you doin' with this jive-ass white man? You got some need to kiss white butt or somethin'?"

Riley said nothing, but crossed the intervening space in a single step and, temper flaring, hit the younger man so hard he was knocked to the pavement. Riley jumped on him and the two men began wrestling and scuffling over the ground. Both Vannevar and Hayes moved to intervene, but were stopped when a shot rang out behind them, echoing loudly through the tunnel.

Nickolai ran straight at them, a .45 automatic extended in his hand. Vannevar heard a low growl and turned back to see Hayes, his face now distorted and bestial, a thick mat of fur sprouting up from the back of his neck, bristling.

Nickolai was now up even with them. "Silver!" he shouted at the werewolf, holding the automatic pointed straight at Hayes' chest. "Don't move!" Nickolai had taken the precaution of loading his weapon with something Hayes had cause to fear — silver bullets.

Hayes calmed down, the thick fur on his neck lying back down. His face relaxed, slowly becoming more human again.

Riley and his opponent were separated; Riley's eye was bruised but the younger man had suffered worse. The meeting ended quickly but not without Vannevar making his intentions understood. He warned Hayes before he left that if he ever caught him in San Francisco again, he would be forced to kill him. Hayes said nothing.

During the ride home Riley sat in the back seat with the prince. He seemed abnormally quiet, despite Vannevar's obvious pleasure over having successfully thwarted Hayes; it was clear to him that his threat had left an impression on the reverend.

"What's the matter?" Vannevar finally asked Riley. "You're awfully quiet." It suddenly dawned on Vannevar what might be bothering his friend. "You're not letting what that young jackass said get to you, are you?" he asked.

Riley shrugged, as though it didn't make a difference.

"You don't really feel like that, do you?" Vannevar asked him, puzzled by all this, but at the same remembering that he'd brought Riley along specifically to make a statement to the racist Hayes.

"Maybe," Riley said. "Just every now and then." His face was turned out the window. "You use people sometimes, you know. I'm not sure I always like it."

Vannevar could think of nothing to say. The two longtime friends rode the rest of the way back home in silence.

■

Virgil's appearance before the prince had been rescheduled for two nights later. Nickolai and Vannevar were in the penthouse as the time neared. The room was darkened; the lights from the aquariums were the sole source of illumination. The two stood near one of the great windows overlooking the city, watching Virgil as he toiled up Nob

Hill, dragging one foot after another, certain he faced imminent doom.

Vannevar's anger had cooled since the night he'd seen Virgil on television. He no longer felt compelled to punish the man seriously. But he had agreed with Nickolai that he could not let this breach of authority pass unremarked. Nickolai had suggested something severe but Vannevar, remembering Iwo's admonition to follow the middle path, desired something less drastic. Together the two had come up with a plan they felt sure would touch the Toreador's Sicilian heart.

A few minutes later Virgil reached the hotel lobby, where he was shown into Vannevar's private elevator. Upstairs, he entered the penthouse apartment to find the prince waiting for him, seated in a great chair of carved wood. Nickolai stood just behind him, almost hidden in the shadows.

Virgil entered, cowed and fearful, holding his cap in his hands.

"Kneel before the prince," Nickolai spoke from the gloom.

Virgil dropped to his knees.

"I'm sorry, your grace," he apologized, twisting his cap, knotting it in his hands. "I didn't realize—"

"Silence!" Nickolai cut him off.

Vannevar now spoke. "You have violated the Masquerade, endangered our secret, and deceived your prince. What do you have to say for yourself?"

"I beg your mercy," Virgil implored, now on hands and knees, head almost touching the rug on the floor at Vannevar's feet. "I had no idea this would happen. Serata promised me it would be all right." He was sobbing now.

"Serata has been warned," Vannevar told him. "Now rise." Virgil wobbled back to his feet, cap still in hand. "Come forward," Vannevar commanded.

Virgil staggered up a step or two. Vannevar extended his hand. On his third finger was a heavy gold ring, set with a single blood-red stone.

Without further invitation Virgil took the prince's hand and began bestowing noisy kisses on the ring. Vannevar allowed the vassal his penance, then gently pulled his hand away.

"Now," he told Virgil. "Go back to your home. Do not let us meet under such circumstances again."

Virgil backed out of the room, bowing, thanking the prince repeatedly, then disappeared out the door in a flash. Vannevar, chuckling to himself, stood up and, pulling the ring from his hand, tossed it back into his desk drawer, convinced he would have no further problems from Virgil.

15

1967: Purple Haze

Nickolai arrived at the penthouse shortly before midnight, bearing with him a briefcase stuffed with papers. Vannevar met him in the outside hall, at the door of the private elevator.

"Come in," Vannevar told him.

The two entered the penthouse. Nickolai went straight to Vannevar's desk, where he immediately began unpacking the briefcase, stacking papers in separate piles atop the desk.

"These are the shipments consigned to the Family?" Vannevar asked the Russian, picking up a thick stack of papers and thumbing through them.

"All the shipping manifests from the last sixty years," Nickolai told him. Any earlier records had been destroyed by the earthquake and fire of 1906.

Vannevar pawed through the stacks, his eyes scanning over the figures, shipping dates, and ports of registry.

"Find anything linking Delfonso to the Family?" Vannevar asked, not looking up from the papers he studied.

"Nothing solid," Nickolai told him. "But there's enough circumstantial evidence that I feel sure of his involvement." Nickolai, knowing about the long-ago meeting between Delfonso and the Family, now suspected the Spaniard of collusion with the Grandfather.

Vannevar and Nickolai were running thorough checks of

the Family's shipping interests over the years. The Grandfather had long been active in the illegal immigrant/slave trade, over the years bringing thousands of Chinese into the country. Vannevar cared little about this, but worried what else the Family might be smuggling in along with the illegal immigrants. They had been lucky when Dirk tipped them off about the spirit jars thirty years ago. They could not count on such luck a second time.

"What about the Dowager?" Vannevar asked.

"Nothing evident," Nickolai said, now picking up a stack of papers himself. "She's up to her usual tricks, but I think there's little chance that she and the Grandfather are in cahoots."

The Dowager and the Grandfather still respected the Chinatown treaty they'd hammered out in the late nineteenth century. Profits from opium dens, fan-tan parlors, brothels, and fireworks were still divided between them. From time to time the two had clashed, but never again had they engaged in the extended violent warfare of the earlier days. The Dowager looked clean.

But suspicious evidence had been found. Illegal shipments — some of them patently innocuous — were on the increase. The Asian threat was still alive.

"Can we force Delfonso to talk?" Vannevar asked his security chief.

"Probably, but I don't think he knows much," Nickolai answered. "He's just a dupe for the Family. Better to leave him in place for now. I'm encouraging Benedict to make friends with him."

Vannevar nodded agreement. "Have you explored the possibility of a meeting with the Grandfather?" he asked.

"I have," Nickolai told him. "I've been in contact with the ghoul, Chi."

Vannevar, though concentrating on the problems at hand, couldn't help but remember the old ghoul fondly.

"And?"

"It can be arranged," Nickolai capitulated.

"Good," Vannevar said, stacking the papers back on his desk. "See to it."

Nickolai wrote it down in his black notebook. Then, changing the subject, asked: "Any word from Margaret?"

Nickolai knew Vannevar was worried about her. She'd not made it to their annual birthday celebration a couple nights ago, despite her repeated promises to show up. She, along with Dirk, had become heavily involved with the so-called "hippie" crowd down on Haight Street. Illicit drug use among the hippies was rampant, Vannevar knew, including a new psychedelic called LSD which, Nickolai had discovered, was being brought into the city by Dirk's motorcycle gang. Margaret and Dirk were living a wild lifestyle and Vannevar worried for her safety.

Vannevar shook his head. "No. I'm afraid not."

Nickolai left a short time later. Vannevar stood at the southern window of the penthouse, looking down Nob Hill, over the Civic Center, to the mountains beyond. The fog, driven by the cold ocean breezes, was rolling in over the mountains, spreading down the mountainsides, trickling through streets walled in by row houses, descending to the lowest parts of the city. From his high vantage point Vannevar could see the lights of distant Haight Street. He went to the phone and called for his car and driver.

Forty-five minutes later Vannevar was prowling the Haight on foot. He'd had his driver drop him off a couple of blocks away, in a place where his limousine would not be spotted. He didn't want to attract attention.

Vannevar had not visited this neighborhood in many years. The area had long been a lower-middle-class district, the streets filled with Victorian redwood row houses populated by the families of streetcar conductors, accountants, and other low-level professionals. Haight Street was the commercial strip, lined with stores, shops, and a few bars and restaurants. By eight o'clock at night Haight Street had traditionally been dark and quiet.

Now it was thronged with people — long-haired, gaudily dressed, playing guitars and harmonicas, high on drugs, simultaneously protesting a war and turning the area into one big all-day, all-night block party. The delicate Victorian facades of the old buildings had been repainted in bright combinations of colors; multicolored flags and pennants flew from rooftops and hung from upstairs apartment windows. Stores and coffeehouses were open late, and crowds clustered around the open doors of neighborhood bars, now doing business at a rate previously unknown.

Vannevar sniffed at the air. It reeked of incense and marijuana. The flower children had taken over.

Vannevar had planned to slip through the streets unnoticed, using shadows and small tricks to avoid being spotted by the crowds. But dressed in his immaculately tailored Brooks Brothers suit and expensive topcoat from Gump's, he stood out like a sore thumb. Despite the attention he continued to draw, he felt surprisingly little animosity from the self-proclaimed "antiestablishment" crowd. He heard a few sniggers, and a couple of disparaging comments, but generally the hippies impressed him as a friendly lot — though, he reasoned, probably all high on drugs.

He stopped a pair of young girls in ankle-length dresses and asked them about Dirk and Margaret. They couldn't help him. He declined their invitation to join them at a party somewhere and continued his search. He finally found a young man with shoulder-length hair playing guitar on the corner. The hippie pointed Vannevar up the street, to an apartment over a hardware store, just a few doors down from the intersection of Haight and Ashbury, the very heart of the hippie scene. Vannevar thanked him, dropping a dollar into his guitar case before leaving.

Once at the spot, Vannevar hesitated, lurking across the

street from the building, trying to decide whether to go up or not. Then he heard the ground-shaking roar of motorcycles coming down the street. It was Dirk, leading his pack.

Dirk had evolved his image the last few years. Gone was the soft cap and zippered leather jacket, replaced now by a headband and Levi's jacket with the sleeves cut off, the back displaying his biker gang's personal colors. He wore a pair of wire-rim glasses with blue octagonal lenses. The rest of the gang dressed similarly, their hair uniformly long and straggly — except for one whose head was shaved clean.

The group parked their chromed and polished bikes in front of the hardware store, then trooped loudly up the narrow stairway leading to the apartments above. Vannevar watched them go, then, after waiting a moment, followed.

The enclosed staircase was brightly painted, decorated with rock posters from the Fillmore and other rock ballrooms. Vannevar followed the staircase up two floors before he found himself at a door. From the other side he heard loud music. He stepped up and knocked.

The door swung open, revealing a long-haired man in his early twenties. A blast of music assailed Vannevar and flashing strobe lights momentarily blinded him. The air inside the apartment was thick with smoke from cigarettes, incense and joints.

"Hey, man," the young man said, smiling broadly when he saw Vannevar. "What's up?" His blue eyes were bloodshot and watery. His eyelids drooped. He held up two fingers, making the "Peace" sign.

"I'm looking for Margaret," Vannevar said.

"Come on in, dude," the youth said. "She's in the back — asleep, I think."

Vannevar followed the man inside. The front room was crowded with people sprawled on makeshift furniture. Vannevar had to be careful stepping through the mess. He felt all eyes on him.

One of the sprawled-out hippies, seeing Vannevar, asked the man who'd answered the door: "Hey, Freddie, who's your friend? A cop? Or the Mafia?" A laugh went round the room.

Vannevar shot an angry look at the young man. The outspoken hippie lying in the bean-bag chair caught it and, wishing to make amends, scrambled to his feet, grabbing a smoldering brass pipe from a nearby table.

"Cool, man," he said, bouncing up to Vannevar. "Here." He thrust the pipe in Vannevar's face. "Have a toke."

Vannevar slapped the pipe away, hissing deep in his throat. The hippie was surprised, then angered.

"Hey man!" he said, aggressively stepping up to Vannevar. He was a good three inches taller than the prince.

Vannevar put his hand on the hippie's chest and gently shoved him back. The young man stumbled over the edge of a bean-bag chair and sat down hard, in the process upsetting a cluttered little table next to him and sending pipes, carved wooden boxes, and plastic guitar picks scattering across the floor.

Vannevar took a step back himself and accidentally tripped over someone's outstretched feet, nearly falling down himself. Shouts went up around the room.

Dirk suddenly appeared in the doorway leading to the kitchen. "Hey! What the fuck!" he shouted, finding the room in a stir. Then he saw Vannevar, standing in the middle of the room, dressed in his dark suit and tie.

"Shut up!" Dirk hollered at the hippies and the room fell silent. "Hi," he told Vannevar, cautiously. "Good to see you again."

Vannevar glared at him.

"The dude was startin' trouble, man," complained the hippie Vannevar had pushed down. He was angry, but hadn't yet dared to get back up from where he'd fallen.

"Shut the fuck up, man," Dirk told him, and the hippie fell silent.

"I'm here to see Margaret," Vannevar told him, glaring around the room.

"Sure," Dirk said. "She's in the back bedroom, resting."

Vannevar pushed his way past Dirk and went up the hallway.

He found Margaret asleep on a mattress spread on the floor. The dark bedroom's walls were plastered with posters of rock bands and handbills. Vannevar knelt down and tried to wake her.

"Vannevar," she squinted up at him through puffy eyelids, after he'd finally brought her around. "What are you doing here?" Then, remembering she'd missed their birthday get-together, she put her hand to her head and groaned. "Oh, man. I'm sorry," she told him. "I lost track of things, I guess." She was still getting over a three-night drug binge she and Dirk had enjoyed. Stalking the Haight, finding hippies dosed on the best acid, they'd fed from them, sharing the high.

"Look at you," Vannevar scolded her. Margaret had lost weight; her skin was sallow, jaundiced. "What are you trying to do to yourself?" he asked.

"Never mind," she said, still groggy, running her fingers through her hair. Vannevar noticed it was greasy, unwashed.

"I think it's time you straightened up a little, young lady, don't you?" Vannevar said.

She looked up at him, her eyes suddenly angry. "Don't tell me what the fuck to do!" she shouted at him, ignoring the pain it caused her already throbbing head. "You don't fuckin' own me, you know."

Her language shocked him. Vannevar expected such talk from a castoff like Dirk, but Margaret? He stood up, stepping back.

"Well," he said, angry but controlling his temper. "You do what you like." He turned and left the room.

"I will!" Margaret shouted after him.

Vannevar stalked back out of the apartment, a swirl of black anger that passed through the living room without acknowledging the hippies still lounged around. Dirk watched from the side, nervously, saying nothing.

Vannevar yanked open the door and headed down the stairs, slamming the door behind him so hard a hinge broke, leaving the door hanging askew.

"Shit!" said one of the hippies. "Did you see *that*, man?"

■

Deep in the smoky, humid chambers of the Grandfather's lair deep beneath Chinatown, Vannevar stood facing the creature feared by so many, seen by so few.

The Grandfather squatted — or crouched — on a broad pad spread on the floor. He was huge, but his bulky form was hidden beneath the voluminous silk robes he wore. He kept his arms folded in front of him, his hands hidden in the loose sleeves. His face was covered by a grotesque mask carved out of black wood. Only the Grandfather's eyes and mouth were visible, and then just barely.

"I am very glad..." the Grandfather began, speaking slowly in a hollow, basso voice, pausing in the midst of sentences to draw deep breaths that caused odd rustling sounds from beneath the robes. "...that we meet...at last."

Chi, the ghoul, stood close by the Grandfather's side, occasionally whispering in his ear. Loo stood a step in front of the Grandfather, his glinting axe at the ready.

Vannevar nodded acknowledgment. Nickolai stood on his right, Don Benedict on his left.

"I, too, am glad we finally meet," Vannevar agreed.

Nickolai had agreed to arrange the meeting between Vannevar and the Grandfather, but had insisted on accompanying the prince. Benedict was invited along to keep an eye on Chi. The ghoul was a powerful magician and deserved watching.

Chi lifted the cover from a brass brazier next to him, adding fresh incense to the burning coals. The pungent fumes that emerged only partially masked the odor of decay that seemed to surround the squatting Grandfather. Benedict watched the old ghoul's movements closely.

"We must talk," Vannevar said.

"We...must," the Grandfather agreed.

Vannevar began discussing their differences and their common goals. He spoke of brotherhood and friendship between them, knowing the Grandfather believed none of it, but still trying to be diplomatic.

The Grandfather, in response, was evasive, never admitting to any wrongdoing, not even his numerous illegal shipments. Nor would the Grandfather actually admit to any struggle between the two of them, stating only that the Family wished to live well, prosper, and bring no harm to others.

The talk dragged on, further slowed by the Grandfather's labored speech. An hour later the meeting had accomplished nothing. The temperature and humidity in the cramped, smoky chamber steadily increased. The visiting vampires grew tired and uncomfortable.

The Grandfather was currently speaking, his words long and slow, his sentences dragged out by his continual need for breath, when Vannevar felt the first wave of dizziness pass over him. It might have been the heat, but the sensation left him uneasy. He shook it off, trying to concentrate on what the Grandfather was saying. The creature shifted his bulk, exposing a bit of its arm under the sleeve. Vannevar saw ancient, yellowed flesh, and a black beetle that ran across the monster's arm to disappear inside the Grandfather's sleeve.

"...and you are accompanied by...the childe of Delfonso...so you must know...I speak truth..." The Grandfather claimed that Don Benedict had been sired by Delfonso, something the Tremere had begun to suspect, but never known for sure.

Vannevar was losing track of what the Grandfather was

saying. It wasn't quite clear to him what the creature was referring to. Another wave of dizziness sent Vannevar rocking on his feet. His vision blurred; the Grandfather suddenly swelled up enormous and disproportionate. He saw the old ghoul once more lift the cover of the brazier and feed the flames, and watched as a great cloud of lavender smoke issued from the brazier, filling the room. Vannevar felt as though he was losing his balance.

Then Don Benedict stepped in front of him, said something unintelligible to Vannevar, and the room rocked backwards. There was bright light, then darkness, then Vannevar was jarred as his feet struck the earth. He swayed drunkenly, grasping at a lamppost that suddenly swam into view, at the last second saving himself from falling to the ground. He heard Nickolai, saw Benedict again, then lost his footing, collapsing to one knee but still clinging to the lamppost.

"Are you all right?" Benedict said, hurrying to the prince's side.

They were outside, on the corner of California and Grant Streets, near the entrance to Chinatown. Vannevar went down on his hands and knees, retching. He vomited — the first time since his Embrace — spattering the sidewalk with black, bloody gobbets, horrid in their implication. But they were safe. Benedict had whisked them out of the Grandfather's clutches just in time.

"The ghoul tried to poison us," Benedict told the prince, helping him back to his feet.

Vannevar continued to cough and spit but, with Benedict's help, managed to get his feet under him and stand upright. He looked around for Nickolai. The Russian was nearby, leaning up against a wall.

"Thank you, Don Benedict," Vannevar told him. "I owe you my life."

"Think nothing of it, milord," Benedict told him, bowing slightly. "I don't believe there will be any lasting ill effects."

"Gentleman," Vannevar said to the two men. "I believe the die is cast."

The three went home their separate ways, Vannevar stepping aboard a passing cable car and riding it to the top of Nob Hill.

■

Vannevar awoke the next evening still suffering from the aftereffects of the previous night's poisoning. His head was achy, his limbs stiff. He had not fed in two nights, but food was the last thing on his mind. He looked at the clock and discovered he'd overslept by two hours. He crawled out of bed quickly. Tonight he intended to catch up with Margaret and see if the two of them could patch things up.

He tried to dress more casually this time, in loafers, cotton pants and a shirt with no tie. Tossing on a sporty, brown leather coat, he checked himself in the mirror, then telephoned downstairs to the desk and had the clerk call a taxi.

The cab driver dropped him off at Haight and Ashbury, right across the street from Dirk and Margaret's apartment. He paid the driver, then crossed the street as the taxi pulled away.

He entered the building and mounted the stairs, carefully stepping over a pile of trash and dirt someone had dumped on the sidewalk near the entrance. Soon he was knocking at the door again, noticing the shoddy repairs that had been made to the broken hinge. As before, music pounded away from the other side.

The door opened, a little more slowly tonight. It was the same hippie that had answered the door a couple nights ago. His eyes grew wide when he recognized Vannevar.

"Oh," he said. "It's you, man. You wanna come in or somethin'?"

Vannevar thanked him and stepped inside. Most of the loungers recognized him from his past visit. No one said a word. Vannevar nodded around the room, then turned to the hippie who'd let him in.

"I'm looking for Margaret," he said.

"She's out," said a young woman sitting nearby.

"Where'd she go?" Vannevar asked her.

She shrugged. "Beats me," she told him. "She just came running out of the bedroom around noon and went flying off down the stairs. She and Dirk were doing some heavy acid."

"She said she was a *butterfly*, man," chimed in another. "She was trippin' hard."

It took a moment for the words to sink in, for Vannevar to realize what he'd been told, to remember the dusty pile of ash he'd seen outside at the bottom of the stairs.

"When did you say?" he said, turning back to the young woman.

"Around noon, I told you," she said. "What difference does it make?"

"In the sun?" Vannevar asked?

"I told you, *around noon*," she responded, as though talking to someone feebleminded.

"Where's Dirk?" he demanded.

"He got up after dark. I told him Margaret left and he blew out of here in a hurry — went lookin' for her, I guess."

The tall hippie that had let Vannevar into the apartment approached him now. "Hey, man. Peace," he said, waggling his fingers in Vannevar's face. "Just *maintain*, okay? It's all right."

Vannevar grabbed the grinning fool by the shoulders and threw him back across the room. Two more hippies stood up and tried to grapple him, but Vannevar, now enraged and roaring, tossed them off like puppies. One fell over the crowded, battered coffee table, breaking it in half. The hippies, now afraid to approach Vannevar, backed off, but shouted at him, demanding that he leave the house. Vannevar yanked open the door and flew back down the stairs.

On the sidewalk outside he found the mound of ash and dust he'd stepped over on the way in. Stirred and dispersed by the evening breeze, little was left of it now — no more than a handful — and as Vannevar reached out to touch it, the swirling winds picked it up and blew it down the street. Margaret was no more.

Vannevar caught up with Dirk down at the seawall overlooking Ocean Beach, on the city's far west side. His motorcycle was parked near the curb. Dirk leaned over the wall, looking out over the dark ocean. The new Cliff House, much smaller and far less grand than Cyrano's old castle, gleamed warmly, invitingly, from a mile away, perched on the rocky headlands to the north.

Dirk heard Vannevar approach but didn't turn to look at him. Vannevar stopped a few feet away, standing silent, his hands thrust in his coat pockets. The roaring ocean breakers pounded on the sands, filling the air with their sound.

"Satisfied?" Vannevar finally asked Dirk.

Dirk ignored him at first, continuing to look out over the ocean. He spit over the side, then turned his gaze on the prince. "Fuck you," he said.

Vannevar said nothing, nor did he move. Dirk looked back away.

"Don't think you'll get off that easy," Vannevar told him. "Despite what you think, I didn't come here to kill you."

Dirk said nothing and, picking up a pebble from the top of the seawall, he pitched it out toward the waves. It fell a hundred feet short of the waterline. He slowly turned back to look at Vannevar.

"Why not?" he asked. "I deserve it. I don't want to live, anyway."

"I know," Vannevar said. "And that's why I won't kill you.

I'll let you live and think about it. You can spend your immortal life racking your mind over it."

Dirk said nothing, only glaring at the prince through swollen eyes. He'd been crying. "Why?" he asked.

"Because that's all you deserve," Vannevar told him. "And you deserve it every bit as much as I do."

The prince turned on his heel and walked away, leaving Dirk alone with his own bitter thoughts.

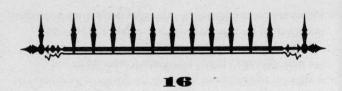

16

1975: Flesh and Blood

Iwo bent over, peering into the huge fishtank that separated Vannevar's front parlor from his office. Bright, flashing *koi*, some up to a foot long, swam around the landscaped enclosure. One of the orange-and-silver fish, spotting Iwo, stopped its circling to paddle over nearer the glass. It begged at the little magician for food, making kissing faces at him. Iwo puckered up and made fish faces back at the *koi*.

The two other men sitting in the living room paid scant attention to Iwo. Vannevar sat cross-legged on the couch, while Benedict occupied the chair across from him. The two were talking about Delfonso. At the prince's request, Don Benedict had befriended the old vampire in an attempt to learn what the old Spaniard and the Grandfather were up to with their recent smuggling activities.

"Well," Benedict began, "it looks like the usual — drugs and illegal immigrants. From China they bring in heroin and a little bit of opium and morphine. From Mexico and South America — Delfonso's connections — they're getting marijuana, cocaine, and brown heroin."

"Sabbat?" Vannevar asked him. It was well known that the Sabbat had made serious inroads into the illegal drug trade during the last few years.

"Almost certainly," Benedict told him. "At least

Delfonso's connections are — though I don't think he really guesses that. He personally finds the Sabbat distasteful."

"Then it's through Domingo?"

Domingo was Delfonso's childe, a former felon and draft-dodger on the run from Los Angeles during World War II. Delfonso had discovered him hiding in San Francisco's Mission District garage and taken him for his own. Domingo was a heavily built, powerful Mexican whose most striking feature was his large gold front tooth. Vannevar judged him an unreliable cutthroat.

"Without a doubt," Benedict told the prince. "Though with Domingo I think it's strictly a business arrangement. I don't think he looks for any real affiliation with the Sabbat."

Vannevar nodded. Nickolai's investigations had revealed much the same information. There seemed to be no ulterior motive to Delfonso's alliance with the Grandfather — save the obvious one of profit, of course. Delfonso, for the most part, looked innocent of wrongdoing. Nonetheless, Vannevar suspected the smuggling operation was merely a smokescreen orchestrated by the Grandfather. He knew the Asian forces were readying themselves for another assault on the city. Once again he found himself suffering from recurrent dreams of a black, hulking, red-eyed beast. Vannevar guessed the long-term smuggling operation was intended to lull him into a sense of complacency, leaving him and the city unprepared for the invasion when it finally came.

Vannevar, through Nickolai, had increased his monitoring of the U.S. Coast Guard patrols off the West Coast. Radar reports came in automatically and were regularly screened by Nickolai. They kept a constant watch on the coast.

Iwo, growing tired of the fish, moved over to Vannevar's desk, taking a seat in front of the personal computer that sat on the corner. Vannevar had purchased the machine a few months ago but was not really sure what to do with it. Iwo now turned it on and began pecking at the keys.

"How's Delfonso doing otherwise?" Vannevar asked Benedict, ignoring Iwo.

"Worse all the time, I'm afraid." He looked upset.

Delfonso had dusted off an old torture chamber hidden in a secret basement underneath Mission Dolores. He now regularly sacrificed victims — most of them illegal immigrants — on a bloody rack, in bizarre rituals reminiscent of both Catholicism and Aztec blood rites. Quasi-Inquisitional torture was followed by tearing out the victim's heart and drinking from it. The very thought of such activities carried on in his domain sickened Vannevar. He remembered all too well the events that had taken place in the St. Francis Hotel nearly fifty years ago.

But poor Benedict had actually been forced to witness these horrific rites, unable to stop the old vampire out of fear of jeopardizing the relationship he'd taken so long to cultivate. The prince needed Benedict in his current position as Delfonso's confidant in order to keep an eye on the activities of the old Spaniard and, ultimately, the Grandfather.

"I'm very sorry to put you through this," Vannevar told him. "I can't imagine what it must be like."

Benedict merely looked at the floor, shaking his head. Other things were on his mind, as well. All evidence now indicated that Don Benedict had actually been sired by Delfonso — the Grandfather had been right. No less a personage than Hortator himself had pronounced Benedict "of the blood" — a descendant of an ancient Aztec priest named Nezahualcoyotl, who had sired Delfonso. The strange mixture of blood had apparently driven Delfonso mad, and Benedict feared it would do the same to him.

Don Benedict had been killed and Embraced while kneeling at the altar of the great cathedral in Mexico City, never seeing the creature that had attacked him from behind. Benedict had awakened later, in his monk's cell, under the care of a Jesuit Tremere vampire, who had raised Benedict as his own.

Iwo claimed Benedict's strange heritage had much to do with his persistent rejection of Western ways, a subconscious attempt to flee his own past. Iwo had tried to convince Benedict there was no such thing as "pure" blood and that everybody's was "mixed," noting Benedict's Spanish heritage consisted of European Goth, African Moor, and Asian Arab. Furthermore, he pointed out, American Indians themselves were merely transplanted Asians. Iwo claimed to have somewhere at home a set of calculations that proved that no one in the world could be anything less than twenty-second cousin to anyone else — and that most people were even more closely related than that. It was all one and the same to Iwo and he claimed not to understand what all the fuss was about.

But right now Iwo was busy with Vannevar's computer. He had an abacus on the desk beside him, using it to race the machine, trying to beat it to the solutions of mathematical problems he posed to it.

"Holy Jiminies," Iwo shouted, mixing his expressions, as the computer once more put him to shame. "It *is* faster!" He beamed a smile toward the two men in the parlor.

Vannevar smiled back at Iwo, then glanced up at the clock with a frown. "Where's Nickolai?" he asked, getting up from the couch and walking to the window overlooking California Street.

The Russian had left a little more than an hour ago, promising to return soon. He was supposed to bring a young girl for questioning — the sister of a man who'd been missing several years but was now rumored to be back in town. The man's name was Joseph Cambridge.

Cambridge had once been a business partner of Robert Foster, a fifth-generation descendant of Davey Foster, one of a number of family members now working directly for Vannevar. Though Cambridge had known nothing of the

Foster family's ties to the Kindred, it was believed Cambridge had been kidnapped as retribution against Vannevar.

The kidnapping had occurred in 1971, on Castro Street, in broad daylight. Witnesses claimed to have seen a gang of "Asian youths" pull up in a green van and snatch Cambridge off the street. No trace of him had been seen since. The Grandfather, of course, had been the primary suspect.

Cambridge, though nearly six and a half feet tall, could not fight the kidnapers. His legs were withered and weak, left nearly useless by a childhood case of polio. He could walk, but only with the aid of braces and canes.

Lately, a dark, hulking form had been seen lurking around some of the Foster family residences at night, and some of the family members reported receiving threatening phone calls. It was believed that Cambridge was now a vampire, seeking revenge against the family for what had happened to him.

Joseph's fifteen-year-old sister, Donna, had already been questioned by Nickolai — under hypnosis — but she had been able to tell him nothing about her older brother. She apparently knew nothing of Cambridge's recent reappearance in the area.

Vannevar had asked Nickolai for an opportunity to question the girl himself. There was no pressing reason for it — Vannevar was confident Nickolai knew his job — but having once seen the young girl from afar, he now wished to view her at closer quarters. Nickolai had chuckled knowingly when Vannevar made the request, realizing the prince had an ulterior motive. He told Vannevar he would bring her before the prince in a hypnotized state, then, after the prince had satisfied himself she knew nothing, return her home safely, her memory of the evening's events wiped clean. Nickolai had planned the interception for an hour ago, while she walked home from her weekly jazz dance lesson at the high school.

But it was well past time for Nickolai to have shown up

and Vannevar was growing concerned. It was not like Nickolai to be late.

Vannevar picked up the phone and dialed Nickolai's flat. The phone rang once and then the answering machine picked up. "Leave your message," said Nickolai's flat voice. Vannevar hung the phone back up.

"Nothing?" Benedict asked from the chair.

Vannevar shook his head. "No. And I'm starting to worry."

He waited a few minutes and tried the phone again, but with no luck. This time after hanging up he dialed a different number.

"Pallazo?" Vannevar said, when someone picked up the phone and said hello.

"Yes, sir?" the man on the other end of the phone answered, nearly coming to attention at the sound of the prince's voice. Tommy Pallazo was a tough young Ventrue who worked directly for Nickolai. For a time he'd been a spy within Dirk's biker gang but, after his cover was blown, Nickolai had to pull him out. Pallazo now functioned as the Russian's lieutenant, specializing in jobs requiring extra muscle.

"Something's up," Vannevar told the young vampire. "I want you to go over to Nickolai's and see what you can find. Call me back right away and let me know."

"Got it," Pallazo said, and hung up.

Vannevar waited, standing by the desk, too impatient to sit down. Pallazo lived close to Nickolai, no more than five minutes away. Benedict watched the prince, saying nothing. Even Iwo ceased playing with the computer.

A couple of minutes later the phone rang. It was Pallazo.

"You'd better get over here right away," he told the prince. "Something bad's happened."

Nickolai lived in a large Victorian home in a fashionable neighborhood overlooking the narrow easternmost strip of Golden Gate Park known as the Panhandle. Vannevar and

Benedict rode over in the limo, while Iwo remained behind at the penthouse. Pallazo met the two at the front door and showed them in. Six feet tall, heavily built, he wore a black leather coat over a white shirt open at the collar. His black hair, slightly thinning, was slicked and combed straight back. The pendant on the gold chain he wore around his neck was nearly lost in the thick, black mat of hair on his chest.

"Come on in," he said, ushering the pair into the living room. "But I gotta warn you, it ain't real pretty."

The house was a shambles: Furniture was smashed, pictures knocked down, lamps overturned. Messages had been scrawled on the walls in blood.

"Pig"

"Blood Lust"

"Freedom"

"Fuck You"

It was the work of the Sabbat. Despite all Nickolai's efforts, they had never been able to learn the location of the sect's headquarters, or even the name of their leader.

"I've already checked through the house," Pallazo told them. "There's not much left."

Judging from the wreckage downstairs, Vannevar understood.

"I'm surprised they didn't torch the place," Vannevar said.

"They wanted us to find it," Pallazo told him.

Vannevar felt at a loss. Lacking his security chief, he was suddenly unsure which way to turn. He had relied on Nickolai too long. "Where do we go from here?" he asked Pallazo.

"Chin's" he said.

Marty Chin ran a bookstore down on Haight Street. Chin specialized in rare and antique volumes in addition to more normal fare. He also dealt in information. He had connections everywhere and no doubt had learned the secret

location of Nickolai's haven. Pallazo figured Chin had sold
Nickolai out.

Several years ago, after first learning of Chin's business
practices, Vannevar had wanted him shut down; Nickolai,
however, had argued against it. The prince could take
advantage of this source of information as well as anyone
else, while simultaneously using Chin to disseminate false
information of his own. Vannevar had finally agreed and
Chin had been allowed to remain in business. But now the
human information broker had obviously sold Nickolai out.
He wondered what the price had been.

When they arrived at the bookstore it was dark inside.
Nearly midnight, the store had been closed for hours and
only a few yellow lights were left burning inside. Chin slept
in the back of the shop. Pallazo, reaching the door first,
hammered away at it. Vannevar and Benedict stood behind
him, waiting.

A minute later Chin shuffled out of the back toward the
front door.

"We're closed," he shouted through the glass at the three
men standing outside, then, suddenly recognizing them,
hurriedly began unlocking the door.

As soon as he turned the latch Pallazo booted the door
open, causing Chin to jump back out of the way. The three
dark, looming figures stepped inside, followed by a cloud of
fog from the street. Pallazo walked right past Chin, ignoring
him, while Vannevar and Benedict turned and waited until
the human closed the door behind them and relocked it.

"What can I do for you gentlemen?" Chin turned and
asked them, his eyes darting nervously back and forth
between the angry prince and Tommy Pallazo, now standing
near a shelf of books. Pallazo pulled out an expensive,
leatherbound volume and began flipping through the pages.

"Where's Nickolai?" Vannevar asked Chin.

"Nickolai?" Chin stuttered, suddenly looking more
nervous than before.

Pallazo, now finished with the book he was holding, let it fall to the floor, landing on its face.

"I...I don't know." Chin answered. Pallazo picked up another book, looked at it, then dropped it on the floor as well.

"Hey!" Chin said, calling over his shoulder at Pallazo. "Don't do that."

"Look at me!" Vannevar shouted. Chin's head snapped back around. "Where is Nickolai?"

Pallazo was now strolling along the length of the bookcase, casually tipping all the books off the shelves one by one, letting them flop down on the floor atop one another, cracking spines and bending pages.

"I don't know," Chin insisted. "I really don't know."

There was a sudden loud crash and Chin jumped. Pallazo, discovering a glass-enclosed case of extremely rare books, had tipped the whole cabinet over on its face. Broken glass lay everywhere. Chin said nothing. Vannevar spoke.

"Then I'd suggest you make a real good guess," the prince told him, his sinister and dark.

Chin looked back and forth at the three vampires, eyes wide. Pallazo picked up a large potted plant — a palm in a brightly decorated terra-cotta urn — lifted it over his head and smashed it on the floor. Chin was already talking.

"There was a woman in here yesterday, asking about him," he said rapidly, hoping he could stop the devastation Pallazo continued to wreak on the shop.

"You gave her Nickolai's address?" the prince asked him.

Chin nodded, his head bobbing up and down rapidly. "I'm sorry," he said. "I shouldn't have."

"What's her name?" Vannevar cut him off.

"I don't kn—"

Tommy Pallazo, sneaking up behind Chin, grabbed his arm and, twisting it up behind the man's back, forced the shopkeeper over his own desk, pressing Chin's face into the hard wooden surface. Chin grunted but couldn't get away.

"The name!" Vannevar demanded.

Chin didn't answer. Pallazo jerked the man's arm and there was a snapping sound. Chin screamed.

"We've got more time than you've got fingers, Chin," Pallazo told him. "Give her up, you sonofabitch."

"Her name's Misty. Misty Halls," Chin suddenly began spouting. "She used to work porno films. She's runnin' a topless club up in North Beach now."

"What's the name of the club?" Pallazo asked him, twisting the man's hand again, threatening a second finger.

"Christo's," Chin gasped. "Corner of Broadway and Kearney. They say she lures the johns upstairs and drinks them there. She's Sabbat."

Vannevar nodded and Pallazo released the shop owner, shoving him to the floor and launching a kick at Chin's ribs before turning and walking away. Together, the three vampires left the half-ruined shop and the battered human.

Benedict had been shocked by the violence he'd witnessed, but said nothing to the prince as they rode across town. He knew how important Nickolai was to Vannevar. All things considered, Chin was lucky to come out of it alive. Vannevar had proved a fair and equitable ruler, often nearly noble, but his rule could be harsh. He demanded and expected loyalty from his subjects, and those who failed him paid dearly.

Vannevar had himself been surprised by Pallazo's actions, but he had no time to worry about it now. He only knew he must find Nickolai.

Pallazo rode up front with Vannevar's driver. Meanwhile, in the back seat, Benedict prepared himself and the prince with disguises. By the time they reached North Beach the two of them looked like no more than the average pair of financial-district businessmen out for a little quick action after work before heading home to the wife and kids.

The beatnik scene at North Beach had years ago

deteriorated into little more than a tourist attraction and popular nightspot. The coffeehouses were still here — and City Lights Bookstore — but with the coming of the late sixties and the "free love" movement, the neighborhood, as though in memory of the old Barbary Coast it had been neighbors with, had bloomed into a brightly lit strip of topless clubs, porn outlets and raucous bars. A myriad neon signs blazed the message: "Live Naked Women." Action on the street was heavy all night long.

The driver let them out a block from the club. Vannevar now appeared as a slightly chubby figure in a blue suit, his hair short, curly and blond. Benedict had dark hair, cut long enough to hang over his collar. His suit was also dark, his Italian shoes gleaming like mirrors in the bright nighttime lights. Few would be able to penetrate the illusions Benedict had cast upon them. After letting them off, the driver would circle the block, then stop again to drop Pallazo off. The young vampire was known about these parts and his visit to the club — if unaccompanied by strangers — would draw little attention.

At the entrance to Christo's, two women dressed in bikinis and high heels sat waiting on stools near the front door. At Vannevar and Benedict's approach they slid off their stools and strutted up to the two apparent businessmen.

"The night's young. Come on in," one of them said, sidling up to Vannevar. The other took hold of Benedict's arm, guiding him toward the doorway. "The girls inside'll show you a good time," she promised him, winking slyly.

The two allowed themselves to be ushered into the dark club. The place reverberated with loud jukebox music; the only light came from blue and red neon tubes decorating the walls and the dim lights over the bar. On the stage three women, stripped to G-strings, writhed and crawled for the pleasure of the hooting, drunken businessmen seated around the edge of the stage. The place reeked of stale beer, old cigarette smoke, vomit and urine.

A tall, bearded man stepped out in front of them as they walked in. "Five bucks cover," he told them, sticking his hand out. He wore sunglasses and a tight Ban-lon shirt; his belly hung over his belt in a huge fold. Vannevar discovered he'd come without cash. Benedict had to pay for both of them.

They took a table away from the stage, in the dark, watching the action under the lights. Men were tucking money in the dancers' G-strings. One of the woman squatted down and let a man suck her breast. He'd given her a ten-dollar bill.

A waitress appeared, wearing little more than the dancers. Vannevar and Benedict ordered a couple of drinks, then Vannevar said: "We're here looking for Misty. Is she in tonight?"

"I can check," the waitress told him, and slipped away to the bar. There, she said something to the bartender, who in turn made a phone call. Vannevar and Benedict watched as the bartender talked to someone on the phone, his eyes occasionally glancing over at the pair sitting at the dark table. Then he nodded and hung up. He said something to the waitress, then fixed her the two drinks the vampires had ordered. The waitress carried them back on a tray.

"Here you go," she said, setting their glasses on the table.

Benedict handed her a ten-dollar bill and told her to keep the change. She thanked him.

"Misty's upstairs," she said. "She says you guys can go up anytime you want. Take your drinks with you."

They thanked her and, after she'd left, got up from the table and crossed the club to the narrow staircase she indicated on the other side of the room. Another bouncer in a striped T-shirt stood at the stairway, arms folded, but hardly gave the pair a second look as they stepped around him and began climbing the steps. Just before they ascended out of sight they caught a glimpse of Tommy Pallazo entering the club, the burly doorman merely nodding as Pallazo stepped inside without paying the cover. None made any sign of recognizing the other.

At the top of the stairs Vannevar and Benedict found a long hallway, again dimly lit. Narrow booths lined both sides, accessed by equally narrow doors. Inside, television sets ran continuous porn loops. Many of the booths were occupied and from within came moans, grunting sounds and occasional thumpings against the wall as customers paid for and received sexual favors.

At the far end of the hall stood a door beyond which, according to the waitress, lay Misty's office. Benedict knocked, a little tentatively.

A woman's voice said: "Come in."

They opened the door and stepped through.

From out of nowhere, arms and clubs descended upon them, trying to beat the two to the floor, grappling at them, pulling them down. Benedict fought furiously, arms and legs flying, but even his deadly martial skills were of no avail against the sheer weight of numbers. Vannevar heard Nickolai — somewhere — shout: "Flee!" but someone began beating Vannevar over the head and he soon lost consciousness.

Both men awoke at nearly the same time to find themselves half stripped and bound by heavy chains to a pair of huge, iron I-beams that ran from the floor below up the second-floor ceiling. The room was dark, walls painted black and decorated by grotesque paintings glowing eerily under ultraviolet lights. Movie screens were set up in a half-dozen locations, even on the ceiling, and images from porn films played over them. Vannevar noticed that most of the loops featured a tall, statuesque blond, whom he figured to be Misty. Shadowy figures milled about in the surrounding darkness: horrid-looking specimens of vampires with matted hair, rotting teeth, and dark-encircled eyes.

Misty herself stood in front of the prince, dressed in a pair of tall black leather boots, a few leather straps, and little else. Her blond, nearly platinum hair was pulled straight back, knotted in a long ponytail that streamed down her naked back. She laughed when she saw Vannevar awake.

"So, prince," she leered. "I see you've finally decided to come pay a little visit to my establishment." She brandished a cruel-looking short leather whip in her hand. "So nice of you to come."

Nearby, a dirty, destitute vampire crawled out of the shadows toward the Sabbat, reaching out for Misty's leg. "Mistress?" the creature begged.

"Beast!" she hissed at the pathetic creature interrupting her, and laid into him with the whip. The vampire screamed in pain, scrabbling to get out of her way. Vannevar noticed the creature smiled as it screamed.

A groan came out of a darkened corner of the room. Vannevar recognized the voice.

"Nickolai?" he called.

"Your friend is here," Misty said, striding across the room to where a bank of light switches stood mounted on the wall. She snapped one of them on and the far corner was suddenly filled with light.

Nickolai hung upside down from chains, vicious hooks thrust through his ankles. He had been stripped not only of his clothing, but of his skin: It had been largely flayed from his body, leaving him little more than a red mass of ridged muscles. Two women, naked but for their high heels, stroked and massaged the quivering Nickolai, licking at the tiny rivulets of blood that issued from his torn muscles. Vannevar, despite his centuries of existence, closed his eyes.

"Look at me!" Misty demanded, slashing Vannevar across the face with her whip.

He opened his eyes and glared at her, feeling the wound in his cheek and the blood running down his face. She lashed out a second time, striking the other side of his face, opening another wound, but Vannevar kept his eyes open.

"That's better," she smiled. "I like men who obey."

A door opened somewhere, and Pallazo was dragged struggling into the room.

"Quiet him down!" Misty ordered her crew.

The Sabbat vampires grappled with Pallazo, holding him tight despite his ferocious attempts to get free. Out of the shadows ran a haggard figure in stinking robes — male or female, Vannevar could not tell which — giggling madly, a sharpened wooden stake raised above its head. It ran straight for Pallazo and leaped upon him, plunging the stake down into the henchman's chest. Pallazo roared like a bull as his heart was pierced; then he stiffened. His captors released him to fall with a crash to the wooden floor.

Instantly a half-dozen Sabbat fell upon the stricken vampire, lapping at the blood, squealing in delight even as they fought with one another for the spoils. Misty watched as her brood quickly exsanguinated the helpless Pallazo, leaving only a withered corpse upon the floor.

Misty then ordered Benedict unbound and carried to the same corner where Nickolai was hung. Benedict struggled with them, but their numbers were too many. They rammed another pair of hooks through his ankles and hauled him up, suspending him next to Nickolai. Then they tore his clothing from his body.

"I want to give you a little demonstration," Misty explained to the prince. "I want you to see what happened to Nickolai, and what will happen to you. I intend to introduce you to the sweet delights of pain — firsthand."

Vannevar bit his lip as the first cuts were made across Benedict's naked chest. Don Benedict refused to scream when the razor bit his flesh, but when the flap of skin was ripped up and torn away from his body he could hold back no longer. A shout of agony tore through the room. The Sabbat holding the razor smiled, then prepared to make the next cut.

But just then they were interrupted by a frantic pounding

at the door across the room. The Sabbat all turned to look; then someone on the other side kicked at the door, knocking it off its hinges and sending it flying. A heavyset, swarthy Mexican plunged into the room, armed with a machete. Behind him strode Delfonso, dressed all in black, sword flashing in his hand.

"I've come to put an end to your heathen practices," Delfonso announced to Misty as he dashed into the room. "I demand you release the prisoners!"

His voice was strong, his eyes bright and clear, his mind unclouded. Once again he was the nobleman of old, a knight, a righter of wrongs.

Misty saw Delfonso's look as well and took a step or two backward, hissing dangerously. Delfonso continued his bold advance toward her, taking advantage of her surprise, the tip of his sword flicking this way and that as he closed in on the Sabbat leader.

Domingo, aided by a band of ghouls, fell on the Sabbat minions around the bleeding prisoners, chopping with his huge machete, cleaving flesh and bone, severing limbs. Two of the ghouls rushed to aid Vannevar, still bound by his chains.

Misty continued backing away from Delfonso, bewildered by the swift feints and lunges of the old vampire's blade, much the way Vannevar had been the night he'd first met Delfonso so many years ago. As always, Vannevar could not help but admire the man's skill.

Misty bumped into the wall behind her and Delfonso thrust forward, trying to drive the blade into her heart. She arched her back, as though ready to meet the blade, but even as she did so her form began to change, expanding in size, altering in shape even as the tip of Delfonso's blade penetrated her flesh. Delfonso, surprised by the sudden event, jumped back, pulling his sword out. The Sabbat's skin became black and scaled, and she reared up over him. She had become a gigantic serpent, its head nearly the size of a horse's.

The snake arched high over the Spaniard, flickering filmed images of a naked Misty playing over its shiny scales, then it struck down at the vampire. Delfonso stepped lightly aside, easily avoiding the lightning-fast monster. He turned to prod it with his blade, but already the serpent had risen back up, preparing itself for a second strike. Behind them a burning brazier overturned, upset by the giant snake's thrashing tail. Flames ran rapidly up the gauzy curtains decorating the wall.

The serpent struck again. Delfonso once more danced out of its way, but this time the snake's gigantic fangs missed him by only inches. Then Delfonso spun around and, before the serpent could lift itself, rose up on his toes. With all his strength brought his blade straight down, piercing the serpent's skull, penetrating its brain, driving all the way through and pinning the monster's head to the floor.

The snake writhed and coiled wildly, trying to break free, its thrashing tail tearing down pictures and movie screens, overturning projectors and sending them crashing to the floor. Delfonso used all his strength to hold the monster down. The flames behind the battling pair meanwhile burned higher, consuming a movie screen on which a red-headed Misty serviced three men simultaneously.

The rest of the Sabbat were now dying, dead, or fleeing down a back stairway. Domingo, leaping atop a table next to Nickolai, had hacked away the chains holding the two men; now, while the ghouls broke Vannevar loose, he raced to Delfonso's side. With a single, powerful swipe he brought the machete down, severing the serpent's head from its twisting body.

The room roared with flames, and thick smoke filled the air. Vannevar, at last freed, ran to Delfonso. The power blew out, dimming the lights and silencing the last projectors.

At Vannevar's approach, Delfonso bowed deeply from the

waist, blade held out straight behind him. "At your service, my lord," he said.

"Let's get him out of here," Vannevar told Domingo. "This place is going up fast."

The Mexican needed no encouragement. They took the old Spaniard by the arms and began hustling him toward the back stairway. Benedict was already ahead of them, supervising the ghouls carrying the nearly lifeless Nickolai away from the scene.

"I sensed trouble," Delfonso told the prince as they hurried down the warped wooden stairs toward the alley below. "We came looking for you, afraid you were in need."

Vannevar thanked him, most sincerely.

Outside, in the alley, they found the neighborhood swarming with police and fire trucks, sirens screaming, lights flashing. They headed down toward one end of the alley, only to find their way suddenly blocked by a police cruiser. Reversing their direction, they headed out the other way, where they were met by Vannevar's big black limo. The escaping vampires flung open the doors and piled inside the car, loading the bleeding, naked Nickolai into the back seat. The driver then reversed, backing up out of the alley and cutting off a driver in a blue sedan, who blew his horn at him before racing away from the scene.

It was nearly five o'clock in the morning before Vannevar finally returned to his penthouse. Shortly after leaving the club they had hooked up with Delfonso's driver and dropped off Delfonso and Domingo before taking Nickolai to a place where a makeshift infirmary could be set up. The Russian was still alive and would recover, though it would be several weeks before he completely regenerated all the tissue he'd lost. Vannevar had then dropped Benedict off before returning home.

He found Iwo asleep on the couch, snoring gently. He woke the man.

Iwo sat up, grinning and rubbing his eyes. "What time is it?" he asked.

Vannevar told him, then sat down to recount the details of the night.

"You have destroyed the Sabbat leader, then?" he asked.

"Yes," Vannevar said, but then reminded him that they still hadn't unearthed the secret Sabbat lair. That still existed somewhere in the city and as long as it remained the Sabbat would continue to be a problem.

"No matter," Iwo said. "At least not for now. The end game draws near and the cards are nearly played out. Only a few possible conclusions now remain."

Daybreak was approaching and Iwo said goodnight, leaving Vannevar alone to ponder Iwo's words. Only a few cards were left to be played, Iwo had said. Vannevar hoped that when the time came, he would play them right.

He fed his fish and went to bed.

■

It was several weeks later, after Nickolai had recovered and recuperated, that Donna Cambridge was brought before Vannevar.

Vannevar had found himself awaiting the meeting a little anxiously, a bit embarrassed to find himself distracted by thoughts of a woman so young. But he could not deny his fascination for her, a fascination he'd enjoyed since the first time he'd seen her.

The young Donna proved to be everything Vannevar had imagined, despite her youth and still somewhat angular, undeveloped female form. From the moment that Nickolai brought her into the room he was overcome with a nearly overwhelming desire to take her in his arms and crush her to him — but he did not.

He remained seated in his chair, studying the groggy captive, showing no emotion. He interrogated her for nearly an hour, but failed to learn anything. As Nickolai had already ascertained, the girl knew nothing of the whereabouts of her brother, Joseph Cambridge. Finally, reluctantly, Vannevar sent them away, Nickolai promising to return the girl safely to her home.

Vannevar once again found himself alone.

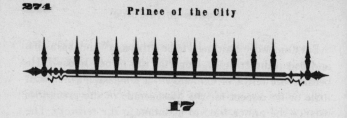

17

1980: Donna

Joseph Cambridge was brought to bay just a few months after Vannevar's meeting with young Donna. Caught while peering through the front window of Jason Foster's home in the suburban Sunset district, he was captured and brought before the prince.

Cambridge was terrible to behold. Not, as they had guessed, a childe of the Grandfather, he was instead the offspring of Chinatown's Dowager, and thus Nosferatu. That clan's curse had twisted him terribly: He had become a gigantic monster with a swollen, misshapen head and putrid, corpselike complexion. The blood of the Nosferatu had also affected his legs, regenerating the formerly shriveled limbs, but also encasing in skin the heavy iron leg braces he still wore. He now stood nearly seven feet tall, a towering monster shackled by a stiff-legged gait.

An innocent victim of the Kindred's wars, he had been taken by the Dowager for no better reason than to annoy the prince. Maddened by his unwonted condition, Cambridge was left obsessed with a desire for vengeance, his anger turned against the Foster family for their involvement with the Kindred. The prince, discovering the truth, had demanded the Dowager order her minion away from the Foster family and she had obeyed, prohibiting Cambridge from further contact with the family.

But Cambridge continued to be a thorn in Vannevar's side, and began directing his anger at the prince himself. He became the terror of Chinatown, a rampaging killer with little or no respect for the Masquerade or the precarious balance the prince tried to maintain in the territory. The Dowager continually promised better behavior of her Blood Bound childe but Cambridge went on seemingly unchecked until Vannevar found himself forced to intervene. The prince had once again been making friendly overtures toward the Grandfather and didn't need any trouble from Cambridge.

Cambridge was once again snatched off the streets, this time by Nickolai and his men, wrestled into the back of a truck and hauled off to an empty warehouse along the south shore. Here, in a long and painful ceremony witnessed by the prince himself, Don Benedict broke the Blood Bond that held Cambridge loyal to his sire, the Dowager. Before being allowed to leave, Cambridge was forced to swear fealty to the prince. Vannevar hoped that once freed of the Dowager's influence, the angry Cambridge would adjust to his condition and new life, and eventually settle down.

The hope proved overly optimistic. Cambridge continued to cause problems in and around the city, including a roaring fight with Sullivan in the middle of the Tenderloin one night. The obvious solution was to destroy him, but Vannevar hesitated. He felt sympathy for the man's plight, and at least partial responsibility for it. It was then that Nickolai suggested that Vannevar make use of Cambridge's sister, Donna, in an effort to control him. The elder Cambridge was known to be extraordinarily fond of his younger sister, and had recently finally revealed himself to her, explaining to her his fate and condition. If Vannevar Embraced Donna and made her his childe, Nickolai suggested, Cambridge could finally be brought to bay. Nickolai, well aware of the prince's ongoing fascination for the woman, secretly felt the plan might have other benefits for his beloved prince.

Vannevar was intrigued by the idea and readily agreed. Hardly a day had passed in the last few years that he had not thought of her.

He thought of her now as he and Nickolai sat in the back seat of the limousine, parked outside San Francisco University in the hills just south of Haight Street. Donna was attending an evening class tonight.

Vannevar looked at his watch.

"She should be out in a few minutes," Nickolai said. He was keeping an eye on the time as well. He had tracked Donna's movements and knew her routines. "Are you ready?" he asked the prince.

"Yes," Vannevar said. "I'm fine."

Nickolai knew the prince was hesitant to go through with this. After his initial acceptance of the idea, he had experienced second thoughts about subjecting the innocent girl to eternal life as one of the Kindred. When the idea was first suggested, Nickolai had planned to snatch Donna off the street and bring her before the prince, but Vannevar had objected. If this thing was to be done, he'd told his advisor, then he should do it himself. This had led to tonight's plan.

They would wait until Donna emerged from the school building then, meeting her in the street, Vannevar would incapacitate her before carrying her off to his apartment. There he would Embrace her.

"There she is," Nickolai said, nudging Vannevar in the ribs.

Vannevar looked to the top of the steps and saw her emerging through the building's front doors, accompanied by a young man her about own age. It would be Nickolai's job to take care of the young man, making sure he didn't interfere. When it was all over the man's mind would be wiped of any memory of the kidnapping.

"Let's go," Nickolai said, opening the left-hand door.

Vannevar opened his own door and stepped out on the sidewalk. He could see Donna and her companion coming toward them, about fifty yards away. He waited for Nickolai to join him; then the two began walking toward the couple.

Vannevar was on the left, facing Donna; Nickolai was on the right, ready to take the young man. The evening was dark and quiet and aside from the young couple, and Vannevar and Nickolai, there was no one on the street. Everything looked perfect.

Vannevar looked the woman over as they drew nearer. She was taller than the last time he'd seen her — at least a couple of inches — and she had filled out a bit, though her figure was still on the slim side. She was wearing a pair of tight jeans and an overly large sweater that, intriguingly, fell off one shoulder. She carried a bundle of books across her chest and chatted brightly with her companion. Vannevar was struck by the way her hair tossed as she spoke animatedly on some subject. Her eyes were flashing with energy, full of life.

Life.

"Vannevar?" Nickolai whispered to the prince as they drew nearer. He sensed something was wrong. The prince was hesitating. "Are you okay?"

Vannevar didn't say anything at first. Then he shook his head. "No. Not here, not now."

By this time they were only twenty feet away from the couple. Nickolai wanted to object, to encourage Vannevar to go through with it, but it was too late.

The two vampires stepped to the side, letting the couple pass between them. The pair of students paid little attention to them but after they passed, Vannevar saw Donna glance back at him once.

Vannevar and Nickolai continued walking straight ahead until the couple was out of sight. They then turned around and walked back toward the limousine, Nickolai saying nothing about Vannevar's failure to carry through. Vannevar ordered the driver to drop Nickolai off, then had himself taken home.

Hours later, Vannevar paced the floor of his penthouse, his thoughts all on Donna. Seeing her again had renewed his passion and more than ever he found himself obsessed by thoughts of her. Everything else was secondary to the problem facing him now.

Around midnight, still unable to concentrate, he left the penthouse, stepping out onto the open terrace that overlooked his city. He raised his hands to the sky, disappearing in a swirl of black mist.

Donna woke up at the sound of something at the foot of her bed. Opening her eyes, she saw a tall, dark figure, surrounded in black mist, standing nearby. She opened her mouth to scream but the dark man waved his hand, inexplicably silencing her. She could not make a sound.

"Please, don't make any noise," the man said, leaning forward, bringing his face into the light from the bedroom window. "I am not here to harm you." Vannevar's eyes glowed slightly in the dark.

Her mouth still open, Donna tried to speak, but nothing came out.

"Can I trust you not to scream?" he asked her, his voice calm, reassuring.

Donna nodded up and down, finally closing her mouth. The dark man waved his hand in another smooth pass and Donna felt life returning to her vocal chords.

"You're the man I saw in front of the school tonight," she said.

"Yes."

"Why are you here?"

"To see you. To speak with you."

"I know you," she said.

"You do?"

"I've seen you in a dream," she explained. "You sit in a chair in front of me, asking me questions." She'd been having the same dream over and over since she was fifteen, a fuzzy memory of her one previous encounter with the prince.

Vannevar said nothing.

"I've been waiting for you to come," she said, pushing the covers aside and slipping out of bed. She was naked, her body gleaming in the moonlight. "I always knew you would." She stood up and crossed the room.

Vannevar took her in his arms. The bond was sealed.

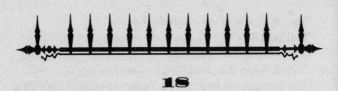

18

1995: Sullivan's Wake

Vannevar sat behind the large desk in his office, elbows on the table, head pressed between his hands. His eyes were tightly closed, his lips compressed. Don Benedict stood nearby, surrounded by sticks of burning incense, his right hand marking time as his lips silently formed the words of the chant.

"Grandfather?" asked Vannevar, barely speaking, his voice low, inaudible.

The prince, with Benedict's aid, was attempting to establish a mental link with the Grandfather, deep in his lair in Chinatown.

"Grandfather?" Vannevar asked again, concentrating harder, trying to form a mental picture of the Grandfather, as Benedict had instructed him. Then he heard a soft voice, not with his ears, but only in his mind.

"Yes, my lord?" It was the Grandfather, responding to his prince's call. "I am here." The Grandfather's telepathic voice was strong and even, not labored.

"We begin now, as we have planned," Vannevar said, willing the words rather than speaking them. "It is time for the Spaniard to take his leave."

"Yes, my lord. We must put an end to Delfonso before it is too late."

"You have chosen your agent?"

"Yes. A childe of mine will do the job."

"Sullivan?"

"He is my choice, my lord."

"Good. Then it is done."

The contact was broken and Vannevar relaxed, dropping his hands to the table and looking up at Benedict. The Tremere, seeing the prince finished, stopped his chanting.

"Everything is ready?" Benedict asked Vannevar.

"All is in place," the prince said, sitting back in his chair and rubbing his temples with his fingertips. "The end game draws near," he said, quoting Iwo. "And Delfonso's life is forfeit."

The prince, in an effort to learn the secrets of the Family, had spent the last few years making overtures to the Grandfather, finally gaining at least the creature's partial trust. Now, together, they planned to dispose of Delfonso.

The old man had become an increasing problem in recent years. The depraved acts he committed in his torture chamber were known to nearly all the Kindred of the city and, even worse, rumored among some of the members of the human community as well. This in itself would be reason enough for the prince to eliminate him, but Delfonso's secret dealings with the Family — smuggling drugs and illegal aliens into the country — only added fuel to the fire. Still, Vannevar felt guilty about planning an old friend's execution.

Benedict saw the look of concern on the prince's face.

"I know how you feel about this," he said. "But there is no choice. Delfonso's fate was established long ago. We do nothing more than take part in what is otherwise an act of fate."

"Humph," was the prince's only comment. Delfonso had years ago witnessed the murder of Snake Whitcomb in the Family's chambers and observed the augury spoken by the slain vampire's head. In the smoke and flames Delfonso had seen a portent of his own doom — his fate that of

Whitcomb's. Learning this, Delfonso had given up, choosing
to live his unlife in a manner that almost guaranteed the
horrid end he feared. Toward the end he had even allied
himself with the Grandfather — his potential executioner
— as though somehow compelled to play with fire. Delfonso
had never realized there were other choices he could have
made — choices that might have led to different
conclusions.

"He did it to himself," Benedict said, flatly.

"I know," Vannevar said. But the prince wondered if it
hadn't been within his own power to turn events in another
direction. He now found himself coldly calculating the
Spaniard's death — signing his death warrant. Was such
drastic action truly necessary? Had not Iwo always warned
Vannevar to choose the "middle path" whenever possible?

Benedict was less bothered by the decision. Though he
knew Delfonso was his sire, he despised Delfonso for what
he had allowed himself to become, and hated him for the
nightmarish torture sessions Benedict had been forced to
watch while ingratiating himself with Delfonso. Benedict
felt that whatever end the old Spaniard faced, he deserved
it.

"Sullivan's going to be the one to do it," Vannevar told
Benedict. The Tremere had not been able to hear the private
mental conversation between the prince and the
Grandfather. "Either Sullivan will manage to kill Delfonso,
or it'll end up the other way around. Either way, it will be
in our favor."

By conniving with the Grandfather, Vannevar actually
hoped to weaken the Family. Regardless of the outcome of
tonight's agreement, the prince and the Camarilla would
come out ahead. If Delfonso died, Vannevar would be rid of
a potential future problem, and the Grandfather would lose
his one Camarilla ally. If Sullivan died, the Grandfather
would lose one of his best childer, one on whom he depended

for protection. In the latter case, Vannevar could find some other way to take care of Delfonso.

Though he professed not to care, privately Vannevar hoped that it would be the old Spaniard who'd die. Vannevar found he still held feelings for the thick-headed Sullivan. The prince had once wanted to make him a childe of his own.

"He'll send Loo along, I'm willing to bet," Benedict said, knowing the concern the prince felt for Sullivan. Sullivan was no real match for Delfonso but, aided by Loo, the odds were more nearly even.

■

A few nights later Vannevar and Nickolai were walking quickly down the slope of Nob Hill toward Chinatown. They moved silently, nearly invisible to most, speaking to each other in hushed tones.

"Sullivan has the head, then?" Vannevar asked Nickolai.

Sullivan and Loo, laying a trap in the chambers below Mission Dolores, had succeeded in killing Delfonso. Ironically, the old vampire had died bound to his own rack, after a grisly torture scene that lasted hours. At the orders of the Grandfather, Loo and Sullivan had carried off Delfonso's head — in order that the Family might perform an augury upon it. Sullivan had insisted on keeping the head himself, only to lose it a few hours later when one of his whores stole it and tried to hold it for ransom. Sullivan had spent a panicky evening the next night trying to track it down and retrieve it.

"It's in his possession again," Nickolai answered. "Though he nearly got killed in the process."

The head had turned up in Oakland, in the hands of Vannevar's old nemesis, the werewolf Reverend Hayes. Sullivan had barely escaped Hayes with his life.

Tonight the two would attempt to undo the Family, dividing them against themselves. All evidence, including Vannevar's own nightmares, pointed to another attempted invasion by the Asian powers. Vannevar and Nickolai agreed that now was the time to destroy the Grandfather. Their plan called for using methods they hoped would avert an open war.

Honerius and Benedict waited for them in Chinatown, in a seedy fourth-floor apartment above a dirty back street. The one-bedroom apartment had been acquired by Nickolai a couple of weeks ago and overlooked the butcher-shop back door that served as the entrance to the Grandfather's underground chambers.

Entering the apartment building and going upstairs, Nickolai knocked on the door at the far end of the dingy hallway. Benedict opened the door and let them in.

"Good evening," he smiled when he saw the two.

Vannevar and Nickolai stepped inside while Benedict shut the door behind them. They found Honerius standing in the middle of the room, obviously waiting for them, looking more nervous than usual. He spoke up, greeting the prince.

"Good evening, my lord. Sullivan has not yet arrived, but all is ready."

Nickolai went straight to the window, taking up a spot beside it, peering out through the gap between the curtains and the wall, keeping an eye on the alley.

"Everything is in place?" Vannevar asked Honerius.

"The spell will go off without a hitch, I assure you," Honerius told him.

Tonight Sullivan was scheduled to bring Delfonso's head to the Grandfather's chambers, where it would be prepared and burned upon a brazier. From the smoke and fumes, the Family would read their future and their fate.

But, unknown to them, the augury would read false, altered by magicks cast by Honerius. The Family would interpret a future that would show one of their own turning

against the Family and slaying them one by one. Sullivan
— the Family's only Anglo and the Grandfather's least
favorite — would most likely be blamed and the others
would turn against him. Sullivan would probably die, but
the Grandfather would be left weaker, an easier target for
the prince.

"I think I see them coming," Nickolai said from his spot
near the window.

The other three tensed, waiting.

"It's him," Nickolai said, a note of triumph in his voice.

Sullivan, accompanied by Loo and Chi, came down the
alley, a dark-stained bundle tucked under his arm.

"And he's got the head," Nickolai added.

"Ready, Don Benedict?" Vannevar asked.

Benedict nodded and got up from his seat. His job was to
telepathically monitor events in the Grandfather's chamber
down below, waiting for the ceremony to begin and letting
the others know when the time was right. Honerius had to
cast his spell at the proper moment if it was to be effective.

Kneeling next to a pentagram already chalked carefully
on the floor, Benedict closed his eyes, quickly slipping into
a trance. Opening his mind, Benedict freed himself of all
thoughts, leaving himself sensitive to impressions emanating
from the powerful magical rites that would take place
underground nearby.

Nickolai remained stationed at the window, keeping an
eye on the alley, while Honerius and Vannevar sat down on
a worn couch to wait, knowing it might be an hour or more
before Benedict told them the ceremony was beginning.

Nearly an hour later Benedict took a sudden, sharp breath,
and a shudder passed through his body. It was time.

Honerius got up quickly and immediately began chanting
the spell intended to confuse the Family's augury. Vannevar
stood as well; however, his attention was not on Honerius,

but on the shivering Don Benedict kneeling on the floor in front of them. He did not look well.

As Honerius began the second stanza of the chant, Vannevar glanced over at him, a question in his eyes. Honerius nodded to the prince, assuring him the spell was working properly and having the desired effect.

Vannevar's attention was drawn back to Benedict when a muffled moan unexpectedly came from the kneeling man's lips. Then, racked by a sudden spasm, Benedict's body twisted painfully and he fell over on his back, legs kicking and scraping against the bare wooden floor.

"Merciful God in heaven!" Benedict cried. "I am repentant for my sins!"

The voice was Delfonso's. Don Benedict had been seized by the old vampire's spirit while the head cooked and sizzled somewhere down below. Linked to Delfonso by blood and telepathy, he now suffered the other man's torments.

"Have mercy on my soul," Benedict shrieked, rolling across the floor, legs and arms thrashing. Vannevar threw himself on top of Benedict, trying to hold him still. "I burn in the fires of Hell!" Benedict shouted.

Nickolai ran from the window and tried to help Vannevar. Honerius, a look of fear gathering on his face, stepped away from the scene, his chant faltering.

"Keep going! Keep going!" Vannevar shouted back at him, struggling with Don Benedict. "Don't stop, dammit!"

Honerius regained his rhythm, maintaining his chant without interruption, but his eyes were on the three men struggling on the floor.

Benedict suddenly twisted an arm free and, flailing it about, upset a table, knocking it over with a crash. "Save me from my torments!" he cried. "My soul! My soul!" The sound of Delfonso's voice coming from Benedict sent a chill through Vannevar.

Someone below them banged on the ceiling: an angry tenant objecting to all the noise from above.

"Hold him still," Vannevar told Nickolai, as the two wrestled with the man.

Then there was a loud pounding at the door. Someone in the hall yelled something at them in Chinese. It was the manager, come to investigate the disturbance.

"Get the door," Vannevar told Nickolai, who spoke Cantonese. "I'll take care of Benedict."

Vannevar grabbed Benedict by the legs and dragged him into the bedroom. He threw him on the bed, then shut the door before throwing himself atop his shouting friend.

Meanwhile, Honerius slipped out of sight, into the tiny bathroom, closing the door behind him, never missing a beat of the chant.

Nickolai waited until everything was clear, then opened the front door. Outside stood the building's manager. The two men exchanged a few quick words, then Nickolai handed the man a fifty-dollar bill. The manager took it and went away, accepting Nickolai's promise of no further noise.

Nickolai quickly shut the door and then called to Vannevar, "Is he okay?"

Vannevar appeared, coming out of the bedroom. "He's quiet now. I think it's all over."

Honerius emerged from the bathroom as well, looking tired and drawn. He no longer chanted. "It's finished," he said. "I think it's been a success."

All three moved to the window where they stood watching out over the alley, waiting for any sign from the butcher shop below. They figured that the Family would try to kill Sullivan immediately but, if Sullivan was fast enough, he might be able to escape their wrath — at least for tonight.

A moment later Sullivan burst into the alley, knocking the butcher shop door half off its hinges. He looked around desperately — right, then left — then raced off out of sight. Hot on his heels appeared a Chinese butcher waving a cleaver at the retreating figure, shouting something after Sullivan.

"Everything goes to plan," Nickolai said, a cold smile on his lips. Vannevar and Honerius nodded agreement.

It was still a few hours before dawn when Vannevar finally returned to the penthouse. Donna was waiting up for him.

"How'd it go?" she asked, after he'd come in and hung up his coat.

He sat down on the couch next to her. "As well as we'd hoped for, I think," he said, sounding a little weary. "Sullivan is out and on the run." He'd said nothing to Donna about his concern for the man, though she'd guessed as much anyway.

"Good," Donna said, pleased to hear Sullivan had not died on the spot, as the prince had feared he might. She moved over, sitting closer to him, distracting his thoughts. He smiled down at her and put his arm around her shoulder, drawing her to him. She nuzzled at his neck, then lifted her head to nip his chin, drawing a tiny drop of blood.

A snarl sounded deep in Vannevar's throat. Then he took her on the couch, sinking fangs deep into her white throat.

■

Much to the surprise of Vannevar and his fellow conspirators, Sullivan managed to stay alive for several weeks, despite the Family's best efforts — including offers of a reward — to put him out of circulation. It seemed that whatever the Irishman lacked in cunning and common sense, he made up for in sheer guts and unflagging determination.

But that was due to end tonight. Sullivan, exhausted from being continually on the run, had been lured out of his hiding place to a meeting with Loo and Chi. Vannevar knew the two planned to assassinate him. Though he regretted this affair, Vannevar knew it would provide him with the opportunity he'd been waiting for. With both Loo and Chi away from the Grandfather's lair, the creature was left virtually unprotected. In his haste to secure Sullivan's demise, the Grandfather was willing to drop his guard.

Vannevar and Benedict now waited for the moment to come. They sat in the back seat of Vannevar's limousine, parked on a narrow Chinatown street. From their vantage point they could see the alley that led to the Grandfather's chambers. Once assured by Nickolai that all was ready, the two powerful vampires would enter the underground chambers and there, hopefully, destroy the Grandfather once and for all.

An hour ago Nickolai had called Vannevar to tell him that Loo and Chi had left Chinatown and were on their way to the meeting place. The prince and Benedict had immediately moved into position. Now they waited for Nickolai to capture Loo and Chi as the pair returned from the meeting, holding them securely until Vannevar and Benedict could accomplish the task before them.

"Sullivan should be meeting up with Loo and Chi right now," Benedict said, glancing at his watch.

"It's about that time," Vannevar said absently.

His face was grim. Benedict knew how Vannevar felt about Sullivan. The prince had been almost elated a few weeks ago when the Irishman first escaped the Grandfather's clutches, but since then he had several times remarked to Benedict his regrets regarding the matter. Vannevar had expressed unhappiness regarding his role in the death of Delfonso, but had agreed with Benedict that the old Spaniard had brought much of it upon himself. But Sullivan was an innocent, mostly oblivious to the whirl of events around him. Vannevar had looked long and hard for some way to help the man escape his doom, but had found none.

Vannevar now glanced at his watch, noting that by this time Sullivan was almost assuredly dead.

The cellular phone in the back of the limousine buzzed once and Vannevar picked it up.

"Hello?"

It was Nickolai.

"Something's gone wrong," he told the prince. "We haven't spotted Loo and Chi returning from the meeting."

"What about Sullivan?" Vannevar asked.

"No sign of him either," Nickolai told him. "Stay in place. I'll phone you as soon I know anything."

Vannevar thanked him and hung up.

"Something wrong?" Benedict asked.

Vannevar shook his head. "Don't know yet," he said. "We've got to wait for Nickolai."

Vannevar grew impatient. He wanted this over with. He looked at his watch. It was only a couple of hours before dawn.

A little less than an hour later the phone rang again.

"Sullivan's alive, I think," Nickolai told the prince.

Vannevar's heart jumped. Though he immediately realized their scheme might be threatened, he was nonetheless excited by the news. "We found Loo's body down by the canal," Nickolai said. "No sign of Chi, but we think he's dead too."

"What about the Grandfather?" the prince asked. Time was growing short. They would have to go in soon or postpone things until tomorrow night, giving the Grandfather a day to prepare for them.

"Sit tight," Nickolai told him. "We're trying to track things down now."

"Never mind," Vannevar told him, looking through the windshield, focusing his eyes on the alley across the way. "I think I see him coming now."

Sullivan, accompanied by a female impersonator known as Eddie the Angel, was creeping down the alley towards the butcher shop door. While Angel stood watch outside, Sullivan kicked in the flimsy door and entered the shop.

"Oh, hell," Vannevar said into the phone as he watched.

"What? What is it?" Nickolai asked, excited.

"Sullivan just kicked his way in. I think he's planning something stupid."

"Keep an eye on things," Nickolai told the prince. "I'll be there as soon as I can." He hung up.

Vannevar set the phone back down on its hook and waited to see what would happen next.

A few minutes later a slim, blond woman showed up in the alley. She spoke with Eddie for a moment then, apparently over his objections, entered the shop.

"What's going on?" the prince asked Benedict, not taking his eyes off the alley.

"I wouldn't hazard a guess," was Benedict's reply.

A moment later Benedict nudged the prince with his elbow. "Look," he said. "Up there." He pointed toward one of the building's upstairs windows. A trickle of dark smoke curled out around the opening.

"Oh, damn," Vannevar muttered. He could see smoke rolling out the downstairs doorway in the alley now, as well. "What has he done?"

As if in answer, Sullivan, soot-covered, staggering and half-carried by the blond woman, stumbled out of the smoky doorway. Angel moved instantly to their aid, even as a car suddenly pulled up at the far end of the alley. Vannevar saw two people jump out, calling to Sullivan and his friends.

Smoke was now pouring out of the building as flames jetted from the windows.

"Let's get out of here," Vannevar said, watching as the strangers, some of them human, helped Sullivan toward the waiting car. "This one's over," he told Benedict.

As Vannevar's driver backed the limo up and pulled away from the scene, they heard a muffled thud behind them as something inside the building exploded. The sound of sirens already filled the early morning air.

Sullivan, in his own way, had managed to kill the Grandfather, but the resultant blaze had destroyed any evidence of the monster's plans as well. Nickolai sifted the ruins the following night but, as they'd guessed, found nothing of value among the ashes.

When and how the inevitable attack from Asia would be mounted, they could only guess, but they knew the time drew near. And somewhere out in the city, against all odds, Sullivan was still alive.

■

A few weeks later Vannevar awoke from a deep sleep, stifling an outcry. He sat up in bed, his eyes wide open.

"What is it?" Donna said, rolling over and looking at him. His shout had awakened her.

"Nothing," Vannevar told her, trying to regain his composure.

"Another dream?" she asked.

Vannevar had been recently plagued by recurring nightmares of an old ship at sea, crashing through the waves. Something stood on the ship's bow, peering down at Vannevar with huge, red, glowing eyes.

"Hmm? No. Nothing," he said. He didn't want to upset her.

Evening was falling, the light from the shuttered bedroom window gray and shadowy. Vannevar, climbing out of bed, got dressed. Donna followed, catching up with him in the living room a few minutes later. Vannevar was already on the telephone.

She sat down on the couch and waited as the prince made call after call. She was worried about his health. The last few weeks had nearly worn him to a frazzle. The long, intricate plan to undo the Grandfather had succeeded, though some of it had gone awry, causing additional difficulties Vannevar had not prepared for. And now members of the primogen council were acting up as well, taking advantage of the prince's distraction to undermine his authority. He slept badly, and Donna couldn't remember the last time he'd eaten properly.

Vannevar hung up the phone.

"More problems?" she asked.

He turned, looking at her darkly. Then his countenance eased. "Sure," he said. "The usual." He didn't share his troubles, an annoying habit she had more than once complained about. Remembering this, Vannevar offered: "Nickolai says the *Festivo* has gone off well — at least, so far."

Donna nodded and smiled. The Mexican-American festival planned for tonight had originally been backed by the Sabbat. Canceled once by the prince, it had been reinstated over his objections by other members of the primogen, using city councilors under their influence. But, since the Sabbat lair had been destroyed accidentally by the fugitive Sullivan, the parade no longer posed a threat. From the penthouse they could see the lights of the parade, miles away on Mission Street.

"Any word on Sullivan?" she asked.

"He's still somewhere on the loose," Vannevar said, frowning.

Following the death of the Grandfather, Vannevar had offered Sullivan the opportunity to join with him. Sullivan had at first agreed but then changed his mind, hooking up instead with Dirk and the anarchs. Soon after, following an embarrassing public episode at the Vampire Club, Sullivan and Dirk had gone their separate ways. Reports from Nickolai indicated that Sullivan, left to his own devices, had unwittingly fallen into the hands of the Sabbat. He had only recently escaped them, destroying their secret lair in the process. Unfortunately, the Sabbat leader — a traitorous Tremere named Selena — had managed to escape.

What Sullivan was up to now was anybody's guess. Nickolai's men had temporarily lost track of him. Sure that Sullivan would be apprehended soon, Nickolai had advised making an example of the wayward vampire. But Vannevar hesitated to be too harsh, despite the numerous crimes Sullivan had committed during the past few weeks.

Tonight two visitors were coming to the penthouse to plead Sullivan's case: Kathy, the thin, blond ex-whore Vannevar had seen in the alley the night the Grandfather died; and Chi, the seemingly immortal ghoul who had survived both the encounter with Sullivan and the fire at the Grandfather's lair. The two hoped to make some sort of peace with Vannevar, and would likely ask that he find some way to spare Sullivan.

Nickolai, always careful for the prince's safety, wanted to attend tonight's meeting, but he had his hands full trying to monitor the *Festivo* while at the same time searching for the escaped Sullivan. Vannevar had promised him he would be careful. Don Benedict would be at his side, keeping an eye on the wily old ghoul.

The intercom on the wall buzzed and Donna answered it. It was Don Benedict, notifying them that the two visitors had arrived. Donna told him to show them up.

Vannevar met the three at the door, betraying no sign of surprise when he saw the tall, thin ghoul shuffling painfully off the elevator, his spine bent and twisted and one hand burnt into a blackened, twisted claw. Chi, arriving back in Chinatown just as Sullivan had made good his escape, had tried to save the Grandfather only to be caught in the ensuing explosion.

Vannevar showed the three inside and had Kathy and Chi take a seat on the couch. Vannevar remained standing, facing them.

"Well?" he said, when no one spoke.

Kathy sat on the edge of the couch, clutching nervously at the hem of her short, tight skirt, intimidated by the prince's commanding presence. She looked toward Chi, silently begging him to say something.

"We have come to plead for Sullivan's life," Chi finally

said. He tried to rise from the couch. His efforts looked painful.

"Remain seated," Vannevar told him. "This is not a formal audience."

The ghoul eased himself back down. "He is a good man, my lord," Chi went on. "He has always tried to do the right thing, sir."

"I know," Vannevar countered. "He's too stupid to actually do anything wrong on purpose. It's the things he does by accident I find so distressing."

The phone rang. Vannevar interrupted their discussion to answer it. It was Nickolai.

"Someone's spotted Sullivan in the vicinity of the parade," the Russian told him. "Should we move in and pick him up?"

Vannevar thought for a moment, then said: "No, let's let him go for now. Follow him and see what he's up to. He might lead us to Selena."

Nickolai agreed and hung up.

Chi, guessing the subject of the conversation, spoke up. "He's after Selena, I'm sure." Chi told him. "He wants revenge." Selena had been responsible for seducing Sullivan away from the prince. Though nowhere near as dangerous as Misty Halls, Vannevar knew Selena was smart and crafty — and a powerful magician in her own right. Sullivan had no business tangling with her.

Vannevar shrugged as if he didn't care. "So why is it you think I should extend the friendly hand to Sullivan? And why should I trust you at all? You are, after all, the advisor of my old enemy."

Chi bowed from where he sat. "The Grandfather is dead," he said. "And the oaths that bound me to him are likewise dead. I live now to serve the Family — Sullivan, and his childe." Chi looked over at Kathy. She smiled a nervous grin at Vannevar then, seeing him still glowering, dropped her eyes. Sullivan, after accidentally nearly killing his ex-whore, had then Embraced her and made her one of the Kindred.

The phone rang again.

"What?" Vannevar said, angered by another interruption.

"Sorry, my lord," Nickolai apologized. "I thought I'd better let you know that Reverend Hayes has been seen around town."

"At the *Festivo*?" Vannevar asked.

"Not yet. He was spotted downtown earlier today but my guess is he's somewhere around in the area of the parade."

Vannevar put the phone back down. He looked at Chi, eyeing him closely. He had always respected the old ghoul. Should he trust him now?

"Benedict?" Vannevar asked, turning to look at his friend. He raised an eyebrow, silently asking his advice.

Benedict nodded approval. "I think so, my lord."

Vannevar buzzed downstairs and called for the limo. "It's time to go out," he said. "Kathy and Chi — come with me. Benedict — stay here and hold down the fort. Keep an eye on Donna."

The three left the apartment and rode the elevator downstairs.

Outside, they got into Vannevar's limo. He ordered the driver to take them down into the Mission, toward the Festivo. During the trip, Vannevar got hold of Nickolai on the cellular.

"What do you mean you lost him?" Vannevar demanded.

"He was on foot and we had him tailed, but then Dirk showed up out of nowhere. Sullivan hopped on the back of the motorcycle and we lost them. We found a dead Sabbat punk in an alley nearby. We think Sullivan got him."

"Try to find him," Vannevar told Nickolai. "We're nearly at the parade now — I can see it from here. Anything on Hayes?"

"Nothing," Nickolai said. "But I'm sure he's down here too. Word is he's looking for Sullivan."

"Call me back." Vannevar said, and hung up the phone.

They cruised a side street a block away from the parade,

pacing the route, searching for some sign of Sullivan.
Vannevar craned his neck around, trying to see through the
crowds. He wondered if they shouldn't abandon the car and
go on foot but, remembering the crippled Chi, decided
against it.

"Look! Down there!" Kathy shouted, pointing in the
direction of the parade. "That's him!"

Vannevar looked and saw a man clambering up the side
of a moving float, apparently after a woman standing atop
it, dressed in a skimpy samba outfit. Police were all around
the float as well, trying to apprehend the man. At first
Vannevar thought the stranger might be no more than a
drunk out for a good time — until he saw him backhand
one of the police officers off the float and nearly ten feet
into the crowd. The woman must be Selena, the Sabbat
leader.

"Turn here!" Vannevar shouted at the driver, his voice
betraying his excitement. "Head toward the parade."

The driver swung left, up the side street, and began
inching his way down the crowded street toward the festival.

As they crept forward Vannevar watched Sullivan climb
to the top of the float, nearly getting his hands on Selena
before she knocked him back with a sudden burst of magic.
Sullivan tumbled off the float, landing on the street with
an audible thud. Selena, meanwhile, hopped down the other
side, landing lightly and running down an opposite street.
Dirk sprinted up from somewhere and helped Sullivan to
his feet. They argued a moment; then the Irishman took off
after Selena, Dirk following closely behind.

"Follow them," Vannevar shouted at the driver, pointing
at the two retreating figures.

"I can't," the driver said. The crowds blocked the end of
the street ahead of them. Beyond, the parade crossed their
path.

"Blow the horn!" Vannevar shouted.

The driver leaned on the horn, edging the big limo

forward, pushing his way gently through the tightly packed crowd. Protesting loudly, the people moved aside, but once at the parade's edge, the driver again hesitated.

"Just pull through," Vannevar told him.

The driver waited for a float to pass, then inched the big car out onto the street, blocking the path of a group of marchers following behind the float. The revelers, incensed by the intrusion of the limo, shouted at the car's occupants. Some banged on the limo's roof and hood. A beer can flew out of nowhere, bouncing harmlessly off the windshield. Then they were through, crossing the parade to reach the street on the other side.

"Where'd they go?" Vannevar asked, having lost sight of their quarry.

"I saw them go down that alley," Kathy said, pointing toward the next block.

The driver punched down the gas and the limo accelerated. Reaching the alley he slammed on the brakes, bringing the car to a halt, tires screeching.

"There they are!" Kathy said.

But Vannevar was already out of the car and running down the alley. Selena, the Sabbat Tremere, lay dead on the ground, torn to shreds. Dirk and Sullivan were both down as well, knocked off their feet by the huge, snarling werewolf that now stood over them.

The bristling monster sensed Vannevar's approach and turned to face him.

"Devil!" the werewolf snarled at the prince. It was Hayes.

Vannevar slowed to a walk. "You have no business here, Hayes," he said, his voice steady, as he continued to approach.

Swearing death to the prince, the werewolf leapt at him. Vannevar merely raised his hand, and Hayes stopped in his tracks. The prince's eyes burned with a fierce, unnatural light.

"You know what I promised you," Vannevar told the werewolf, menace in his voice.

Then the werewolf suddenly twisted about, snarling. Dropping to all fours, it began running in tight circles. As it did so, it slashed and chewed at its own belly, ripping through flesh and muscle, tearing at its own entrails until, weak and exhausted, it collapsed and died. Within seconds the body transformed, assuming the form of the Reverend Hayes from Oakland, eyes open and glazed, staring toward heaven.

Dirk staggered slowly to his feet, leaning against a wall to support himself. Sullivan was still down, his leg and arm so badly injured he couldn't raise himself from his sitting position. Vannevar bent down and examined his wounds.

"They're pretty bad," the prince told Sullivan. "But nothing that will kill you. You should heal."

Sullivan nodded, unsure of whether he should thank the prince or not.

Kathy and Chi appeared, hurrying to Sullivan's side, anxious to learn his condition. Once assured he would be all right, Kathy helped the prince get him on his feet, Together the two walked him down the alley toward the waiting limo, Chi hobbling behind. They put Sullivan inside, then the prince turned and asked Dirk if he needed a ride.

"We can drop you off at home," Vannevar suggested.

"No," Dirk answered. "I'm fine." He turned and walked off into the night.

Vannevar watched as the anarch disappeared. He knew that, like himself, Dirk had sought Sullivan's loyal friendship. In the end, Vannevar had won.

The following week, after Sullivan's wounds had mostly healed, he was formally conducted into Vannevar's family during a private ceremony performed in the prince's penthouse apartment.

Vannevar was particularly anxious to complete the ceremony. His nightmares continued unabated, growing stronger daily. But though he'd lost the chance to learn details of the Asians' plot when the Grandfather's lair was destroyed, Vannevar was glad to have Sullivan at his side. He was sure his newly won minion would serve him well when the fast-approaching day of truth arrived.

There were but a few cards left to play and Vannevar hoped he was playing them right.

19

1995: Mystery Ship

A cold rain drizzled down from a gray sky, streaking the tall, broad windows that ringed Vannevar's penthouse. It was April, still the rainy season, a time of damp, cold and fog.

A group of men were gathered at the apartment, the same group that had met here every night for the past three weeks. Numbering five vampires and two ghouls, they anxiously awaited some sign of the impending Asian invasion.

Vannevar paced the floor, pensive, his mood dark. Occasionally stopping to talk to Benedict, he consulted with the Tremere about details of possible upcoming events. Nickolai stood next to the fax machine, pulling off Coast Guard reports as they came in, interpreting them and relaying the information across the room to Hortator who, sitting on the couch, entered the data into his laptop computer. The machine was modemed direct to Coast Guard radar screens, providing him with graphic displays. Riley sprawled on a nearby couch, while Sullivan sat across from him, next to the crippled Chi.

Nickolai pulled a fresh fax off the machine and scanned it, at the same time relaying the information to Hortator, hunched over his keyboard.

"Aircraft called in. Weather heavy. Air search temporarily abandoned."

A Coast Guard helicopter on patrol had gone down an

hour earlier, dropping off the radar screens some forty miles off the coast, just south of San Francisco. The Coast Guard was recalling the rescue searchers, for the offshore storm made searching too dangerous.

"Any ID on the target ship?" Hortator asked, flipping the computer through a selection of radar displays. An unidentified freighter had been spotted steaming north, heading up the coast in their direction. The missing helicopter had gone down in its vicinity.

The lack of identification in itself was not startling. The sea lanes off San Francisco were always filled with ships heading back and forth between North America, Asia, South America, and Australia. Cruise ships also worked out of San Francisco, and the several naval bases in the bay serviced an array of submarines, destroyers and aircraft carriers. Add to all this the many Coast Guard patrols and private pleasure craft, and the color-coded blips on Hortator's radar simulations looked like so much confetti. Unidentified vessels were colored white. The mystery freighter was one of these.

Hortator had tracked her all the way up the coast, watching as she now neared the Farralon Islands. Still miles offshore, she continued steaming north, apparently intending to pass the city by.

"I still think she is the one," Chi said from the couch. "I feel it in my bones." The coffee table in front of Chi was littered with shipping reports. The mystery ship matched none of the vessels listed in the port registries.

"There she goes," Hortator suddenly announced. "She's turning toward the bay." The white, unidentified blip had suddenly turned to starboard, setting a course straight for the entrance of the bay.

The room became a flurry of activity, everyone crowding around Hortator and the glowing screen in his lap. The Aztec pointed his finger at a blip on the screen. "That's the one," he said.

Chi had told them all he knew of the secret plans long brewing in Asia. Vannevar now suspected a variation on the plot he had defeated in 1936 with the removal of the city's cemeteries. This time, however, instead of using the city's dead, it was believed the enemy was shipping in its own cargo of special corpses, along with the spirits used to animate them. Local airports had been put under close scrutiny but all believed the attack would inevitably come by sea. It was beginning to look as though their guess was right.

"What do you think, Don Benedict?" the prince asked his most trusted advisor.

"There's no way to be sure," Benedict answered him, not taking his eyes off Hortator's screen. "But all the signs seem to point that way."

All agreed this vessel was most likely the one.

"Everybody get ready," Vannevar finally said, then asked Hortator, "How many miles out?"

"Looks about twenty miles off the coast right now," the Aztec answered him. "Still headed straight at us."

"How much time do we have?" the prince asked Benedict.

Benedict would use magic to transport them to the invading ship. But his power was limited; they had to wait until the ship was close in order to make the jump safely.

Benedict made a quick calculation in his head. "We should board in about ten minutes," he said. "Give or take a couple." The ship was slowed by the storm but, riding the flood tide, was still making good time. They had to stop the ship before it reached the coast.

"Get ready," the prince said, then he turned and left the room.

The prince intended to board the freighter and face his enemy head-on, despite objections from the others. He had ignored their advice to stay safe in the city while others assaulted the attackers. He would go, and he had chosen Riley, Sullivan, and Benedict to accompany him. Riley was

his oldest, most trusted companion; Benedict would provide
the prince with magical expertise; and Sullivan was the only
one of the group with any experience at sea, knowledge that
might prove valuable. Nickolai and Hortator would be left
behind, manning the penthouse headquarters and keeping
track of the ship on radar. Chi would remain here also; his
physical condition prohibited his joining the boarding party.

Vannevar reappeared in the room a moment later.
Strapped to his hip was his old cavalry saber. Riley had
donned a leather shoulder holster with a revolver, and
Sullivan wore his big sheath knife. Don Benedict would rely
on martial arts for protection.

The time drew near and the four assembled themselves
near the center of the room, Benedict facing the other three.
Outside, the rain beat down steadily. Benedict raised his
hand, gestured, and said something in a soft voice. Vannevar
felt a familiar rocking motion, a snapping sound, a bright
flash of light, and they were gone.

Vannevar's feet hit the ship's pitching deck at an angle,
throwing him off balance and sending him skidding across
the iron plate into the ship's rail. Rain soaked him as he
clutched at the rail, hanging on for dear life as the ship rose
high atop a rolling wave. The wind screamed, driving the
rain at nearly right angles to the deck. A wave broke over
the rail, washing over Vannevar and drenching him to the
skin.

Sullivan was suddenly beside him, steadying the prince
with one arm while holding onto the rail with his other.

"Are you all right?" Sullivan shouted over the howling
gale.

"All right!" Vannevar yelled back, looking around for their
other two companions. Don Benedict and Riley stood
nearby, also clutching the rail. Only Sullivan, his sea legs
serving him well, seemed unperturbed by the rolling, rocking
ship.

"Are you two all right?" Vannevar shouted over the storm at Benedict and Riley.

They acknowledged they were.

"Which way's the bridge?" Vannevar asked Sullivan, still shouting.

Sullivan pointed forward to a dimly lighted cabin above the deck, a hundred yards away. "There," he said. The superstructure looked unoccupied.

"Let's go," Vannevar said, leading the way, moving hand over hand along the rail toward their goal. Sullivan followed behind him, his legs carrying him steadily, keeping a hand on the prince's shoulder.

Without warning, a black form leaped out at them from the darkness, springing high, landing on the prince. Hissing, the thing went for Vannevar's throat, hands clawing at the prince's eyes.

Vannevar tried to fight it off, but slipped on the deck and fell down beneath the thing. Then he felt the monster pulled away from him. He saw Sullivan lift the writhing black form high over his head and pitch it over the ship's side. The thing fell, still hissing, into the water, disappearing instantly beneath the dark waves.

Sullivan helped the prince back to his feet.

"Thank you," Vannevar shouted to him over the roaring winds.

One hand clutching the rail tightly, the prince drew his sword. The others readied their weapons as well.

Reaching the superstructure, they found a ladder leading up. To reach it would require them to cross an open expanse of rolling deck. Sullivan went first, smoothly crossing the rain-slicked surface, reaching the ladder and climbing straight up. Vannevar went next, wobbling uncertainly over the rolling deck but reaching the ladder safely. Benedict and Riley followed behind, not much steadier than the prince.

Topside, they found themselves outside the cabin. At a nod from Vannevar, Sullivan booted in the door and the four piled inside, quickly closing the door behind them, relieved to be away from the soaking rain and incessantly howling wind.

The bridge was lit only by the glow of its instruments and a single small radar screen. No one manned the wheel but as they watched they saw it moving slightly left and right, adjusting the ship in its course.

"Someone's at the helm below," Sullivan said, pointing at the moving wheel.

"Can you turn it?" Vannevar asked.

Sullivan stepped up to the wheel and, putting both hands on it, tried to twist it left. The wheel wouldn't budge. He made a second effort, this time planting his feet wide apart and putting his back into it. The wheel barely moved.

"Shit!" Sullivan swore, letting go with a grunt and stepping back. "I can't budge it."

Vannevar had hoped they might simply turn the ship about and send it back out to sea. He was not surprised when it proved impossible. The others waited for Vannevar to decide what they should do next.

Vannevar walked across the cabin and looked out the front windows. He could just barely see the line of the lights that marked the coast a few short miles away.

"Time's running out," he said, turning back to face the others. "I want Sullivan and Riley to stay on the bridge and keep watch," he told them. "Benedict and I will go below and see what we can find."

Riley and Sullivan, water still streaming down their faces, agreed, though reluctantly. They would have preferred staying with the prince.

Vannevar and Benedict opened the door and stepped out into the howling gale. Riley and Sullivan, closing the door behind them, watched through the windows as the two men made their way over the windswept forward deck toward a large hatch.

Reaching the hatch, they knelt beside it. It was barred

and locked, but they managed to pry up a corner, bending
the heavy metal back on itself. Vannevar squeezed down
first, finding an iron bulkhead with his feet and quickly
scrambling down to land on the cargo deck below.

Benedict joined him at the bottom and together the two
men scanned the ship's cargo hold. It was empty, dank and
cold. The rocking of the ship was less violent down here,
and they could hear the steady thrumming of the ship's twin
steam engines echoing up through the hull from the ship's
stern.

"There's nothing down here," the prince said as his eyes
adjusted to the dim light.

"They're in here somewhere," Benedict whispered. "I can
feel it. I sense their presence."

Benedict moved toward one of the bulkheads and put his
hands on it, sliding his palms up and down. "Here!" he said.
He beat a fist on the metal. It made a hollow, tinny
reverberation. "This is false," he announced.

They searched the hold for iron bars and, finding them,
attacked the phony bulkhead, gradually prying it loose,
popping the light rivets that held it in place. Curling it back,
they found concealed behind it five narrow shelves arranged
in a tier. Each shelf held a single, desiccated corpse.

"Bingo!" Benedict smiled.

The dead things appeared only vaguely human. Bald,
completely devoid of hair, they had large, round eyes and
terrible fangs that protruded from their closed mouths.

Vannevar and Benedict went straight to work, the
Tremere kindling a small fire with which to destroy the
corpses while Vannevar went to work prying open the next
bulkhead. By the time Vannevar had the second panel off,
Benedict was already igniting the first five corpses.

Meanwhile, Sullivan grew anxious waiting on the bridge
with nothing to do. Riley watched him as he took hold of
the wheel and once again tried to turn it. Riley joined to

help him this time, but even their combined strengths could not move it.

"It feels like something's holding on to it," Riley said, as they stepped away from the wheel."

"Something's controlling the rudder from below," Sullivan agreed, wondering at the strength the unknown steersman must command. He looked out the window. "Shore's less than five miles off," he said, spotting the glowing lights of the Cliff House that lay just south of the entrance. "We're heading right toward the Golden Gate. We'll be there in less than ten minutes."

They both looked out the window toward the partially opened hatch on the forward deck, through which they'd seen the prince and Don Benedict disappear into the holds below.

"Think we should go after them?" Sullivan asked Riley.

"They told us to wait here," Riley answered, but it was obvious he wasn't happy with the situation. There was no telling what kind of trouble Vannevar and Benedict might have run into down there.

"I'm going back toward the engine rooms," Sullivan suddenly announced. "I'm gonna try and shut this ship down. You stay here in case the wheel frees up."

Riley wasn't sure he wanted to stay alone on the bridge, but finally agreed. "Okay," he said. "Be careful."

Sullivan went out the door, back into the teeth of the storm, scrambling down the ladder from the superstructure, then dashing across the deck toward a hatch on the ship's stern. Riley saw him kneel to open the hatch, then slip down out of sight, disappearing into the dark hold below.

Back in the forward hold Vannevar and Benedict toiled away at the task of breaking open the compartments and destroying the corpses hidden behind them. As more and more of the corpses were consumed by flames, the air in the hold began filling with a thick, black, oily smoke. In a few minutes Vannevar had opened all the compartments on the port side, exposing fifty corpses, then began working on the starboard bulkheads, where he guessed they would find another fifty of the creatures. He left Benedict alone on the port side, disposing of the last few corpses Vannevar had uncovered.

Vannevar had the first starboard compartment nearly opened when a shout from Benedict made him drop his iron bar and run to his friend's aid. Pulling out his sword, he rounded a corner to find Benedict facing three black-clad creatures similar to the one they'd met above decks. Hunched nearly double, swathed in black silk, they hissed and growled as they warily shambled toward Benedict, fanning out in an attempt to encircle him. Benedict turned slowly, positioning his back to the bulkhead, his open hands poised, eyes flicking back and forth among his opponents.

Vannevar shouted when he saw them, waving his sword above his head. The ghouls, distracted by Vannevar's shout, looked away from Benedict. The Tremere took the split-second opportunity and, stepping sideways, caught one of the ghouls in the side of its head with a single, chopping blow. It fell dead, slumping to the deck with a broken neck. In one smooth motion, Benedict swung around and caught a second ghoul unawares with a swift kick to the chin. It too fell dead.

The third ghoul, seeing his comrades fall, had no time to react before it fell under Benedict's furious onslaught. All three ghouls were dead before Vannevar could even reach his friend's side.

"There are more!" Vannevar shouted as he joined Benedict, pointing toward the lighted doorway at the far end of the hold. At least a dozen of the black-swathed ghouls were pouring through the open valve, charging straight down on them. The two vampires prepared to meet them.

Once through the stern hatch, Sullivan plunged deep into

the ship's bowels, climbing down darkened ladders, running
through passageways filthy with trash and garbage, searching
everywhere for a way to the engine rooms. He'd not been
at sea since the middle of the last century and, unfamiliar
with a ship of this size and type, he was amazed by its
complexity. But he followed his ears, tracking the steady
thrum of the ship's engines, following the sound to its source.
Breaking through a valve, he emerged onto an iron catwalk
suspended high above two huge, throbbing steam engines.
Never hesitating, he hopped off the catwalk, dropping a
dozen feet to the deck below, landing with a splash in six
inches of dirty bilge water. He immediately began searching
for the steam valves that controlled the engines.

Sullivan was operating without orders, but he knew the
prince wanted the ship stopped before it reached the coast
— even if it meant disabling the ship in the midst of the
storm, and at its mercy.

He ran through the engine room, popping open valves and
pressure releases wherever he found them, hoping that one
or the other would somehow shut down the complicated
machinery that hummed and beat all around him. Finally
he found the great clutches and, without a thought,
disengaged them both, cutting power to the twin screws that
powered the ship. Without them the ship could not be
steered.

Still not satisfied, he then opened the bilges, allowing
torrents of water to pour into the hold before hurrying back
up a ladder to the catwalk. He abandoned the engine room
to its fate. The cold seawater flooding the hold would soon
reach the engines — and their hot boilers — putting them
out of commission, permanently.

Riley kept his post on the bridge staring out over the water
toward the distant shore until he felt the ship lose power.
No longer was the vessel plunging forward, cutting through
the waves toward San Francisco. Now it instead rode atop

the waves, driven forward only by the storm. A huge wave caught the ship in the stern and he felt the freighter tilting forward until he thought the bow would submerge and they would plunge straight down to the bottom. Then the wave passed under them and the ship's stern turned about, leaving the helpless vessel lying broadside to the waves. The lights of the Cliff House burned on the shore, dead ahead and less than half a mile away. Riley realized the wave had lifted them away from the bay's entrance, pushing them south of the narrow opening. Through the gloomy mist he could just barely make out the twin conical peaks of Seal Rocks, lying right in their path.

Riley grabbed the wheel, surprised to find it now turned easily in his hands but, spinning it back and forth, he found it did no good. The ship didn't respond. Riley then decided to leave the bridge. He must get word to the prince, wherever he was. Charging back out into the storm, he carefully made his way down the ladder and then across the forward deck toward the hatch he'd seen the prince enter earlier.

Below decks, in the forward hold, Vannevar met the first charging ghoul head-on. A powerful swipe of his saber caught the monster in the midriff, nearly cutting it in half. A second ghoul fell beneath his blade, its skull split by a powerful overhand stroke.

Benedict stood nearby, fending off his own wave of attackers, snapping necks and limbs with swift kicks and blows he delivered with his hands and feet.

But the horde of snarling ghouls pressed down on them, forcing them back against the bulkhead. One leapt at Vannevar, dodging past his defense to sink his teeth in the prince's shoulder. Vannevar tore the thing loose and, with one hand, tossed the snarling ghoul halfway across the ship's cavernous hold. Back to back, he and Benedict continued to fight off their attackers, slaying them one by one.

Sullivan was still finding his way through the ship's myriad passageways when he heard the muffled thump from behind. The cold seawater had reached the boilers and they were now cracking, blowing apart. He felt a creeping panic as he desperately tried to find a route to the ship's forward holds. He had to get word to the prince that the vessel was crippled and out of control.

Coming to a large valve, he spun the handle and yanked it open, stumbling upon a scene he'd not expected.

In the large compartment in front of him he saw a second helm, complete with wheel and engine controls. This wheel, now unattended, spun back and forth, uncontrolled. In the center of the compartment he saw a series of wooden racks holding dozens of earthen jars, their lids sealed with dark pitch. Painted designs decorated the deck around the jars — curlicues, swirls, and strange, complex symbols. And he smelled the air — air that reeked of an odor all too familiar to Sullivan. A chill went down his spine when he recognized the rotten stink that had perpetually surrounded the Grandfather.

Then he saw it — a huge, misshapen thing, crawling painfully and slowly as it squeezed its vast bulk through an opened valve on the far side of the compartment. Only its hunched, retreating back and tiny, almost useless rear limbs were visible. Not giving the situation a thought, Sullivan drew his knife and went after it.

Vannevar and Benedict were dispatching the last of the attacking ghouls when the prince looked up and saw the thing squeezing through the door, its huge red eyes burning like coals.

"Benedict!" the prince shouted. "What is it?"

Benedict looked up and saw a monstrous creature, bulky and nearly seven feet high, crawling toward them on all fours, dragging itself along on two powerful forelimbs while its nearly useless rear legs pushed weakly from behind. The